T0004948

'A compulsive page turner . . . The science behind the author's dystopian vision of the future is impressive, but it's the movements of the heart that mark this book as a standout'   Elspeth Sandys

'A remarkably original first novel, beautifully written, about a future that could be just around the corner'   Julie Christie

'Susannah Wise's first novel is a dystopian triumph: dark, compelling, and all too believable like an extended episode of Black Mirror, it reminds us of the power of love'
Saul David, author of *Victoria's Wars*

'This superbly accomplished debut is dark and compelling but ultimately filled with hope. I couldn't put it down' Ruth Hogan
'Poignant and perfect. This Fragile Earth shows us exactly how breakable-and reparable-our world is. Not to be missed!'
Christina Dalcher, author of *VOX* and *Q*

'I absolutely DEVOURED this book. It has everything I love - great characters, intrigue, action, heart, drama and hope. Cannot recommend it enough. It was so nice to read something so gripping it got me off my phone for two days'   Aisling Bea

'Utterly compelling. Susannah Wise's subtle envisioning of a near-future dystopia is sophisticated, emotionally acute and brilliantly unnerving, but what sets this novel apart is the breadth of the author's inventiveness. This is fantasy with a deeply intelligent heart, chilling, poignant and captivating from the first page to the last. I didn't want to leave the world Wise creates: her talent for understated tension kept me gripped to the end'
Lisa Hilton, author of *Maestra*

This edition first published in Great Britain in 2022

First published in Great Britain in 2021 by Gollancz
an imprint of The Orion Publishing Group Ltd
Carmelite House, 50 Victoria Embankment
London EC4Y 0DZ

An Hachette UK Company

1 3 5 7 9 10 8 6 4 2

A CIP catalogue record for this book is
available from the British Library.

ISBN (Mass Market Paperback) 978 1 473 23234 1
ISBN (eBook) 978 1 473 23235 8

Typeset by Deltatype Ltd, Birkenhead, Merseyside

Printed and bound in Great Britain by Clays Ltd, Elcograf S.p.A.

www.gollancz.co.uk

THIS
FRAGILE
EARTH

Susannah Wise

For my father

'One thing I know, that I know nothing.
This is the source of my wisdom.'

Socrates

Day 1

They cycled past the trimmed hedges of the park and on towards the Inner Circle. Jed was too big for the bike seat now, and she struggled as she stood on the pedals. His knees nudged uncomfortably at her hips; her body swayed but there was simple pleasure in moving at speed with her son.

The sun was bright. Shadows lay sharply delineated against the tarmac.

'Hallo! Goodbye! Hallo! Goodbye!' Jed's hand waved back and forth, greeting his own shadow as it dipped in and out between parked cars.

The back of her neck felt hot; she should have brought sunscreen. They would head to the Fairy Island – Jed's name for it – next to the Rose Garden to play tag. A red tan line would streak his nape. They'd throw stones in the water. They'd share a picnic on the grass by the fountain.

Later she and Matthew would be going out to that new restaurant in Kentish Town. She couldn't remember the name. They'd be with friends so they'd have to get along, laugh at one another's jokes. Maybe they'd have sex at the end of the night.

A couple of cars purred past, her bicycle protected in its own lane between the pavement and the road. She turned left to the Inner Circle, stopped by one of the car-charging ports and attached her bike to the Maglock.

Jed threw the safety-bar on his seat up and dragged his jumper over his head.

'Too hot.'

He held his arm out, the jumper draped across one narrow wrist like a waiter's towel. She stuffed it in her rucksack. When she straightened, the sunlight made her squint.

'Put these on.' She hooked Jed's UV sunglasses over his ears, then put on her own. 'Come.'

Jed took her hand and skipped across the fibreglass road panels, grey and squeaky beneath their feet. He looked ridiculous in his UVs, the mirrored blue lenses too big for his head. Through the black and gold gates they went into the seclusion of Queen Mary's Garden, the landscaping the same as when she had been a little girl, save for the scarcity of leaves on the trees, and the heat for March. Her parents used to bring her here on Sundays to watch the starlings homing at twilight. She lifted her face to the sky. Some things are past, and will not come again.

They turned left into the circular garden, the neat beds a cloud of clone-roses in full bloom. The previous year, the roses had blossomed in February.

'Let's have a sniff!' Jed raced to a flower of darkest red. He stuck his face into its centre. These farmed varieties carried that synthetic odour, like acetone. It set her teeth on edge. Jed didn't know any different. 'Smells like that lady's house we went to one time, with the biscuits and the potty. Where we sang "Good King When's His Lass".'

She giggled; voluntary service never sounded so inviting.

'It wasn't her house, love. It's called a nursing home.'

'But she did live there?'

'Yes.'

They'd been only once, two Christmases ago. Matthew had strummed his guitar while she'd bashed out carols on the electric piano in the home's main reception room. Jed had handed out tinsel, then sat in a plastic chair, bouncing on an inflatable cushion.

She looked at the red rose, its petals thick and lustrous like velvet, its heart unfurling lazily towards the outer leaves.

'Deep Secret,' read Jed from the black lacquer plate in front.

She gazed at the other roses: different shades of reds, pinks, oranges, mauves. Like sweets.

The advanced hybrids sat further off in a separate bed beyond the wooden pergola, wound with climbers. The petals of the hybrids flashed neon and electric blue and onyx through the gaps in a bench where two old ladies sat snacking on bananas. The odourless hybrids held no interest for Jed; this place was all about sniffing until he became light-headed.

She turned to some egg-yolk yellow blooms, around which the pollen-drones were busily doing their thing.

'You know, when I was your age, Gamma and Grandpa's kitchen walls were this colour.' Jed's eyes had glazed over. 'Hey.' She nudged his elbow. 'You listening?'

'Nope.'

'Cheeky.'

'I was thinking.'

'What about?'

'The Golden Ratio.'

'The what?' She knew, but she wanted to hear his explanation.

He dragged her closer to the rose. 'It's where things go in spirals. The number is 1.618, and it goes on forever. Miss Yue said: "look for it in flowers".'

'Like Fibonacci.'

'Yeah. Like that. Except the Golden Ratio doesn't really exist, Miss Yue said. She said Man made it up, to explain the existence of spheres mathematically.'

'Are you sure that's right?'

He frowned. 'Not completely.'

'You're only six. How d'you know this stuff?'

'Learned it in coding.'

'Learned about the Welfare State yet? Have you learned what the Welfare State was and which Prime Minister abolished it?'

'The what?' He grinned, revealing two rows of white milk teeth before escaping to a different flower.

'Music can be Golden too, Jed. Spirals exist in a perfect piece of music and bees hum in it. In the key of C.' But he was no longer listening.

Her gaze returned to the yellow rose, thick thorns poking a warning from its stems. Her parents' kitchen table had been too big for the room. The ridged oak top carried a particular smell, perhaps from the years of meals spilt, ground into the grain by a good scrubbing with a cloth. If she thought hard, in the far corner by the back door she could see the sun refracting off her father's silver telescope.

A pollen-drone appeared, hovered by her chin, alighted briefly on her nose, then flew away.

'Mama, come and smell these pink ones!'

Her GScope rang inside her rucksack: Matthew. She'd assigned him the ringtone 'Lazy Days', which was appropriate, if a bit mean. She swung the bag round to her elbow and found the GScope folded like a paper note in the front zip.

'*Matthew is calling, Signy*,' GQOS' voice began, a little tardily, given the GScope was already ringing. 'Would you like to—?'

'Let me answer.'

Jed snatched the flexuous graphene sheet and flicked it upwards with a practised hand. A green circle of light flashed around the GScope's camera lens. The Holoscreen appeared in front of Jed's face.

Matthew's head was suddenly there; three-dimensional, transparent. His image danced against the backdrop of roses.

'Hey.' She bent low, her face joining Jed's in the tiny window at the corner. Why was her hair so flat? She fluffed it.

'Hi, Dada!'

'Hey, Jed.'

There was tutting from the old ladies on the bench. She swiped her finger downwards through the air to lower the volume.

'Yes?' he said.

'"Yes"? You rang me!'

Matthew's hand passed across his face, as if exhausted by the simple act of listening.

'No I didn't.'

There was a hiatus, in which they both checked their call logs.

'GQOS must be getting old.' His face creased into a smile.

'Weird,' she said. 'We're in the rose garden at Regent's Park.'

'I can see. Why are you whispering?'

'Why are you still at work? It's Sunday afternoon. They are aware you have a family?'

'I'm leaving soon. Forgot to charge the car battery but I reckon I'll make it back in a one-er.' His shoulders sighed.

Jed elbowed her out of the way. He stuck his tongue out at the screen.

'Oh, my tongue's a funny colour, sort of blue. It's the UV lenses, isn't it? We're busy – going to the Fairy Island. Bye, Dada.'

'Bye,' she said, but Matthew had already gone. They should probably dispense with talking altogether and communicate solely via V-mail.

Her screensaver, a photo of the family on holiday in Scotland two years ago, hovered in the air. Jed tapped her arm.

'You cross?'

And she hadn't had a chance to ask him to pick up pumpernickel. But then he'd have forgotten that too. Matthew forgot almost everything. She couldn't decide if there might be something wrong with his brain, or if he just wasn't interested in what she had to say.

'*You have one new V-mail, Signy. Would you like to see it now?*'

GQOS' voice from the GScope again. You could tell GQOS was an AI system because no human could sound that happy all the time.

'No thank you, GQOS.'

The screen disintegrated. The park landscape stretched out uninterrupted in front of her.

'D'you remember, Mama, when I asked GQOS how many bees there were left in the world and she said, "*I'm sorry, I don't know how many boobies there are left in the world.*" That was funny.'

She laughed.

Jed rubbed his nose. 'Why did the droid cross the road?'

'I don't know.'

'Because the chicken was controlling it.'

'Did you make that up?'

'Nope. Fairy Island.' Jed marched on between the bushes, down the shallow incline towards the lake. Forty feet ahead, on a plinth in the green water, a bronzed eagle signalled the north point of the island. 'Basically,' Jed sighed, 'eagles don't exist here in Regent's Park. There are only two golden eagles left in the world and they're in a special massive cage. Miss Yue told us. It should be a statue of a heron or a pigeon – something more appropriate.'

'That's a big word for a small person.'

'Is it lunchtime?'

'Not yet. Let's get to the island.'

She felt good today – as if she fitted into life and life fitted into her. The question that yawned somewhere around her solar plexus, the feeling that she might be always missing something, was answered by this day: spent with her son and full of light and memory – like an echo. Jed ran ahead, stopping at the short wooden bridge that led across the lake. She followed him, passing the fountain where she'd once gifted a Leatherman knife to a long-ago boyfriend. He'd taken it with shaking hands, saying no girl had ever given him such a masculine present, then burst into tears.

'Go on!' she called now to Jed.

Jed trip-trapped across the bridge and disappeared down one of the island's small gorse pathways. She raced to catch him up.

Day 2

The concrete playground behind Jed's school had claimed another victim. A small girl of two with fat and bloody knees was being comforted by her mother. Or maybe it was her nanny; you could never tell.

Another day, another park. Not anywhere near as pretty as Regent's Park and a tenth of the size. Signy stood in this particular one every weekday, watching Jed and his friends as they climbed the enormous slide from the wrong end, trainers squeaking on metal. They'd reach the top and tumble pell-mell, landing together in a heap. It would be Jed who always hurt himself – his chin, an ankle, a finger.

Today his friends had been dragged home already: to Kumon, coding, Mandarin. She glanced at her wrist, though she could almost always tell the time without a watch now. She thought without resentment that this was one of the premier skills learned from the routine school pick-up. *Snacks! Playground! Holoscreen!* Children's lives, existing entirely in the vocative.

The asphalt around the fountains in the corner was dry. The fountains never worked, except for one solitary month in autumn when it was too cold. By summer, when hordes of sweating kids would stamp fretfully on the buttons, willing them to cool their hot little bodies, the jets would have given up.

The buzzing of a police drone above. Or one of those environmental ones, testing for any remaining trace of beetle-blight spores. She wasn't sure which was more depressing. The buzzing went up in pitch as the drone flew near. There it was: small, blue, property of the police.

Nearly five o'clock.

Jed was sprinting the perimeter of the roundabout. He was a fast runner; she'd give him that. He came to a halt and put his hands on his hips.

'Need the loo.'

She took his arm and led him to the dismal toilet by the railings. The exterior had been painted green, as if Conglomerate North's decision to colour-match it to the few trees made it somehow less offensive. The lonely tolling of a church bell up the road. Monday: she wondered what time Matthew would be home.

He probably shouldn't be driving today. They'd drunk too much sake last night at that disappointing new restaurant in Kentish Town with Aya and James. Matthew's best friend and Signy's best friend, together thanks to them. Aya had had lipstick on her teeth and talked on and on about their new baby, while James banged a drum for the reunification of Korea and how his stem-cell knee graft made him feel like the bionic fucking man. Signy had chosen the sustainable salmon because it said it came from the Orkneys. Who really knew what was or wasn't safe to eat any more? The WaitreX robot had fiddled with the lighting all night and Signy's tinnitus had been bothersome, especially when James leant forward to kiss Aya right in front of her. Signy had said 'Get a room' and no one had laughed. She'd grinned at everyone all night, crossing her eyes as heat built between her ears, finishing her boozy lychee dessert with a spoon that was too small for the job.

'Hurry up, I'm desperate.' Jed was tugging at the button on his jeans.

The playground toilet stank of pee. On the floor, matted balls of loo roll. Some things, she reflected, never changed. It was almost unbearably hot with the door closed. The light in the windowless cubicle made her face, tinted blue by her UV glasses, ghoulish in the scrubby mirror.

On their drive home after the meal, just the two of them, she'd joked about Matthew's never wanting to marry her and resurrected the argument about a second child. He'd told her off for being drunk, flicked the car into driverless mode and stared out of the window with his arms folded across his chest, until the road told the tyres that told the car that told them that the tyres needed pumping, and they both shouted for the car to shut up.

'Ugh, Mama, there's nothing to wipe with again.' Jed held up the palms of his hands. It was a gesture of comical hopelessness. He cantilevered himself off the seat. 'And it's not flushing.'

'You don't need to wipe, it's only a pee. And why won't you stand up to do it?'

'Then it goes everywhere.'

She lifted the lever on the sink tap. No water. Odd. The tap's silver plating was dotted with a suspicious white crust.

'Broken,' she said. 'Fabulous.'

'You're being sarcastic.'

'We'll have to do without clean hands. We'll wash them at home.'

Something thudded against the outside wall of the toilet. Again, then again.

'What's that?' said Jed.

They re-emerged into daylight and followed the wall around

its edges. The small police drone was bashing itself repeatedly against the breeze blocks.

'What's it doing?'

'Covering more ground than a hundred beat officers, apparently.'

They watched it dash its own camera to pieces, its delicate leg-spindles splintering, dangling like snapped limbs, until the broken drone fell to the ground, lifeless.

'Droney!' Jed lamented, dropping to his knees. 'Why did you kill yourself?' He looked at Signy. 'Why did it do that, Mama?'

'I don't know, love. A malfunction?'

The playground had emptied. Odd how she hadn't noticed. She'd never make a decent spy.

Two other police drones – which didn't look to be committing suicide any time soon, but fingers crossed, you never knew – hovered above three teenagers on the AstroTurf football pitch.

Clouds were moving slowly across an increasingly white sky. No birdsong. The city hung over the park as if disappointed somehow; at the balding trees, the absence of wildlife, the endless drones.

'Time to go.'

She took Jed's hand and began the slow trundle back. An electric bike whizzed past on the cycle path, nearly sending Jed flying as he tried to balance on the raised barrier. She called out but the cyclist was already far away.

They crossed the Holloway Road. Driverless cars purred silently up the hill. On the southbound lane, a phalanx of Magtrams and one of those mobile hologrammed car ads, all shining chrome and big wheels.

'That H-car is sage!'

Jed craned his neck to get a last look as the hologram car accelerated, zooming right through the body of a tram and into the distance.

She chuckled. 'Sage?'

'What?'

'Your lingo. It's funny.'

'No it isn't.' Jed was tapping each electric charging port along the street with his hand. He whipped his fingers away. 'Ouch, this one's hot.'

She loved his hands. They were soft and warm and fitted perfectly into hers. He was singing. She leant in closer. It was a commercial jingle she'd composed a long while back: '*At Icestar check out faster, use your palm, it's smarter!*' The melody was catchy but irritating. He was bang in the key of E flat major. She ruffled his head.

'That's my boy.'

'I am your boy.'

'It's an expression. When are you going to start piano lessons?'

He sighed. 'Mama, not *again*.'

They were on the other side of the A-road now; the street with the pastel-coloured houses, the original windows long gone. The solar-blue acrylic made her think of mirrored aviator shades. She missed being able to see into gardens beyond living rooms, imagining other people's lives, greedy for ones she hadn't lived.

'I'm thirsty.' Jed smacked his lips.

She brought out the bottle of water. She always carried one in her bag. Her mother liked to call her a 'waterholic'; the phrase had been coined with a smile, but Signy had detected subtext. She handed Jed the bottle. It looked enormous in his arms. He unscrewed the cap and drained half.

Tinnitus whined in her ear. She shook her head.

'That's better.' Jed had a water moustache.

She grabbed his hand. 'Let's have a race.'

They ran fast along the pavement. He was nearly quicker than her now, his legs scissoring back and forth like a film in fast-motion. Freeing his hand, he surged ahead, glancing back now and then over his shoulder. He liked to win. She couldn't bear to disappoint him.

'I was first!' He gave a victory jump.

They turned into their street. Long lines of grey-brown terraced Victorian houses stretched left and right, reflections of clouds floating in uneven rows of more blue acrylic.

'Nearly there now.'

'Is Dada home? Can I do my palm?'

'No. And yes.'

Palm-plates were touched, doors opened, coats dumped on the backs of kitchen chairs, UV glasses removed and piled with all the spares on the shelf above the sink.

'I'm actually really hungry, Mama.'

He was always hungry. She hoped he'd grow to be taller than his two granddads, who'd both been dismally short.

She pulled out the brand new book of blank music manuscript from her bag, bought in town this afternoon on a promise to herself, and without knowing quite why, hid it beneath the piles of Mozart and Beethoven on top of the piano.

Jed shrugged his school bag from his shoulders and tipped it upside down. A muddle of pale sticks scarred with blight and shards of bark now decorated the living-room floor.

'Jed!'

'What? It's for mine and Dada's house! For the roof!'

They both glanced at the small wood-blight house, sitting on its own little worktable in the corner. It was more of a log cabin, a tiny circle at the front for a door, beautifully crafted. Matthew called it *a work in progress*, an *eco-project*.

'You can't argue with that.'

Jed picked up his sticks and carried them to the house.

She went into the kitchen. It smelled odd. She'd only been gone for four hours. Perhaps the bin needed changing. She hit the swing-lid and peered inside. Carrot peelings and an empty packet of biscuits greeted her. There were pumpernickel crumbs on the table, the remains of breakfast. She was a sloven. She wiped them up and dropped them, unthinkingly, into her jacket pocket.

'Oh, for God's ...'

The pocket was already occupied by a piece of card. She pulled it out.

A flyer: a glossy rectangle of white paper with a moon-in-a-night-sky graphic. 'A silent five-day meditation retreat,' it promised, 'in the beautiful Welsh mountains in sunny June.'

Vicky had invited her: a parent from school, one she actually liked. They'd bumped into one another, Vicky with her daughter Cassidy in tow, a few days ago. Signy had stared at the words on the card while Jed had stared longingly at Cassidy's hoverboard. 'A relaxing and restorative time for reflection.' She'd wondered if she'd manage to not talk for that long. June: it was ages away.

That smell; she scanned the kitchen for an unwashed plate or other guilty party. Jed entered and opened the freezer. The mulchy odour of thawing frozen veg filled the room. He was undaunted.

'Breaded prawn tails here. Can I have some for dinner?'

'Oh God, no.'

'Why not?'

'They've defrosted by themselves, love.' And should have

been chucked because they were recalled by the manufacturer for mercury testing, she wanted to say, but didn't.

The freezer drawers were swimming in water. A crashing sound of something hard hitting plastic made them both step away. A miniature iceberg calved itself from the freezer roof.

'It's broken. Let's call someone.' He looked at her. He reminded her of an owl.

She opened the door of the fridge; the light was off inside. Beads of water trickled down the walls, forming a small pool around an already-open box of synthetic chicken thighs and some rambutan on the bottom shelf. She pulled the synthetic chicken out and stared at the label on the side. Past its date by two days.

'Pooh.' Jed held his nose.

She chucked the packet in the bin, feeling guilty.

She wandered to the fuse box in the hall. The lighted panel of virtual switches had gone blank. She slammed the lid shut, wandered back to the kitchen. She clapped her hands.

'On!'

Nothing. She tried the hob. She flicked the light switch on the wall. Jed was sitting at the kitchen table, crestfallen.

'Power cut!' she said.

'So I can't have any supper and I can't use the VR.' The corners of his mouth went down.

'Let's go to the shop at the end of the road, and you can have a real meat spring roll, and I'll cut up some veg and you can have that raw.'

'Okaaay.'

She grabbed her bag, their glasses.

On the street, an older man from the house opposite called to her from his upstairs window.

'Have you got no electric?'

It was the first time he'd ever spoken to her. She longed to correct his grammar.

'It's probably the whole street. I'm sure it'll be on again soon.'

The man went back inside.

They marched to the little Malaysian café at the end of the road. Ahead, pollution was visible in a sky turning milk-pink at the edges. She nudged her UV glasses further up her nose. The spindly branches of birch trees that once populated the whole of Whitehall Park poked at lonely intervals above rooftops.

Through the café windows, two women whispering behind the counter, heads together. They looked up when Jed and she entered.

'There's no electric,' said one.

'I just thought we could buy a spring roll or something?'

'There's only synthetic-meat spring roll now. Is that okay?'

Jed scowled. Signy ignored him. 'Synthetic is fine. Two, please.'

They were wrapped in paper. The woman smiled at Jed but he was still sulking about the prawn tails.

'Here.' The other woman thrust some orange juice and yeast milk into Signy's hands. 'The fridge is broken. We're giving it away for free.'

'Oh, thank you.'

She left the shop thinking that Jed and Matthew would need to drink the yeast milk tonight or it would curdle. She hated all milk, animal or vegetable; even the smell of it made her gag.

She chopped cucumber and carrots into little sticks while Jed played upstairs. She'd better call Matthew, tell him about the electricity. She unfolded the GScope from her bag, swiped her fingerprint and flicked the screen on to the kitchen wall.

'Matthew,' she said.

Matthew's profile photo appeared, all sunglasses and movie-star cheekbones. He was smiling; you could see the gap between his two top teeth. There was silence while GQOS tried to find a connection.

'*Hi. This is Matthew. Please leave a message after the tone.*'

'Hey, love, it's me,' she said into the empty kitchen. 'Just wondering where you are – there's no electricity on the whole street. Do you have any, wherever you are? Where are you? Call me.' She added, 'Please.'

He'd probably be on his way home in the car, enjoying the silent traffic, singing along to Radio G with the window down.

'Track in GPRS. Matthew.'

'*Tracking in GPRS,*' said GQOS. A map appeared on the wall. The little blue dot hovered and pulsed over her location. '*Sorry, Signy. GPRS is not available at this time.*'

'Track in Drone-Cam.' At least they were good for something.

'*Sorry, Signy. Drone-Cam is not available at this time.*'

Fine. She'd call the electricity board and find out when the power would restart. The battery life on her GScope read fifty-five per cent. What if she used it all up waiting on hold?

'Electroscene, North London,' she instructed.

She was patched through surprisingly quickly. A photograph of wind turbines popped up, morphing into the interior of a bee silo, thousands of farmed bees busy making honey out of sugar-syrup. Tinny muzak played. It was algorithm-composed, she could tell: the computers always left unnatural gaps between the end of one phrase and the beginning of the next. How noisy would it be to stand inside a bee silo? Like an extreme version of tinnitus, but deeper, louder. Thrilling.

An automated message: 'We are sorry, electricity and gas

services are currently out of order but will be restored as soon as possible. We apologise for any inconvenience. Your custom is important to us.'

'Well,' she said.

'*I'm sorry, Signy – I don't understand what you would like me to do,*' said GQOS. '*Repeat your command.*'

'Go away, GQOS. I mean, turn off. Jed – supper's ready!'

Jed galloped down the stairs; he made a great deal of noise for such a small boy. He climbed onto the chair and balefully eyed the meal on the table.

'Come on, eat up and then you can have ice cream.'

'Freezer's broken.'

'Okay then – chocolate.'

He shovelled cucumber into his mouth. She poured a glass of water from the tap and gave it to him.

'This tastes weird,' he said.

'Don't be silly, it's absolutely fine.' She took a sip. 'Ugh.' It did taste strange: sort of metallic, warm. The internal filter must be on the blink. 'I'm sure it's all right, just drink it.'

The boiler wailed from the back room. She went to inspect it: the pressure dial had dropped to zero. Hydrogen was far more combustible that the old carbon boiler, surely? What was it that engineer had said – the one whose breath smelt of too much time spent in a van? When there's no gas going through the system the boiler will make an awful noise, but it's not dangerous.

No gas. She flicked the switch. The wailing stopped. Good.

Someone in the street was leaning on their horn. She marched down the hall, passing the painting of an old man, sketched in charcoal by one of Matthew's many relatives. It was hanging askew. Matthew liked symmetry. She had a peculiar fondness for objects on the diagonal – pictures, rugs, ornaments – the haphazard nature of things at angles, as if they'd arrived there by accident.

Through the bay window in the living room, she could see a car out of charge a short distance along the road. The driver was trying to push it to the kerb. Other cars waited behind, the drivers watching through windscreens with arms crossed like Olympic judges. Eventually they took pity and climbed out of their vehicles. Together they helped move the broken car out of the way. There now, she thought: teamwork.

'Everybody's cross.'

Two feet below and behind her stood Jed. He was chewing.

'You made me jump. What are you doing leaving the table?'

'I don't like the carrots. They're warm.'

'How else are you going to see in the dark?'

'I don't need to see in the dark, Mama.'

He would tonight if they didn't get the electricity back on.

They were in the centre of that Venn diagram between night and day.

'The only decent torch, Jedster,' she said, 'is locked in the camping box in the attic.'

'*I'm* not going into the attic in the dark,' said Jed.

'Well. Neither am I.' She laughed. He did too.

Jed fetched the small plastic torch from his bedroom but it had run out of battery. It had been hers as a child. She must buy some AAAs, if she could find a shop that still had any. They found some long white candles in the back of the kitchen's Drawer of Doom that contained all the small things they could never find a specific home for. There was also a half-melted FOUR in sparkly blue.

'When was I four?' said Jed. 'That was ages ago. I wanna use this one for bedtime.'

'You can definitely use it because it's yours.'

He punched the air.

She quite liked being without light to begin with, then later on, she didn't. The noises of the house, the feeling they were being watched from corners where the flame from the single lit candle couldn't reach. No. Silly. The whole area was in blackout.

She and Jed played Dinosaur Top Trumps until it was too dark to see. She extinguished the candle and ushered him upstairs for a bath. The water spluttered and coughed from the tap. It ran for a minute. She dipped her hand in: freezing cold.

'I forgot – the boiler's broken. No bath for you tonight.'

'Yesssss. Let's light *my* candle.'

She pulled out some matches and lit the FOUR. The bathroom filled with shadows. Jed made animal shapes with his hands against the wall.

She tried calling Matthew again; nothing. Perhaps his car had run out of power, like the car on the street. She wondered if public transport was working.

She tucked Jed into bed and read him a story in the flickering light. When the candle was out the room was darker than it had ever been.

'Ooh, spooky. When's Dada going to be home?'

'I don't know, love. Soon.'

It *was* spooky. She didn't like it.

'Love you, Mama.'

'Love you too, my darling. Sleep well and sweet dreams.'

'I wish the hall light was on. Can you switch the bunny on with the battery?'

She'd forgotten about the plastic bunny. She hunted on hands and knees until she found it at the bottom of his toy basket. She placed it carefully on the bedside table where its weak pink glow brought relief to both of them.

'Phew,' said Jed. Like every other thing in the house, the batteries were old. 'Will the electricity be normal tomorrow?'

''Course, don't worry.'

She felt her way carefully down the stairs. The halogen street lights were off. Two foxes hollered to each other in the back garden. The house was pitch black. When she looked behind herself, she couldn't see a thing. She had never experienced darkness like it apart from weekends at the cottage in Warston. Though the sky there was illuminated by stars, the moon. This city darkness had a heavy, crackled quality like black foil.

She searched with her hands for the other candles in the drawer. There were six in all, white, greasy, bought in expectation of dinner parties that never happened. She lined them up on the kitchen table and relit the extinguished one with a shaking hand. She hadn't had anything to eat since a sticky supermarket rice ball at lunch. She went over to the mantelpiece to examine her wrinkles in the mirror: too dark. The GQOS-assist sat in its corner.

'On!' she said.

Stupid thing. She'd never liked it anyway.

'Mama?' Jed's voice echoed on the stairs.

'Yes, love?'

'A pollen-drone's trapped behind my bed and now it's come out and it's bashing itself against the window.'

She returned to his room, candle in hand.

'Okay, where is it?'

'Ssh. I don't know. It moved. Listen.'

The soft buzz of the pollen-drone in flight. She stared at the ceiling. Silence. The buzz began again.

'There!' he cried. It was by his bookshelf.

She waited until it had settled against the wall and scooped it up with one hand, closing her fingers around its glossy black body, its tiny propeller. She must be careful or she would break it.

'Is it tickly?' he whispered.

'Yeah.'

'I love that,' he said. 'And they can't sting. *Sage!*'

The propeller stilled. She opened the window and freed the drone to the elements. The propeller jumped to life and it took off.

'There you go.'

'What's it doing here? Why isn't it back in its cosy home?'

She laughed. 'Drone-hub. It's called a drone-hub.'

'I like cosy home better.'

'Me too. With real bees, it was the females who were the workers and the *drones* were the lazy males who sat in the cosy home all day impregnating the queen.'

'Like Dada,' he said, and they both giggled a second time.

Back downstairs and ruminating on the second synthetic-meat spring roll, she sat on the sofa, pulling her laptop towards her, flipping the lid. It was working. Weird. She squinted in the flare of unnatural light, throwing the SOLA roof panels a brief prayer of thanks. Though why they were able to sustain a laptop, and not lights or a boiler, was beyond her. The icon at the top of the screen read twenty per cent. She sighed. So much for the nanowire battery. She typed: 'BBC News electricity blackout London'. Somewhere at the top of the house, the floorboards were making a snapping sound, contracting as the night cooled.

'*London has been plunged into darkness today, as several utilities have been cut to at least six million homes across the capital. Conglomerates have been left without heating and light. The government has assured concerned citizens that it is working to resolve the problem as soon as possible.*'

Beneath this, a recorded interview with the managing director of Electroscene, the electricity provider, apologising for the inconvenience. Yes, people would be compensated. Old people should stay in – some of them may be able to remember the blackouts as far back as the 1970s. Let's keep this in perspective.

She would keep this in perspective. She closed the laptop. The room dipped several hundred lumens. The candle flame quivered.

She couldn't think of a single thing to do. She flicked a guilty eye at the piano. Her new music manuscript pages were waiting, safe in their hiding place. No, the sound of playing would wake Jed.

Yesterday's *Gelos News* lay folded next to her. She must be one of the only people left on Earth still reading hard-copy. Though she didn't really *read* it, she reminded herself, so much as do the puzzle pages, tut over the music reviews. She searched for anything by Gethin Jones, but the science section was a pull-out and it had either gone missing or dropped en route from the shop. Never mind.

Her childhood friend from Warston; whenever she thought of Gethin, it was as a small boy running around naked save for a pair of brown cotton shorts and red wellies, lambing sheep and fruit-picking. Gethin's hands had always been grubby and he'd smelled of margarine. Now he was science editor at *Gelos*. He'd modestly told his mum, who'd told Signy's mum, that working for *Gelos* was better for his soul than working for the *Reference Daily Online*, but only fractionally.

She turned to the concise crossword. Seven down, five letters: 'Destiny, Fate'. She searched her brain. Nope.

She barely saw Gethin any more. He lived just fifteen minutes away, but they'd lost touch and she'd never bumped into him in London, not once. Only on the rare occasion that they'd return to Warston across the same weekend would she set eyes on him.

Something caught in her throat, as though she'd swallowed a badly shaped piece of puzzle.

The street below was silent. Behind the blued-out windows opposite she could see outlines: three sets of shoulders hunched, faces illuminated by the glow from a computer screen. Young people: far younger than her. She wondered what careers they were dreaming of. The computer cast its light beyond them to a wall-poster behind their heads: the word LANIAKEA curled around a drawing of a drone. Something about it was familiar. A place, perhaps? A Chinese youxiu band? Whatever.

Perhaps she'd try to contact Gethin tomorrow if the power hadn't come on. He'd have an idea about what was happening.

She tried Matthew's GScope again. Still nothing. She stared into the candle flame and twiddled her thumbs as her father used to, to make her laugh.

'Hey, Dad,' she said.

Time passed. She was playing Grandmother's Footsteps with her watch. After an hour she gave up waiting for Matthew and went to bed feeling anxious. This was character-building: everything would be all right in the morning; Matthew would be home soon.

In the bathroom's blackness she brushed her teeth in the odd-tasting tepid water. Some instinct made her go back down to the kitchen, where she filled three large saucepans with water from the sink. She dipped a tumbler and drank a glass to check if it tasted different but it was still horrible.

She climbed into bed, congratulating herself for being good in a *situation*, which was what someone in a story would call what was happening to her right now.

★

She woke with a jump to the crunchy sound of the lock sliding back on the internal door to their flat. It was still night. She lay motionless, heart beating hard. Her breath grew shallow. Footsteps mounted the stairs. Her body stiffened.

There was the familiar creak on the seventh tread. He cleared his throat. Matthew. She'd known it would be him, of course she had. She felt her way to the door of the bedroom in her T-shirt, calling his name softly in case she woke Jed.

Matthew's body appeared larger in the darkness, solid like the trunk of a tree. His mouth brushed hers in greeting.

'Sorry. The car died on me somewhere along the frigging A40. I've walked all the way from Chiswick in the dark.' He put his head into Jed's bedroom. 'How come there's a light on in here?'

'The camping bunny.'

He went to rearrange Jed, who would be caught in a tangle of sheets. She waited on the landing, hearing Jed's childish breathing deep and fast like an animal, before returning to the room and crawling under the duvet. Matthew came in and closed the door. He removed his jumper, trousers and pants and dropped them all in a puddle on the floor, his glasses escaping his pocket, clattering across the floorboards.

'Bonkers, isn't it?' he said. 'How was your day?'

Naked now, he hid his crotch in his hands and hopped in beside her.

'Why d'you do that? I do know what you look like without clothes on.'

'Dunno. Feels safer.'

'Weirdo. My day was … There's no electricity, no gas, Matt.'

'I am aware. Thank you.'

'Also, the water tastes weird. You're weird. It's all weird.'

'Don't worry, it'll be fine by tomorrow.' His eyelids clicked as he rubbed them.

There was silence. They lay side by side like corpses.

She said, 'You know, the electricity's out over all of London, not just our area? That's what I read on the BBC.'

'Yeah. The Underground is out. The trams. The Maglev is out.' In a pastiche of the 1940s World Service he said, 'This little London lady is having a crisis. Her husband's shirts lie unironed and no one has done the dishes. What's a gal to do?'

Matthew had executed an excellent impression of a dog barking in the distance when they'd first met. Then he'd spoiled it by barking every time she'd arrived at his door.

'Jed brought more blighted sticks for your wood house,' she said.

'Bless him.'

They were silent for a moment.

'Bloody computer systems,' she whispered. It sounded like the right thing to say.

'This is what happens when the UEC votes to abolish nuclear power. They're imbeciles. What do they expect? This is it. Ta-da.'

'The laptop's working, but nothing else. And what are you going to do about the car?'

The mattress dipped as his body turned towards her. He spoke close to her ear, breath warm on her hair.

'Collect it tomorrow. With the portable charger, if there's any juice in it. I mean, it was totally chaotic.' He chuckled.

'It's not funny.'

'Sorry. You sound tense. I'm just trying to cheer you up.'

He felt for the radio on the bedside table, switched to battery-power mode, and tuned into the news.

'*How do you feel about this situation?*' a broadcaster was asking someone.

'*Oh, not so bad. I'm not worried about owt.*' A woman with a Hull accent.

'*Do you remember the blackouts in the seventies?*'

'*I do.*'

'*And if you don't mind me asking, how old are you?*'

'*I'm a hundred and one.*'

'*A hundred and one. Do you worry about being cold tonight? Falling over in the dark?*'

Matthew laughed. 'Oh God, don't make her feel worse than she already does.'

'Ssh. You'll wake Jed.'

'*Oh no, lad. Cold? Ha. It'll take more than a temperature of eighteen degrees to put me in danger.*' The old lady's breath blew a gale into the microphone.

'*Thank you. I'm moving on to someone else now. Yes, you.*'

The sound of leather soles on wet pavement.

A young man's voice. '*This United Ecological Congress ought to be ashamed of itself. Everyone knew that closing down nuclear power plants, killing jobs and creating one mainframe that's responsible for all energy, all utilities, was a recipe for disaster. We didn't vote for this. Get it fixed.*'

'A man after my own heart,' said Matthew.

More talking. More opinions. It all added up to very little. After ten minutes Matthew yawned.

'Heard enough?'

'Yeah.'

He lowered the volume and picked up his in-ear phones. He liked to listen to the World Service while he slept.

'Shouldn't you save battery?'

'Sig, it'll be back to normal tomorrow.'

'Aren't you worried?'

'No. I'm fine.'

'"No, I'm fine."'

He leant up on one elbow. 'What?'

She sighed. 'Nothing. Just ...' She tried to think of a nice way to say it. 'Boarding school boys.'

'That's me,' he said with satisfaction.

He rolled onto his front, earphones in, and dropped immediately into a deep sleep.

She stared at the ceiling, wide awake now, listening to Jed's rhythmical breathing in the next room and the beginning of Matthew's snores. Sometimes he'd moan on the exhale; it was almost musical. She would have quite enjoyed it if it hadn't kept her awake.

Her breath was uneven, her chest a cloth bag tightened by a drawstring. In the street below she heard the voices of two teenage boys discussing the increased probability of getting laid now there was no power. She smiled in spite of herself and turned away from Matthew.

Day 3

'Mama. Mama.'

Jed's face was close to hers, his nose touching her forehead. When her eyes opened, she saw his polar bear pyjama-top had ridden up, the whey-coloured skin of his tummy illuminated by a thin shaft of sunlight creeping its way through the blinds.

'Is it morning?'

'Sshh. Yes, whisper, or you'll wake Dada.'

Matthew was face down in the pillow, one leg spread out, as if he had fainted in the night and been placed into the recovery position.

'He looks dead.'

'No he doesn't, Jed, don't say that.'

'Why not? That's how he looks.'

She hoped this day was going to be all right. She hoped for lights. And gas. Solar power. Electricity. Cars. Trams. Normal things.

'Time is it?' Jed asked, squinting at the window.

She switched her GScope on: 7.15 a.m. The battery had run down another few per cent.

School.

She padded out of the bedroom, Jed in tow, and climbed the stairs to the bathroom. The shower spluttered and hissed.

Cold water flowed. She jumped in and out of the jet, freezing. Jed stood outside the shower cubicle, laughing at her through the glass.

'Bollocks,' he said. 'I can't write steam letters.'

'Jed! How d'you know that word?'

'You say it. Is it a schoolday?'

'Yes.'

'Will school be open?'

'Yes. No. I don't know.'

She'd better call Mum, and see if she'd made it to the DoctreX. She shivered her way back to the bedroom, dressed Jed, dressed herself, scooped up her GScope.

'Morning.' Matthew yawned expansively.

'There's still no electricity or gas or anything.'

'It'll be fine. It *will* come back on today. Seriously, don't worry about it.'

She frowned but he didn't notice. Jed threw himself on the bed.

'Dadaaaaa!'

Matthew tickled him under his armpits. The two of them could barely breathe for laughing.

'Stop! Can we build the wood house, Dada?'

'When you get home from school.'

Another squeal. She liked watching them. She put her fingers to her lips.

'The neighbours.'

'Why are you always telling us to be quiet, Mama?'

'Yeah, Mama. Why?' Matthew was grinning at her.

She took her GScope downstairs to the kitchen and dialled her mother's home tag in peace.

'*The tag you are calling is temporarily unavailable.*'

She tried her mother's GScope: switched off. Would Warston

have electricity? There was nothing there except houses and a church. Her parents' cottage did have two big gardens back and front full of flowers, but you couldn't use a rose to light a house.

Thoughts of Warston were always rich with fondness and melancholy and an almost imperceptible piercing in her heart, like a tiny needle that has skidded off its thimble for a moment. On Signy's last visit her mother had brought her dad's telescope, relegated to the attic, into the playroom. She imagined it there now on its tripod, pointing skywards, hopeful.

Mum wasn't taking care of herself, she knew. The last time they'd Scoped, the conversation had gone like this:

'I'm going back to the DoctreX tomorrow about my kidney. "*DoctreX*". "GQOS". Listen to me.' She pronounced it *Jee-koss*. 'Whatever happened to human diagnosis?'

'Ma, you know how to say it – *GEH-kose*, like the lizard. *Gelos Quantum Operating System*.'

'Well.'

Signy had softened. 'And you've been forgetting your meds. I told you not to send back the MediX.'

'He was always bossing me about, telling me to take this, take that.'

'It's a robotic medical system. That's what it's supposed to do.'

'He's a can on wheels. He couldn't save your father.'

'Don't say that. It's self-learning. And DoctreX is far more accurate than any human. Let me know what it says. And remember to drink more water.'

Her mother's voice had lowered to a whisper. 'And I didn't send him back. He's in the shed.'

'You can speak up. It's an "it", not a "he", and it can't hear you.'

'Oh, but he can. I switched him off but his little eyes keep blinking. He's recording me each time I go in there.'

'Recording you what? Pulling out the wheelbarrow? You're hardly MI5 material.'

'No. Well. Your father's observatory papers.'

'His research is old and out of date now, Ma.'

'Barely three years he's been gone, and already you're telling me this?'

'Science moves fast, Ma. I'm just saying.'

'Well, don't. Tell Jed I've got a new hose for the garden he'll like. It's got a trigger.'

When the call ended, Signy had told Jed about the hose and he'd actually been excited.

'What's for breakfast? I'm starving.'

Matthew slid into the kitchen. In his hands, the battery-powered radio was spitting out static.

'Pumpernickel with warm and slightly rancid Yeasterine. Cereal with warm and slightly rancid yeast milk. Rambutan and apples.'

Matthew grinned. 'I'll only eat them if they're warm and slightly rancid.'

'What's wrong with the radio?'

'Not working.'

Matthew opened the fridge and carefully pulled out the melting Yeasterine as if it might escape between his fingers. He looked a bit less relaxed than he had last night. She was glad: she didn't want to be the only one worrying. He fiddled with the radio frequency, tapped the back panel. The radio crackled. The sound of blurry voices, as if someone were speaking underwater, against a high-pitched mechanical hum.

'For Pete's sake. What is going on?'

He threw the radio onto the table. It lay there wobbling,

silver, like the rejected spratlings she and Gethin would leave at the side of the brook as children.

She'd always tried to throw the fish back into the water before they'd died, but Gethin would shout at her. It was funny, she thought, that someone who had been so mean to animals as a child had ended up at a newspaper covering the big scientific stories – the beetle blight, algorithms in charge of utilities, nanobiotics, Trinculated coding – the list went on and on, she could barely keep up. Jed seemed to absorb information about these things like a plant via osmosis. Or maybe it was school where he learned it. She felt suddenly old.

She went to find her own GScope and returned, sitting herself at the table.

'GQOS. Open LiteWallet.'

'*I'm sorry, Signy, but LiteWallet is temporarily out of service. No funds available at present.*'

'No bloody money?' she said. 'What the fuck?'

'Mama!' Jed admonished, through a mouthful of cereal.

'Eh?' Matthew peered over her shoulder. 'You're kidding me?'

'That's what it's saying. The system must be down.'

'That is fucked *up*.'

'Dada!'

'Well, everyone's in the same boat, I suppose.'

She punched out a message on the GScope.

'There's still the ATM on Junction Road.'

'That dinosaur?'

'Also, there are some Litecoin cards in my pants drawer,' he said, which made her laugh. 'What? For emergencies. Take some. What are you doing now?'

'Texting.'

'Old-school. Who?'

'Gethin.'

He might be at work. He might be at home staring at his GScope, just like her.

'Your boyfriend?'

'To ask him what's going on.'

'Ooh, Gethin –' Matthew's voice went up an octave – 'you're so clever with all your *science*.'

'Bugger off. He's an old friend, that's it.'

Matthew snorted.

'Mama's got a boyfriend?' Jed asked.

'No.' Matthew ran the water from the tap, filled a glass and downed it. He winced. 'This water's disgusting.'

Jed nodded. 'That's what I said!'

She fed them pumpernickel with melted Yeasterine and silo honey. She ate her slice with honey but without the Yeasterine. The honey was gritty and tasteless. She put the pumpernickel down and stared at it.

'When are they going to improve this stuff?'

'Mama, you should be thankful there's food on your plate,' said Jed. 'Some people in the world are starving.'

'Yeah, Mama,' said Matthew, his eyes crinkling.

They had an apple each.

'Matt, we shouldn't empty the saucepans of water I filled last night. Okay?' Something dark inside her opened its wings. '*Hey!*'

He looked up. 'What?'

'Did you hear me?'

'Yes.'

'What'd I say?'

'God, calm down.' He blinked. 'You said – water – don't throw it away.'

'Sorry. I'm edgy.'

She put the plates into the sink and washed them in cold water.

'You're telling me.'

Normal things. She left Matthew with his head bowed over the faulty radio, grabbed a twenty Litecoin card from his pants drawer and walked Jed to school.

Their street was quiet. Rounding the corner onto Holloway Road, it seemed to her as if everyone had come out this morning, most of them walking in the car-lanes. The whole place had been inadvertently pedestrianised. Cars that had run out of charge sat abandoned by their owners on the fibreglass road panels like tortoises. Adults held the hands of children; no rush, meandering, squinting in the day's glare despite their UV glasses. It actually looked rather jolly. She grinned and raised her eyebrows at a man with two little girls. He grinned back.

She crossed into the park. On the grass by the playground with the broken toilet were the remains of yesterday's suicidal drone.

A young woman approached from the side, taking Signy by surprise.

'Sorry love, d'you got a Scope with battery? Mine's run out. I've gotten stuck here last night. I've slept in the park and I need to call my boyfriend to let him know I'm okay.'

Signy shrugged. 'Sorry. I haven't got battery either.'

The woman's eyes narrowed. Signy hurried away, taking Jed with her. Far behind her now, the sound of the woman trying someone else.

'That lady had actual hard money in her pocket,' said Jed.

'She did?'

'Yep. I saw a whole roll. Probably a million.'

Signy smiled. 'Maybe not quite that much.'

The school gates were closed. Several sets of parents stood in front of a note taped to one of the metal rails.

THE SCHOOL IS SHUT TODAY DUE TO UNFORESEEN CIR-CUMSTANCES. SORRY FOR ANY INCONVENIENCE. WE LOOK FORWARD TO SEEING YOU ALL SOON!

Next to it, the half-ripped poster with instructions on how to spot Bovine Staph in children.

She sighed. 'Bollocks.'

'I told you you say it,' said Jed happily. 'Can we go to the playground in the park?'

Her child. Her throat felt full and empty at the same time.

They'd better not go to the playground. No. What they'd better do is go to the Lianhua supermarket further up the road to get food that didn't require refrigeration. Just in case.

She turned to a dad who, on occasion, she'd exchanged smiles with across the rubberised green moguls of the school yard.

'Any idea what's going on?'

'I'm supposed to be delivering a presentation at work in thirty minutes.' He shook his head. 'Instead, it's colouring in and cold beans for lunch. What are you going to do today with your kids?'

'Kid,' she said. 'Singular.'

The dad gave her a funny look. She instantly felt tired.

'Remember Raymond Briggs' *When The Wind Blows*?' said someone.

They began the journey back the way they'd come. Into the park they went. She'd better try her mother again, check in. She spoke to GQOS, unfolded the GScope. The call hadn't even connected when the young woman without her phone was back, a finger in Signy's face. Signy threw the GScope into her bag.

'I'm calling my mother,' she snapped. 'She's elderly and lives by herself in the middle of nowhere. I have barely any battery left. So—'

'*I'm sorry, Signy, but I don't understand the command,*' GQOS bleated from her bag.

People were staring. Signy slalomed through the cycle barriers at the park's edge, hands shaking.

'Lying slag!' the woman yelled as she turned the corner.

Halfway up Holloway Road, Jed said, 'What does "slag" mean?'

'Someone who isn't nice.'

There were scratches on the lenses of her UV glasses. She pushed them onto her head. Sod the UV. She looked up. High above, police drones were buzzing.

Jed followed her gaze. 'Are they watching us?'

'No, love.'

'Who are they watching then?'

'Everyone, maybe?'

Ahead, a crowd of people waited at the Magtram stop outside the supermarket. They were going to wait a long time for a tram. They passed the newsagent, the self-drive office and the little hairdresser's next to the Maglev station. Closed, closed, and closed. Ten yards from the stop she saw that the crowd wasn't waiting for a tram at all; they were queuing to get in to Lianhua's. The line began in front of the beautician's, hidden behind its metal grille, and serried around the tram shelter. People looked disapproving as she and Jed jumped the queue. The automatic doors were no longer automatic, but jammed open with two wedges of wood.

Inside, the neon strips were out. Natural light exposed a grubby floor. The refrigerator sections had dirty white blinds drawn down. It smelt of yeast cheese. The shelves were almost empty.

She didn't know what she had expected exactly, but it wasn't this. An elderly man helped himself to the last box of Milletbix.

Instead of stacking shelves and manning the two non-self-checkouts, the CheX robots were motionless mid-aisle, heads drooped like flowers in need of water. Four harassed human employees had been drafted in to add up prices on paper. She could tell by their concentrated expressions they were struggling with the mental arithmetic.

'You know there's a queue?'

A tall man with eyes like raisins. He stared over her head. Everyone was being terribly unfriendly. She led Jed out and back down the road, holding tightly to the twenty-Litecoin card in her hand.

'Why aren't we buying anything, Mama? Where's all the food?'

'It's fine, Jed. We'll find another shop.'

The small green-fronted fruit and veg shop optimistically titled 'Premier Foods' beckoned, back up the hill eighty metres away. She wheeled about. Jed ran to keep up.

'Are we going back to Lianhua's?'

'No. We're going there.'

'Where?'

'Jed, for goodness' sake. You'll see in a minute.'

His lip went out. There wasn't time to care.

People crowded the tiny shop. The odour was entirely of olives. She took whatever she could find: a packet of dried lentils, some halva with pistachios, a jar of chillis, two enormous lemons, a tin of water chestnuts.

'Hold that, Jed.'

'What is it?'

'A yam.'

'What's a yam?'

'A sort of tuber, like a potato.'

'What do we do with it?'

'I don't know.'

'Why are we getting it, then?'

'Jed. Please.' He was silent. After a moment, there was a tapping at her thigh. 'What?'

'Sorry, Mama.'

Tears dripped from his eyes. They landed on his red jumper, blossoming into large circles.

'No, I'm sorry, monkey. Don't cry. It's not your fault. Things are all a bit weird. Stick with me and do what I say, okay?' She planted a kiss on the crown of his head.

Behind the counter the owner was talking. She waited in the queue. Her GScope bleeped.

Two messages: Are you alright? Fen, her violinist friend.

The other was from Gelos, the network provider, apologising for the reduced service. Now she thought about it, she'd quite enjoyed not being bothered by the endless GQOS alerts. At least people were looking at one another – even if it was to argue about food – rather than their devices.

Yes! Are you? she wrote back to Fen.

The message failed to send. She switched the GScope off. Important to preserve battery. Still nothing from Mum.

It was her turn to pay. She plonked her goods on the counter-top. The shop owner took her Litecoin card and grinned at her wonkily.

'You hear the news, my friend?'

'No. We don't have power.'

'Word on the street is the CheX are all broken, everywhere the robots busted – WaitreX, DoctreX, MediX, BinX. FTSE broken. Now rich people are the same as everyone else. Everyone's acting funny. Like it's the end of the bloody world.

Stupid. I sold out of my shop in four hours. Better with human workers now, innit.' He laughed, head nodding.

She nodded in return, the two of them like bobbing plastic dogs at the back of a car.

She left Premier Foods with one heavy-duty paper bag full of produce. There were only three Litecoin credits left on the card.

They weaved through the streets until they reached the old machine in the wall at KoreaBank on Junction Road. Signy stared at the blank screen. She put a finger to the recognition pad. Her shoulders sagged.

'I'm an idiot.'

'What is it, Mama?'

'The power cut. Obviously the machine's not working.'

'What are we going to do?'

She thought suddenly of Jed's fire-engine money box. Two people queued behind her.

'It's not giving money out,' Signy said, stepping away. 'I mean, there's money in it, but it won't work because everything's shorted.'

The man behind her approached the machine. He wiped his hand on his trousers before trying his finger on the pad.

'Not working,' he said, looking up. She wanted to shake him.

They trailed past the flats where the Boston Arms had once stood. The building that replaced it was one of those 3D-printed things. Her teenage years had been spent in that pub, dancing in the cavernous clubroom at the back to darkwave classics, protected by a gang of school-friends. Now she missed the shabby Victorian grandeur of the Boston, the nights of sticky floors, the smoking on the street outside in uncomfortable shoes texting boys on an iPhone, but people needed homes.

They crossed over the hump of the bridge for the Maglev

line. The 3D ad hoardings above were black. Only a couple of days ago, a good-looking man had shone down from there, all silver hair, tears in his eyes, holding a shabby dog, a baby cradled in his arms. BECAUSE YOU NEVER KNOW WHAT THE FUTURE HOLDS. Life insurance: was the man meant to be happy or sad? Was he thrilled to have a new baby, or had his wife had a tragic accident, leaving him alone with a child and a husky?

'When can I have a hoverboard?' sighed Jed.

'Soon. Let's go home.'

She took his hand.

They found Matthew sitting on the sofa in the living room, laptop on knees.

'Oh,' she said when she saw him, which made him glance up, then down. His hair was greying at the edges. Funny how she'd never noticed.

'What?'

'I thought you'd have gone to work. Or tried to collect the car.'

'On what? There's no public transport. Met texted saying don't bother coming in, the computers are down and no one else has. Look at this.' He gestured to the screen. 'I can't connect to Ra, LiteStix, Blackstar. Just news.'

'No social media? What *are* we going to do?' She came to sit beside him. 'At least there's news.'

'But it's all bullshit.'

Jed tutted. Matthew hit a key on his laptop. The pixels of light made Signy's pupils contract. The connection was slow. Eventually they linked to a site.

Matthew read out, "'*A temporary problem with centralised computer systems ... some unrest across the United Kingdom ... advice is to stay close to home ... normal services are expected to resume imminently . . . backup generators being used . . .*" blah "*. . . all flights in and out of the UK suspended.*'"

The written report ran into a streamed interview with the Prime Minister. Three minutes passed before it even started. The PM's voice was reedy, insistent.

'*The government's actions during this situation have been swift and appropriate.*'

'Ha. Yeah,' said Matthew. 'It's never your fault, we know.'

'What actions does he mean? See if there are any other reports from out on the streets,' she urged.

'But it takes so long to load. Honestly.' He yawned. 'Storm in a teacup, Sig. People's lives are boring – they just want to inject some drama.'

'Please,' she said.

She had a morbid desire to see how bad it was, even if it wasn't actually that bad.

'We could build the house?' said Jed, tapping Matthew's knee.

'In a minute, love.'

'Couldn't get any money out of the ATM,' she said, 'so now at least everyone will be broke.'

'Or liberated.'

'Don't go all Marxist on me.' She took control of Matthew's laptop and connected to some shaky camera footage of people breaking into an electrical store in Regent Street. 'How liberated does that look?'

'Depressing,' said Matthew. The picture froze. 'Could you use your own laptop, please?'

She opened her computer and sent an email to her entire contact list: Hi. Everyone ok? Anyone have a clue what's going on?! It appeared to send.

Encouraged, to her brother, she wrote: Elis, what's happening over there? Anything weird? Or at least, weirder than normal for Oz? The electricity's cut out, but laptop and Scope still working – just! I'm worried about Ma – can you get hold of her?

After a second, she sent a separate email to Gethin: 'Hey G, I've texted you but no response. Do you know why everything is kaput?

An out of office autoreply popped into her inbox from an old tutor at music college. A response, albeit automatic, was something. Twenty minutes later, a second email arrived. It was Aya.

We're ok! James thinks the Chinese have built viruses into our computer systems! Do you know what the cause is? Really hope it gets sorted soon. The baby's running a temperature. James has been counting our baked bean tins, ha. Stupid London. Let me know if you hear anything. Look after yourselves, love to Jed and Matt.

Aya making contact, making jokes. Signy's shoulders relaxed. She reread the words. Why did everyone mention baked beans when they talked about food shortages? She didn't even like baked beans.

No further responses. What was her brother doing? It was night in Australia.

Matthew was typing his own email. She heard him hit the Refresh button.

'Has it even sent? Why the hell is nobody answering me?'

'It's payback time?'

'Funny.'

She walked into the kitchen with her bag of groceries.

'Where's the water in the pans?'

'I chucked it,' he said.

'Why?'

'There's plenty of disgusting water in the tap.'

She filled the pans again and replaced them on the hob. Her temples throbbed, signalling the start of a migraine. She drank some cold boiled water left in the kettle and climbed three floors to the bathroom at the top of the flat in search of aspirin, while Matthew got to work on the wooden house with Jed.

The rain upstairs plopped onto the Velux. The sound was comforting. It hadn't rained, not properly, for weeks. She knocked back a couple of tablets with the horrid water from the bathroom tap and put her head into the spare room, where a second Velux was open and dripping water onto the bedspread. She hopped onto the bed and looked out. Nothing to see, just endless sloping rows of slate-grey tiles. There was the sucking sound of air being squeezed between the seals as she pulled the window shut.

She glanced sideways at the two low doors leading into the small storage attic – also open; Matthew had misplaced the key soon after they'd moved in and now the doors would drift apart of their own accord. The attic gaped, dark inside. Half-full boxes of childhood belongings, underused tents and piles of sheet music covered in Signy's scrawl. That was all that was in there. And the torch. The good one. She mustn't forget that.

She wandered downstairs. Jed's latest sticks and the wooden house littered the living room floor, the two boys marooned in the centre.

'We've decided, Mama. It's going to be a bee-house, for when all the bees come out of the farms.'

'That's nice, monkey. I think you might have to wait a while.'

'No. Miss Yue says it's going to be soon.'

'She did?'

Miss Yue sounded like a person with whom she'd want to share a sake.

'Yup. We're going to put the house up on the wall in the back garden.'

'Great. Matt, the attic doors are open again.'

'Don't worry, it wasn't a ghost,' said Matthew. 'I found the camping stove in there when you were out. The cylinder's full. It's in the back room.'

'Oh yes, of course. Brilliant.'

Hot food. She felt much better suddenly.

'Survival skills, baby.' He grinned.

She fetched the stove and gas canister and lugged them to the kitchen table. A ping from her computer. She checked her emails: Gethin.

Sig. I've an idea about what is going on, yes. I can't write about it here. I need to tell you exactly the

She hit the Refresh button. She waved at Matthew.

'Look at this.'

He came over. 'An email from the skinny midget?'

'What does he mean, "exactly the"?' she said. 'Why does it end in the middle of a sentence? And he's not a skinny midget. Please don't make fun of Crohn's, Matt.'

'I don't know why it ends like that. He got distracted? His battery died?'

'Why does he say he can't talk about it via email?'

'I don't know, Sig. Send him one of your famous texts. Call him?'

Gethin's GScope rang and rang. No voicemail option. She sent him another text: Are you ok? Your email cut off in the middle. Please make contact. S x.

She spent the next ten minutes burning the battery on the laptop, relaying the visuals to Matthew – who had stationed himself on the floor again – as further news arrived, the connection increasingly sluggish with each passing second. A report from Oxford city centre: a hand-held V-screen showed children playing on the street. At the end, a small cardboard box was thrown at the journalist's head by someone out of shot. A fresh report: looting in cities across the country, in other countries too; Europe and the States, the Middle East.

Matthew left his gluing and came to sit beside her. She found his hand, gripped it. The screen suddenly went white: OOPS! GELOSNET CANNOT CONNECT TO THE WEB AT THIS TIME.

They fiddled with the connectivity icon and the power button.

'I thought you said we were on the SOLA network when the Raydem had stopped working?'

Matthew stared upwards, as if the solar panels might be visible through the ceiling.

'It was a guess, not a fact.' Signy woke Matthew's laptop. Another blank screen. 'Oh, for God's *sake*!'

'Maybe the connection will come back later?' he suggested.

'I bet it doesn't. Bloody *Gelos*. I told you we should have gone with Hen Kuai.'

'This whole thing stinks.' Matthew stared out of the window, grim-faced.

'What's the matter?' Jed was holding four wooden twigs in one hand and a glue gun in the other.

'It's okay, love. It's fine.'

A small pool of dried blood had gathered at the cuticle of her left thumb. She experimented with rubbing it. The pain was comforting somehow.

She picked her way across the flotsam of sticks, and placed herself on the edge of the white lacquer piano stool. Too low. The knob at the side squeaked when it was turned. She tried to imagine the piano's weight on the floor. She opened the lid's folding leaf, careful not to snare her fingers, and inhaled the smell of home: wood, varnish. There was possibility in the black and white keys. A four-bar phrase formed in her ear. What did Gethin mean when he said he knew what was going on? The music dissolved.

Somebody was knocking on the door to their flat.

'Michelle,' she said. It couldn't be anyone else. Matthew didn't move. Signy sighed. 'I'll get it.'

Their downstairs neighbour stood on the top step, barely visible in the gloom.

'Hi,' said Michelle. She was eight months pregnant. Her belly stuck out like the prow of a ship. Her bleached hair was growing out, the roots black and shiny. Her hand went to her head, as if reading Signy's thoughts. 'Heard you pootling about up here.'

'Sorry,' Signy said. 'Was Jed making too much noise with his sawing and gluing?'

'Oh no, it's not that.'

Signy hoped the washing machine hadn't leaked again. The landing was small; Michelle took a step back as Signy opened the door fully.

'Oops. Don't fall off the stairs! How's the bump?'

'Yeah, not bad. D'you have any water?'

'Yes, but it tastes horrid.' Signy's smile wavered. 'Why? What's wrong?'

'Mine's stopped.'

There was a whooshing in Signy's ears like waves breaking. She steadied herself on the door frame.

'Really? Oh God. Please don't worry. You can use ours. Twenty minutes ago I drank from our bathroom tap. I swallowed some aspirins. Headache.'

Michelle looked confused by the level of detail.

'Thanks.' She sniffed. 'I don't wanna bother you, you know.'

'It's fine. You can help yourself whenever. It tastes horrible, so boil it before you drink.'

'I can't boil it, can I? No electric.'

'Oh yes, sorry, 'course.' Signy laughed.

Michelle was looking at her. 'So. Can I come in?'

'Yes. Sorry.'

She must stop apologising. She stood aside to let Michelle enter but the hallway was too narrow for two people to stand side by side. There was a dance while they negotiated who would go first.

'Hi, Jed. Hi, Matthew.'

Michelle waved flaccidly as she passed the living room. Signy followed her into the kitchen. Jed ran forward, launching himself around Michelle's knees, almost tipping her sideways, his nose level with her crotch.

'We're building a house out of sticks!'

Michelle's hand went out to the wall. 'Sounds lovely.'

On Michelle's feet were Nikes with gold and pink flowers decorating the uppers. Michelle caught Signy's eye.

'Customised them myself.'

'I can see. Nice.'

'Made from recycled ocean plastic.' Michelle spotted the camping stove. 'Portable cooker?'

'Yeah.'

She hoped Michelle wouldn't expect to borrow that as well.

The two women stood in the middle of the kitchen, Michelle's eyes roving. Her gaze fell on the saucepans of water sitting on the hob.

'Filled those up already?'

'Well. You *know*.' Signy waved a hand in the air. She nodded at Jed, who was busy retrieving a rubber-tipped arrow from beneath the table. 'Go and play in the other room, monkey.' She

48

chivvied him out. Her voice dropped. 'I'm worried, honestly.'

'Yeah. Me too.'

'Anyway, here's the tap – I'll fill you a bucket. It's been sterilised. Our cleaner, Vesi, is amazing.' She wished she hadn't said that.

Signy fetched the bucket from underneath the sink and hit the tap. Water spat and coughed, then gushed out. When the bucket was half-full, the water pressure weakened. She watched as the stream became a trickle, a steady drip, then dribbled away to nothing.

'Matthew!'

He entered the kitchen fast, Jed in his slipstream. They clustered around the sink, Jed shifting foot to foot at Matthew's flank.

'What's wrong, Mama?'

'Nothing, love.'

'Is it no water?'

'No. I mean, yes. It is no water.'

'That's not good, is it?'

Michelle was curling her fingers around the handle of the bucket and lifting it from the sink. Signy had that whooshing feeling again. She put a hand on Michelle's arm.

'I'm so sorry.'

Michelle's eyes were big. 'What d'you mean?'

'I didn't know ours had run out. You can have one glass. But we'll need the rest of that for Jed. I'm sorry.'

'But you've got three saucepans on the oven.'

'Yes, but there are three of us living here, including a child.'

'But I'm pregnant.'

There was silence.

Matthew and Signy stood next to one another, shoulders touching. Michelle frowned.

They all stared at the bucket.

'Have you got apple juice?' Jed's voice, like a bell.

'No, sweetheart, I haven't got no apple juice.'

'We have.'

He went to the fridge. He handed Michelle some warm, fermented juice.

Signy scooped up a glass of water from the bucket, swallowing the lump in her throat.

'Like I said, I'm really sorry, Michelle. I think we'd all just better get on now.'

Why was she being so horrible? Why wasn't she *sharing*?

'Okay. Sure.' Michelle stared out of the kitchen window at the sky.

Matthew laid a palm on Signy's shoulders. He took a step forward.

'I'm so sorry we can't be of more help, Michelle. I really don't think this will go on long. We'll make it up to you when it's fixed.' He smiled.

Michelle left with the apple juice carton and her one glass of water. Signy's hands shook as she closed the door.

'We need to go to a shop and buy water, *now*.'

'Calm, Sig.'

'I am calm, for fuck's sake!'

'Mama, you sound really angry.'

'I'm not angry, I'm worried.' It was herself she was furious with, for not sharing, for not thinking of a possible water shortage before. 'We can't drink from streams or rivers. It's got to be bottled.'

Both boys were looking at her.

'Why?' said Matthew.

'Hallo? Bovine Staph?'

'Where do you think our rainwater condenses from?' he said. 'And yet we're all still alive, amazingly.'

'Yeah, but we're not drinking rainwater, are we?'

'Well, perhaps we should start?'

'No, too risky. There's clean water in the shops. And – "we're all still alive"? I think you'll find several million dying people in far-off countries would disagree with you on that.'

'Yeah,' added Jed. 'And all the beetles that brought Bovine Staph here, Dada. We don't want to get it. Miss Yue said your skin gets boiled.'

'Boils,' she corrected. 'I—'

'And then your blood's poisoned. That's what's happening to thousands of poor people in other countries where they have no medicines and it's hot. Because of the beetle blight, because of us.'

'We know, love,' she said. 'Matt—'

'Because grown-ups chopped down the rainforest and used too many chemicals everywhere and made nuclear leaky and ate animals they shouldn't, and now the sun is burning everything through the great big hole in the sky and it's really hot everywhere, especially over Asia.'

'We *know*, I said. Jed, I'm trying to speak.'

Matthew gave her a look.

'See?' He put his hand on top of Jed's head. 'Sweetheart, don't worry, we're not at risk here. There are nanodrugs in the UK, environmental laws. Now, we'll go to the shop and it'll all be *fine*. We need to think *slowly* and *clearly*.'

'*Thank* you.' She slipped her UV glasses on and helped Jed to put on his. 'Matt.' She held a fresh pair out for him.

'No.'

Matthew walked out of the door. Fine; let him go blind.

They exited the flat and turned towards Hornsey Road.

Rubbish gathered around bins in front gardens. Bits of paper wrapping and cardboard cartons were blowing about. Someone had placed an empty can of beer on top of the next-door neighbours' garden wall. It sat there glinting, the wind making a faint whistle across the opening in the lid.

The little Malaysian café where they'd bought the spring rolls was closed but the mini-market opposite was open. A queue of people waited outside. People wanting things. She took Matthew's hand. It felt dry, reassuring.

They stood at the back of the line.

'I'm sorry,' she said. 'I should have thought to buy water earlier.'

'It's not your fault.'

The queue crawled along until they were finally inside the shop, moving at a snail's pace between aisles until they reached the lane with the cleaning products. At the end, by the disinfectant, were three five-gallon water containers on the floor. Signy tried not to push as two were snaffled up by the man just ahead.

'Greedy.'

Matthew shuffled forward. He clapped a hand on the remaining one and spun it out of position in front of the bottles of Alibaba.

'For God's sake, this lot have got the last one,' said a woman behind.

'Sorry,' said Signy, shoulders lifting, but she wasn't sorry. Not at all.

The container slid along the floor between Matthew's legs until it was their turn to pay at the till.

'Forty-five Lites.' The woman behind the counter had a poker face.

Signy laughed. Matthew said, 'Don't be ridiculous.'

'High demand. Take it or leave it.'

'Let's go to another shop.'

Signy turned towards the door.

'Get it here, love,' said a man on his way out. 'It's more expensive in the garage. Just been. And at Auchan up the other end.'

'Excuse me.' The woman waiting directly behind Signy tapped her on the shoulder. 'You don't want to share, do you? That way it's half-price.'

'Sorry, we need the whole thing,' Signy said. 'We've got a *massive* family.'

The woman looked away.

Matthew dug in his jeans pocket and brought out a wad of coin-cards, sliding them with exaggerated care across the countertop. He reached forty-five Lites. The last card teetered at the counter lip, before flipping over on to the woman's feet.

'There's your money.' Matthew hoisted the water onto his shoulder. 'Hope you enjoy spending it.'

They walked home in silence. Her mind was tired, as though it had spent all day solving problems.

'I forgot to get batteries for the torch!'

'Forget it,' said Matthew.

At the front door, Jed touched the palm-plate.

'Ouch. Plate's hot.'

The door didn't open. Jed stared at his hand, rubbed it on his trousers a few times and slapped it back on the plate with force. He turned to her.

'Broken.'

'Hang on.'

Signy placed her palm onto the plate: it was as hot as the car charging-ports yesterday.

Matthew tried his palm. Nothing. They stepped back a couple of paces, squinting at the roof.

'The solar panels aren't cracked, are they?' she said. 'If the mechanism is broken, why is the plate hot? Hot means power passing through, right?'

She really didn't want to have to speak to Michelle again after the episode in the kitchen.

'Fuck's sake.' Matthew rang Michelle's doorbell.

'Fucksake,' said Jed.

'Jed!'

'Dada said it.'

Michelle's doorbell chimed out its five-chord structure. The notes ascended into a saccharine antepenultimate cadence. Every time she heard it, Signy longed to put her fingers in her ears.

She jogged from foot to foot on the doorstep.

'Waiting for front doors to open always makes me want to pee,' she said.

'Me too,' said Jed.

Matthew snorted. 'You both need your bladders testing.'

Behind the pebbled acrylic panes in the door, a bobbly shadow moved. The lock sprang from the inside and Michelle stood in the door. She was frowning, her arms wide. Signy stepped forwards.

'Sorry to disturb. The lock's died on the communal door.'

Michelle shook her head. 'Oh.'

Matthew said, 'We've bought some water from the shop – you can have some if you like.'

'Oh. Right. Thanks.'

Michelle reversed down the hall and disappeared behind the door to her flat, emerging a few seconds later with a large saucepan. Matthew unscrewed the cap on top of the water container. He poured it out carefully into Michelle's saucepan until the pan was almost full. Michelle thanked them again and went back into her flat. She kicked the door closed behind her.

Signy climbed the stairs. How would they manage to go in and out of the house safely without a working lock? Matthew was on the top step, peering at the palm-plate on the door to their flat.

'Ours is locked too. Stupid bloody thing.'

'What?'

'I'm hungry,' Jed said.

'Don't panic. We just need a screwdriver.'

Matthew went back down the stairs and knocked on Michelle's door. Michelle poked her head out.

'Yes?'

Matthew explained. He went into Michelle's flat. He came back with a red-handled Phillips, a medium-sized penknife and a tin of WD-40. Signy raised her eyebrows. He smiled.

'You never know.'

She watched him being busy, his body bent in an L-shape, face pressed close against the lock. She stared at the strip of skin exposed above the line of his jeans. What if they weren't able to get in? Where would they go?

There was a loud cracking sound and the front of the palm-plate flew off into Matthew's chest. He fiddled with the wires inside the console. The lock moved inside the door frame. The door opened.

'Well done!' She patted him on the back. 'How did you manage that?'

'I have my uses.'

'Dada, you are brilliant.' Jed covered Matthew's arm in kisses.

Michelle's door opened again.

'Oh, you done it.' She stared at the broken palm-plate. 'I meant to say, have you had any drones been coming round?'

'Drones?' Signy's jaw tightened. 'Pollen-drones or police drones?'

'Them blue police ones. Normally they're higher up, aren't they, unless you've done a crime. Now they're right outside my window.'

'What? When?'

'When you were out.'

'We saw one in the park killing itself,' Jed said. 'Didn't we, Mama?'

Matthew looked at her. 'Did you?' He turned back to Michelle. 'Let us know if you see them around our house again.'

Michelle nodded and left them to it.

In the kitchen Signy opened the camping stove.

'Why are the drones hanging around *our* house? What's special about us?'

Matthew shrugged. 'Beats me.'

She attached the rubber nozzle to the gas canister and poured a small amount of water into a pan to boil. They ate noodles with tinned water chestnut, tinned dace, and oil. It tasted good.

Without thinking, she went to the sink and pushed the lever up. She stared at the silent tap. A fresh bud of anxiety blossomed in her chest.

'We can save that water for another meal,' said Matthew. 'Put a plate over it.'

'And yet ...'

'And yet what?'

'You were the one who chucked away all those pans I'd filled. Luckily, I filled them up again.'

'Sig. Please. The dirty stuff can go out onto the terrace and be washed by rain.'

'If we have any more.'

She carried the plates out to the back, grumpily. She heard

Matthew send Jed upstairs to play. He joined her on the terrace, an empty bucket in his hands. He put it next to the plates.

'Rainwater,' he said, 'for drinking. Just in case.'

'Buckets for dodgy rainwater. I can't believe this is where we are. It's nuts.' She sniffed the air. 'What's that smell? Like a men's urinal?'

'Our loo,' he said. 'Let's sit in the garden.'

They descended the uneven concrete steps to the tiny square of garden they shared with Michelle, and sat beside each other on the wooden bench. She rested her face in her hands, enjoying the feeling of her elbows digging into her knees.

'We should call my brother, and your sister, and try your parents, Matt.'

And Gethin, she thought but didn't say, for information.

Matthew grunted.

'What?'

'Don't you think we should keep the Scope for an emergency?' he said.

'What about the extra police drones, their weird behaviour, not just around our house but everywhere?'

'What about them?'

'What do you think they're up to?'

He sighed. 'I dunno. Checking everything since it's gone odd.'

They fell silent.

A buzzing sound. Six drones flew overhead, arranged in two triangles of three, and disappeared into the estate behind them.

'See? Checking up.'

'Well, I don't like it,' she said.

Matthew pulled out a cigarette. A proper one, with tobacco in it. She stared.

'A fag? Where'd you get that relic?'

'Work. Met knows a guy who knows a guy.' He lit the cigarette with an old disposable lighter and inhaled deeply. 'Seemed like as good a time as any to have it.' He looked good when he smoked.

The afternoon was passing. A second night without light approached. Tinned water chestnut churned in her stomach. She held her hand out.

'Give us a puff.' The cigarette made her head spin. 'Disgusting.' She handed it back to him.

Matthew took another toke. 'We need to stay positive. Trust me, I'll look after you.'

'Oh. Thanks. And I'll look after you.'

'Women's lib.'

'Jeez, Matt, it's not the twentieth century.'

He grinned when she said that.

The sun came out from behind a cloud, shining light on the back of his head, and for a moment he had a halo.

'We just need to stick together,' she said. 'I wouldn't want to be alone during something like this.'

'Yeah, who would you argue with then?'

That made her laugh. She reached over to kiss his cheek, her arms curling around his neck. When she moved to sit on his lap, the gesture seemed to take them both by surprise and it was a second before he returned her embrace. He broke away first.

'Please don't worry,' he said, 'it's—'

'All going to be fine. I know.'

He kissed her briefly on the mouth. He tasted strongly of tobacco. She waited in case he would try to kiss her again. Her decision to be loving towards him had brought out a latent entitlement in her, an expectation she'd be loved in return. She would have to do more to earn it.

'I'm going inside to try Mum again.'

She went back into the house.

From the living room, Jed's woeful American accent drifted down the stairs. 'I carn't help you, Spidermarn. I'm jurst the Green Arrow, it's harrrd being me.'

She sat sideways on the stool and called her mother. She ran her finger over the film of dust that still resolutely clung to the piano lid.

'*Relaunching your career? Tune in your head? Gonna make us some money?*'

Matthew's voice, his teasing on any normal day, if she'd brought out her new music pad. Perhaps not now. That had been why she'd hidden it, she realised. Perhaps she needn't have bothered.

'Mamaaaa!' came Jed's voice. 'Can we play hide-and-seek?'

She sighed. 'Yes, love, okay.'

He appeared at the living-room door holding a Lego car he'd designed himself and wearing a blue Batman cape. A black plastic knife was stuffed into the top of his jeans, the handle just poking out of the top.

'Smooth criminal,' she said.

Jed's nose wrinkled. 'How can a criminal be smooth, silly? I'm hiding first. Count to thirty. No, forty. No, wait … Thirty-three point six recurring. It's my favourite.'

He dashed back up the stairs. She waited.

'Coming, ready or not!'

He wasn't in the kitchen.

'Where could he be?'

She mounted the stairs, looking in Jed's room, under his bed and in his cupboards. She went into her bedroom. Jed liked to hide under their bed too, but not today. She opened the cupboards, pushing her hand noisily through the hangers. She listened for the usual rustle, Jed's sound-trail, like a poltergeist.

'He must be upstairs, then!'

She walked up the final flight into the bathroom, in case he was hiding in the shower cubicle. No.

In the spare room she peered under the bed. He wasn't there. She went to the attic doors.

'Hallo? Jed? You in there?' He couldn't have gone out of the house without her knowledge, could he? It was hot in the attic. 'Okay! I give up!' It was the first time ever that she'd failed to find him.

'Mama!' His voice crowed through the attic hatch. 'Look where I am!'

He was buried under a mess of sleeping bags and sheets and invisible behind a baffle of boxes.

'Good place.'

'I think I heard a mouse,' he said.

'Well, that's okay.'

It was not okay if he'd heard a mouse.

'Come and lie in my den. We can pretend we're bears.'

She didn't want to lie down in the attic but she nodded. Jed pulled her in beside him. His breath tickled her ears. Cobwebs swagged from the pitched roof. She wanted to reverse out but Jed dug his torso further under the sleeping bags, trapping her. She kept her breathing slow and deep.

'Gosh, it's dark.'

'I know,' he giggled. 'Grrrrr. I'm hibernating.'

The attic smelt of unwashed canvas. She heard Matthew's steps on the stairs.

'Hallooo?'

'We're in here! We're in our den! Watch out, we're bears.'

Jed popped his head from under the nylon, his hair sticking up with static.

She crawled out from the blankets. Dust floated in the slanting light. Matthew's head was in the attic.

'Very good, guys.'

Jed growled and pulled the plastic knife from his jeans. He charged at Matthew, who retreated. The two of them rolled around the spare room bed.

'I stabbed you, Dada. You're killed!' Matthew pretended to be dead for a long time; too long. Jed prodded. 'Dada. Dada? Wake up, Dada.' He shook Matthew's shoulder.

'Come on, Matt, don't tease him. He's worried.'

Signy rubbed the dust from her jeans and breathed in the cool fresh air outside the attic. For a moment she forgot about the lack of water, the dead laptops, the empty shops, and was swallowed by the immediate present, her two boys play-fighting and laughing. She hadn't realised she'd been smiling until a red-faced Jed said he was thirsty and asked her what was funny. He left his plastic knife on the bed and they plodded downstairs to the kitchen, where they drank sparingly from the water container, after which all three of them got to work on the little wooden house.

Day 4

During the night her sleep was interrupted by two helicopters flying overhead. Then much later, near dawn, shouting in the street. She woke first, nudging Matthew's shoulder. He grunted and went straight back to sleep.

She nudged him again.

'*Matt*. What's happening out there?'

'Out where? You've woken me up.'

'There's something happening. Can you have a look?'

'Now?'

'Yeah.'

He sighed but felt his way to the window.

'Okay. There's a fight going on between a man and two women. They sound drunk.'

She went to join him, a T-shirt in front of her chest. She leant over the sill and looked down. The early light was dim and chalky.

A man in a baseball cap, the letters NYPD stitched in white above the peak, was wrestling a bottle from a woman. Another woman stood beside him, a passive accomplice.

'... scrounging. Warren told me that ain't even his flat!'

Signy's neighbours peered out of windows.

'I will *cut* you!'

'Fuck's sake.' Matthew drew his head inside.

'Why don't you say something?'

'They're off their faces.'

Signy made a noise.

'What?' Matthew glared. 'They don't look like the nicest people. Okay, fine.' He leant far out, tummy expanding across the sill. 'Excuse me! Some of us are trying to sleep. Can you be quiet?'

'Come down here and say that, you posh cunt.'

Signy dodged out of sight behind the wall.

Matthew glanced sideways. 'Happy now?'

She shrank further into the shadows. 'Not my fault.'

The pigeons squawked in the gutter next door, disturbed from their sleep, just like them.

'I see you! You at number ...' A scrabbling of feet and the man's voice shouting with such intensity that his voice split. 'I will fucking *do* you!'

One of the women yelped like an animal. Matthew threw on his trousers.

'What are you doing?' Signy whispered. 'You're going down there?'

'They've got her in a headlock. The one with the bottle. He's punching the living daylights out of her. Fuck. For God's sake, a minute ago you were telling me to get involved. Stay here.'

He left the room, pounded down the stairs.

'Let *go* of her!' Matthew's shout bounced off the buildings opposite.

Scuffling.

The woman: 'I'm all right. Fuck off.'

'You're not all right. He was punching you!'

The man in the NYPD cap: 'Yeah? You want some? Come on then.'

Matthew: 'Woah, woah, woah. Mate, slow down.'

Shit shit shit. She should go and help him. No, she mustn't leave Jed alone.

Things went quiet.

Signy waited in the dark, ears straining. Matthew again: 'Look, I'm sorry. Let's all calm down and go home.'

The sound of footsteps going away, returning.

'I won't forget you!'

'Right. Great,' said Matthew. 'Look forward to it.'

The front door slammed. Matthew stomped up the stairs. He entered the bedroom, breathing hard.

'He still out there?' Signy was shivering. 'You all right? Fuck. Now they know where we live.'

'Where *I* live.' Matthew marched to the bedroom window. He slammed down the sash. 'He's a fucking nutcase.'

He got back into bed.

She stood listening as the argument moved off down the road. She climbed in beside him, pulling the covers around her chin.

'I'm sorry. For making you do that.'

''S okay. I'm fine.'

'What will we do if this doesn't get better?' Matthew didn't answer. 'I can't stop thinking about Gethin's words. I mean, should we try to get to Warston and stick it out with Mum? Gethin might be there, we could—'

'All right, shut up about Gethin now.'

'Warston's much more' — she searched for the word — 'remote. And Mum's kidneys. We could come back when everything has calmed down.'

'How do you think we're going to get there? It's ninety miles away.'

'Eighty-four.'

He gave a short bark of laughter. 'All right, eighty-four, for God's sake.'

'Ssh. You'll wake Jed. It was just an idea.' Her voice had gone all small.

'Don't think it's one of your best. This will be sorted. Okay?'

'Okay. Matt?'

'Yes?'

'Do you think the internet carried on working for a while after everything else went wrong because whoever, or whatever, has taken control of our systems needed it to control the drones?'

'I don't know. Maybe. What difference would it make if it had? Sig, stop thinking. You're supposed to stop thinking at night.'

'I can't. I'm scared.'

He touched her arm closest to him under the covers.

'I know, love. Hold your nerve for Jed.'

'Okay.'

'Don't worry. I'm going to take care of us.'

'Yeah.'

He kissed her on the forehead, squeezed her leg. She stroked the top of his arm with her fingers. The flesh felt soft, unhoned. He fidgeted for a while, sat up to try the radio again – more static – and fell asleep with one earphone hissing in his ear.

She longed to sleep. She lay there looking at him, his breath releasing through his mouth, his lips making a puffing noise.

Her toes felt cold.

An hour passed without sleep. Feeling thirsty, she crept downstairs, the day still at half-light, for a glass of water. Her head was full of shadows. Drinking the water supply when neither Matthew nor Jed were there to have their share felt somehow wrong. She'd have only one glass.

A black and white advert from an old magazine hung on the wall, proof of her mother's short-lived modelling career. A studio shot, her mother's body, thin and elegant like a ballerina. The product was a black dance leotard for a long-gone company. On a dark-coloured mat her mother knelt, hands resting on her kneecaps. Her blonde hair had been tied at the side, a smile that reached beyond the lens right into Signy's core as she stood now in this kitchen, more than forty years later.

She was still thirsty.

She took herself out to the back terrace. Michelle's white cat sat on the uneven stone steps.

'Hey, Oscar.'

She beckoned to him but he wouldn't come.

The city was quiet, the sun rising on the other side of the house, a soft wind blowing the shrubs in the garden. Pink aquilegia fronted up to the sky at the edges of the raised beds, wildly out of their traditional flowering time. In the last five years, the seasons had changed as quick as the wind. She still couldn't fathom it.

The chocolate-brown estate that backed on to their house was disconcertingly still. The small back road, the one that separated their garden from the estate, was empty. She thought she could hear music somewhere, but couldn't work out which direction it was coming from. It sounded like upstairs. She should count out the time signature, recognise the key – she should use her skills.

She should, she should, she should. What should she? Music college, moderate success, then Jed. She'd let it all float away. She should have trained as an electrical engineer. That way, she'd be good for something now, be useful, have made a sodding living.

The acrid scent of burning rubber. What might have caused such a smell? Looters; a car; a shop on fire; someone's house; a bonfire to get rid of rubbish. None of this was good.

She looked down at her toenails, square and neat, painted red by Pru at Top Spa & Massage on Holloway Road only two weeks ago, beginning to chip now. What was Pru doing at the moment? Not pedicures.

A police drone was close; she could hear it – too close. It rose up from behind the wooden slats of the terrace fence – the micro-sized version of a helicopter appearing over the horizon in a film – and hovered right in front of her face. She could see herself reflected in its eye.

'Hallo?'

She waved, as if the action could somehow convert the strangeness of its presence into something ordinary.

Then it was gone, shooting directly into the sky, taking a sudden right turn in mid-air. Now it was just a speck. Spying on her. Spying on everyone.

'Sig!' Matthew's voice carried down the stairs. 'I've got reception on the radio!'

She ran up to join him. Jed emerged from his room, meeting her on the landing with his hair all over the place.

'Is it morning?'

Signy pulled him into her bedroom and they waited on the edge of the mattress next to Matthew, heads turned, listening to the radio.

'Is it music?' said Jed.

Open-throated 'voices' ululated atonally over a sustained bass. A throb that came and went, a pulsing heartbeat of a sound. The close harmonies moved through F sharp major and C sharp minor. Nine-eight time. The pulse was too fast. Her heart seemed to increase speed to keep up with it.

'Weird,' breathed Matthew.

'Weird,' said Jed, looking at his father. A second later, she felt his hot little hand on her arm. 'Wait! I know this. It's code!'

'What d'you mean, monkey?'

'It's TrincXcode.'

'No, love. I've heard TrincXcode. It doesn't sound like this. It's much more digital-sounding.'

'That's the *old* version. We use the new one in CDT for 3D-printing. It sounds like people singing, but it isn't. You have to programme it in with the app – it looks like a set of piano keys and everything.'

'But why would TrincX be playing on the radio?'

'I don't know,' he said. 'But I know that's what it is! It's lines of code that come out as sounds and beats instead of numbers, running all at once, over each other. That's why it's actual music.'

She looked at Matthew.

Her palms were wet.

'At school, we built that copy of Tower Bridge with Miss Yue using TrincX. I got "Good as Gold" for programming the top. Remember?'

Gethin had given her a demonstration of TrincX a few years back, when they'd bumped into one another in Warston.

'See, Sig?' he'd teased, holding the GScope to her ear. 'Computers that make music *and* do jobs. Your lot'll be redundant before you know it.'

Your lot. The artists. The dreamers.

'I should have been an engineer,' she said out loud.

Matthew and Jed looked at her, brows drawn down.

The radio went silent. GQOS spoke one or two sentences in an Asian-sounding language. More static. Then, fuzzy and indistinct, a human voice.

'X-ray, Delta, Charlie, ... grss ... shut ... ssss ... perrni ... sss ... override. Over.'

'Who the hell is that?' She put her ear close to the speaker.

'The police? Military?'

The radio went silent again. They waited. Nothing.

'A police drone just appeared right outside the back door,' she said. 'It was nose to nose with me, Matt. I think it was filming me.'

'Why would it be filming you?'

'I don't know!'

'Paranoia.'

'A blue drone? Here, in our house?' Jed looked terrified.

Matthew stood suddenly. 'Okay. Things are getting silly. We need to keep calm. We need to get hold of our friends.'

She shook her head. 'No. We should go and get the car.'

'Not yet. We'll be safer when there's more of us. I need to do something. I'm going to James and Aya's.'

'Now?'

'Yes. What time is it?'

She looked at her watch. 'Seven-thirty in the morning. I don't think you've thought this through, Matt. What are you going to do when you get there?'

'Bring them here.'

'We don't have enough food and water to share.'

'Please don't argue,' said Jed.

'We're not arguing, monkey.' She ruffled his hair.

'They have a little baby, for God's sake,' Matthew was saying. 'Anyway, they might have food and water of their own. To share. With us.' He was buckling his belt.

'If we go to get the car, there's a whole stash of nanobiotics and VireX in the boot left over from Dad. I didn't throw them out.'

He stopped then. 'Right. Why in your madness do you think we need nanobiotics now? Who's ill?'

'No one. I'm saying *in case*.'

'You've got your priorities wrong. Someone's hacking our systems.'

'Yes. Okay. That's what I think.' She mustn't cry.

'Who's hacking our systems, Mama?'

'No one, love.'

Matthew's shirt went on.

'We won't find answers sitting here. We have to stay strong until it passes. Which it will. And we'll be even stronger as a group. You're the one always moaning at me to behave in a more dynamic fashion.'

'It's just ... my instinct says we should leave London.'

'One thing at a time. We have to approach this logically.'

'But what about the car? Shouldn't we fetch that at some point soon? We need it.' Her voice had gone all high.

'We can get it tomorrow.'

'Can I come with you, Dada?'

'No, sweetheart. You stay with Mama. I'll be back soon.'

'We could all go?' she said. Everything was happening too fast.

'It's better if you stay here. Look, Sig, I know you don't think I behave like *that* kind of person very often, but now I need to do things that a person who does things like that does.' He took her hand and smiled. 'If you get my drift? Don't be scared. It's going to be fine. Okay?'

She nodded. Jed mustn't worry about her being worried. Downstairs, she filled a Thermos with water, pushing it at Matthew on his way out. He put his hands on her shoulders.

'I'm a big boy. I can look after myself.'

'Jed and I will have to stay in the house while you're out or we won't be able to get back in.'

'No you won't. Ask Michelle.'

She wasn't going to ask Michelle. She wasn't going to rely on anybody else.

'Try to get some batteries,' she called.

'I will.'

'Don't forget!'

He hugged Jed at the front door.

'Glasses!' she shouted as he walked away. 'You forgot your UVs!'

He was already gone.

She closed the front door.

'I'd like to watch something on the Holoscreen now,' Jed said, hands on hips.

'You can't, darling, remember?'

'Oh yeah,' he laughed. 'Silly me.'

She picked him up and kissed him, as if her fears were hidden in his face and she could spirit them away.

'Ugh. Too much!' He wiped his cheek.

'I'll get you some breakfast and read you a story.'

'Mama. I might … might … be able to read you a story.'

He wanted Millet Crispies. She filled the bowl with cereal, then added a small amount of water. Matthew's old red lighter was on the table. She put it in her pocket.

'This tastes yucky without milk,' said Jed. They shared a browning rambutan. 'We should cook that today –' Jed pointed at the yam – 'for lunch.'

He fetched a book from his room: Beatrix Potter's *The Tale of Peter Rabbit*.

'I don't like Mr Mack Wrecker,' he said, climbing onto her lap. 'He's nasty to Peter.'

71

'*Once upon a time ...*' she began.

When she reached the part about five currant buns, Jed said, 'I don't like raisins, which are the same as currants, aren't they? Peter's a thief, isn't he, Mama? He steals vegetables from Mack Wrecker and that's not right.'

'I suppose so, but he *is* very hungry,' she said.

She continued until Mr McGregor searches for Peter in the tool shed. Jed hid his face behind his hands. She stroked the curve of his back.

'It's not real, you know.'

'He runs and runs, doesn't he? And doesn't look back until he gets to his cosy home?'

'Exactly.' She tried to think where Matthew might be.

She read to the end and closed the book. Jed looked at her.

'Have we got any blackberries?'

'Jed, you know the new version of TrincXcode you were telling us about? What else can it do?'

'Nothing. Just building. And it sounds nice. Sometimes we make tunes with it when we have Golden Time.'

'But how does it work? How does music make code? How is it different and more advanced?'

He sighed. 'Really? It's complicated.'

'That's why I'm asking.'

'The way the notes are arranged, Miss Yue said. It's called a constellation. It creates a ...' His forehead wrinkled. '... Quantum field which allows the system to work out infinite possibilities.'

'What do you mean, "infinite possibilities"?'

'The system can work out in milliseconds every possible outcome that can happen from any action it takes in multiple universe models and make the best choice.'

He hopped off her lap and went to the door.

'Wait. Best choice for whom? For what?'

'For whatever it's been programmed for. So, if it's a MediX, it's for the person they're looking after. If it's a CheX, it's for Lianhua or another supermarket. If it's an Agrico-bot, it's for the field or wherever it's been programmed to work.'

She thought for a second. 'So the algorithm for gas and electricity and water – who or what is that programmed to make the best choice for? Planet Earth? The homeowner, the electricity company? Or what?'

His shoulders shrugged in frustration. 'I don't know. We didn't learn about them.' He went back upstairs. A moment passed and he called from his room, 'Mama, did you know TrincX was invented by a woman? She's called Lau-Chen and she lives in Scotland. That's good, isn't it?'

'That she's a woman?'

'That she lives near us.'

That unknown language in GQOS' voice. Perhaps it was terrorists. Perhaps it was that *Shǐluò zhǐ* group.

Jed brought down a five-hundred piece puzzle called 'Carolling at Christmas with Santa'. He picked out the reindeer feet and antlers, she found the edge pieces. She glanced at the sky. It was so blue, it made her want to weep.

They went into the garden to play, Signy wary in case the drone returned. Dirty plates greeted her on the terrace. To her left she found her neighbours sitting on plastic chairs in their garden: the two old brothers – Ken and the other one.

'Hi.' She waved.

The men looked up, nodding sleepily.

'Hallo, darlin'. We trying to relax, stay calm. This thing gonna pass. The sun rise and the sun set, d'you know what I saying? Soon come. We sit here and wait. We stay nice.'

'It nice to be nice,' the other brother said. 'You okay?'

'Yes,' Signy said, because it's what you say when someone asks if you're okay. Then she said, 'Has your water gone off?'

'Yeah. The church bring us some spare, you know?'

Ken blinked in the bright sun. 'You hear about them cleaning machines coming over to work for the police now? Them BinX.'

Jed giggled. 'You say it "BinZ" with a Z at the end, like in "Xylophone". Like we say "iCanZ", instead of "iCanX".'

'Really?' Ken frowned. 'But it an X. Why we got to say it like that?'

He shrugged. 'That's just how it is.'

'Make no sense.' Ken turned to his brother, who was chuckling. 'You know that? Anyway, the "*BinZ*" all been pimped. Church say the police using them now. It all futuristic.'

'I saw that on *Newsbites*!' exclaimed Jed. 'But I haven't seen one with the police in real life yet. My mummy doesn't like the BinX.' He gave her a smile.

'Well ...' she said.

'Me either,' said the other brother. 'Even the spelling you can't trust.'

'Exactly.' She picked at the crumbling brick on the terrace wall.

'How old are you?' Jed asked Ken. 'Are you a hundred?'

'Jed!' she said.

The two old men started laughing hard then.

'Yes, pickney. We ninety-eight and ninety-nine respective. Seen the world spin long time. Seen a few thing.'

BinX machines: when they'd appeared last year at the very end of the blight, they'd given her the shivers. They were large, seven feet or more, shiny, black and completely silent as they moved about sucking up rubbish from wherever, with their huge hoses like elephants' trunks. Most disconcerting of all, like the Magtransport, the BinX didn't touch the floor but floated several feet above the earth. Why were so many things detached from the ground these days? What was wrong with being earthed?

'We going in now, darlin',' called Ken. 'It nothing you said, we getting something to eat. You take care, you hear? Anything you want, just come knocking. Door open to you twenty-four hour of the day.'

'Thank you. I will,' she said.

The men got up slowly and went indoors.

'The BinX are working with the police?' said Jed. 'That will be *sage*.'

'Yeah. Come on.'

They made their way down the uneven stone steps and perched on the wooden bench in the garden, squinting into the sun as Jed pushed his Hot Wheels around the edge of the raised bed. Michelle's washing hung over a drying rack in the side-return: hot-pink sports socks, hot-pink lacy pants. She pushed away the image of Michelle in them.

Low voices whispering too close to the wooden fence at the back of the garden and a scratching sound. The ivy shook. Two hands appeared, gripping the splintered slats. She leapt into the centre of the garden and took Jed's hand. The edges of his toy car dug into her palm. Someone's head was at the top of the fence: a man, red hair matting his forehead. For one irrational second she thought it might be Gethin.

'What are you doing?' Her voice was too loud.

'Oh, sorry, love. I'm looking for Frank.'

'Well, no one called Frank lives here.'

'Frank doesn't live here? Sorry to bother you, love. I thought he lived here.'

'I know. You just said. He doesn't.'

The head disappeared. She heard his body slither down the other side of the fence. Whispering. There must be two of them. Signy stayed still, legs trembling. The sound of feet shuffling off down the back road.

'Are they gone, Mama?'

She put her fingers to her lips. They crept up the steps onto the terrace. She had a good view from there. The men had gone. She went inside and slid the bolt across the back door.

Jed insisted they cook the yam for lunch with pinto beans. She peeled, chopped and used as little water as possible to boil on the gas stove. Maybe it was a good thing the BinX were working with the police? Maybe they'd control the looting, the weirdness.

The yam emerged from the pot twelve minutes later, starchy and sweet. They were running low on clean plates. After one mouthful, Jed put down his fork.

'I can't eat this tuber. It's *disgusting*.'

'Well, that's what there is for lunch, so you can eat it or go hungry.'

He made a face but ate it anyway, smothered in ketchup. Her GScope said eighteen per cent. She placed the dirty plates out the back with the others.

There was a throaty buzzing noise at the front of the house. They ran to the living room. A Kawasaki petrol bike streaked down the street, weaving between cars, metal thorax fat like a hornet.

Gethin's old bike. Her heart lurched. He'd come to find her after all. He would tell them what to do. She leant out of the window.

'Gethin!'

The bike would be around the corner any second. He wouldn't remember the house number she lived at and he'd miss her. She skidded down the stairs, through the front door and onto the street, Jed racing after her.

'Where you going?'

But the bike had gone.

She waited for it to return. Jed pulled at her sleeve.

'He was breaking the law, wasn't he, Mama, using petrol? The police are going to tell him off.'

'No.'

'Why not?'

'The police will be too busy.'

'Doing what?'

They went back inside. She sent Gethin a message: Was that you I just saw in Archway on your bike? Please answer. We've heard something peculiar on the radio this morning and I'm scared.

The day's heat was escaping up beyond the ceiling of blue sky as the afternoon scudded by. They pulled on jumpers and an extra pair of socks each. Later, she tried video-calling Gethin. The network wouldn't connect. She tried her mother. The battery made a dying sound. GQOS warned, 'You need to charge, Signy.' Seconds later, the screen went black.

'Fuck!'

She threw the GScope on the sofa. It disappeared between a crack in the cushions.

Matthew called up from the street. She went down to let him in. He arrived home without James and Aya, any food, or batteries.

'They weren't there.'

'What? Where would they have gone?'

He shrugged. She led him up the stairs.

'My Scope's dead. Are you okay?' He didn't answer. 'Matt?'

'I'm fine.'

He frowned at the kitchen window. If it was something bad, he didn't want to say in front of Jed.

'What's wrong, Mama?'

'Nothing, love. Dada couldn't find James and Aya. They've probably gone to see other friends.'

'What friends?'

'Just friends,' said Matthew.

She handed him a glass of water. Jed told him about the disgusting yam and how a man had looked over the garden wall. She didn't mention the motorbike; Matthew would think she'd gone mad.

'Are *you* all right?' he asked. His face was pale. His eyes looked very blue.

'Yeah. Feel slightly sick.'

'I need to wash my hands, they're filthy.'

She shook her head. 'We can't spare the water. You'll have to wait for a puddle in the bucket out the back.'

He turned his palms to her. They were coated in black oil.

'How did that happen?'

'Leant against a wall. It's gonna go over everything.'

'We can't use water for things like that. We can't. I'm sorry.'

'We can, for God's sake. I'll use a tiny amount. It's not hygienic.'

'Since when did you give a shit about hygiene?'

She stamped upstairs to the bathroom, annoyed now that she'd taken the care to pour the extra glass of water back into the container that morning when she was still thirsty. She returned with a packet of facial cleansing pads and threw them at Matthew's chest. They missed and hit the wall next to the photo of her mother in a leotard. A wet trail led in a straight line to the floor.

'I don't like it when you argue,' wailed Jed.

She turned her head away.

Jed went to bed wearing pyjamas and socks. He had a belly full of noodles, millet sticks, tinned dace and halva. She was shocked at how much water they'd used from the container already. Jed cleaned his teeth with a dry toothbrush, pinching his nose as he leant over the toilet to take a pee.

'Ugh. Mama, what are these insects?'

Blackflies. She slammed the lid down.

'Get into bed, love. Matt, there are bloody insects in here!'

Matthew's voice travelled up the stairs, echoing against the white tiles.

'If it rains heavily, we can tip a bucket of water down the cistern.'

'Can I have the bunny light on?'

Jed was sitting up in bed holding his favourite teddy, an otter he'd named XO.

She flicked the switch on the plastic night-light. The glow was imperceptible.

'Dada forgot to get batteries for the torch,' Jed said.

'I know, love. I'm so sorry. You'll be fine without a bright light. Daddy's here, and Mummy. All safe. Nothing to worry about.'

'Mama?'

'Yes?'

'How d'you know you're real? I mean, how d'you know?'

'Oh. That's an interesting question. Because, I suppose, I can feel inside myself that I'm real.'

'But how?'

'I don't know. How do you know *you're* real?'

'I just do.'

'Well, it's the same with me.'

'But are we not going to be real any more now everything has stopped working?'

'What d'you mean, sweetheart?'

'I don't know.'

'Jed, people have existed without light and Holoscreens and internet and GScopes for millions of years, so that's just what we'll keep doing. Existing.'

'Existing,' he repeated. He settled beneath the covers. 'Grandpa said God's mummy is Gaia and God's daddy is Time. They're still alive, Grandpa said. They might look like they're sleeping, but they've always got an eye open and one day they're going to get up.'

'And do what?'

He shrugged.

'But Grandpa didn't believe in God.'

'Yes he did – the cosmos.'

'You two had some good chats.'

'Yes. And I was only *very* little. Mama?'

'Yes?'

'My throat's sore.'

'I'm sure you'll feel better in the morning, love. Try to get some sleep.'

She went downstairs. Matthew was sitting at the kitchen table. Two of the white candles had been lit. She sat opposite him. His Light-Camera was on the tabletop. She tried to catch his eye.

'I'm sorry about earlier.'

''S fine.'

She pointed at the camera. 'You took photos? Can I see?'

He shook his head. 'I forgot to empty the cache.'

There was one solitary photograph: two homeless men grinning into the lens. Around the two men, shards of acrylic.

'Near that restaurant we went to the other night. The broken glass is from the shop behind them, which is for second-hand clothes. Why are people stealing old clothes, for fuck's sake?'

'Because they're scared. No one knows what's going on. It won't just have been us who heard those voices and the code on the radio today.'

'I didn't see any police when I was out. Not one, human or bot.'

'That's not possible. The brothers next door said the BinX machines are being repurposed for police use.'

'Well, I didn't see any of those either,' he said. It was almost a relief. 'There were some volunteer officers. They said the Police-X bots are all down, so I guess the BinX will be too, and the human police are completely overwhelmed. There's been a massive fire in South London, and a lot of what they call "civil unrest", surprise, surprise. They said there are people still stuck underground on the Tube. The fire services are trying to get them out.'

'But if the Police-X are down, and all the other bots, how come the drones are still working?'

'I have no idea. Maybe their juice lasts longer 'cos they're small?'

'But didn't you ask? I mean, did they say anything about a systems hack?' She changed position to get more air in.

'They were a bit cagey, to be honest. Maybe they didn't know. I don't think anyone's actually *sure*, Sig.'

They both considered this. She looked at the photo again. Something caught her eye.

'There. Look.' She put her fingernail into the far left corner of the picture, where the sky met the buildings: three dots in the sky. 'The drones again, but in a triangle shape. That's what I've been noticing. They're moving in triangles.'

Matthew stared. 'So? They're always out, checking on us. The little people. They're probably built to keep going for-ever.'

'But the way they're moving. It feels different.' She reached for his hand. 'Do you think James and Aya are okay?'

'They might have gone to that uncle of hers.' He nodded. 'Or the one she calls Auntie, the one who lives in Stoke Newington with the funny eye, who's not really her aunt.'

It made her think of Mum.

He smiled and stood, rubbing his eyes.

'What?' she said.

'Nothing.'

She kicked him gently on the shin. 'Jed says he has a sore throat.'

'So?'

'So. The nanobiotics and VireX are in the boot. I think we should go and get the car tomorrow. We can take the spare charger with us.'

'Nanos and VireX for Jed? Are you being a hypochondriac?'

'No. We need the car anyway.'

'Car's not going to work, Sig.'

'Please.'

''K. I'll go.'

She shook her head. 'We'll come with you.'

'No.'

'Yes.'

'We'll see.'

'Do you think Gethin meant *Shīluò zhī*, when he said he couldn't talk about it? Do you think he's all right?'

'I don't know, Sig. I'm sure he's fine.'

She was silent for a second. 'You forgot to get batteries for the torch.'

'Don't give me a hard time about that. I'm not in the mood.'

He left her alone in the kitchen with the candles burning.

She thought of her dad's hands. His palms had been square-shaped. She always pictured him sitting behind his telescope in his leather swivel chair, smiling at her through his half-moon glasses.

'Come here, darling,' he'd say in that soft Eastern European accent. 'Look through the lens. The universe is two mirrors, see? Look into one and you're reflected all the way to infinity. Somewhere out there are millions of "yous". Not all the Signys will be getting ready for bed, though. Now, have you brushed your teeth? Show me. I have a sixth sense for knowing if you're telling the truth.'

Day 5

Just outside Camden they came to a fork in the road.

They'd travelled fast to get here, on bikes. It had felt good to begin with, safe somehow, the sense of freedom growing as she pushed against the pedals. Still, after a while everything around her seemed to move fast too, catching her up, sealing her in with it all. Holloway Road had been a blur of people, a reedy rendering of 'Jerusalem' from a choir of women outside Upper Holloway Maglev station; the Fortess Road ice cream parlour, with its last splotches of melted blackcurrant and lemon swirls dripping into a kerbside drain; Kentish Town Road messy and broken; no police presence; trams stalled side by side in the road; a group of old men extorting food from passers-by under the guise of charity, their scam having a depressing inevitability to it; overhearing that police were attending a riot; so many drones everywhere, like a constantly shifting dot-to-dot against the sky; worst of all, James and Aya still not being in when, en route, they'd knocked a second time.

'Mama?' Jed's voice was weak.

'Yes, love?'

She wanted everything to be normal. She wanted answers. It wasn't good enough. This was supposed to be a civilised nation.

'When can I go back to school?'

'I don't know, monkey. Soon.'

He began to sing. For once, he was fantastically off-key.

He'd woken with a fever and problems swallowing. There'd followed a lengthy argument about the wisdom of carting a sick child across London on the back of a bike, but Signy had insisted. She'd had no desire to stay by herself in the flat with Jed. She wanted to be out in the world on her bike. Apart from the drugs inside the boot to help him, the car was their best chance of getting to Mum's. Jed, hot and swaying at the bottom of the communal stairs, had held tight to his toy otter, XO.

'No,' she'd told him. 'You might lose him. Then you'll be sad.'

'I won't.'

'XO stays here. It's non-negotiable.'

'I don't even know what that *means*.'

He'd dragged himself up the stairs and dumped XO on the landing.

Just before they'd left they'd knocked on Michelle's door; she'd asked for a bottle of Lucozade, if possible. They'd then discovered Ken and his brother on the pavement, boarding up their house, departing for some place safe with members of their church, which had made Signy feel sick inside, even though she'd told them she was happy they'd be safe.

Now here they were, near Camden, with Matthew carrying the rucksack, the extra car battery and a Thermos of water inside, Jed drooping in his seat behind her and she staring at the white lines on the fibreglass with a funny sensation growing inside her, a sort of homesick feeling, as if she were missing something, had left something behind. To the right, an ancient yellow diesel bulldozer was pushing abandoned cars to the side with its massive metal flat plate. Its caterpillar tracks moved steadily. The hydraulic arm created an ear-splitting crunch. She turned her head away and upwards to the broken traffic lights: they were now just three dull bobbles, dangling over the road at right angles on their pole.

'Let's go the other way!' Matthew had to shout to be heard. 'We can cut around the big Lianhua and head out up Parkway!'

Parkway was one-way, but she didn't suppose that mattered any more.

'Mama?'

'Yes, love.' She glanced over her shoulder. 'You okay?'

'I feel cold.'

A helicopter chopped overhead. The deafening noise ricocheted off the buildings.

The enormous Lianhua windows were empty metal frames surrounded by a sea of broken acrylic. Signy's arm went back for Jed. She could feel him shivering.

She looked at all the people. New tribes springing up. A headache bloomed. Only three in her tribe: Matthew, Jed and her. It wasn't big enough.

She glanced round; Jed was taking it all in, eyebrows pulled together more in puzzlement than alarm. Perhaps he was enjoying the change of routine. Beads of sweat around his hairline darkened his fringe. She wanted to say something, to make it all right for him, but she was floating above herself.

'You okay?'

Matthew's hand found her elbow. The helicopter's blades thwacked at the air above.

'This is too awful,' she said.

Matthew leant towards her. 'What? I can't hear you!'

'Oh, for God's sake, will that thing shut up?' She lifted her face to the sky.

Two flaps in the helicopter's belly opened. A snow-flurry of papers tumbled out. Hundreds of them, fluttering and spinning, blown downwards in the vortex like sycamore seeds, until they touched the ground or were captured by people in the street. The helicopter banked to the left. It headed towards King's Cross. She watched it dump another batch further off. The pavement was now completely white. One had stuck to her boot. A black insignia at the top: a shield inside a circle with a crown above. She picked it up.

> A STATE OF NATIONAL EMERGENCY HAS BEEN DECLARED. WHILE THE GOVERNMENT IS TRYING TO RESOLVE THE CURRENT SITUATION, WE KINDLY REQUEST THAT YOU STAY CALM. WE HOPE TO HAVE NORMAL SERVICES UP AND RUNNING WITHIN 24 HOURS. MILITARY PERSONNEL WILL BE DRAFTED INTO YOUR AREA. YOU ARE REQUIRED BY LAW TO COMPLY WITH THEIR ORDERS. WE APOLOGISE FOR ANY INCONVENIENCE.

'Ministry of Defence' was written underneath. There was an accidental fingerprint in ink at the corner. She wondered who it belonged to.

'Why is the army being drafted if they plan to have everything fixed by tomorrow?' she said. 'Is this propaganda?'

'The MOD is on it, Sig.' Matthew read through slitted eyes. He whistled through his teeth. 'That's definitely what all the extra drones are about, as I said. Keeping eyes on us. It's gonna be sorted.'

'By tomorrow? You believe that?'

'I'm *optimistic*,' he said, as if the word might be unfamiliar to her.

'But they haven't explained anything.'

A family with four children carrying little rucksacks passed in front of them.

'At least it isn't raining,' she said.

They cycled on.

They passed the iCanX shop. The home-help humanoid robots virtually no one had ever been able to afford had been removed from the window display. In their place were female mannequins of varying ethnicities, their arms where their legs should have been and vice versa. Around their necks hung printed signs: *Burple Simp*, *Redarmande*, *Roycroft Briss*. Curious. She rolled the names silently across her tongue. They were unfamiliar to her eyes, though the feel of them in her mouth lit a pathway in her brain. Then she was past the shop too quickly, all thoughts taken with navigating the road before she could recall where she'd come across them before.

Past Camden Underground station, up Parkway. The bulldozer had done its work here already; cars were squashed against the kerb – glass, twisted metal. There was room on the road now to drive a vehicle. She had a sudden fantasy of them bringing their car home in a few hours, Jed's fever cooling with the VireX, travelling in the correct direction down this road like any normal day.

Matthew made for Regent's Park.

'What a bloody mess.'

They entered the park through Gloucester Gate. It suddenly went quiet. Carpets of green stretched left and right. Beneath the flat sky, crows and river gulls scattered and regrouped, pecking at litter. In the long avenue of balding trees a lone Jack Russell snuffled the grass near its owner.

'Where have all the pollen-drones gone?' said Jed.

How had she not noticed they'd disappeared?

'Maybe they've been recalled.'

'What for?'

'I don't know, love. None of us know.'

They stopped by a bench for a breather.

'Thing's heavier than it looks.'

Matthew plonked the rucksack on the path. They drank from the Thermos they'd brought from home, the water inside unsatisfyingly tepid. Jed had several gulps, then collapsed against her shoulder.

'All right, sweetheart?'

'Yeah.'

'Don't worry, we'll have medicine for you soon.'

Tired, she rested her neck on the top slat of the bench, put her face to the sky.

'If it's because the computers are out, why can't some boffin get it fixed?' The white clouds were almost blinding. 'Maybe we should get Jed on it.'

She fell into silence, enjoying the peace. A shrub poked up through the arm of the bench beside her. A solitary jewelled drop of moisture rested on its leaf. Where had it come from? She touched it with her finger. The water separated like mercury, spreading along the leaf-face. It dripped onto the cement and left a tiny circular stain. She longed to lick it from the pad of her finger. It might taste sweet. Sweet, but toxic. She wiped it on her jeans.

Jed sat up. 'What's that noise?'

A group of men walking past came to a halt in front of the bench. Far off, a sound like distant thunder. Matthew stood.

'Look,' Jed whispered.

'Fucking hell,' said one of the men.

Over a ridge in the landscape, a phalanx of mounted police cantered towards them, Perspex shields clipped to the front of the horses' faces. She couldn't remember when she'd last seen such a thing. Jed's mouth hung open.

'Horses?'

She held out her hand. 'Get up, Jed. Quick, love!'

The horses raced past just metres away, dark flanks glossy with sweat, surging towards Primrose Hill. They split into two groups by the park's perimeter hedge and exited from separate gates.

'Men on horses! Who are they? Where are they going?' said Jed.

She stared at the empty space they'd left behind.

'Police.' The chirruping of the birds returned. 'Finally.'

She turned towards the men who had been standing with them but they'd left, heading down the path and out of the gate on Chester Road.

'But why are they on horses and not the new police BinX?' Jed persisted.

'Horses don't run out of juice,' she said.

Matthew turned to Signy. 'Listen to him. He's anxious and hot. I think you'd better go home.'

'What? No way.' She picked up her bike, lifted Jed into his seat. 'If you go on alone and can't get the car moving it will be hours before I can give him the VireX.'

Matthew was looking at the floor. 'Where's the rucksack with the charger?'

'Where you put it.'

'No, Sig, I mean it. It's not here. I just had it. It was by my feet.'

She leant her bike against the bench and hunted about. It wasn't anywhere.

Her heart thumped. 'Those guys. The ones who were watching the horses with us just now.'

'Stay here.'

He ran towards Chester Road. His body stretched into a sprint. She'd forgotten what a fast runner he was. He disappeared out of the gate.

'Where's Dada going? He might get hurt. Let's catch him up.'

'No, love. He'll be back in a minute.'

Matthew reappeared a couple of minutes later, shoulders hunched, head low. He was empty-handed, his neck an angry red. She wheeled to meet him on the path.

'They had the bag.' He was breathing heavily. 'I told them to give it back. I told them the bloody thing was encrypted. One of them grabbed me by the throat.'

'Oh God. Are you okay?' She put her arms around him, but he was too pumped to notice.

He picked up his bike. 'Fuck it. That's it then. Car's buggered. We're going home.'

'What? No, we can still get the drugs from the boot.'

'Mama, I'm really cold.'

'Sig, you're like a stuck record. How many times? He doesn't need drugs, he needs to lie in bed.'

'No. He needs—'

'Anyway, the only override key was in the side pocket of the rucksack, so we can't get into the boot.'

'What? You should never have put the bag down!'

'What's that supposed to mean?'

'I'm just saying, if you hadn't put it down, if you'd kept it on the bench, we'd still have it.'

She hated herself. She wanted to take the words and stuff them back inside her mouth.

'And if you'd stayed at home with Jed, I'd have been there by now and this would never have happened.' His eyes met hers.

In silence, they remounted their bikes and headed back the way they had come.

They pedalled through Kentish Town, Tufnell Park and Archway. A great lump swelled in her throat. She tried to swallow, but it kept rising up. She wanted Mum. She wasn't going to cry.

When they reached home, the windows of their flat and everyone else's had lost their blue opacity. Like when she was a girl. Like the old days. Funny. Not funny.

Matthew threw his bike against the wall. Signy tapped Michelle's window. The blinds were down. Michelle came to the door.

'Everyone can see into my flat.' She pointed to her bay window. 'People keep walking by and looking through, asking for water. Them bloody drones have been back and all.'

'Somebody stole our car battery. Jed's ill. We had to come home.' Signy's voice held a tremor.

'No sign of Lucozade?' Michelle said.

They'd forgotten completely about Lucozade.

'No. I'm so sorry,' Signy said. She couldn't quite meet Michelle's eye.

'Never mind,' sighed Michelle. 'That's bad about the charger. What then, you just gotta wait until this is all fixed and then go get your car?'

'Car'll be crushed for scrap before then. If it hasn't been already.'

Matthew pushed his way past to get in.

Signy was about to tell Michelle about the police horses but Michelle seemed strangely relaxed. She didn't want to frighten her. She apologised for Matthew's rudeness, thanked her again and headed upstairs, Jed trailing behind.

★

Much later, after she'd tucked Jed into bed with a glass of warm water and silo-honey heated on the camping stove, she came into the living room. Matthew was kneeling, his back to her, head bent, gluing sticks on to the wooden house. The light from the candle shone coral through the skin of his ears.

'Are you okay?'

'Yep.'

He was doing one side of the roof. She watched him until he'd finished. He breathed out heavily, pulled himself to his knees and came to sit on the sofa some distance from her. His skin was pale, his beard had grown. There were violet bruises under his eyes.

Climbing onto his lap, she leant her head against his shoulder.

'I'm sorry. About the rucksack. It wasn't your fault. Don't hate me.'

She started crying. Matthew was warm. Her crying was loud and she couldn't stop.

'I don't hate you. Ssh. I love you.' There was a pause, then with a low chuckle he said, 'Even if you are a massive hypochondriac.'

She needed him now. They needed one another.

'Please, please can we leave here and go to Mum's?'

'Sig. Yes.'

'When? Tomorrow?'

Matthew put his arms around her. He squeezed her ribs. It felt good. He rubbed her back.

'Can we wait another day? We can leave the day *after* tomorrow. I promise.'

'Why? That's too long.'

'In case things change, like the leaflet promised. It's only been forty-eight hours.'

'It's ... Has it? How are we going to get there?'

He smiled. 'We'll find a way. Jed's going to be fine. It's all right, Sig, please don't cry.'

When they went to bed that night and she bent to take off her socks, something buzzed in one corner of the room, too loud for a pollen-drone. They hunted behind the chair that was drowning in Matthew's clothes.

'It can't be ...?'

It was a bee. A honeybee. Far from a silo. They captured it in a glass and examined it in wonder. Its orange-and-black furred thorax, its glassy wings.

'Hallo, Mrs Bee,' she said. 'Welcome. You are very welcome here.'

Matthew opened the window.

'I don't want to let it go,' she whispered.

'We have to,' he said. He threw it out to the night.

'Are they swarming, making a break for it?' she said, once they were in bed. 'Are they being reintroduced? Is that why all the pollen-drones have gone away?'

'*To make a prairie it takes a clover and one bee*,' Matthew intoned. '*One clover, and a bee,*

And revery.

The revery alone will do,

If bees are few.'

She sat up. 'That's ... Who wrote that?'

'Emily Dickinson.' He grinned. 'Learned it at school. Not just a pretty face, see? That's shut you up.'

'Your expensive education wasn't entirely wasted.' She lay back down. 'Good to know. A-star.'

'Night.'

'Night.'

A bee. They'd seen a bee in the wild. Well, '*the wild*'.

London was hardly the prairie. Still. She could feel something. Change. Change was coming. It should have felt good.

She turned onto her side and fell asleep.

Later there was more shouting outside. She didn't get up to look. That same smell of burning rubber found its way into her nostrils, waking her briefly, but she was too exhausted to worry.

Later still, Matthew called out something unintelligible in his sleep.

Day 6

She dreamt of Gethin – although it was more a memory than a dream. He and she and also Raquel, who was thirteen – a year older than her and already with magnificent boobs – in Warston, creeping around the outside of Dolly Darker's static caravan. Gethin's granny said Dolly was a witch. They stood on the breeze blocks that kept the caravan off the grass, eyes over the grubby metal windowsill. It was hard to see through because the glass was flecked with bird poo. Dolly Darker was not inside. It was just a messy tabletop covered with blue, red and silver milk-bottle tops threaded together on string. Raquel was taller and therefore had a better view. There were open tins of tomato soup by the sink, she said, but no witchy business going on.

They dropped back into the long grass and sprinted to the safety of the humpback bridge. Gethin said Dolly must be hunting crows to eat. Raquel told Gethin he was an idiot, produced a packet of salt and vinegar Hula Hoops from her pocket and counted them out carefully between three. They sat munching silently in the sunlight. In the dream, the crisps grew fronds and became poisonous, closing their throats and making them choke.

She woke in a cold sweat, her tongue welded to the roof of

her mouth. She could smell herself: uric sweat, hormones. Her legs ached from cycling yesterday.

Outside she could hear a bulldozer engine banging and crashing along the Holloway Road. Jed might be worse today. He might be better.

She tried to conjure the journey from her parents' Victorian terrace in London to the cottage in Warston: her London home's familiar smell of upholstery and cooking; her father's Eau Sauvage aftershave trailing as he packed up the car; the drive up the M1 and the sudden silence as they'd turn off onto country lanes; the way the light came diamond-shaped through the leaded windows of the cottage.

The bulldozer was closer now. They would leave for the cottage tomorrow if the electricity didn't return today.

She looked at Matthew sleeping beside her. She wondered if he'd remember what he'd dreamt of in the night – the thing that had made him call out.

She stared at the wall, at the painting of the three horses galloping in a row, manes tossing in the wind, tails flying, the two horses on the outside looking in at the horse in the centre. The colours were dark green and gloomy, but the image itself was full of joy. Lucky horses.

The bees were out of their silos. Some. One.

Why was Matthew insisting they wait? Even if the utilities were restored as promised, it would take weeks for life to return to normal.

A list began to take shape in her head: *Tent, water, food, torches.* It was a stupidly long journey even without a child, let alone a child with a fever.

She must relax. What *was* that TrincXcode on the radio? She let the top line float towards her: F sharp major, C sharp minor. Was it nine-eight? Or seven-four?

Tinnitus in her ears.

Carry mats, map, waterproofs … Burple simp, Redarmande, Roycroft Briss … No, that wasn't right.

Matthew's eyelids fluttered. Outside, the grinding of the bulldozer faded.

… First aid box, Jed's teddy, penknife.

There was nothing left in the first aid box except scissors and two plasters, it was that old.

Somewhere on the street a child shouted in Polish. A helicopter thundered overhead, then away. The buzzing of a drone.

F sharp major. C sharp minor. The TrincXcode notes refused to leave her. It was like being forced to listen to the vitals of a peculiarly digital person. She put her fingers in her ears. The tinnitus grew louder.

… Bin bags, Trangia stove plus meths …

The faintest smell of burning still drifting in. Matthew grunted. He sat up very straight in bed.

'What time is it?'

'We need to get stuff,' she said. 'I've made a list. In my head. We need to go out again.'

6.30 a.m. She flicked the light switches. No matter. It was too early for gas and electricity to be fully restored, surely. Jed was feeling better at least.

'Just my legs are a bit achy,' he said.

'See?' said Matthew as they ate the last of the pumpernickel for breakfast. Jed was allowed to eat a packet of Quavers with his dry cereal, which he thought excellent. 'A good night's sleep is all that was needed.'

'I still think it's important we have medicines for when we go,' she said.

'At least we won't get scurvy,' said Jed, wiping orange flecks from his lips.

It had rained heavily overnight – a small miracle – and the plates on the terrace had been given a superficial wash. She scrubbed at them with a cloth, trying not to think about precipitation and beetles and spores of Bovine Staph dropped into rivers and streams. The plates now looked serviceable. Matthew used rainwater collected in the empty bucket to flush away the waste in the loo. She poured in disinfectant and examined the fresh white bowl. After breakfast they sat in the kitchen, waiting.

'Everything will come on again today, you'll see,' Matthew said. He looked pleased. Hopeful. 'We saw a bee last night, Jed, in our bedroom. A real honeybee.'

Jed looked confused. 'A bee? What does that mean? Why was he here?'

'She,' she corrected. 'I told you, the workers are shes.'

'We don't know what it means,' said Matthew. 'But it's good. Definitely.'

'Does it mean the poisonous chemicals on the crops have gone away, finally?' How could a six year-old sound so like an old man? 'Did the beetles do their job eating it all up? I thought the beetles were baddies?'

Matthew chuckled. 'It's not as simple as that, love. The beetles were good to begin with – we introduced them everywhere, to eat the nasty chemicals on the crops – but then they reproduced too rapidly, and they morphed into baddies.'

'Yeah.' Jed rubbed his nose. 'Miss Yue told us when we went on the school trip to the bee-silo in Richmond. The beetles ate all the leaves on the trees and dropped Bovine Staph into the water.'

'More or less.'

'And now the bees are coming back. Excellent.'

He disappeared upstairs.

She perched on the stool edge at the open piano and depressed five notes in a row. It sounded crunchy. She ran a chromatic scale. To Jed it was goodies and baddies. She wanted to be six again. Her fingers stumbled.

There was galloping and he was back in the room, pushing his bottom next to hers, leaning on the keys with the whole of his upper body.

'*You* play then.'

She whipped her hands away but her foot stayed on the sustain pedal. The notes flung themselves against the walls. Jed looked hurt.

'Sorry,' she said. 'It's not you. It's everything else.'

She left him there.

The large water bottle they'd bought from the shop was in the corner of the kitchen, already half-empty and too heavy to lug all the way to Warston. She went to find Matthew.

'We need to find a better way to carry water on our journey. The CamelBaks that are packed away in some godforsaken box who-knows-where are full of mould. And we need batteries.' She flicked the light switches again. 'And medicines.'

'Stop it,' said Matthew. 'You're doing my head in.'

'I'm going to tell Michelle we're going out.'

She knocked on Michelle's door. No answer.

'Matt, can you come here?' Matthew came down with Jed. 'Do you think she's all right? You don't think she's sick or passed out or anything?'

Matthew gave the door a gentle shove with his shoulder. It opened easily.

'Hallo? Michelle? Anybody in?'

They stepped cautiously around her flat.

'Michelle?'

Signy peered into the tiny damp bedroom at the back. The cupboard doors were open, the cupboard empty. Metal hangers dangled from the rail. The duvet was missing from the bed. A pair of Michelle's customised trainers were lined neatly against the skirting board.

'And she didn't even tell us,' Signy said.

Gone. First the brothers next door, now Michelle. James and Aya too. Perhaps Gethin had left his home in Crouch End and headed back to Warston.

'Dada, what about the cats?' Jed went to the back door. Signy had forgotten about Michelle's two cats; they lived outside during the day. 'There's empty tins of cat food in her part of the garden, Mama, but I can't see them.'

'I saw Oscar just the other day, love. We can feed them if we see them.'

'But we haven't got any cat food,' he wailed.

Matthew lifted him into his arms. 'Come on, little one. Let's go and find batteries and stuff with Mummy and worry about the cats later.'

'Okay.' Jed rubbed his eyes.

'We should make a lock for the front door so we can get in and out,' she said.

Matthew looked at her.

He found a hammer and two small loops of metal and banged one into the door, one into the door frame. They would use her ancient heavy-duty bike lock – she still had the key – to secure it from the outside. Matthew tugged experimentally to check if the loops would hold.

'Doesn't look particularly safe,' she said.

'The drill's out of battery. The only other option is you stay here and I go out.'

'No, I want to come.'

'Yeah,' said Jed, crossing his arms. 'We want to come.'

'Okay, how about you two go, and *I'll* stay back?' he said.

'Are you mad?' she said. 'No way.' She busied herself with the laces of Jed's walking boots. 'And I don't want to cycle. My legs are aching too.'

'You're going to make your son *walk*?'

'*Our* son. We're travelling eighty-four miles tomorrow, so he may as well get used to it!'

'I don't get it,' Matthew said to himself as she stood up. She didn't either, but she was damned if she'd tell him.

'What's in your rucksack, Mama?'

'Tinned dace and sweetcorn sandwiches and a Thermos of water.'

'I *love* dace sandwiches!'

'That's why I made them.' It was only partly a lie. She stepped onto the pavement. 'I've just thought, Matt – Michelle won't be able to get in if she comes back.'

'She's not coming back.'

He secured the bike lock and they walked towards Holloway Road. She felt sick.

Here they were, the three of them: out on a hunt for *batteries*.

There were fewer people than yesterday on Holloway Road and everyone who was seemed to have retreated psychologically, as if by doing so they could pretend nothing was actually happening. A digger had cleared all the cars to one side. Someone shouted near Archway station. The small blue drones were out in force, in their odd triangle formations. An object smoked in the road a few hundred metres down the hill. She pulled Jed away up St John's Grove. Matthew had to run to catch up.

The sun came out. Seagulls flapped their wings on the roofs

before nose-diving into the overflowing bins. They crossed Junction Road. More drones. The throbbing of another helicopter. This time a green Chinook, two sets of propellers spinning, almost invisible. People in the street came to a stand-still. Jed waved to it.

'What's it doing, for God's sake?' She stared hopefully at the chute in its belly. 'You'd think they'd be dropping food parcels by now, wouldn't you?'

'Not in Archway, apparently.'

Matthew shook his head as the Chinook passed overhead towards central London.

Every single shop they passed was closed. They headed up the sloping streets, then downhill on the approach to the Heath, broken cars on narrow roads blocking any hope of driving anything other than a digger through. The charging ports stood sentry-like along the pavement edge. Jed didn't bother tapping them.

She thought of Mum on her own in Warston. Mum would be worrying about her, Signy, because that's what mothers did. She imagined her brother, Elis and his family, across the wide ocean, climbing into bed after a day at the beach. He wouldn't be doing that. He would be doing what she was doing now: looking for supplies. But then, everyone in Australia was look-ing for supplies, for water certainly, all the time. Perhaps the change wasn't so marked for them?

They rounded the bend on Swains Lane, the shopfronts cloaked in sheets of protective steel.

'Damn it.'

No supplies. Nothing.

She turned on her heel to lead them to the shops in Tufnell Park for anything worth foraging, but her eye was caught by the leafless trees that edged the Heath. It seemed that some held the very beginnings of buds. Thirty feet up, their branches swayed in the wind, delicate, strong. A yellow and green grassy oasis waited beyond those trees, away from the chaos. Jed sped up beside her as if reading her mind.

'Let's go for a walk on the Heath! Please, Mama?'

She looked at Matthew, raised her shoulders, as if Jed's word was king, as if that was that and there was nothing either of them could do about it.

'Just for a bit. Okay, Matt?'

Matthew was silent; the decision had already been made. She felt suddenly sorry for him.

They stepped onto the Heath path. A man with headphones attached to his ears was swinging a metal detector over a hillock. Every few feet, he would bend and dig into the earth with a trowel. Behind a clump of trees at the side of Parliament Hill, the blue-green nylon of a tent, still in the heat of the day. The prospect of camping here was actually appealing.

They strode out. How could everything natural look so normal? Jed skittered across the grass. She thought it remarkable how fast children recovered.

'There are those parakeets!' shrieked Jed. 'There's a kestrel, I bet it's hunting for a mouse!' He ran ahead. '*Cass!*'

Coming along the path towards them were Cassidy and Vicky, and Steve, Vicky's husband. Friendly people, people she knew. Signy rushed forward, arms wide. She threw herself on Vicky's shoulder, their UV glasses clacking as their heads glanced against one another. Vicky's arms went around Signy's back, her hair across Signy's face; she smelled of cooking and soap. Her hug was reassuring, like home. Jed and Cassidy chased each other in circles.

'We're so pleased to see you!' Something vulnerable in Vicky's smile. 'We've been drinking from the water butt in our garden but the UV stick is running out. Did you see the leaflet-drop yesterday? Wasn't it surreal?'

'My mummy and daddy saw a bee!' cried Jed.

'A bee?' Vicky looked at Steve. His face was angled at the sky.

'Ssh a second. You hear that?'

'I can,' whispered Jed.

She could too. Drones.

They arrived en masse, fifty at least, hovering twenty feet above the grassy expanse, cameras angled down. They descended slowly in groups of three, each group focusing on a particular area or group of people.

'Move in together,' Matthew instructed, grabbing Jed and Cassidy, putting them in the centre of the four adults as the triangle-formation of drones circled slowly. Signy felt the hairs rise on her arms.

'Go on, bugger off!'

Steve shooed the drones away but they hovered out of reach, too fleet for human hands. A second later the entire set of fifty lifted into the air. They flew off in the direction of central London.

'Got to get out of here,' Signy breathed.

Matthew was still staring at the sky. 'Yeah.'

'The heck?' Steve let go of the children's hands.

'They're keeping tabs,' Matthew said. 'I think they're checking on people's movements.'

'But why? And *who* they're keeping tabs on is entirely random, it seems,' said Signy. 'At least, I hope it is. Have they been flying around your house?'

Vicky folded her arms around herself. 'No. And who's controlling them, anyway?'

Signy turned to Matthew. 'They haven't had them around their house, Matt.'

He shook his head at her. 'I think it's the MOD. Random checks,' said Matthew, with a short laugh. 'Though I don't fancy them following us tomorrow.'

'Following where?' Vicky said.

'Sig wants us to travel to Northamptonshire. To stay with her mum, check she's okay. She has health problems.'

Vicky put a hand on Signy's arm. 'But we're going to Steve's dad's in Leicester tomorrow! We could travel together?' Her face was hopeful.

Steve said, 'Six of us will be safer. We've our own tents, firelighters, safe water from our water butt, medicines – more than enough to share with you if you'll shoulder some of the load?'

This was good: travelling with friends, people they could trust.

'Yes,' Signy said. 'Yes, definitely.'

'We're going to walk the Maglev line to Rugby and up. We could separate there?' said Vicky.

Signy's hand went to her head. 'Wait. But do you have bikes?'

'We're cycling?' said Matthew. 'I don't remember that conversation.'

A flush spread across her cheeks. 'Matt. Of course we're cycling. It's faster and safer.'

'With the tiny panniers you own? And Jed on the back, too?' Matthew turned to the others. 'Sig's got an outdated pedal-bike from like, 2018, with pimped up road-panel appropriate tyres. It weighs a ton and makes her legs ache.'

Vicky and Steve had gone quiet.

'Walking is even slower. The longer the journey takes,' Signy insisted, her voice rising, 'the more danger we put ourselves in. You said this morning that Jed wasn't strong enough to walk.'

Pressure built in her throat. The children had stopped running and were looking at her. Vicky stared at the ground.

'Why?' said Jed. 'I'm fine.'

Matthew exhaled heavily. He reminded her of a bull.

'They saw a bee?' Cassidy whispered loudly to Jed. 'A honeybee?'

'Uh-huh. In their bedroom.'

Cassidy tugged on Vicky's sleeve. 'That's good, isn't it, Mum? A bee?'

Vicky smiled. 'It's really good.' That made Signy smile, as well.

'I think your fella might be right,' said Steve, at last. 'If we take the Maglev line, which is by far the safest and most direct route, we won't be able to bike on the tracks. Best to avoid motorways and any obvious routes, I think.' He shrugged his shoulders. 'Especially if you don't own a graphene electric.'

'Walking is the only realistic option, Sig.'

She caught Matthew mouthing a silent *thank you* to Steve over her head.

So they were walking – a tribe of six. Of course they couldn't carry a tent and water and large rucksacks on her bike – on any bike; of course they couldn't cycle over Maglev sleepers. Surprised to find she felt only relief that this important decision had been taken out of her hands, that she hadn't been the one to have to make it, she smiled at Matthew. He did a double take.

The two families walked on beside the ponds, flooded and bloated despite the intensive damming decades before. At the edge of the water, a few hardy saplings pushed their way towards the sun, evidence of the blight's end. The seas of dead beetles had disappeared now, blown away in the wind perhaps, or more likely, hoovered up by BinX. She thought again about Ken and his brother. She thought about the police controlling rioting hordes with BinX. She didn't want to bear witness to any of it.

A discussion was taking place: who would carry what; where they would join the Maglev track; how the children would manage. Vicky and Steve had batteries, they said, lots of them, saved for years in a special sealed box for an emergency. He'd tested them, Steve said, good as new. She was having problems focusing, her thoughts snagging on the swing hanging from the tree above the brook at Warston. Who else might be heading back? Gethin. Her old friends, with children of their own. The next generation pushing each other on that swing, just as their parents had before them.

They made a slow circle over Parliament Hill, the city below like a paper cut-out from a pop-up book. You could see the pine-scented flat-pack houses, the city's 3D buildings, their spiralling fascias pretty from this angle, like Jed's Golden Ratio. Cylinders of dark smoke rising near Crystal Palace. The Shard, the Razor, the tall revolving Quill piercing the clear sky like needles. A cluster of drones, perhaps the same ones that had been only recently above their heads, hovering over central London. She hadn't heard a single shock-trail from a hyperplane since this whole thing started.

They walked deeper into the trees. She missed the waterfall sound of leaves fluttering. Though now they'd seen the bee, who knew what might happen? Perhaps the beetle-destroyed leaves would return. Skidding along a path, Jed and Cassidy called back and forth. The only friend Jed had seen in days.

They stopped on a bench at Kenwood House to share sand-wiches. Long white blinds hung over the Georgian windows of the stately home, the smooth creamy-pink walls like a wedding cake at their backs. Vicky presented the children with some millet-bread and hummous.

'No thank you,' Jed said, always polite. 'If that's okay?'

Vicky smiled. 'Of course, poppet. More for us.'

Signy's hand shook as she waved goodbye. Vicky and Steve would be with them tomorrow morning at 11 a.m. to set off. They promised not to be late.

Signy pulled Jed and Matthew on towards Tufnell Park.

'What about Michelle's cats?' said Jed. 'Will we take them with us tomorrow?'

'Let me have a think,' she said.

Matthew smiled and rolled his eyes at her.

On Hargrave Road the community hall was buzzing.

'Food. Bank. Water,' Jed read from the pen-scrawl on the sheet that was pegged to the railings.

A food bank. There were still good people left. People who cared about others. About people like Matthew, Jed, her.

'This is fantastic!' She looked at her watch. 'What time do you think the army is coming? It's midday already.'

'Soon,' said Matthew.

They headed inside, a bead of lightness dancing in her throat.

'Another queue?' sighed Jed.

Volunteers handed out tins and dried food from behind trestles at the far end of the hall. A separate table was piled with water.

Further along the queue a child waved. She nudged Jed's shoulder.

'Look.'

'Keir!'

Jed ran off. She watched the two boys embracing. Keir's mother caught her eye, gesturing to the trestles, shaking her head. Signy smiled, shrugged her shoulders, weary now.

A voice behind her said, 'Hallo again.' She turned.

The NYPD cap. The man from the fight the other night. He wasn't addressing her, because how could he know who she was, after all? She'd been hidden behind the window frame, a coward. It was Matthew he recognised. Matthew, whom she constantly criticised for not doing enough. He had done something, and now he was in the firing line, and it was her fault.

A red gilet clung about the man's narrow ribs; his sallow skin seemed too tight to contain the person within. He was close enough for her to see the moisture pooling in his tear ducts. Behind him stood the same woman – his accomplice, his girlfriend, whatever.

Tingling began in Signy's hands and feet and travelled up her arms and legs. Matthew was looking the other way, pretending no one had spoken.

'You know I'm here.' The man's lip curled. 'You're that guy who likes a quiet street. Nice little chat at your front door. This your missus?'

Signy could smell alcohol and something else, sweet and chemical, on his breath.

A pink flush spread across Matthew's cheeks.

'Mate, I don't want any hassle. I've got my kid here. Go and get your box of supplies or whatever and take it easy.'

'Me and my missus aren't allowed supplies.' A string of saliva had attached itself between his top and bottom teeth. His finger jabbed the air near Matthew's chest. 'Apparently we were aggressive. They're only for the likes of you. Mate.'

Jed ran into her side.

'Keir's got a new game for his V-Raptor but says he can't play it because his brother broke the solar panel, and anyway now there's no elec—'

His eyes went to the two strangers. Signy pulled him in behind her back.

The woman's face softened. 'Pack it in, D. There's a little 'un with them. Sorry, love.' She looked Signy up and down before moving off. 'He don't mean nothing by it.'

She slapped her palms on her thighs and the man followed her out of the door.

Jed tapped Signy's bottom with his finger. Signy's hand found Matthew's.

'Dickhead little Kitehead,' was all he said.

Jed looked at the exit. Angry red cuts had developed at the corners of his mouth. When had that happened? In the night?

'What's a Kitehead? He smelt horrible.'

'A person who takes Kite. It's a drug. Don't worry, love, Daddy's here and he's stronger.'

They edged forwards in the queue. Her wrists trembled in her sleeves.

Keir's family left with a wave and their box of supplies. Signy and Matthew reached the front of the line. They were asked for their address. It was noted down, Signy mindful of being polite. A box of food and water was handed over.

'Thank you so much,' she said.

'You're welcome.'

The old woman behind the table had white hair in tight curls. She smelt of hairspray and when she nodded her curls jounced merrily.

Matthew lifted the box and the water into his arms and headed to the exit.

'Let's go home.'

Jed skipped along beside his dad, his hand in the box like a lucky dip.

'Ooh, look at these! Noodles!' He licked his tongue across his lips.

The man in the cap was sitting alone on the low wall in

front of the hall, the red gilet straining across the curve of his spine. Signy hesitated but Matthew was already ahead of her, half-hidden behind the cardboard box, talking to Jed. She had no time to warn them. They passed him and he was instantly on his feet, following them.

She overtook and ran to Matthew's side. '*Matt!*'

'Just ignore him,' he said. 'He's not going to try anything.'

She whipped Jed into her arms. Jed's eyes grew round as he stared over her shoulder.

'Mama, it's the man with the kitehead!'

'Shush now.'

They continued in silence, concentrating on the road ahead. Her feet felt strangely disconnected from her legs.

'*Excuse* me. Give us some of your food, boss.'

Her head felt light, her scalp fizzing.

'*Hey!* Don't ignore me.' The slapping of his trainered feet and he was suddenly in front of them, walking backwards. 'Oy. *Cunt.*'

Matthew stopped. 'You can't have any of our food. This is my son and you're scaring him, and you're scaring my partner. I suggest you get out of our way.' He set off again, crossing Junction Road onto St John's Grove. Signy kept close by his side.

Beyond the swooping seagulls, an army truck had stationed itself at the turning where St John's Grove joined Holloway Road. She could have wept with relief.

'Finally.'

She hurried forward. Safety. Order. A symbol that someone knew what they were doing.

Rifled soldiers stood behind a cordon of red and white tape. People waited behind the tape to be let through. Khaki-coloured vehicles thundered down the A-road towards the city.

'They've got guns,' Jed said. 'Oh, I *love* guns.'

'Has the man gone?' she whispered.

Jed peeped around her neck. 'Nope.'

They joined the group of people queuing behind the tape. She pushed herself as far in among the line as she dared and glanced back. The man was still there, hovering twenty metres behind. There were many people queueing ahead. She could smell the jasmine that snarled around the fence of someone's house nearby. No sign of the supposedly repurposed BinX. For once, she wished there were some here, now.

'Follow me,' she said to Matthew, and wriggled her way to the front. 'Sorry. Sorry. Excuse me.'

The young soldier at the tape had paper-white knuckles curled tight around his gun butt.

'We live just the other side of the road,' she said to him. 'Can we cross?'

He gazed above her head as if addressing someone taller.

'Sorry, ma'am. You need to wait until all vehicles have passed.'

A helicopter arrived and hovered directly above.

'My son is only six!' She had to shout now. 'He's asthmatic!' She hoped Jed wouldn't correct her. 'His medication is in our house over there. Hey! Are you listening to me?'

'Are you listening to her, young man? Her kid's got asthma.' An older woman stepped forward.

The soldier's face wavered, uncertain. Signy didn't want him to be uncertain, she wanted him to be in control.

'I'm sorry, ma'am. Wait a couple of minutes and your family can be one of the first to pass through.'

She searched for the NYPD insignia but there were too many people in the way now.

The army trucks flew up Holloway Road, on and on, camo tarpaulins flapping, the last leaving diesel fumes in its wake.

The smell took her back to childhood, to exhaust fugging the road. Funny, she thought, how something so disgusting could acquire a sweetness on reflection. She imagined soldiers inside these trucks, sitting in lines, travelling to ... where exactly? To what? Maybe the new BinX were in there instead?

Some sort of sergeant appeared by the tape. He hopped up onto the running board of a parked truck.

'Please be patient! Stay in line! Have your details ready and any ID.'

The tape was untied. People went through one by one. Her shoulders were killing her. She put Jed down. They were beckoned forward. Matthew took Jed's hand.

'ID card, sir?'

'I don't have it. Can't I use my palm?'

'Palm readers are not functional, sir. Name and address?'

The soldier fed Matthew's details back through the comms near his cheek. Signy felt her stomach turn over. The faintest crackle of voices at the other end.

'You can head across.'

Matthew and Jed set off ahead of her.

'ID please?'

She pulled her card from her wallet. The soldier looked at her face and back to the photograph.

'Thank you. You're free to cross.'

There was a shove at her back and she pitched forward. When she turned, he was right there, inches from her nose: the cap, the awful smell.

'Leave us alone!' She spun back to the tape but it had closed in front of her. 'Wait!' she cried. 'I need to cross! You said I could go!'

Another soldier appeared at her side. 'Ma'am? You're blocking the cordon. Is there a problem?'

'She's with me,' NYPD said.

'No! This man –' she pointed – 'has been following my family. He's threatened to hurt us.'

'I can walk where the fuck I like.'

'Not at the moment you can't,' said the soldier, clapping the man on the arm. She could have kissed him.

Matthew was back suddenly, panting heavily.

'You okay, Sig?' He took her hand. 'I didn't see you weren't behind us.'

The soldier led NYPD away.

'Sorry, mate. I don't know what's going on here, but you're going to have to wait. These people don't seem very keen on you.'

His protestations carried over the road as they crossed to the other side. Feeling safer now, she glanced over her shoulder. He was being questioned. Good. He caught her eye and drew a deliberate slow line with his hand across his throat.

'Matt, he did that thing to me, like they do in films. He said he would cut someone the other night, remember?'

'He's not going to cut you, he's not even going to get through the barriers. You've got the whole army out here. The lights will come back on tonight. Try not to panic.'

'After he *punched* that woman? I am panicked.' She made off down the road with Jed, who was picking his lips. 'Stop that.'

A larger military drone-hailer boomed from Holloway Road. 'REMAIN CALM. MILITARY STAFF WILL BE A CONTINUED PRESENCE ON YOUR STREETS. STAY IN YOUR HOMES WHERE POSSIBLE. YOU WILL RECEIVE A HOUSE CALL AS PROCEDURE. PLEASE COMPLY WITH ALL REQUESTS.'

When she looked round, the large drone was hovering just above one of the flattened cars at the side of the road.

Their own street was full of confused neighbours drawn outside by the noise.

'Mama, look at Ken's house.'

The wood nailed to the brothers' front door had split and the door hung open.

The bike lock. She ran the last few metres. Their door, the lock, was fine.

'Where's the key?'

Matthew patted the pockets in his coat, then his jeans.

'You took it.'

'I haven't got it.'

'Fuck's sake.'

She checked her own pockets. The two of them stood on the porch, patting and searching each other.

'Mama.'

'Not now, Jed.'

'But, Mama, I know where it is. Dada put it in his boot. I saw him.'

'I did?' Matthew bent down. He pulled the key from his sock. 'Our son's a genius.'

'Miss Yue always says that,' Jed said.

They closed the door carefully behind them, locking it from the inside and went upstairs. Matthew disappeared onto the terrace.

'Oh, for God's sake!'

A barbecue had been thrown over the back wall. Its hot coals had burnt a hole in the Living-Turf and the blades of eco-friendly whatever were now scorched and melted together. Michelle's cats chewed on some bones beside the foil casing. An empty bottle of pop lay among the flowers. A fresh dump of rubbish sat in next door's garden. At least the brothers wouldn't be there to see it. She went back inside and flicked a light switch.

'Mama! There's no loo paper!'

She wiped Jed's bottom with the packet of face wipes she'd thrown at Matthew the day before.

'Ouch. They're stingy.'

'I'm sorry, darling.'

'You're hurting me!'

'I didn't mean to, Jed!'

'Stop shouting, Mama!'

He cried then, standing beside the toilet with his pants around his ankles. She got down and hugged him. The wood floor was unforgiving on her knees.

Matthew led him upstairs to play.

'Sig, why don't you take a moment.'

What was *wrong* with her, with everyone?

Then Jed was calling out the height of every superhero in his Top Trumps, with Matthew's interjections: 'Oh really? That's tall,' and, 'Wolverine's tiny'; and Jed again: 'Poison Ivy's the same height as Mama,' and her shoulders relaxed.

She went to sit at the piano, the helicopter blades chopping above. She needed a bath. She wanted to wash away the day, that man's stench. Schubert's *Impromptus* lay at the top of the pile, the book's spine shades of blue, white, yellow. She opened to No. 1 and stared at the black dots wavering on the page. The notes seemed more densely packed than she remembered, like trees in a wood. She needed reading glasses now to see them. Her fingers touched the keys. She imagined the notes flowing through her fingers.

They still didn't have batteries for tomorrow. Medicines.

No, but Vicky and Steve did.

The drone-hailer sounded in the distance.

MOVE ALONG THE ROAD. PLEASE DO NOT BLOCK THE AREA.

TrincXcode: nine-eight or seven-four? Was that essentially the same thing? She was losing her edge.

Mozart; she should be playing Mozart now. His work always came out *right*, like a perfect equation. She pulled out a book of his variations.

Jed appeared in the doorway. 'What's that? It sounds like "Twinkle Twinkle", but all ... busy.'

'It is exactly like "Twinkle Twinkle", sweetheart. The composer made lots of different-sounding pieces from the same song.'

'Can I see?'

She pulled him onto her lap and showed him the music. He stared at the notes.

'It's by a man who lived a long, long time ago.'

Jed giggled. 'What's the difference between a piano and a fish?'

'I don't know.'

'You can tune a piano but you can't tuna fish. Get it? Tune. A. Fish.'

'I get it. That's a good one.'

'It doesn't work so well with dace.'

'No.'

He reached up and pulled out the brand-new manuscript pad she'd hidden some days before.

'What's this? Are you going to be making adverts again, Mama?'

'Ssh. No. I don't know. Maybe.'

She pushed the pad back underneath the Schubert.

'What's that noise outside?'

'Drones.'

118

'How long ago did the Twinkle music man die?'

'About two hundred and seventy years ago.'

'What was his name?'

'Wolfgang Amadeus Mozart.'

'Weird. Did he do "Jingle Bells"?'

'No, he didn't do "Jingle Bells". Would you like to hear the rest?'

Jed nodded. She played the second variation, then the third, and he listened with his head on one side. When she was half-way through the fourth he said, 'Can I have something to eat?'

She went into the kitchen to try the tap. The box from the food bank was on the countertop. Inside, two tins of dace, four packets of dried noodles, two tins of crystallised rambutan, a tin of tomatoes, something grey-looking in a sealed foil bag, a jar of GM nut butter, and a pack of dried pinto beans. They wouldn't eat any of it now. They would take it with them tomorrow.

She found a tin of lentils in the carousel, and an out-of-date tin of synthetic beef consommé that her dad had brought round years before when she'd had the flu. There was half a packet of rice left. Cooking rice used very little water, which was good, but quite a lot of gas, which was not. She weighed up her options.

Her hands felt good after the Mozart. Her tinnitus had gone for now. She twisted the knob on the canister and pressed the ignition on the camping stove. Gas hissed through the pipe. The gas ring sparked and clicked and a weak flame grew around it. She threw some cardamom pods in with the rice.

Matthew came into the room. 'I've been pulling things out of the attic for tomorrow.'

Pleased, she said, 'I'll put on paper the list of stuff that's been in my head.'

He sniffed the saucepan of consommé. 'Boot polish?'

She tried the kettle, the boiler, the light switch; still nothing. She kicked the dishwasher.

'It's been over twenty-four hours since they made the announcement that everything would come back on within twenty-four hours. You know Jed's got little cracks in the side of his lips?'

'Yeah?' Matthew searched for a frequency on the radio.

'It's one of the early signs of Bovine—'

'Sig, stop! There is nothing wrong with him!'

She sat at the table with pen and paper while the rice boiled and wrote everything down. She slid the paper across the table. Matthew studied it.

'I don't think we'll manage all that. We've got to carry Jed's stuff for him. You going to walk all that way with a heavy pack?'

'Yes.'

He looked at her. The food was ready. She called Jed in to eat.

'Salty,' said Jed, struggling with a large spoon. His hand flew to his mouth. 'Ooh.'

'Let me put some lip balm on that.'

'I don't like lip balm. It tastes of plastic.'

The doorbell rang. The sound was unexpected and made them jump.

'The bell battery's working. Cheer up, Sig – something works.' Matthew stood. 'Stay there.'

'It might be the bloke in the cap.'

'Lord have *mercy*.'

He disappeared into the hallway.

She heard the front door open. Low male voices. She and Jed scuttled into the living room. When she lifted the window to poke her head out, the voices were below her and she had to go right over the sill to get a view of the porch.

The top of Matthew's head and two other heads in green berets. Soldiers. Matthew was saying, '... old-school.'

The scratching of pencil on paper as he relayed his name and date of birth; hers; Jed's.

'Yeah. Back to analogue.' The accent was soft; West Country perhaps. She wondered whether Matthew would do an imitation of it later. 'Know your ID numbers?'

'Not off by heart,' Matthew said. 'Why is this necessary?'

'Know the name of the person who lives below you at Flat A?'

'Michelle Brassington, but we think she's gone to stay with a relative.'

'Hallo!' Jed called from the window.

The soldiers threw their heads back.

'Hallo, young man.' They waved.

'What are your names?' asked Jed.

'All right, lad?' One raised his hand in greeting. 'I'm Southwick, this is Waters.'

'You're called Waters and our taps aren't working!' laughed Jed. The soldiers smiled.

'Load of nonsense this, isn't it?' said Waters. 'We're just talking to your dad and then tomorrow we might get you to come to the Sobell Centre to register with us. Okay with you?'

'Will there be trampolining?'

Both soldiers laughed.

'Not at the moment. Maybe soon.'

'Where are the BinX machines?' Jed said. '*Newsbites* said they're working with the police and the goodies.'

'Ah, lad.' Both soldiers shook their heads, rueful. 'They're out of power, like everything else.'

'But they're solar,' Jed insisted.

The soldiers' faces seemed to close, as if Jed had insulted them somehow.

'They're out of power,' Waters repeated. That was the end of that.

Signy leant further out. 'What do you mean when you say "register"? Why do we need to register?'

'Everyone who registers at a local centre will get supplies,' said Waters.

She felt suddenly cross. 'But why don't you just give everyone supplies anyway, without registering?'

The soldiers were silent. Southwick shook his head.

'Look, it doesn't make any sense to me, either. Just telling you what I've been told to. They'll give you more information when you get to the Sobell.'

'It'll all be over soon, eh?'

Waters gave an apologetic shrug. This last was to Jed, whose response was to run downstairs and gift them a plastic soldier each.

'Don't tell them we're leaving town tomorrow,' she called as he left the room. She wasn't sure what view the soldiers would take on that.

They shook Jed's hand and moved on to Ken's house. She watched them reach the broken front door. They called into the hallway and disappeared inside. Waste of time. She felt a bit sorry for them.

She should stop feeling sorry for people. Everyone was in the same boat.

Jed and Matthew were back at the table.

'Finish your dinner, monkey.'

'I'm leaving some for the cats.'

'I'm not sure they'll like soupy rice with lentils.'

'Oh. They will. Come on, Mama.'

He scraped the remains into a shallow bowl and they tiptoed downstairs to Michelle's flat.

Jed miaowed. 'Oscar? Oscar?' he called into the darkening, stale-smelling kitchen. The white cat mewled from the bedroom and padded in. He weaved between their legs, leaving a snowfall of white fur around their ankles. Jed dropped to his haunches. 'He's so sweet and hungry. Where's Pyewacket, Oscar?'

Signy placed the saucepan of leftovers on the floor and watched as Oscar's small pink tongue circled the pan clean. The cat sat back, licking his chops. His spine arched and he vomited on the laminate.

Jed fell backwards. 'Ugh! Oscar! You ate it too fast!'

The head of the black cat appeared through the flap in the back door. There was a scratch on his face. He approached warily, squinting his big yellow eyes, and came to a halt before the puddle of sick. His head dipped and he lapped it up.

'Pyewacket!'

'Come on, love. Let's leave them to it.'

She took Jed upstairs and installed him on the sofa with some books.

Matthew and she went up to the spare room. She gave him a captain's salute.

'An impression of Southwick, sir, if you please?'

She'd made him laugh.

'It doesn't make any sense to me, either.'

She shook her head. 'Terrible. Try Waters.'

'No. It's mean. They were nice.'

She whacked her palm against the light switch. Matthew had laid out the rucksacks and their lightest three-person tent. Up and down the stairs they went, out of breath, ticking items off the list. When everything had been crossed off, she considered their belongings. The bed was invisible beneath it all. She let out a long sigh.

'What?'

She raised her shoulders. 'It's just … it looks like we're going on holiday.'

Matthew's face creased and he chuckled. She hadn't meant it as a joke. She snorted at the ridiculousness of it. Laughter bubbled up through her nose. The sound she was making was grotesque, like a series of piglets escaping, but this only made her snort again. She sat on the bed. Matthew sat next to her. She looked at him through scrunched eyes, enjoying the delicious feeling of letting go. He was studying her. He looked happy she was happy.

He lunged then, grabbing hold of her shoulders and pushing her back until he was lying on top of her. His body was heavy on her tummy. His hair tickled her forehead.

He kissed her. It felt good – better than laughing. He tasted of salt and cardamom.

She pulled her T-shirt over her head and threw it on the floor. The poles of the tent clinked in their canvas bag next to her. She wound her legs around his hips, the edge of the camping lantern caught under her thighs. She wondered if anyone had ever made love on top of so many uncomfortable things.

Everything reduced to only this room, only this bed, only Matthew.

She'd forgotten what it was like to be so close to him. His skin was firmer than she remembered and cool to the touch.

Jed's plastic knife lay between them.

'You came inside me.'

'Well, it wouldn't do to get it on the itinerary.'

He was grinning, his trousers doughnutting at his knees.

'Great time to get me up the duff. The end of the fucking world.'

'Bit dramatic. I thought you wanted a second child?'

She pointed to his socked feet. 'Who says romance is dead?'

'Difficult times call for special measures.'

He got dressed. He looked chirpy.

'Your flies are undone. Again.'

'That's how I like 'em, baby. We'll pack this stuff in the morning.' He fastened his belt.

Jed was calling from downstairs.

'The cats are miaowing outside our door.'

She pulled herself up.

He was waiting for her.

'I tried to glue some of the stick house but it went all wrong.'

'Oh, love.'

Oscar sat outside in the hall, one paw raised. Pyewacket was behind, eyes peeping from below the top step.

'Can we let them in? They look lonely and scared.'

'Okay. But only for tonight.'

'We *can* take them with us?'

'No, they're not dogs, they won't follow us.'

'I can carry them in my rucksack,' he said.

'No.'

His face fell.

The battery in the plastic bunny had almost run out. For Jed's sake, adorable in his polar bear pyjamas, Signy made a big show of flicking the *ON* switch, but it was hardly worth it.

'Night, night. Sleep tight. Sweet dreams.'

'Mama?' The moon glowed at the edge of the blinds. His eyes were two wet orbs shining at her in the darkness. 'Will I get to play with Gamma's hose?'

'Yes, monkey.' The mention of Mum made her wince. 'Love you.'

'Love you, Mama.'

Matthew went to kiss Jed goodnight while Signy lit the two remaining candles. He returned to the kitchen.

'Jed told me he'd like a hoverboard for Christmas.'

Christmas: her body gave an involuntary shiver.

'We haven't got any charge for the UV sticks to disinfect water. We can't even clean out the mouldy CamelBaks.'

'The CamelBaks will have to do as they are.'

'*If* we can find them.'

'It'll be fine.' Matthew pretended to roll a cigarette from the paper with her list on it. 'God, I wish I had another one.'

They unfolded the road map on the coffee table. The date on the front said 2011 but, like the CamelBaks it would have to do. The route to Warston spread over ten non-consecutive pages. Perhaps she was getting a headache.

'Looks a lot longer than I remember,' she said.

In the distance a drone-hailer blasted.

They went to bed when it was only nine o'clock. She made Matthew check that the doors, front and back, were secure. She checked the light switches. She checked the taps.

Oscar followed them upstairs, hopped onto their bed and gazed at them in expectation of a stroke.

'Get off, fur-shedding machine.' Matthew made a shooing motion with his arm.

'Oh, come on. Let him sleep here tonight. Poor sod's going to be abandoned tomorrow.'

She climbed into bed and watched as Matthew took his clothes off.

'What you looking at?'

He jumped in beside her and blew out the stub of candle in the ramekin.

She sat up. 'I feel nervous. About the journey.'

'For crying out loud, it's you that wants to go! We'll be fine. There's still time for the lights to come back on.' He leant towards her, struggling to find her mouth in the dark. 'Love you.'

'Love you.'

She lay thinking until first he, and then she, fell asleep.

She was woken by a rocking motion. It dragged her from far off in a deep, peaceful place. She tried to ignore it; oblivion beckoned, but the shaking was urgent, persistent and she rose to the surface too quickly.

Her eyes fluttered. What time was it? Dawn was coming through the blinds. Someone was whispering.

'Signy. *Signy!*'

Matthew was leaning over her, one hand near her face, his voice so quiet she could hardly hear it.

'What?' Her muscles trembled from being woken too fast.

'*Sssh.* There's someone in the flat.'

She bolted upright. 'Where?' There was a ticking, then a ringing in her ears.

'I think they got in through the back door. They're in the kitchen. Take Jed, get into the attic and hide.'

'What? You're coming with us.'

'I'm going to see them off.'

'What if it's that guy in the cap?'

'*Signy.* Take Jed upstairs. Now.'

He was flinging on his trousers. She leapt up, naked from the waist down, and ran in to Jed's room.

Jed was half-hidden in a sheet. She scooped him up as quietly as she could. He hardly stirred. Throwing him over her shoulder, she struggled up the flight of stairs to the top floor. She didn't look back.

She heard Matthew's voice calling deep and loud, 'Hey! What d'you think you're doing? Get out!'

She bundled Jed through the open attic doors and flicked them closed behind her. It was pitch black. Jed was awake now, flailing, disorientated.

'Mama*aaa*!'

She clamped a hand over his mouth. 'Ssshh. It's Mummy. You're fine. We're in the attic.'

He shook his head free, his fingers exploring her face. 'What's happening?'

'Ssshh. Some people have come in to take our food. Daddy's going to scare them away.' Jed let out a whimper. 'It's all right. Come and get in behind here, where we hid before. Quickly now.'

She felt about in the dark, finding the pile of boxes and blankets. She covered them both and they lay there, breathing hard. It was hot and airless. Small noises were fleeing Jed's mouth. His leg oscillated against hers.

Footsteps echoed two floors below.

It was going to be that man. He was going to cut them all, like he said he would. She waited for his distinctive voice, but it was a muffled foreign accent that carried up the stairs, maybe Spanish.

'Out the fucking way ...' – something else – '... want trouble for your family.'

How many of them? She clung hard to Jed.

Another man's voice – English. It was him. It was NYPD. '*Move!*'

Then Matthew. 'My family isn't here. You can try …' –
something – '… taking our stuff.'

There was scuffling. Several pairs of feet moved heavily
across squeaking boards.

Matthew shouted, '*Fuck off!*'

Steps thumping up the first flight of stairs to the landing
beneath her, the landing with their bedrooms on it. The steps
went into her and Matthew's bedroom.

'Mama, what about Dada?' Jed was snatching at breath.

'Shut up. You have to. Until they've gone.'

Below, a thud against the wall, more scuffling.

'Fuck *off*! Get the fuck *off* me.'

Matthew's voice was high. She'd never heard it like that
before.

If anything happened to her, Jed was too small to look after
himself. Sweat dripped from her armpits.

Downstairs, quiet. The hairs prickled on her neck.

Matthew's howl came loud and clear from inside the bedroom. She screwed her face into the blanket. Another silence.

'*Fuck!*' said the other voice. He sounded out of breath. 'Shit.
I didn't mean—'

NYPD's voice. 'You frigging dickhead.'

There was a squeak as their bedroom door opened or closed.
One set of feet climbed the next flight of stairs. They were on
the landing. She turned her face into Jed's ear.

'Be very very still and quiet now, monkey.' She found his
hand and held it.

Footsteps entered the spare room. Canvas rustled on the
bed; their belongings.

'Stuff it in that rucksack, mate.' That red gilet. That chemical
smell. 'What's that? Take that. Nah, not that. Hurry up. *Fuck!*
You *idiot.*'

A sliver of torchlight shone through the crack in the attic door, veered away. The whine in her ear was so loud the men would surely hear it.

'What time?'

NYPD was wheezing. 'Haven't got a fuckin' clue, mate. Five o'clock?'

'Take it. We trade for something good.'

'What is it?'

'Water go in it. Like for a long walk. Take. Hurry up.'

There was a pause.

'What about in there?'

She clamped her thighs together, sharply aware of her lower body, its nakedness. Jed made a tiny noise.

'Hear something?'

The attic doors opened. A torch beam swerved across the eaves. The two of them lay like statues. Her ears crackled with the effort. The heat was suffocating.

''S just boxes of papers and old books.' Through a hole in the blanket, she saw the outline of a man. 'He had a missus and a kid, but they're not here.'

'The kid's bed.' The Spanish-sounding accent, whispering now. 'It been slept in.'

'Look, I'm not hanging around here with you and your fucking mistake. Let's go.'

The doors were kicked shut. Footsteps travelled downstairs.

They were on the landing below now. She heard the hinges on her bedroom door creak as it was opened again, feet moving around inside. Matthew must have been knocked out. Yes. No.

The footsteps went down another flight and the men's voices were in the kitchen, too faint to hear what was being said.

The door to the flat banged shut. The house grew thick with silence.

She pulled the blanket from Jed's face.

'Lie still, love. Don't move yet.'

'I feel sick, Mama.'

'Just hold on.' She sucked in cooler air.

'I need water.'

'Sssh.'

'Are they gone?'

She put her arm over Jed's stomach. She wanted to call Matthew's name. She didn't dare.

They lay quiet for what felt like a long time.

She heard Jed's breathing regulate; he'd fallen asleep. She could hardly believe it. She let her head drop back on the floor. Dust flew up her nose. The blackness above her. The ringing inside her head. She was shivering. When would it be safe to come out?

Matthew.

Jed's hot, child's breath touched her ear.

'Mama! Mama! I need a wee.'

She'd lain still in this darkness for hours. Or for just a few seconds. She couldn't tell which.

'Stay here.'

Jed gripped her arm. 'No! Don't leave me!'

She didn't want to.

She must be the first one out of the attic. Something felt stuck in her throat.

She crawled to the attic doors and inched them apart. With one eye, she peeped through the gap.

No one there. It was day. Day followed night. *The sun rise and the sun set.*

She listened for any sound below. Nothing.

She poked the doors with the tips of her fingers, expecting the world on the other side to have changed completely, expanded or darkened or lost its shape, but the spare room was just there through the slit, rich with daylight. The sky floated beyond the windows. The throaty rattle of a magpie. One lonely bird. Its call.

Cool air gusted through the gap. Her forehead was slick with sweat. She grabbed the blanket from the attic and wrapped it around her naked hips, edging herself out of the hatch. Jed followed close, nose touching the small of her back.

'No, monkey. Wait for me in the attic.'

'No.'

She looked around the spare room. Their belongings had gone. Not all, but most. The things that remained were strewn across the floor – clothes, the road map, Jed's plastic knife, snapped in two. Matthew's rucksack had been taken, the tent, other things – she couldn't remember what.

Her rucksack. Still there. Wedged beneath the bed. They'd missed it.

'I need a wee.' Jed's words vibrated in her spine.

'Wait here.'

The floorboards groaned as she edged forward on all fours, bare knees painful against the wood. She put her head out onto the top landing, glancing sideways to the bathroom, then down the stairs.

'Come here. Sssh, quietly.'

Jed copied her, crawling until he reached the door. He pushed himself against her.

'Good boy.'

She clung to the door jamb for support, thirsty and cold. She waited for Jed to finish his pee in the bathroom, then made her way carefully down the stairs, the blanket trailing at her feet. Their bedroom was in front of her now, the door ajar, the dark beyond fat, ominous. Jed clung to her.

She peered over the next set of banisters to the lowest landing. She knew the men had gone; she could feel their absence. She pictured the kitchen, the walls bruised and resonating from the touch of their filthy hands, the cupboards empty now, the box from the food bank gone. The crystallised rambutan. She'd been looking forward to it.

A small thump inside the bedroom, followed by a light movement, sent her racing back up to the top floor, propelling Jed in front of her. She waited, watching the door like a hawk. It was Oscar, pink ears and nose first, his body, his tail. The cat stared up at them. He padded lazily up the treads towards them. Jed bent for a stroke.

'Mama, there's blood on my fingers.'

She crouched beside him. The blood, sticky and fresh, was all around the cat's mouth. He could have cut himself. He could. The thing that had stuck in Signy's throat formed itself into a caveman sound, one simple flat note, as if she were learning to speak.

'Is Oscar hurt, Mama?'

She fought to provide Jed with something, anything.

'I'm going into my bedroom.' Her voice was rough now, foreign-sounding.

'I want to come.'

'You can't, Jed. Stay here.'

'Is Dada okay?'

She took a step forward, then another. Her feet were at the bedroom door. Her fingers belonged to someone else. She made contact with the wooden handle. She pushed the door open and closed it behind her.

Inside the blinds were down, the light dim.

The first thing: a shape, half-on, half-off the bed, legs bent, knees almost touching the floor, belly down on the edge of the mattress, an arm up in front of his head. His face was turned away to the far wall. The position was wrong, but also familiar. She studied his hair.

He could be asleep.

'Matt?'

'Mama?' Jed was directly outside the door.

'Don't come in.'

She waited until she was sure Jed had shuffled further off. She was not herself. She was someone else. She waited for the rise and fall in Matthew's breathing. His body. Still.

She moved to him. She shook his shoulder. He wobbled from side to side. The moths have eaten a lot of holes in your T-shirt, she thought.

'Wake up, Matt.'

His skin, even cooler than usual. She curved over him to look at his face. His eyes were closed, the lids tinged purply-pink.

On the white duvet beside his head, a pool of blood, an inkblot that spread dark red in the centre, lightening to pink at the edges. The blanket at her waist fell to the floor.

She pressed two fingers against his neck. His skin was springy, soft beneath her fingertips, his beard stubble prickly. There was no pulse.

Was it his throat that had been ... cut? She couldn't look. She slid her hand into his armpit.

Dad's armpit stayed warm for three whole hours after he'd died. Matthew's armpit was cooling. Cooler. He was cool all over.

★

'Mama?'

Her head was resting on her elbows, that were resting on the chest of drawers. How long had she been like this?

'Stay there.'

Her voice came from outside herself but also inside herself, too loud, as if she were wearing headphones.

She picked up the blanket and wrapped it back around her, turned and walked out of the room, closing the door carefully.

'What's wrong with Dada?' Jed stood on one leg, arms hugging his chest. She could see the polar bear ear-tips on his pyjamas sticking beyond the curve of his elbows. '*Tell* me.'

'Dada's hurt.'

'Is he okay?'

'I ... don't think so.'

'Is he dead?'

'He ...' Her hand went onto his shoulder.

Jed's face crumpled and he threw his hands to his head, pummelling himself with his fists. She could bear it no longer.

'No, love, he's not dead, he's badly hurt,' she lied. 'But he'll get better.'

She pulled Jed into her. His hands bunched in front of his face. His knuckles dug in to her stomach. He wailed, long and loud.

'It's all right,' she said. Why wouldn't he stop? 'I know. He's going to be okay. It's all right.'

'*Promise?*'

'Promise.'

Her head dropped backwards. She stared at the lightbulb. Her eyes closed.

She must get a grip, take control, she needed to do something.

Focus. Everything has its tipping point. It's only when pushed to the edge that you can see who someone really is.

'Dada. *My daddy!*'

Oscar weaved in and out of her legs. His purring was loud.

Jed was pulling her down. Once more, her knees met the cold wood floor on the landing. The last time she had been in this position had been helping Jed in the downstairs toilet yesterday. Matthew had been alive then. Now he was dead.

She hugged and rocked Jed and buried her head in his neck. He smelt of home. There was a spot of blood on her leg where the cat had rubbed his mouth against it. She wiped it away with her finger, licked it.

Metallic. Matthew's blood. She was going to puke.

'Jed. We need to go.'

She knew what she was going to do and what order she would do it in.

'To get help for Dada?'

'Yes.'

'What about Cassidy and her mummy and daddy?'

'We haven't time to wait for them. I'm sorry.'

Jed nodded. She led him to his room to collect his things. They were on their own now.

Day 7

Jed's eyes were fixed on the pebbled acrylic panes of the front door. In the dim light of the communal hallway, she tried to get him settled in his child seat at the back of the bike. Her hands shook so much that she struggled to click the catch on the safety belt. Her rucksack lay at her feet. Those men might come back.

'Where are we going?'

'To get help, my love.'

She felt drunk. Her lips tried to make themselves into the correct shapes.

'To get help,' Jed intoned, XO in his lap.

'Yes, monkey.'

The front door hung open a fraction. Through the gap, the metal hooks dangled from the door frame, the ones that had secured the bike lock. That must have happened when the men left the house. Matthew had put that lock there.

She cleared her throat. The sound rebounded in the narrow hallway as though there was someone else with them.

She loaded the rucksack on her shoulders: bulky. It would stick out behind her and Jed wouldn't have room to turn his head properly. Never mind.

Minutes ago, she'd led Jed to his bedroom, knelt in the

middle of the blue rug patterned with foxes, seen herself reflected in his pupils as he waited like a statue while she dressed him. She'd taken his binoculars from the toy basket, the old torch and picked up the plastic bunny light. She'd emptied his money box.

She had not gone back into her bedroom.

She must have gone upstairs to the spare room to put on her walking boots and outdoor gear because she was wearing them now. She'd taken the road map and her penknife and some matches that were hidden in the Drawer of Doom. Matthew's lighter was still in her pocket. The men had stolen the UV glasses from the shelf – every single pair. She'd taken two tins of food, a packet of dried noodles and the one bottle of water that had been left behind. She'd found a packet of rice cakes too, and offered one to Jed as they'd stood in the empty kitchen, but he'd said no. She hadn't wanted one either.

Someone must get help. That someone was her. Things must not collapse inwards. Life was happening. This was real.

She pulled the safety bar down in front of Jed's knees and wheeled the bike out of the hallway before pulling the front door to.

It was cold outside. Her eyes smarted against the glaring, clouded day. Jed squinted. Everything was dangerous, even daylight. She should have brought a hat for him.

Matthew's bike had gone. They'd had that too.

She didn't recognise the people on the street. Any one of them could be that other man, could have broken into her home last night. Any one of them might try to take something from her.

She glanced back at the house, bumped the bike wheels off the pavement into the road, Jed's head bouncing like a dolly in his seat. She should have listened to Matthew. A graphene electric: that's what she needed. She looked up at the bedroom windows, then down. He was behind them now. She put her leg over the crossbar. She headed towards Hornsey Road, past the Malaysian café which had once had spring rolls.

Matthew's walking boots had been on the bottom stair in the hallway, the red laces tied in bows. There was mud cut in patterns from his soles on the carpeted treads.

To her left, a man was stapling black plastic bags over the windows of his house. A roadblock had sprung up overnight at this end and Hornsey Road was now divided in two, one side leading down to the police station, the other side leading up Crouch Hill towards Crouch End. She was on the Crouch Hill side. She must pass through the taped cordon to reach the police station. That was who she needed: the police.

An enormous queue swelled on both sides of the tape, people moving through the cordon one by one, soldiers controlling the flow.

He could be here: NYPD. Waiting.

She recognised Southwick and Waters. They had knocked on her door yesterday. They had spoken to Matthew.

She joined the queue and nudged the bike wheels forwards.

'Please,' she said, the words a surprise, even to her, 'I need to get past.'

She pushed a little. The woman in front spun round.

'We all need to get through. You're hurting my legs.'

'You don't understand.'

Let the old bag's legs fucking hurt. Signy pushed again. The woman squealed.

She was gripped hard at the elbow, so hard her eyes closed. The image of the man in the NYPD cap right there behind her lids.

'Listen.' Her eyes flicked open. A man, a different man.

A deep voice. A beige raincoat. 'Wait your turn like everybody else.' He let her go.

Jed said, 'My daddy's ...' but the man had turned away.

They needed help. Her toes were cold inside her walking boots. Jed stared at his hands. The police station was just out of reach. The sentence she needed to say, that would get them there right away, was at the front of her mouth. She must get it out.

'Hey.' She tapped the raincoat man, leant towards his ear. *Say it.* 'Burglars broke into our house last night. Something happened to my partner. I mean, something terrible. For my son, help us get through? Please.'

That was it. Those were the right words. Good girl.

The man stared into her eyes. Then he was pushing the people in front of him to the side.

'Could you let this woman through? This lady urgently needs to get through.'

They were going to the police station. People could be good. People could be friendly, helpful. One thing was leading to another in a neat straight line. Yes. She wheeled the bike through the small corridor that opened up.

Southwick and Waters were busy ahead. The rucksack dragged. Something inside with sharp corners was digging at her ribs.

A high-pitched buzzing above their heads. A larger drone-hailer surrounded by many smaller ones.

ONCE THROUGH, PLEASE MAKE YOUR WAY ALONG THE ROAD. DO NOT BLOCK THE PASSAGEWAY. IF YOU NEED ASSISTANCE, PLEASE ASK A UNIFORMED OFFICER.

She was three people deep from the cordon. There wasn't enough air here. Too slow. She waved at Southwick, but his eyes were studying someone passing through the tape and he didn't notice her. She jumped up and down. The bike wobbled. Somebody shouted for her to keep still.

Behind her, towards Crouch Hill, the sound of a truck pulling up. A bleeping signalled its reversing and the engine was killed. The drone-hailer stopped giving orders. A peculiar lull, as if the lights had dimmed before a spectacle. The ticking of the engine cooling.

'*Southwick!*' she yelled. More words. Do it. Southwick glanced up. His eyes locked on to hers. 'You spoke to us! I need your help!'

There was another noise: a rolling, squeaking sound from the truck. Southwick's hand cupped his ear. She mouthed, '*Police!*'

Southwick nudged Waters next to him. Waters looked at her, recognition dawning. He beckoned her forward.

The drone-hailer began again. IF YOU WISH TO QUEUE FOR SUPPLIES FROM THE EMERGENCY TRUCK, PLEASE DO SO IN AN ORDERLY MANNER.

She tried to move towards the soldiers, the bike heavy with Jed, but she was pushed backwards. People wanted supplies from that truck. They wanted them now. This wasn't her plan. Shoving, shouting. No. A terrible thing had happened to her. She was entitled to order.

Southwick's body disappeared downwards suddenly, as if taken by a shark. That wasn't right either. This was a road, not an ocean. Waters and the other soldiers split up and fanned out along the road.

She was being taken further from them. She was going to faint. If she fainted, there would be no one to look after Jed.

The bike chain snagged on its cog. Someone shoved her in the ribs. Her hands lost their grip of the bike and it fell sideways away from her and she was falling too. Her palms flew out to meet the fibreglass. The road was warm, unyielding. People were climbing over her. The bike wheels spun, Jed still tied in his seat, suspended perpendicular to the ground, the seat's casing protecting him.

'Mama!'

He was crying out for her. Beyond, through a blizzard of legs, she saw the enormous black tyres of the truck.

The drone-hailer buzzed. PLEASE STAY CALM. DO NOT PUSH.

She picked herself up and reached for the bike.

'Jed! My son! Stop!'

Her elbows went out. Someone staggered backwards. A young woman. Signy didn't care. Now she was standing over Jed.

She hauled up the bike, checked he was unhurt. She tried to move, thrusting the wheels at the people in front of her, but she was wedged in. A heel on her foot, the pain sharp. She let her body yield to the great swell ploughing them to the left and back to the right.

'Hang on, Jed! It's going to be all right!'

Arms were crossed over chests for protection but she had to keep hold of the bike. It dug into her stomach, pain radiating from her belly button. She was nose to nose with her fellow humans – the nurses, the civil servants, the artists, the burglars, the murderers.

The supplies truck had rolled up its canvas at the rear and the inside swarmed with her neighbours, her community. So many. Ants crawling on the roof to get the water bottles and boxes of dried food being thrown out. Someone screaming, '*Danny!*'.

She had to get back to the roadblock. She had to get to the other side and the police station. The bike was her only weapon.

She looked back at the cordon. Troops in riot gear were

approaching, and further down the hill, mounted police. The clattering of hooves. Horses sliding on the road surface. Small canisters arcing through the air. A hissing sound. A line of fog rising from the ground. People clutching their eyes, fleeing past her.

She was looking through a telescope. She was going to stay calm. She was the Pacific Ocean on a windless day. The fog-smoke hissed towards her.

Calm. A change of plan.

She let herself be taken up Crouch Hill with everyone else. She was adapting. Drifting. This was good.

The bike felt heavy. The rubber handlebars burned her palms. The rucksack. She was panting.

'Don't worry, monkey.'

Past the unkempt recreation ground, past the new flats towards Crouch End. Was there a police station there? She was sure there wasn't. Gethin lived in Crouch End. Matthew in the flat. They were moving away from him. She and Matthew's son. His son. She was going to be sick.

They were nearing the crest of the hill.

'Dada!' Jed wailed. 'Mama, are we getting help?'

'Yes.'

Why was the hill so steep? Her lungs burned, her breath came swift and shallow. The bike pedal caught on her shin again, again.

She must stop.

A gap materialised in the crowd ahead. She seized her chance, steering the bike sideways into a front garden. She wheeled it up to the front door. Her reflection stared at her from the bevelled acrylic. Widow. No, not even. Never married. Behind her head, the reflections of people moving right to left. Behind that, the scrub of land next to New Era Academy School.

That scrub of land. Yes.

She navigated the bike swiftly across the road to a wooded copse. The copse had a path behind it to the Parkland Walk, following the disused Victorian railway line. There was an entry point here, she knew it from childhood. She stood in the copse among the trees listening to the sound of the crowds moving along the main road, her ears still ringing.

Between the densely packed tree trunks, the path was visible below. Overgrown thickets kept it well hidden from passers-by. She unclipped Jed from his seat and wheeled the bike down the steep slope towards some low railings. She had to run to keep up with the wheels.

'Where are we going?'

'You'll see.'

'What about Dada?'

An old sign over the railings was partially obscured by an overhanging oak branch. She rested the bike against two wooden stobs and parted the leaves:

'*Welcome to the Parkland Walk. Please respect the environment by taking your litter with you.*'

Someone had written MATTHEW NEEDS A HAIRCUT, in black Sharpie over the word '*litter*'.

No. It was MAZZY. MAZZY NEEDS A HAIRCUT.

A small map in the bottom left-hand corner indicated the route; it had been designed in cosy greens and browns, with cartoon leaf trees and an interrupted line in red that marked the path's distance in metres. She wanted to disappear into that map. She wanted sunshine and cups of tea, and chats about stars with her dad.

She traced the line with her finger; the route went as far as West Finchley, where it faded to a pale green haze as if nobody knew what happened after that. She and Jed would be able to rejoin the road at Finchley. There was a huge police station there next to the Tesco, you couldn't miss it.

Matthew had always hated Finchley. She looked to the sky.

Jed was rubbing his middle. 'I feel sick.'

'You're hungry, love.'

'No I'm not.'

'Let's go down here where it's quieter. I'll find something for you to eat.'

She led the way between the railings, bumping the bike down shallow steps cut into the earth, onto the track. The path was full of potholes. On either side, trees rose from the banks. There wasn't another soul here, only the vibration from the people on the road and a lone wood pigeon calling, sending her mind to Warston. She closed her eyes. The air smelt of earth.

'Mama?'

She shrugged the rucksack from her shoulders. It slithered backwards along her arms and hit the ground. Please let nothing have broken inside. She untied the drawstring. She, too, needed to eat: optimal performance was determined by calories-in equalling calories-out.

A tin of baked beans lay at the top of their belongings. She tugged at the ring pull. The silver lid peeled back in one smooth roll.

She hadn't brought a tin-opener. She'd need one. Most foods stored in aluminium didn't have a ring pull. She had only the blade on her small penknife. That was a mistake. That, and the hat to protect Jed.

The neon beans gave off a vinegary smell. She rooted in a side-pouch and found a plastic spork left over from a camping trip.

'Sit here, monkey, next to me.'

'I'm not hungry.'

'You are, you just don't know it.'

She handed him the tin. He held it in both hands, balancing it between knees drawn close to his chest.

'Cold,' he said, mouth full of beans.

Salt trails streaked his cheeks. The corner of his right eye had a red dot in it. He was holding himself together. She stroked his hair. His lips had gone orange.

'See? You were hungry after all.'

'Do you think Dada's crying?'

Jed dropped the spork to the floor, where it collected soil crumbs. She brushed them away with a finger.

'No, he knows we'll be back soon.'

She shovelled beans into her mouth to stop herself saying more.

'Do you think he'll finish the wooden house without me?'

She dug one fist into the earth.

The beans were sugary and salty and felt like sponge in her mouth. She forced down half the tin and pulled out the bottle of water. The liquid met the measuring line at the one-litre mark. It would last until they reached the police station. She would have to file a report – how long would that take? The police might want to transport them home in one of those army trucks. Her head throbbed. She repacked the rucksack. One thing at a time.

A soft noise, like wind. Jed nudged her. She looked up.

Thousands of tiny pollen-drones were stationed on the path twenty metres ahead.

'Don't move,' she whispered.

They watched as the drones took off, forming a black-balled mass low in the sky. They swarmed away as one entity.

'What were they doing?' Jed said.

146

'Let's go.'

She pulled the rucksack onto her back, returned Jed to his seat and they set off down the track. The wheels bumped in the potholes. Faster and faster they went, the landscape blurring: an adventure playground; a broken fence; a bin overflowing with cans.

She cycled between two raised concrete train platforms, Anthropocene fossils overgrown with nettles, ghosts of Victorian children waiting in plus-fours and hats.

The rucksack scratched noisily against the corners of Jed's seat.

'Mama?'

'Yes, love?'

'When will we be there?'

'I don't know, sweet pea. As soon as we can.'

A man in a baseball cap and a woman, riding mountain bikes on the path ahead. A flare of adrenaline in her stomach.

It couldn't be. They hadn't had bikes. Had they? They hadn't had anything, not even all their teeth.

Except Matthew's bike now. Head down, *keep going*.

The bikes passed one another. She kept low, hardly breathing. Navy jackets. Her eyes darted to their faces. It wasn't the NYPD man. He was bad. The bad ones were him, and also the other who had a funny accent. Where were they now? Looking over the spoils of last night. Washing the blood from their clothes.

The little wooden house. Oh God.

Keep moving.

The track had an almost imperceptible incline. Another twist in the path and a road emerged, running above them on the left bank. It looked quiet up there. She'd lost her bearings with the frequent weaving, but they must be heading in the right direction.

At Highgate the track was interrupted by the Maglev line. Focus. She would come up on to the street and walk along the road to Queen's Wood, then back on the Parkland Walk at Muswell Hill Broadway. She wheeled the bike up the exit ramp.

'Where are we going?'

A cordon had been set up at the junction of Archway Road and Muswell Hill Road. People queued on both sides. The Parkland Walk had been kind to them, had spat them out on the correct side for Queen's Wood. Now they wouldn't have to waste more time standing in line.

Jed stared. 'Do you think they're all going to the police station?'

'No.'

She weaved her way along Muswell Hill Road, shards of blue acrylic like scattered jewels in the road. The skeleton frame of a broken tram stop.

'Are we nearly there?'

'No.'

The entrance to Queen's Wood was in the dip of the hill and hidden behind a battery of flattened cars. She wheeled the bike through a small gate and along the path between rows of giant trees. A watery sun sat in the sky. It lay uncertain rays across the few leaves and cast column-like shadows on the ground from the chestnuts and oaks. The *chok, chok, chok* of a woodpecker echoed off the bark as they travelled deeper in.

'XO's sad.'

She stopped and turned. Jed in his seat, legs dangling above the back wheel.

'Is he?' she said. 'Why is he sad?'

'Because he wants to go home to see his friends.'

'Home to a river where otters live, or home to our house?'

'Our house. He's missing Paddington.'

She squeezed him gently in the crook of her arm.

'Tell XO, "Don't worry, everything will be okay".'

'Don't worry, XO, everything will be okay.' He kissed the toy on its plastic nose. 'You give him a kiss, Mama.'

She kissed the teddy's ear.

'Did you kiss Dada before we left, Mama?'

'Yes.'

Another lie. So many.

'I didn't.'

Her watch said 10.30 a.m. There would be silence in the bedroom now, the day's light pushing at the edges of the blinds.

They passed a rope swing.

'That's what Dada and me play on.'

'Yes.'

'And we build dens out of branches and then use the Aerobie.'

'Jed, how about you count to a thousand in your head?'

'Why?'

'Just do it.'

Queen's Wood led to Muswell Hill Broadway. She emerged onto the busy street, its closed shopfronts, its air of controlled chaos. A man standing on a crate with an old megaphone shouting about a capitalist conspiracy. Next to him, four men and a woman were handing out water and tins from plastic sacks.

'Live well for less!'

One of them was actually laughing, lobbing out the tins overarm like cricket balls. She watched him – his mouth, his eyes crinkling. Laughter.

SUSANNAH WISE

She couldn't get close enough to take any food; there were too many bodies in front of her. What was she thinking? She should go back, go home.

Home.

Far far away, the wail of an old air-raid siren. People glanced up, then down. It didn't matter to them; wherever it was, it wasn't here.

She pulled Jed from his seat.

'Go and ask the lady for some tins. Remember – just the lady. And say "please".'

'But I've only got to three hundred and five.'

'It doesn't matter.'

'Where will you be?'

'Right here. I promise.'

Jed pushed his way between legs. She lost sight of him briefly, then he reappeared at the front next to the woman. He tapped her thigh with his finger in that way he had. The woman bent, smiling as Jed whispered in her ear. She thrust two tins and a packet of noodles into his hands. More food now, in their kitty. That was good.

He found his way back.

'Well done, monkey.'

'Shall I carry on counting?'

'Yeah.'

The tins were dented – synthetic beef and lychee chunks in syrup. The taste of tinned lychee was inextricably linked to her childhood, but her mind went instead to the pudding she'd eaten at that new restaurant with Matthew and James and Aya. The fruit had been drowning in baijiu. She'd been upset about something important; she couldn't remember what.

'Could you move out of the way, please?'

She stepped sideways to let a woman pass, stashed the tins in the rucksack and they crossed the Broadway's central round-about towards the next leg of the Parkland Walk.

Jed was running to keep up. Yet another taped cordon to get through, another queue. Time was passing.

'My legs ache,' he said. She put him back in his seat.

The soldiers seemed confused about protocol, some people walking straight through the tape, others taken aside for questioning. It was her turn. The female soldier looked weary.

'Name?'

She wanted to tell her. About Matthew. And yet ... A dead stare. An unyielding set of the shoulders. Not this one.

'Mary Made-Up.'

This was how she would get taken aside and speak to someone official, someone who would meet her eyes, be willing to help.

'Address?'

'1 Made-up Street, Made-up Land, M1 1MM.'

The tape opened. She hesitated.

'Look, love,' the soldier said, 'do you want to pass across or not?'

Signy wheeled the bike through.

A steeply wooded area. There didn't appear to be an entry point. She took them backwards and forwards along the railings running beside the path below. Jed's weight made the bike skid across the loose earth. She tried to picture the map in her head.

'Mama! There's the gate.' She looked but it was all trees. 'Further,' he urged.

A section of railings ahead, bent flat to the ground as though something heavy had years before driven into it from higher up the slope.

'Well done, love. Not far now.'

'I need a poo.'

She picked her way across the twisted metal and down onto the path. A low-roofed breeze block shed with an open door sat to one side. She leant the bike against the shed wall and pulled Jed from his seat.

He jogged on the spot. 'Quick, I'm desperate.' He nodded at the shed. 'Can I do it in there in case someone comes?'

'There's no one here, monkey. It's better to go outside.'

'You keep lookout.'

She led him into the shade of a chestnut trunk. He pulled down his trousers and his pants and crouched low.

'Don't peek.'

She turned away, listening to Jed's straining and the wind swishing in the branches. The sun disappeared. She looked at her watch: 12.05 p.m. An hour and a half it had taken them, to go nowhere.

'Finished.'

She grabbed a handful of grass. It absorbed nothing and smeared everything. She threw it away from her.

'I've got pindles and needles.'

'Nearly done.'

She pulled him up and kicked a mound of sticks and earth over everything while he buttoned his trousers.

'Wild animals might track our scent,' he said.

'Don't be silly. We're in London.'

'Bears?'

'No.'

'Leopards?'

'No.'

'Monsters, then?'

'No monsters.'

152

The light from the torch swinging through the attic.

Her eyes found the ground. Her bootlaces had come undone. She bent to tie them. When she raised her head, Jed had gone. She spun around, her throat closing.

'*Jed?*'

'Here, Mama.' His voice echoed inside the shed. There was a brief silence, then she heard him say, 'Hallo?'

She raced through the open door into darkness.

'Are you alive?'

Jed's outline dimly visible in the centre of the room. Her eyes adjusted: a pile of blankets in the corner. The blankets shifted. A bald head, tufts of grey hair sticking out either side. She screamed.

'*Mama!*'

She was yanking Jed by the scruff of the neck, dragging him to the rectangle of light at the door. The body rose to standing.

She flung Jed back into his bike seat, threw the rucksack onto one shoulder and sped away.

'That man could have been a ghost,' said Jed. He was hard to hear over her breathing.

'He was very much alive.'

'I don't like it when you're scared, Mama.'

'I don't like it when I'm scared either.'

He was quiet for a moment.

'Was he homeless? His hair was just like Grandpa's, all sticking out at the side.'

'That's right.'

'I got to a thousand.'

'Start again.'

They snaked along the path, a curious roaring sound like waves on the sea coming from somewhere in the distance. The route came to an abrupt end where a thicket of brambles blocked the way. Through the tangled sticks, two sets of rusted iron buffers: the old terminus.

'We've missed the exit.'

Jed's eyebrows lifted.

'We'll just go back a bit and find it.'

They retraced their steps a hundred metres, high banks either side. No path to lead them out. She pointed the bike at the hill.

'Up there?' said Jed.

'Up there.'

The incline grew with each step. The brakes squeaked.

'You'll have to get off, love.' Jed climbed out and bent to pick up sticks. 'No. Not now.'

He straightened. 'For our collection. Dada will—'

'No.'

He let the sticks drop.

That roaring sound was growing. It might be inside her – heart pounding in her chest.

'My legs are still achy, Mama.'

'Nearly there. You're doing really well.'

They reached the top of the bank. She took a slug of water from the bottle and passed it to Jed. He gulped so fast, he sloshed liquid over his shoes. He burped and gave the bottle back.

'Thirsty.'

Green railings stretched unbroken in front of her, high as her chest.

Her heart felt bruised. No. She felt nothing.

On the other side, the remainder of the hill leading to the road. She shrugged off the rucksack and lifted the bike. It was heavier, dirtier than she remembered, the blackened cog thick with miles of road-dust inches from her face.

Some things change, some stay the same.

She hitched the front wheel, jammed herself beneath the frame and hoiked the back end over, throwing it away from her. The bike clattered to the ground on the other side. She looked through the metal bars, assessing the damage. The chain had come off but otherwise it was all right. The chain oil was black blood, tacky on her palms, with a sensation that set her teeth on edge.

'Okay, monkey, you're next.' She gave Jed a leg-up. He grappled with the bars, jumped over. 'All right?'

He brushed himself down. 'What's that noise?'

'It's the sea. We're going to the seaside.'

'Are we?' His expression lifted.

'No, monkey, sorry.'

'Why did you say it, then?'

'I don't know.'

The rucksack followed next, an ominous clanking inside as the bag hit the ground. Jed held the straps.

'I'll guard it for you, Mama.'

She threw herself over and replaced the bike chain on its cog.

'Messy job.'

'Here.'

It was Jed's turn to hold out grass. Grateful, she wiped her fingers clean.

They continued up the last part of the hill and out of the treeline onto the verge of a dual carriageway. The North Circular. She hadn't expected to be here, at this road. It was busy – pedestrians, push-bikes, motorbikes moving in both directions between lines of static cars. More police drones.

Jed looked left and right. 'Where's the police station, then?'

'In Finchley.'

'Is this Finchley?'

'It's near here.'

'How near? Why do you keep saying that?'

'Jed.'

His face wavered and he turned away.

'When will Dada be better?'

'Soon.' She put her hand on the back of his neck and studied the road. 'I'm not cross with you, I promise.'

Finchley must be there, where it curved to the north-west. She stepped out onto the concrete lanes and headed left, the distant roar increasing.

The bike was a shark cutting through water. The road was the current carrying them along. The concrete was smooth beneath the wheels, better than the stubbly Parkland Walk.

This was what shock was like. A great nothing, a universe of darkness from the tips of your toes to the ends of your hair, each hair like an aerial that streamed the lack of sensation up, up and away.

Focus.

The unbroken white lines kept company beneath her, lulling, muzzing her brain. It was all right. Everything was going to be …

Her feet missed the pedals. She fell onto the crossbar. Her boots skidded on the road and the bike juddered to a halt.

'Mama? You okay?'

Her legs quivered. 'No. Yeah. Missed my footing.'

They arrived at a junction allowing them to cross on to the opposite carriageway. No military cordons here, but a turning: *Avondale Road.*

It was as good as any and took them in a northerly direction.

NYPD. That man had never been to New York. He and his friend had taken Matthew on the journey of a lifetime.

A one-way ticket. It was what people said in films. Perhaps she was in one.

She turned the bike into a long stretch of detached houses. Pollarded plane trees lined the pavement on both sides. The roaring sound grew closer still.

At the end of Avondale Road, Ballards Lane ran at right angles. Finchley police station was on Ballards Lane. She turned left onto it.

A few hundred yards ahead, a mass of roiling bodies, backs to her, surrounded by soldiers and police officers in a sort of roped corral. What fresh hell was this? Police drones, large and small, hovered overhead. A chant rang out – '*Open up! Let us in! Open up! Let us in!*'

In the middle of it, two men had climbed a lamppost.

'What is everyone doing?' shouted Jed.

What were they doing? Waiting? For something to open? The police station? Her body, so recently numb and clumsy, felt suddenly fleet, charged like an electric rod. More people arrived, swelling the crowd. She steered the bike away, then back again. Someone should tell her what to do. She needed the police. So did everyone else. She needed Matthew. To tell her.

Jed fidgeted in his seat. 'Can I get out?'

'No.'

'My bum's aching.'

She pulled him from the bike and offloaded the rucksack into the empty seat. Relieved of its burden, her back seemed to float upwards. So much noise.

Then, among the faces in the crowd: Gethin. He was in profile. A green coat, his red hair. He was right there. Right *here*. Her *friend*. Blood rushed to her cheeks.

'Gethin!'

A deep, rich clap of thunder. She ducked her head, pulled Jed into her, shielding him with one arm, curling them both into a ball with her eyes clamped shut. The sound pinballed between the buildings. The air throbbed. Her ears rang.

A peculiar silence, a moment of suspension. Around her the shouting had stopped. She was okay, Jed was okay. Safe.

She raised her head.

Clouds of black smoke billowed in the distance, half a mile away. Not thunder. A fire. Something. An explosion.

A jumble of panicked screams. She could no longer see Gethin. A wall of people headed her way.

PLEASE STAY CALM.

She threw Jed onto her hip, swivelled the bike and belted back the way she'd come. Her feet sent the road away. Jed clung on like an animal.

She streaked for metres and metres, keeping ahead of the swell along Ballards Lane, and skidded the bike wheels to the left into a side road. On and on she ran, the bike in her free hand like an extra limb, groups of people running beside her now, overtaking as she fell behind.

The side road seemed endless. She ran until she'd drained the power from her legs and let Jed drop to the ground. The rucksack was still in his seat. She doubled over, panting, one hand on the bike.

'Mama. Come on! We need to help Dada.'

'Just ... give me a minute.'

She found a low cement wall in front of someone's house and collapsed onto it. The bike fell against her. It was heavy as a cow. She let it stay there. Her mouth was parched. Her eyes closed and the world disappeared. Blissful, blissful nothing.

There might be another explosion. A bomb planted by *Shīluò zhī*. Fuel going up at a gas station.

Gethin. He had been there. She must stand. She must take them elsewhere.

Pink rings flashed on the inside of her lids. Her face was brushed with warmth. The sun.

She listened: footsteps, a drone-hailer far away, shouting in the distance.

Not safe to return to the centre of the city. She couldn't go to the police station. Her head sagged, too heavy for her neck. Matthew.

Gethin had been right there in front of her.

They would have to travel further out.

'What if Cassidy's waiting at our house?' Jed's voice was soft.

Cassidy entering their unlocked flat with Vicky and Steve, searching for Jed but finding Matthew instead. The wooden house, unfinished. Oh.

'Maybe they can get help for Dada?'

This was too hard. She wasn't sure she could do it.

'Who would want to blow everyone up, Mama?'

'I don't know, love. It might have been an accident.'

'Is the world ending?'

'No.'

'We have to go to Gamma's.'

She shook her head. 'Too far on our own.'

'It's not, Mama! We can go on this.' He stroked the frame of the bike as if it were a pet. 'It's all nice there. She's got the hose with the trigger.'

She looked at his face, small and round, clear eyes shining.

'That's where we were *going* to go. Before,' he said.

A lump in her throat. If she opened her mouth, the lump might drop like a stone onto the pavement or she might collapse, sink into the cold paving slabs, never get up. What would Jed do, then?

Something was happening, something bigger than her. She wasn't up to it.

She gazed at the sky, heavy with smoke. Above that, a V of police drones travelling left to right. Higher still, another V: seven Canada geese flapping silently in the opposite direction.

The bike wheels had left tread marks on her jeans. She'd forgotten to bring a pump. The hat; the tin-opener; the pump. *I went to the shop and I bought …*

Warston: the light in the autumn evening, the fields sodden with rain, the cold at night. Mum was unwell. She would need Signy's help. Gethin might be heading there. It made sense.

She would go to Warston. She would take Jed there. Since they'd left the house, she had always been going to Warston, she just hadn't known it until now. She was close here to Exit 2 of the M1. Warston was at Exit 18. How long it would take to cycle roughly eighty miles up the motorway? Two days, possibly. They had enough food to last until they got there. They would find clean water along the way. They would.

Protect Jed. It's what Matthew would have wanted.

The thought of tackling that distance by herself made her want to sleep.

2.30 p.m. now. It would be dark at seven. They'd need to find a safe place along the way for the night.

She unfolded the road map. Her eyes couldn't focus. It was squiggles of different colours leading nowhere. The paper shook in her hands. Why was the writing so small? All the streets would be blocked soon and there would be people everywhere and they would be trapped.

'Jed, can you read the roads out loud for me?'

He said the names as she sketched a back route to the motorway with her finger. She needed a pee.

Specks of ash landed gently on the map. The air smelled like burned toast. She grabbed the rucksack, put Jed in his seat. They set off.

'Are we going to Gamma's?'

'Yes.'

'Then Dada will join us when he wakes up?'

'Yes.'

'Wahoo!'

Jed raised his arms in the air. Perhaps he was pretending they were on a roller coaster.

They flew along. Her back had that tingling feeling. Past a line of low-rent shops, their fronts smashed, acrylic and sheet metal on the pavement. Travelling was comforting. Time folded around her like a cape, propelling her forward, keeping her mind from dark corners.

Oscar and Pyewacket.

Three toothbrushes sitting in the blue china cup on the bathroom sink.

Creased rolls of Christmas wrapping and tinsel bagged beneath her bed.

The wooden …

Her fingers held fast to the steel brakes; cold, numb again. Better than feeling.

She swerved left onto Totteridge Lane – a long tree-lined road. Her bladder was bursting, her brow prickling with sweat. Where another tributary road joined the lane, a small triangle of grass had been planted in the centre like a miniature village green. In the centre of the grass was a clump of low shrubs. She stopped. It was quiet here. Safe.

'I need to pee, Jed. I'll get you out and we'll go into those bushes there.'

'But the bushes are just in this little patch of grass and it's right in the middle of the road. Someone might see.'

'Tough.' She wheeled the bike into the centre of the grass. 'You keep lookout.'

She crept in among the shrubbery and crouched. Her quadriceps burned. How would she ever make it all that way? Her pee splashed onto the earth, dark, strong-smelling. She needed to drink more water.

Jed's voice carried from the edge of the bushes.

'Mama, my mouth's bleeding.'

She found her way back to him. He held his fingers out, fingertips stained red. She took his chin in her hand and angled his mouth up towards her. The small line at the left corner had split. He needed drugs for it.

'Is it Bovine Staph?'

'Jed. No.'

The revery alone will do …

That poem. The Emily Dickinson. She couldn't remember it. Oh God, she couldn't remember.

What did she remember? Toothbrushes in the blue pot. Matthew's blue shower gel. The bathroom so white.

'Mama?'

'Does it hurt?'

'Only when I open it.'

He made an O of his mouth. Pinpricks of blood oozed afresh.

'Here.'

She found the small tin of lip balm and smothered it over his lips.

She let her legs fold beneath her and her bottom met the grass with a thump. She'd fallen from a horse once in Warston. It had felt just like this.

The houses here were pale-coloured, still with their original 1930s exteriors. Front doors with neat panes of old glass. An empty square on a roof where a missing solar panel should have been. The curtains below were drawn. A tree in the front garden with tiny orange berries on it.

She needed sugar. She found the tin of lychees in the ruck-sack. She stared at it, dumbly. No ring pull.

She stabbed at the lid with the small blade of her penknife until she'd pierced a hole and sawed a circle around the tin's radius. Wrapping her fingers in her jumper, she flicked the lid up. There – done it.

She could smell the fruit from here.

'Don't cut yourself.'

She handed it to Jed. He fished inside the tin. Her mouth watered. A lychee, white and smooth. Like an eyeball. He pushed it carefully between his lips.

The blood on his fingertips had found its way into the syrup. It floated slick on the surface. She agitated it, watching the red turn pink, swirl and spread. A good source of iron. His blood was her blood anyway, more or less.

She ate three. They were delicious: sweet and cold, as if they'd arrived straight from the fridge. The syrup ran down her chin.

Jed thrust his hand back into the tin.

'This lychee's very stingy. How long till my birthday?' His mouth was full.

'Two months.'

'What day is it today?'

The tinnitus began in her ear. 'Saturday 24 March,' she said. 'I think.'

'Saturday 24 March.' Jed pulled up the grass with his hands. 'I'm missing ballet. What day did Dada get hurt?'

'Today, monkey.'

'Oh.'

In the house opposite, the one with the missing tile, a child's face appeared between the curtains at the upstairs window. A girl, no more than three years old. Signy waved. The child waved back. A grown-up's hand slipped between a break in the material and pulled the child out of sight.

'What does "passed away" mean?'

'It means passing out, you know? Fainting.' She threw the empty tin into the bushes. 'Let's go.'

Three miles on, the route widened. It curved slowly, a slip road that became a flyover, rising into the air in a sweeping arc, the lanes lined with cars and lorries. At the far end the road would slope downwards, taking them onto the M1 proper at Exit 2. Four lanes leading north to Warston. From behind, Jed's hand curled around her cheek.

'Sweetheart, I can't see when you do that.'

'Where has everyone gone?'

The little child, waving at the curtained window. Everyone crowded into areas or hiding at home or at a leisure centre waiting to register. She and Jed were here.

The bike looped round the last bend. She stopped at the bottom of the flyover, shielding her eyes with her hand against the glare of white sky.

'Uh-oh,' sang Jed.

At the apex of the ramp, a military cordon blocked entry to the motorway. A spike chain, angry metal teeth pointing up, lay across the road panels ahead of a line of armed soldiers, bellies slunked over belts. They gazed stonily in her direction, still as waxworks. Parked behind the soldiers were two military trucks and a yellow hurdle barrier that reached across the entire road to the hard shoulder. Three drones buzzed, two small, but one startlingly large. She'd never seen a drone so big. In contrast to the smaller ones, the lone giant hovered silently, casting its glossy shadow on the fibreglass road below. Its body swivelled on its axis, several circular holes puncturing its smooth exterior at intervals. She watched as six black barrels extended, one from each hole, reaching far and wide. Six long metal pipes protruding in six directions.

This was not a watching drone, a guardian drone. This was a weapon.

A sweat broke across her belly, gluing her T-shirt to her skin. A soldier began a slow amble down the ramp towards her. His hand went up to shield his eyes, the action a curious mirror of hers. Angry grey clouds gathered in the north.

They wouldn't allow her past. That drone was on high alert. The soldiers would send her back into London. She wheeled the bike around quickly.

'What are you doing? That man wants to talk to us.'

'Ssh.'

She cycled back along the slip road and turned left.

From back on the ramp, there came a sudden green flash, followed by an amplified noise like a blowtorch burning through a crisp-packet. She pulled up, looked back over her shoulder.

'That's the drone,' said Jed, as if it were obvious. 'That is sage. That's the big quiet one, with the lasers. But why did they fire it?'

'Lasers?'

'But why—'

'Which drones use lasers?'

'The new army ones. They don't make any noise. You never know they're coming. *Newsbites* said, "weapon technology's improved tenfold in the last year".' He was speaking fast and she knew he wanted to get to the end so he could ask his question. 'The lasers are sixteen times more powerful and twenty-five times more accurate than bullets, it said. But why did they fire—'

'I don't know.'

They weren't going to find out. Not today. Not any day.

'If we'd had them at home, then Dada wouldn't have been hurt.'

'Yes.'

She was on an A-road now, running parallel to the motorway and sandwiched between modern housing developments. A mile further on, a fallow field stretched away to her left-hand side. In a far corner, a stockpile of tall, thin blue Agrico-bots, their rubbery digging and sprinkling arms hanging at their sides, their netted langlauf feet parked in an upright position at the front, making them look faintly comical, like penguins. At the far end, the M1 slashed through the land.

A metal gate cut into the hedge. It opened easily.

It was so quiet. Extraordinary that no one was here, had not attempted this route. Perhaps hundreds of thousands of people were already miles ahead of her, escaping to Birmingham, Scotland, Leicester. Perhaps Vicky and Steve. Perhaps she'd meet them on the way.

Or maybe they were locked in a registration centre. Doing what they'd been told. She wasn't sure which – here or there – made her feel more safe.

Through the gate, across the clay soil. Her boots grew heavy with mud.

'What do the funnels do?' said Jed.

'What?'

'The funnels in the Agrico-bots' bellies? What do they do?'

He knew so much, yet he did not know this simple thing.

'When they've done their seeding, they use the funnels to pour liquid compost in. To help fertilise the soil.'

'Is that how it works with mummies and daddies?'

'Not exactly.'

The bike juddered across the soil.

'Where are we going now?'

'Finding our entry another way.'

'That's against the law.'

'Quiet now.'

Laser drones might have protected Matthew. They hadn't been there when she'd needed them. She hated them for that.

Jed hummed tunelessly, his voice vibrating with the bumpy ground.

'Mama,' he whispered. 'Wouldn't it be good if the Agricobots woke up?'

'Not really.'

'Yes, because then Dada might wake up too.'

'Ssh, I said.'

'Why ssh?'

'For God's sake! *Because!*'

She pushed up the slope at the other side.

There was a pause, then Jed said, 'Is it shush in case of that laser drone?'

'What?'

'In case it comes to get us?'

'Why would it come to—'

'Don't worry,' he whispered. 'They're intelligent. They can train themselves on your body and know all your information straight away. It wouldn't hurt us.' He raised his hands. 'There's no reason. We're the goodies.'

'Yeah.'

A laser that pulls information from your body without asking. Her child could accept that, easily, as natural as a bee collecting pollen.

Her child could accept he has a father who might sleep for an indeterminate number of days while she worked out how to break the news to him.

Eight lanes of motorway stretched out in both directions, an endless line of vehicles. Some had barely an inch between bumper and tail. No movement inside. It gave her goosebumps.

She pulled Jed from his seat and lifted the bike over the metal barriers. They walked through the gaps in traffic on the southbound carriageway. A large green coach with white paper bibs draped over the headrests in the fast lane. The door was closed but the luggage section underneath was open, the luggage all gone save for a fire extinguisher and a gurney. The sign up front read, 'Steadway Academy'.

They climbed the central reservation and stood on the northbound carriageway, staring up the straight lanes that led away. Lorries towered in the slow lane like standing stones. To her right, a hatchback. Inside, a baby seat covered in crumbs; an empty water bottle; a pair of UV glasses with the arms missing; a book on cooking: *Delicious for Little Ones*. The jacket cover, a picture of a steaming sweet potato with cheese. She tried the doors: locked.

Not a soul around. She stamped on the fibreglass. Mud from her boots flew off in pellets.

'This is the road to Gamma's?'

'This is it.'

Grey clouds lowered, closer now. Miles ahead, the sky a blueish-white. She chose the hard shoulder – fewer cars – pedalling slowly. A red estate car, doors open. A trail of empty crisp packets, coffee cups and foil paper led away to the verge.

Further ahead, belongings, people's rubbish littering the road like entrails.

She took off again. That feeling as the landscape slid back. *The further we go, the more we leave the ugliness behind.* Who used to say that? Was it Dad?

'If you see anyone,' she said, eyes fixed on the road ahead, 'tell me immediately but don't shout, whisper like I'm doing now.'

Each revolution of the pedals was another yard further from home.

And also, to home.

Matthew, Matthew, far behind.

She had no idea of the distance they'd travelled. The motorway's digital exit signs were haughty blank plaques that rose from the hard shoulder. Why couldn't they have printed the bloody numbers in the corner with actual reflective stickers like they used to? She could cycle right past Exit 18 and not even know it.

Four lanes away, a jeep, all doors shut. A shadow in the driver's seat. The outline of a person. She squeezed hard on the brakes.

'Mama?'

'Wait.'

The shadow wasn't moving. Someone trapped in their car. They could have had a heart attack. A dead body.

She would put herself ahead of it, get a glimpse through the windscreen. No; this angle was worse. The entire thing was just a reflection of white sky.

'Mama, is there someone? I'm scared.'

She reversed, veered closer.

Their mouth and eyes would be wide open, a zombie, the shadow still half-alive, she'd—

It was a coat.

The hood had been placed over the headrest and the sides of the coat hung down around the seat, creating the illusion of a fully rounded body.

'Why are you making that noise? I thought we were supposed to be being quiet.'

'What noise?'

'Like a cat. Can we go now? I want to get to Gamma's. Dada might get there before us unless we hurry. Can I have some water?'

The bottle was empty.

The Watford bee-farm silos were visible from the road. She must be at Exit 5. There was no sign of the army. Though the soldiers could be hidden at the end of the slip road with their weaponised drones. Trying to catch people out.

Droplets of rain pattered onto her coat, a light stream growing steadily heavier. The sky opened and the landscape dissolved.

'XO's going to get wet!'

She felt Jed's body curve over, his head pushing against the rucksack on her back. The water arrowed onto the fibreglass and bounced back around the pedals.

She skidded to a halt, pulled Jed from his seat, dropped the bike onto the road and ripped open the slippery-wet rucksack. She pulled out the only other food tin with a ring pull, the one from home, and peeled it open: chickpeas. There was a clean dry-bag at the bottom of the rucksack. She emptied out the tin's brine, poured the chickpeas into the dry-bag and gave it to Jed.

'What are you doing? Let's hide under something.'

'Wait!'

She put the empty tin on the road, held it steady with her fingers. The rain beat against her spine. The feeling wasn't unpleasant.

The tin filled, the raindrops making a hollow pinging sound against the metal. Water dribbled into the gap between her boots and her socks.

'We can't drink that!' Jed yelled.

Matthew had been right. She was a hypochondriac. Now she'd created a hypochondriac in her son, too.

'It's for emergencies. We might not have a choice, love.'

The rain stopped suddenly. The sun emerged and the air softened. Water plopped rhythmically from the ends of her hair onto her jacket. The dry-bag of chickpeas lay at Jed's feet. She sealed the top. The empty tin was sitting by itself on the road, with bubbles on its surface.

Matthew's hands fixing a puncture on her bike. Watching the bubbles float up.

She decanted the water carefully into her bottle. When she put Jed back in his seat, the foam seat-cover squelched beneath his bottom.

A sound. Like her own voice inside her, but on the outside. They both froze. Jed grabbed her wrist.

They stared at the lines of wet cars. Jed lifted the safety bar and hopped out of his seat onto the road. She shook her head. He pointed to a white van over on the fast lane.

'That one.'

The voice was coming from inside. Perhaps someone was trapped in the back, had been sealed in when everything ground to a halt.

'Oh,' Jed moaned. 'I want Dada.'

'Wait there.'

She gave him the bike and went to listen at the rear doors.

The sound was coming from the front seats. She crept around the side, stood on tiptoes and peered through the passenger window.

Dolly Darker's caravan. The three of them on tiptoes, looking for a sign Dolly was a witch.

The radio. The dials were alight. The music, the TrincXcode, spooling out its peculiar time signature, and overlaying it, a benign woman's voice: '... *aurora, auscultation, auspice, auspicious, Aussie, austere, austerity, austral* ...'

She ran back to Jed.

'What is it?' he whispered.

'It's GQOS talking.'

'What's she saying?'

'She's running through the dictionary, I think.'

'But why?'

'I don't know.'

'She's been hacked.'

'Yeah.'

They took off, the road slick now. Puddles shone on the fibreglass.

A radio. A second one that worked of its own accord. It might mean nothing.

'But it doesn't make sense,' Jed pointed out. 'How can just a single radio be working on the motorway? Why not all of them?'

What would Matthew have said?

'I don't know,' she said. Not that.

'You don't know anything,' Jed sighed.

She was shivering. They would have to sleep in wet clothes tonight. Everything inside the rucksack would be wet too.

The bike tyres had lost air. In spite of their deep treads they slid unnervingly over the white lines.

'I want to go home,' Jed said.

The metronomic bump of each cat's-eye marked pace as they rode over it. After a time, she almost enjoyed the mindless repetition.

Warston was coming closer. Her mother would be expecting them. Three of them. There would be only two.

Steam rose from the road panels. The smell of wet road-dust and damp grass in the air. Jed had been quiet. She imagined his child-brain trying to make sense of this. A dull pain in her chest.

More exits: 6, 7. Or was it 7A? They'd stopped several times to check inside cars for food or water. Nothing except a strawberry chew, which she'd given to Jed, and a pair of women's purple leather driving gloves. No more radios talking. It was all right. The matches in the rucksack had gone sodden in the rain, but Matthew's lighter still worked. They were okay. They had a plan, somewhere to go. She longed for a warm arm around her shoulders.

'How long now?'

'Long.'

'But how long? I want Dada.'

'Count to a—'

'No.'

Aya teaching a yoga class in that bright white studio, the one with the stained glass panels in the windows. Signy lying supine on a mat, Aya's hands pushing at her shoulders, relaxing, sinking into the floor.

Traffic cones dotted the fast lane. Their luminous internal lights had lost charge and were now dull and grey. The cones went on for miles like rows of dunces' hats. Several had detached themselves from their road fixtures and were on their side, rolling gently in the breeze.

How had she been cycling for so long? Her crotch was stinging.

'Mama, my eyes are sore.'

'Use your arm as a shade.'

'Too achy.'

They descended into silence.

An exit loomed. She needed water. It was quarter to seven and the light was fading. She should think about finding a car to sleep in. She stopped.

On the grass verge beside them, a large shit. It smelt strong.

'Is that a dog's?'

'Or a human's.'

Life had been reduced to intervals between excretions and finding others' excretions left behind.

'How long has it been here?'

'I don't know.'

'I'm scared.'

Buzzing above. Hundreds of police drones circling in their strange triangulate formations. She'd never seen such a large number. They looked like birds wheeling in thermals. They went round and round for minutes, then flew away.

'I don't like it,' said Jed.

'Let's get going.'

'Yes. That's what I want to do.'

A section of the motorway where the hedges at the top of the sloping verges lowered and the land opened out. She left the bike on the road and led Jed behind a bush to pee, her urine pale-coloured now. It trickled downhill between her feet.

'I've wet my boots,' said Jed.

'Me too. Never mind.'

'Yeah, who cares?'

He rolled his eyes. It made her smile. He did it again. She forced a laugh. Jed copied the sound of it.

She straightened up and fastened her jeans, glancing back down at the road over the top of the bushes. Her throat closed.

On the southbound carriageway a man, a woman and two children on fancy SOLA bikes. They were studying her rucksack and her own bike lying on the hard shoulder.

'What is it?'

'Ssh.' She gripped the back of his neck.

'I want to see!' He strained against her.

The family of four wheeled to the central reservation. The elder child climbed the low metal railings onto the northbound side and made his way towards her things. He picked up her rucksack and opened the top.

'*Hey!*'

The boy looked up. He was only ten or so. Signy ran fast at him down the slope. His body concaved away from her, belly first, but she was too quick for him.

'That's our stuff!'

She snatched the rucksack from his hands.

'Take your hands off my son!' The man's voice bounced on the fibreglass. He dropped the bike and ran at her. 'What the fuck do you think you're doing?'

She backed up the slope, fanning her arms out sideways to make herself bigger.

'Okay! I'm sorry! It's just me. And my son.'

Jed clutched the back of her jacket.

The man grabbed his son, breath rising and falling beneath his coat. He held the boy at arm's length.

'You okay?'

The boy nodded. The man whispered something. The boy nodded again. Perhaps they were going to attack her now, take everything. No; the boy went to his mother. The man looked up.

'What are you doing on the motorway by yourselves? It's not safe.'

'We ...' She ran her sleeve over her face. Be someone. Someone whose partner isn't at home, half-on, half-off the bed. 'I could ask you the same question.'

The woman was climbing the barrier now, walking forward, her waterproofs crackling and rustling.

'We didn't mean to scare you. Everything's upside down. We're all jumpy.'

Signy went further up the slope until she had backed herself against the bushes. The woman's hand was extending, Signy shrinking back. The woman smiling.

'Please,' she said, waggling her arm. 'I don't bite.'

Signy took it. The palm felt warm, soft.

'I'm Madeleine.'

Madeleine was tall. She had a nice voice, kind. Black hair. Her shoulders looked as if she did a lot of swimming.

'Signy.' Her voice sounded weak and wavery. 'This is Jed, my son.'

'Six, my husband.' Madeleine pointed at her children. 'And these two idiots are Tom and Zinia.'

'Your name's *Six*?' Jed stepped out from behind her legs.

'Yes.' The man's eyes creased.

'Like the number?'

'Yep.'

'That's funny.'

'It is, isn't it? It's Chinese.'

'Is that yours?' Zinia was staring at XO, fluffy, still sopping wet and sitting in the bike basket.

'It's an otter, don't touch him, he's mine!' Jed ran down the slope.

'Jed, come back!'

Jed snatched XO. 'I don't want him anyway,' Zinia said, 'Beavers are far cleverer.'

'*Beavers?*' Jed let the teddy hang at his side. '*Really?*'

'Yeah.'

The two children became involved in a conversation.

Six let his rucksack fall to the ground. He walked up the slope, pulling his son with him.

'Signy, is it? I'm sorry. Everything's terrible. Where are you travelling to?'

Matthew in her head: *It's going to be fine.*

'To my mother's. In Northants. You?'

Madeleine hugged her arms about herself, lifted her chin to the wind.

'To London.'

'That's where we've come from. It's not safe.'

'Nowhere's safe,' said Six.

The ground seemed to shift beneath her feet.

'What do you mean?'

'Some weird shit going on in our home town,' the boy said.

'Tom.' Six frowned.

'Weird how?' Signy persisted.

Tom scuffed his toe against the road. Madeleine shook her head at him. Zinia's chat with Jed ended. A silence. Then far away, very faint, the sound of a truck. Signy gripped Madeleine's arm.

'Hear that?'

'I don't hear anything.'

Another silence. They listened. Six shook his head again. 'Nothing.'

'We saw an explosion in London.' Jed's voice was soft.

'An explosion? A bomb?'

Madeleine turned to Signy, then to Six, shoulders raised as if to say: *See?*

'I don't know,' Signy said. 'People were running. The army was there.'

What would Matthew make of these people? It didn't matter any more.

'In our town it's the same,' said Tom.

'Not exactly the same,' Zinia said.

'You two. Enough.' Six produced a packet of crisps from his rucksack. 'You hungry?'

'Oh *yes*,' Jed said.

'Youngest first.'

Jed took a handful of crisps and passed them round: cheese and onion. She took one. The familiar flavour returned her to childhood. Her body felt a deep, deep ...

'Have you seen anyone else on the motorway?' said Six.

The day was failing. To the east, a dark line blackened the sky.

Signy said, 'No. I thought there'd be loads of people, but the army was blocking the entry point. We snuck on. I don't think many people have tried to leave London. Or they're stuck in registration centres. Or they've already gone, you know? Before the government sent the military in.' How was she managing such long sentences?

Good girl. That was Dad's voice. Everybody who was gone, talking inside her head, telling her what to say.

'They'll all be coming soon,' said Six. 'From London. You'll see. Everyone will want to get out.'

'But you want to get in,' she said.

'Precisely.'

It had a logic to it.

'Have you heard GQOS on any car radios on the motorway?' Jed asked. 'We have.'

'We have too.' Tom picked up a stone, threw it across the road. It bounced tinnily off the side of a car. 'Haven't we, Dad?'

Dad. She looked at Jed but he was staring at Tom.

'You have? Was it running through the dictionary?' said Six.

'Yes!' she said.

'Bizarre.'

There was silence. Zinia touched her father's arm.

'I'm freezing.'

'I'm starving,' said Tom.

'Me too!' That was Jed. He had an appetite.

Good boy. If her father's voice kept repeating this, everything might be okay.

Six blew into his hands.

'We have food,' he said. 'Would you like to share?'

'Are you sure?' She couldn't stop the shaking in her hands and feet. 'We have some horrid decanted chickpeas if you're game?'

He laughed. 'Save your chickpeas. And of course I'm sure. We haven't entirely lost our minds.'

'Yet,' she said. When Six didn't laugh again, she said, 'Thank you so much.'

The sky was deepest indigo now. Bats flitted between the trees along the verge. Madeleine gestured to the tent at the back of the pannier-rail on her bike and chuckled.

'Home sweet home. We're going to camp here and set off in the morning. The wherever-it-is we're going, now we know about the *bombs* in London.'

She looked pointedly at Six. He turned away.

'Discuss this later?'

They gathered their bikes and belongings together in one pile. Six produced a Trangia stove.

The smell of lighter fluid. St Ives beach. Matthew over the Trangia, trying to get a flame going in the breeze. After they'd eaten, he'd smoked a cigar. She couldn't remember where he'd got it from.

Jed picked his lip. She nudged his hand away from his mouth. No point drawing attention to it. These people might not share their food if they thought he was unwell. *Diseased*. Six pulled out a paper bag with a whole raw chicken inside. She was so hungry she felt nauseous. From another bag he produced carrots, fresh peas and asparagus.

'*Chicken?*' exclaimed Jed. 'And vegetables?'

'They're from our garden,' said Zinia. 'This is Susan.' She held the chicken by its legs. 'We had to kill her. We had another one called Steve, but we've eaten him already.'

Six took some noodles from the bag and placed them in his lap.

She had noodles too. No, she would hold on to hers for now, they would last a long time.

'Are you sure you don't want our chickpeas?'

'Get away with your chickpeas.'

'Okay. Back in a bit.'

She led Jed to hunt for a car to camp in. They walked for a while. She felt more alone in the dark. The night air always seemed to have a greater percentage of oxygen within it, as if the trees were sighing out the day's exertions.

A silvery saloon sat in the middle lane, two front doors open. She poked her head inside and looked at the radio. Nothing.

Something was scrabbling in the boot. A small black shape. Jed yelped.

'Shit!' She whipped her head out.

They backed off. This was a stupid idea. What had she been thinking?

'Ahh, but look, Mama.'

A squirrel. It was perched on the passenger seat; in its claws, a lump of pumpernickel. It considered them with one beady eye.

'So sweet!'

Jed made clucking noises, walking forward with his hand out. The squirrel hopped onto the road and darted away. She didn't feel like sleeping in that saloon. She didn't want to meet any more squirrels.

Further along, an expensive-looking Gatester 4×4, the passenger door ajar, leather interior shining. She could easily push the back down and make enough room to lie flat.

'This is waaaay better than that stupid silver one.' Jed clambered in, trailing dirty boots across the seats. He clicked the glove compartment. 'Hey, Mama. Jelly beans! They're sours, Dada's favourite! And those sucky-sweet things. The ones Grandpa used to have.' He pushed the tin of travel sweets into his face so he could read the label in the twilight. 'Barley sugar.'

She shook the tin. A few sweets rattled inside.

'We can share them with the others.'

Jed held up the packet of jelly beans. He looked at her slyly.

'Let's keep these, for just us.'

'No. That's not fair. These people are sharing their food with us.'

'Susan.'

'What?'

'The chicken.'

'Right. Let's go back to eat ... Susan.'

Before they left the car, she shoved the pack of jelly beans back into the glove compartment, making sure Jed didn't see. They might need them for the journey. The others could survive with a barley sugar. They should count themselves lucky they were getting that.

'Jed.' She grabbed his arm. 'We're not going to talk to these people about Daddy, okay?'

'Why?'

'Because. If Six or Madeleine ask, just don't contradict what I say, all right?'

'What does contradict mean?'

'It means don't say, "That's not true" or anything, if I say something that isn't true.'

'If you lie?'

'Yes.'

He was silent.

'Sorry, monkey. Just trust me.'

She counted the number of vehicles between the Gatester and the others' camp. Ten cars.

Back along the verge, the Trangia flame glowed, the gas hissing like Nana's old grill. The family was arranged in a circle on a tarpaulin. There was a delicious smell of frying meat. Her mouth watered.

Sunday roast. Matthew's mum, down from Scotland.

'I only like breast,' she'd said, smoothing her patterned skirt, and Jed had giggled.

'Hey, look what I found.' Jed held up the tin of sweets. 'We can have them for pudding.'

She waited for him to remember the jelly beans, to ask where they were, but he didn't. She flattened her waterproof on the grass and made enough space for them both to sit down. Her jeans, still damp from the rain, made it hard to cross her legs.

'We'll have to dig into the pot together,' said Six. 'I forgot to bring plates.'

She wasn't sure if it was a joke.

He turned off the flame. The night became oily. She felt for Jed's knee. There was a volley of clicking. Four laser head-torches beamed slices of lemon yellow into the darkness. The lamplight hit her square in the face, momentarily blinding her.

'Sorry,' said Tom.

'I wish I had one,' sighed Jed.

Six removed his torch and placed the elastic strap around Jed's head. Jed looked left, right, left. He leant over the pot, and shovelled in three mouthfuls with the spork.

'Oh wow. This is so good.'

'Jed! You can't do that!'

Madeleine laughed. 'It's fine, Jed, help yourself.'

Signy's turn next. The flavour, the texture of fresh vege-tables, meat and noodles. It was the best thing she'd ever tasted. Matthew would have loved it. Warmth spread from her stomach to her limbs.

'Shame Ocadrone couldn't deliver,' Madeleine said, and Signy smiled.

It went quiet as everyone chewed. Too quiet: questions were coming. She turned to Zinia.

'What's your favourite animal?'

'Guess.'

'Let's play the animal alphabet game?' Jed interrupted. 'I'll start — aardvark.'

'Ant,' said Zinia. This was better.

'Arctic fox,' said Tom.

'Beaver,' said Jed, looking at Zinia for approval.

'Who'd have thought, eh?'

Six stared at the sky. Madeleine put her hand in his. Signy looked the other way.

The pot was almost empty.

'... and my mummy's favourite animal is an anteater because it has a long nose like hers,' Jed was saying.

'Excuse me!'

'Mama, I'm thirsty.'

She pulled out the bottle.

Jed shook his head. 'Not drinking that motorway road water.'

'Jed,' she said. 'Come on. It's all we've got.'

'Here.' Madeleine pulled an unopened mineral water from her jacket pocket. 'We found loads in the service station just off Exit 9. You can have one. That's where we pinched the crisps.'

A service station at Exit 9.

'What exit are we close to now?'

Six looked at her in a funny way. 'Exit 7a.'

'We'll stop at the service station tomorrow, Jed, okay?'

'But how will we know when it's Exit 9?' he said.

Six said, 'No flies on you, boy, are there? Look for three blue triangular signposts on the verge before the next slip road.'

'Triangular?' Jed whispered. 'The drones are moving in triangles.' This was to the children. 'Have you noticed?'

'Yeah,' said Tom.

She saw Zinia tell her brother something with her eyes.

'D'you want a barley sugar?' Jed held the tin out.

The sound of six mouths sucking.

Zinia's gaze went to the long lanes disappearing into blackness.

'We need to get the tent up.'

Six and his children climbed to the flat area at the top of the verge. Jed scurried to help, his voice carrying back to her.

'Why are pirates called pirates?'

'No clue.' Six's voice, distracted.

'Because they *arrrrrr*.'

There was groaning.

She and Madeleine were left by the roadside, listening to the scratch and slide of unfurling nylon, the slippery click of cheap fibreglass tent poles connecting, the children's chatter.

Matthew with her in the top bedroom. On the bed.

'Life. Stranger than fiction.' Madeleine shook her head.

'Are you a swimmer?'

Madeleine laughed. 'My shoulders? No. Inherited from my dad.'

'Oh.'

'Signy's an unusual name.'

'My grandparents were Swedish. On my mother's side. There are tons of us in Norse mythology.'

'You don't look Swedish.'

'My dad's a Hungarian Jew. Was. One of his great-grandparents was Indian. I'm a mongrel.'

'We're all mongrels. Where in London do you live, Signy?'

She pushed her hands beneath her thighs. 'North. Archway.'

'Lived there long?'

'I grew up half there, half in Northamptonshire, at weekends and holidays. In a hamlet. Nothing there except nature. And a church.'

Mum waiting for her, tapping her watch. *What took you so long?*

Madeleine was saying something.

'Sorry?'

'I said, do you and Jed live by yourselves?'

Signy might have flinched because Madeleine said quickly, 'Sorry. Didn't mean to pry.'

'We live by ourselves. Could you tell me about your town? What Tom meant – why did you make him shut up?'

Madeleine gazed at an invisible point. 'Umm. It's hard to ... I don't ... Do you really want to know?'

'I think I should, don't you?'

'The army was there, out of its depth – herding people like cattle to these ridiculous registration centres. People are so good at doing what they're told, aren't they? What's that thing about the bigger a collective grows, the more stupid it becomes? Our electronic devices were behaving strangely. GQOS-assist was talking to us at all hours of the day and night from every room, even though we'd already switched her off. TrincXcode and a strange language – it sounded like Chinese but Six said it wasn't.'

'We heard the same on our radio!'

Matthew, Jed, herself, sitting in a line on the bed.

Madeleine's eyes narrowed. 'The children ...'

'The children?' prompted Signy. 'Please. You have to tell me.'

'Six is a motor engineer in a manufacturing plant. They specialise in onboard computers for the cars' self-drive units and the hardware that surrounds them. I don't understand much of it, to be honest. It's pretty high-end. He has access to every floor in the plant, every room. Two days ago, he and some others returned to the plant to collect bits and belongings – for security reasons, with everything being broken into, you know? The hard drives for the patented systems. He took Zinia with him because we hadn't been out for two days and the kids were going crazy. He got his papers and all the things he wanted from his office. Zinia heard a noise coming from the manufacturing floor in the basement. When they got there, the doors had locked themselves. The locks closed on their own, right in front of their faces.'

'But it's an automated system, isn't it? So that's to be expected?'

'Except the automated systems were down and there was no one else there to action it manually. Inside, on the shop floor, the robotic arms, the machines that make the machines so to speak, were busy building something.'

'Building? What? Car computing systems?'

Madeleine shook her head. 'The curved pieces of material they use – the carbon polymer – were being moved and shaped. Into something. Six stood with the other engineers, trying to work out what and how. Their best guess was someone had taken remote control of the building and its computers. The army rolled up a minute later and kicked them all out. The entrance was barricaded, the main gate closed and the soldiers sent them all home.'

'But—'

'Wait. The next day we went to register at the leisure centre because we're people that do as we're told. We waited forever in a queue. After we'd given our names and addresses the soldiers assembled us in waves, lined us up in the main gym. Someone official came and asked for people with maths, physics and computing skills to step forward. Six volunteered, thinking he could help. They wanted to take him to a separate area with the others, an area with food and water. Obviously, he said he wasn't going without us. They tried to force him but he stood his ground. Eventually, we were told to go home, no food or water for us.'

'None at all?'

'None.'

'That's ...' She was going to say 'awful'. It wasn't as awful as another thing.

'Six thinks a rogue cell has taken control of our entire infrastructure, but it must be backed by a hostile state – there's no way a small outfit could manage all this alone. Once the big boys are involved, it's not as difficult as one might think. Even with a closed system.'

'Okay. What rogue cell, which hostile state and who are the "big boys" in this scenario?'

'Well, a hostile state is a subjective thing, isn't it? So, for the West that might mean some of China, possibly? I don't know, I'm guessing. A rogue cell could be *Shīluò zhī* ... I can never remember their whole name—'

'I don't think anyone in the West can.'

'... for example. They're pretty bloody fired up. If we follow this logic, when I say, "big boys", I mean their allies – Russia, Japan – pretty much everyone that isn't the US, Europe, the Antipodes.'

Signy thought about this. It made sense.

'And what do you mean when you say "a closed system"?'

'One that isn't connected to any other system. States still protect themselves that way against unwanted "visitors". In theory.'

'I see.'

She didn't see, though. She didn't see this part, at all. She thought states had moved on from such antiquated modes of defence.

'Six and I were at a loss. That's why we were heading to London. Hemel Hempstead was a mess when we left it – left home. Some friends headed off the day before us. We were going to meet them in East London.'

'*Hemel Hempstead?* But why would anyone want to take control of Hemel Hempstead?'

'I know. The world's most boring town. It's not just there, though, is it?' Madeleine shook her head. 'We thought, London's where the infrastructure will hold up. London has intelligent people. Some, anyway. Where else can we go? We have to face the fact that every town, every city could be the same.'

Goodies. Baddies. Baddies and goodies.

There was silence.

Something jogged in her mind. Like a flower blooming, the thought expanded, opened.

'Do you remember a blog? Back in 2016? I doubt you do. I didn't. It's a bit niche. We would have been very young. I think it was on Facebook or another old-person social media site. It was called "Lewis and Quark"? Years later, my friend, Gethin –' it felt strange to say his name out loud, here, now – 'wrote a big round-up piece for *Gelos* on the birth of AI, entitled "See How Far We've Come", which included Lewis and Quark's work. The piece went viral and suddenly everyone was quoting them.'

Madeleine shook her head. 'I'm sorry. Remind me.'

'So, Lewis and Quark was a blog documenting a weak AI neural net and its learning attempts. Invented by a student. Lewis. Or Quark. The program learnt from inputted data, came up with its own titles for things – pop bands, recipes, films and stuff. Gethin listed hundreds of them in his piece. The neural net always got everything so wrong – it was adorable.'

'Ah, the piece *Gelos* ran around 2030 after the markets crashed? I remember! Bad titles for novels. Funny recipes for cake.'

'That's the one! There's an iCanX shop in London near our

home. We cycled past it around day three of this. The iCanX had gone from the window display and these upside-down mannequins were there instead, with signs around their necks: *Burple Simp, Redarmande, Roycroft Briss.*'

'And?'

'They're names for paint colours. They were in Gethin's piece. I've only just twigged. Created by Lewis's poor AI.'

'I'm not seeing the relevance?'

'Well. It has to mean something. Doesn't it?'

Madeleine pulled mud from the grooves of her shoe with a stick.

'Well, I suppose if I were to try to make a connection, I would say someone put those signs there ironically. Whoever that was knew what was happening to our systems early on. Earlier than us, certainly.'

'Yes. And that person must be some kind of hacker, or better than a hacker. A virus that's been put into a system – say, the system that controls all our utilities – can be taken out again, can't it? That ironic person might be busy right now trying to undo everything, undo the damage.' It couldn't have been Gethin. 'They might be the ones using GQOS on the radio?'

Madeleine was scratching her head. 'Um ...'

Madeleine was right. Her theory meant nothing. Less than nothing. Of course it wasn't Gethin. The whole idea was nonsense.

'What do you do, for a job?' Signy said after a while.

'I was a microbiologist. Then I had kids and decided I'd rather study my family's Archaea.' Madeleine laughed.

'Archaea?'

'Biologist's joke.'

Signy's limbs went heavy. She stood up too fast. Her head spun.

'Would you mind if I went to bed? We've cycled miles today.'

Madeleine got to her feet. 'Of course. We're all beat. I'm sorry if I've frightened you.'

Signy pitched forward suddenly, threw her arms about the other woman. She wanted to squeeze the life out of her. Madeleine did the same in return. It felt like when Vicky did it, like home. Like the idea of home. Madeleine's arms were strong. Signy closed her eyes; spots of red and black flickered on her eyeballs. She could have been anywhere – in her father's arms, a child. Matthew's.

Madeleine rubbed the base of Signy's skull above her neck.

'Don't worry,' she said, almost sang, 'it's going to be fine. We'll see you in the morning.'

She must escape to the Gatester before she lost control.

'Jed. We're going to bed.'

'Oh-oh. I don't want to.'

'He doesn't want to!' called Zinia.

'*Jed.*' Her voice was sharp.

Jed handed the head-torch back to Six and stomped down the verge.

'You're spoiling everything.'

She hid her bike behind a bush and pulled him away. Four voices called goodnight to them through the darkness.

They retraced their steps to the Gatester shakily, the rucksack damp and heavy on her elbow, feeling their way car by car. She counted ten, then tried the door. It opened.

They climbed in. She pulled the door to quietly.

'You okay, Jed?'

'Yep.'

Machines making things. A hostile state. What would it do once it had control of a whole country?

Half-on, half-off the bed.

It was warmer in the car. No breeze; the stagnant air of a hermetically sealed metal box. She felt around for the catches to depress the back seats.

What had Gethin known? As much as that person who'd placed the signs on the mannequins? More?

Jed was shivering. She removed his wet socks and trousers, covered him with extra pieces of clothing, fashioned a small pillow from two woolly hats. She would make do with what she had on. She took off her own boots and socks. Her fingers were clumsy.

They lay flat on the passenger seats next to one another, separated by the leather armrest. She could hear his eyes clicking as he blinked. Like Matthew's.

'Susan tasted so nice.'

'She did.'

'Mama?'

'Yes?'

'Do you believe in Heaven?'

An empty space opened in front of her. It gaped, dark and hot, like the mouth of an animal.

'No, monkey. Lots of people do, though. Do you?'

He let out a sigh. 'I wish it was true.'

She stroked his hair. He shook her hand away.

'The only thing that's true is Father Christmas,' he said. The leather seat squeaked as Jed rearranged his body. 'And space. Space is true. Grandpa told me when he was ill. And all the stars in it. That's when he told me about Gaia and Time and the cosmos. Although even stars die someday. Grandpa said that when we die, our pieces go back into the earth and grow back as trees.'

'I agree with that.'

'He said we're nothing and everything at the same time and that the body cannot lie, even when the mind does.'

'I agree with that too.'

'I don't understand what it means.' Jed sat up. 'Where are the jelly beans?'

'Oh yes, I forgot. I left them in here by accident.' Her lie. More lies. 'We can have them tomorrow.'

'Share them?'

'No,' she said, carefully. 'Just for us.'

'Good.' He smiled before his eyes closed. 'We have to leave one for Dada otherwise he'll think we've forgotten about him. We haven't, have we, Mama?'

'No, love.'

'Lime's his favourite.'

He fell asleep.

The body cannot lie.

He would find out eventually. He would hate her when he did. She would hate herself.

Outside, a skittering on the fibreglass. She tensed. The bark of a fox.

Warston was full of animals. Gethin's dad, Dylan, had sheep and cows and a vegetable patch in the back garden. There were chickens pecking at Tenny's farm.

Burple Simp, Redarmande, Roycroft Briss.

She stared at the car's pale ceiling: a blank rectangle. A hundred times she'd fallen asleep in the back seat of her dad's Volvo, her family speeding up the motorway. She'd look out at the stars beyond the orange muzz of lights, the low hum of her parents' conversation up front. The memory was just within reach.

What if she forgot what Matthew looked like?

The silence of the night roared outside.

She turned on her side to conserve heat. They were halfway there. More than halfway. Perhaps.

Having to adjust her world. It would be … She felt … Asleep.

Day 8

The sun, stitched across the car's ceiling.

They were here. In a Gatester. On the motorway. She had to get through this day and all the days that followed this one.

She looked at Jed. His mouth was open, the sound of his breath snagging in his nostrils. She leant up on her elbows. His eyelids were twitching back and forth. The corners of his lips were swollen. In the creases, pus. Round red blotches spread across his cheeks.

Pus equalled bad. Equalled a whole new level of infection. Redness spreading.

Infection. Sepsis. Death.

Her hand shot out and she grabbed the handle above her. No. *Hypochondriac.* She simply needed to find something to treat it with. This would be possible if today things happened in a neat order: one, two, three. Like that.

A crow's caw.

She looked through the rear windscreen to see Six's tent, but the angle was wrong.

Outside the sky was blue and cloudless, though she could feel its morning bite inside the car. It would warm up later. That's how it often was in March. Cold first, then heat, sometimes rain. Was it still March? Yes.

Their combined breath had condensed on the windows. She wrote her name backwards in the steam. She exhaled a long hot breath. One by one the letters disappeared.

Jed stirred.

'Hey, monkey.'

His eyes opened. 'What time is it? Where are we? Oh, in the Gatester. Are we going to get Dada now?'

'Not now, love. We're going to Gamma's, remember?'

'Oh, yeah.' His face drooped.

'Let's go and find Zinia and Tom. Shall we see if they want to have breakfast with us?'

'I'm thirsty.'

The night had been too cold to dry their clothes. She slid soggy socks onto Jed's feet.

'Ugh.'

She pulled on her own socks. 'They're fine. We won't notice in a bit.'

She grabbed the rucksack, collected the jelly beans from the glove compartment and pushed open the door. A group of jays took off from the road – a flurry of grey and blue wings, a curl of orange peel between a beak. More birds. Each day, more.

They peed on the verge behind an elm bent by years of resisting the elements. Urine splashed up her trousers. It smelled like vitamin tablets.

They made their way back to the tent. Voices from inside. She called from the bottom of the verge.

'Hallo?'

A tearing sound. Tom's head popped through the flaps and went back in again.

'Mum, they're up!'

Madeleine's voice: 'Don't go without your coat, Tom, please.'

Scuffling. Tom ran down the slope.

'Hey, Jed.'

Jed flung his arms around the boy's waist.

'Can we have some of your breakfast?'

Six stepped out. 'How was your night?'

'Cold. But safe.' Her tongue was thick, sort of sticky. 'Would you mind very much if Jed and I took another tiny sip of your water? Sorry to ask. Please say no if you can't spare it.'

Madeleine joined them on the hard shoulder. She held out the Tibet Spring.

'Help yourself.'

'Thank you.' Signy gave the bottle to Jed. 'Not too much now.' He tipped his head back. The diagonal liquid line got lower and lower. 'Enough.'

'Keep it,' Madeleine said. She rubbed her hands together. 'Fancy baked beans for breakfast?'

'Yes!' said Jed.

'I've got synthetic beef,' said Signy. She smiled. 'I never thought I'd look forward to such a thing.' She lowered her voice. 'Do either of you have antiseptic?'

Madeleine's eyebrows drew together. 'I'm so sorry, we don't. Is it for you?'

Signy hesitated. 'For Jed,' she said finally. 'His cheek. It's swollen.'

'We'll make up some warm salt and water, okay? That should help.'

Signy nodded, grateful.

Afterwards, Six fried the fake beef and beans and they used his pasty-white millet-bread from the service station in place of plates. He wiped his mouth with a camping towel.

'Madeleine and I had a chat last night, Signy, after what you told us about London.'

'Oh. And?'

'And we've decided not to go.'

'Good.'

Was it good?

'We're staying here,' said Madeleine.

'*Here?* On the motorway?'

'It's the safest place right now.'

That might be true.

'What about food and stuff?'

Six said, 'We've got enough for a week, we reckon. There's the service station to go back to if we need more. Would you and Jed like to stay here? With us?'

Jed said '*Yes!*' and Signy said 'No.' She turned to him. 'Jed. We're going home. Gamma's waiting.'

'But Mama, *please?*'

She looked across the motorway at the eight lanes of cars. She could hear the tent blustering. Would it be so bad? They could wait to see what happened in the next few days and then travel to Warston. Or to London. To Matthew. Half on, half off the ...

He might be in the same position when they got there.

A lorry sitting patiently in the fast lane: 'Farmfresh Ltd'. Its massive tyres, at least six rows of them, one of its rear doors ajar. They could wait here with this family until everything had passed. She stared at her hands. It was what her son wanted.

'I think ...' she began.

Her eye caught the lorry again. Both rear doors were closed. She could swear they'd been open. Her skin prickled.

'I'm sorry, Jed. We're leaving. We're sticking to our plan.'

Nowhere was safe. Mum needed them. Signy needed help.

*

'I wish we had something sweet to eat,' said Zinia, as the stove was packed away.

'You haven't got any of that barley sugar left, have you?'

Six chucked the beef and bean tins into the bushes. Jed's eyes went to her.

'No, sorry,' she said. Jed looked at the floor.

They stood in the slow lane, Signy holding her bike. She felt sick, deep in her belly.

'Thank you so much, for everything.'

'Of course. Thank *you*.' Madeleine leant across the bike and kissed her on both cheeks. 'Jed, take care of your mummy.'

Jed tapped Signy's bottom. 'Can I have one of the jelly beans now?' His hand clapped his mouth. 'Oops.' He looked at Signy, cheeks burning. 'Sorry, Mama.'

Signy waved her hand. 'Oh! Well remembered, Jed. I left jelly beans in the car last night. By accident.' She pulled the packet from her pocket. 'Help yourself.'

Zinia took one carefully, eyes slitted.

Signy offered one to Madeleine. Madeleine made an up-and-down movement with her elbows.

'No. Thank you.'

Signy went to hug Six. He stuck his hand out. She shook it.

'Well. Bye then.' She scribbled her GScope tag on a piece of paper and gave it to him. 'For the future,' she said, 'for when it's all better.'

Six took it. He didn't offer his in return.

She concentrated on getting Jed into his seat and pulling on the rucksack. Heat burned behind her eyes.

'Mama.' Police drones buzzed in the sky above. 'They're back.'

Overhead like vultures. Someone was watching, someone was there. An all-seeing eye, a hostile state, a rogue cell, a neural net, a something. A detonating button, waiting to be pressed.

Not Matthew, he was gone. Turned to stone.

'Zinia and Tom didn't wave to me,' complained Jed once they'd cycled out of sight.

The bike wheels had lost more air overnight. She was pedalling through treacle. Her eyes stung. She longed for some UVs.

'You all right, love? Your eyes sore?'

'No.'

'How's your cheek?'

'Okay.'

'Cold?'

'Nope,' Jed said. 'My skin is keeping me warm.'

The road flew away. Think only of Warston. Press other thoughts to a corner.

Matthew laughing at her on a Norfolk beach as she deer-leapt across the sand in walking boots.

Marrow. Beef mince. Gethin's kitchen. Potatoes. Goose dripping. A pinch on her leg under the table. Gethin, annoying her for sport. She squealing. Dylan frowning, saying, 'What's wrong with you, townie?'

She cycled under a bridge. The bike was too slow. Spray-painted graffiti tags in pink: *Doot*, *Sparky*, *Medium*.

The humpback bridge. Under it. Gethin and her, pants down. Gethin's granny finding them, separating them for a week.

Matthew. A red kite. Red. Blue drone. Circling in the gyre …

'Mama!'

A split second. She was tipping. The bike was moving side-ways. That wasn't right. Reflexively, her body fell against the handlebars, one leg acting as a brake. The full weight of the bike went against her thigh. The pain was acute. She screwed her face up to stop herself screaming. A strong wind blew past her ears.

'I must have fallen asleep.'

Her body trembled. She slapped herself gently in the face, had a jelly bean. Lime flavour, or perhaps lemon. Sweet. She felt instantly better.

Jed touched her shoulder. 'What does it mean if you see a blue lady made of metal?'

'Sorry?'

'I'm not supposed to tell you.' His pupils were enormous.

'Tell me.'

'Zinia said she saw a blue lady made of metal. It spoke to her.'

'What? When?' She stepped off the bike, faced him properly. 'What's going on? What do you mean "a blue lady"? Where did Zinia see a lady?'

'In the factory where her daddy works.' He lowered his voice. 'She went to the loo and when she came out there was a blue metal lady there. It's a secret. Tom didn't want her to tell me but she did anyway.'

'What kind of ...? What did she look like?'

He glanced behind himself. 'A big lady. Bigger than Zinia. Like an Agrico-bot, she said. And it was blue. It said things.'

The pain in her thigh radiated to her feet.

'What did it say?'

Jed leant forward. '*You cannot become better than a bird in the future.*'

Signy swallowed. She made a dismissive noise, a sort of cough. It sounded loud on the silent motorway.

Jed's mouth opened. 'It's not funny.'

'I'm not laughing. That sentence doesn't make sense.'

'I *know*.' He glared at her. 'Zinia said grown-ups would say that. That's why she hasn't told any of you.'

'But sweetheart, why would a metal lady say things like that?' Her skin was prickling again.

'I don't know.'

She gazed at the trees. She must reassure him. That was her job.

'Sometimes, when we're little and we're scared and we don't understand what's going on, we invent things to make sense of the world – monsters, ghosts, or metal ladies that say nonsense words.'

Jed was quiet. After a second, he shook his head.

'Zinia said she laughed after she said it.'

'Eh?'

'The metal lady. She laughed afterwards.'

'Why would she do that?'

'Because the lady knows what she said doesn't make sense.'

A philosophising robot.

'No, Jed.'

It was humans they should be afraid of. Men with torches that shone into attics. And rogue cells. And the big boys. And hostile states. They should be afraid. Very afraid of everyone.

She was silent. Then she cycled on.

A series of triangular signs. The service station couldn't be far: Junction 9.

'In a minute we're going to stop, okay?'

''K.' He sounded glum. Glum was better than grieving.

Ahead, a bridge with a covered walkway that crossed the motorway. She could see the blue paint on its interior walls from here.

This was it. Another signpost and dotted white lines curving off onto a slip road. The familiar baffle of conifers at the end of the drive. Behind the trees, the building. Jed huffed.

'What's the matter?'

He muttered something. She stopped the bike.

'What? I can't hear you.'

'I *said*, I wish we'd stayed with Zinia and Tom. It's your fault. You hid the jelly beans.'

'We're going to Gamma's, Jed. If you remember, it was *your* idea to hide the jelly beans in the first place. If it had been up to you, we wouldn't even have shared the barley sugar.'

Jed turned his head away.

'What colour did you eat?' he demanded.

'What?'

'I *said*, just before when you nearly fell asleep and you ate one, what colour did you—'

'Green.'

'That's Dada's one!' His face was puce. 'I saved it *specially* for when he comes! You ate it. You don't care about him!'

She looked straight ahead. She must not say anything. Nothing. Nothing.

'Mama? Mama? Are you all right?'

'Yeah.'

She made a sudden right turn in the direction of the charging garage.

'Why're we going here?'

'You'll see.'

She leant the bike against the large boxed air pump and picked out one Lite-card from among the cash taken from Jed's money box.

She hadn't loved Matthew enough.

He hadn't loved her enough, either, but that didn't matter now. He'd won that competition.

She fed the card into the slot. Nothing happened.

Now he was dead and she was alive.

''S broken,' Jed said.

She kicked the pump hard and it sprang to life. She stared at the pressure gauge. It wasn't meant for bicycles, it was meant for the triple-tube tyres on self-drive cars, though the rubber end fitted snugly onto the nipple of the bike's inner tube. She squeezed the lever. The gauge shot up.

'Shit.'

'You okay?' Jed looked down at her from his seat.

'You'd better get out of your seat.'

'Don't want to.'

'Do it.' She took up the pump again, squeezed the lever briefly. The tyre became satisfyingly solid. She repeated the process on the back wheel. 'Now we have a perfect set.' She patted the air machine.

'What next? I'm thirsty.'

'We're going to look inside this little garage shop.'

Jed ran his fingers over the netted stacks of *BBQ* blightwood as they went towards the shop door.

'Our house,' he whispered. 'We could build a whole new one with this.'

'We can't carry it,' she said.

'Cunt it.'

'*What* did you say?'

'Nothing.'

Magazines and newspapers littered the floor. The shelves were mostly empty. She headed straight for the darkening chiller cabinet.

A few curling sandwiches wilting in cardboard packaging. Blooms of mould had spread across the millet-bread either side and in the middle, rotting crayfish tails, mulched Chinese leaf.

She leant against a shelf. Six and Madeleine said there had been lots of water left. Others had been through here. More than a few.

'Treasure.'

Jed swiped two remaining chocolate bars from beneath the counter at the till. She took a bottle of motor oil to empty over the bike chain. They walked out.

'We're going to look in the actual service station now.'

They pedalled towards it, the bike wheels her friends now.

Cars in the parking bays. Picnic benches on the grass. Everything looked normal. Not one person there. She imagined bodies inside, frozen in time as they walked to the toilets or paid for a burger. That was silly: Six and Madeleine had been here only yesterday.

The sun bounced off the solar panels on the roof. She leant the bike against the wall.

Jed walked between the cars, tugging experimentally on each door-handle.

'I'm sorry for what I said before,' she said.

He stopped, glared at her crossly. She pushed on.

'I'm sorry I hid the jelly beans, I'm sorry I ate Daddy's special one and I do understand why you wanted to stay with Tom. We need to find Gamma, and Gethin too. Gethin can help us. Do you understand?'

'The midget?'

'Jed.'

'That's what Dada calls him.'

'Do you understand, I said?'

'Yes.'

'Maybe we can meet up with Tom and Zinia when things are ... normal. I gave their Daddy our GScope tag. Let's go and find a proper loo, and see if there's food here and a drink.'

They walked towards the entrance. Normal: things would never be normal, not without Matthew. Her reflection approached in the building's long panes of acrylic, hair straggly but otherwise looking pretty much as usual. She was a widow and a liar. She didn't want to know herself. She put her hand against the window to cover her face. Her watchstrap glowed gold. The long hand and the short hand, round and round, the little solar panel shining like a star. Her head ached.

They walked through the jammed automatic doors. The atmosphere in the atrium was flat, peculiar. No humming fridges, no bleeps from the games area. Swing-bins overflowed with wrappers. Trays everywhere strewn with empty burger papers. It stank of rotting food.

'I don't like it here,' said Jed.

The newsagent's sat in a corner in the gloom.

Something flew at them from the ceiling in a long arc, missing her head by inches, and thudded into the acrylic at the entrance behind them. Jed screamed.

'Don't move.' She pushed Jed behind her and turned slowly. It lay twitching on the stone floor, small and grey. 'Oh God, Jed, it's a pigeon!'

They watched the bird right itself, dazed but alive, turn in circles and wobble outside.

Jed's hand was at his crotch. 'I nearly peed my pants.'

'It's all right, love.'

They found their way to the toilets.

'I want to use the gents,' he said.

'Don't be silly.' The hinges on the door of the ladies squealed open. The bathroom was dark and smelled of piss. She wasn't going in there. 'Come.'

They stepped away and the toilet door drifted to a close on its own.

They went outside, peed on the grass next to a picnic bench, then headed back in.

Jed dug his heels in. 'I don't want to go in there again.'

'This is where we'll find things we need.'

He followed her, head down.

They approached the aisles in the newsagent's. A fusty odour of damp paper. Jed headed straight to the toys section. She stepped over things: a pair of headphones; a travel charger for a GScope; a small box of cotton buds. She picked up some batteries and a pack of tampons.

In the refrigerator cabinet: water. She put the rucksack on the floor and filled any spaces with the bottles. There was a solitary can of lemonade. She popped the lid. The liquid fizzed. Jed came to stand beside her. She tipped her head back.

'Oh wow.' Her eyes stung. She belched. Jed smiled.

'My turn.' He swigged. 'Oh. Mama. So sweet.'

The lemonade put a spring in her step.

'What you got there, monkey?'

He held something close to his chest.

'Can I take it?' A colouring book; inside, cheap paper, the outlines of cats tangled in skeins of wool. She knew what he was thinking. 'That one looks like Oscar, this one's Pyewacket.' He stared intently at the drawings.

'What are you going to colour them in with?'

'Gamma's got pens.'

They went to the canteen area. Behind the long counter, empty shelves. A wicker basket next to the pay point, a shrivelled tangerine at the bottom, hard as rock. A pile of coffee beans in the grinder. She scooped up a handful and dropped them into her pocket.

A sound, faint but familiar: a woman speaking, the tone

friendly, official. It was GQOS again. A device. One that worked. Or a radio – a third one.

Or a woman, in here now, hiding.

Her scalp tingled. She scanned the shopping area. It was coming from nearby. In the middle of the service station.

The voice went silent and started again, sounding now like the same person speaking over itself, different words echoing on two channels. Jed pushed himself in close to her. She pulled him down to hide behind a shiny children's ride. A sign above the card slot: 1 × RIDE = 2 LITES. They peered through the plastic seats towards the café area.

The voices were talking – silent – talking – silent. An official broadcast, perhaps. Information, an instruction on what to do, where to go.

'Stay here.'

She left Jed crouching in the shadows and tiptoed around the ride towards the sound.

On a shelf against the back wall of the canteen next to the microwave was a small and very old black radio, its dials flickering.

'What's it saying, Mama?'

'I told you to stay there!'

He shook his head and put a hand inside the back pocket of her jeans.

The radio went quiet. She hopped over the counter and put her ear to the speaker. GQOS began again, louder, startling her.

The dials lit up.

'*Would you like to ... creature comforts ... graft onto the stem ... grate four ounces of cheese ... please stay calm ... I've searched the web for ... ready to pick up ... to your nearest registration centre ... standard practice ... how does it ... means ... the collective ... ward of the state ... water will be provided ... Canadian skidoo ... please attend immediately ... D2 ...'*

Silence.

She pulled the radio from the wall and opened the back panel: no batteries. No solar panel either. Beside the socket on the skirting the plug dangled at the end of its cable, disconnected.

'Why is she talking about a skidoo? Why are there so many of her, and talking about Canada? Are all the people in Canada having the same thing happen as us?'

'Ssh, Jed.'

'Every time ... fan-assisted ... push the nail into the rawl ... gathering leaves ... gradient ... wawawaga ... Honolulu ... treble clef four minims ... che-che-che- ... please stay calm ... rotic tongue ... plasma LED ... to your nearest registration centre ... D5 ... how you feel ... forelock.'

Silence.

'She's stuck in a loop and all broken,' he hissed.

'Ssh.'

Signy picked the radio up and shook it. She stuffed it under one arm.

'Why are we taking it?'

'It might be useful.'

'I don't like it. What for?'

'Be quiet.'

They went to the fast-food hatch. She climbed over the greasy countertop and made a tour of the cooking area at the back. It stank of sour fat. A fridge in the corner, open drawers of putrid chicken fillets and unopened bags of pre-cut fries. The smell made her retch. Jed's voice carried from the other side of the counter.

'Anything?'

'No.'

'Can we go onto the other side? Over the bridge with the cover?'

She hadn't thought of that. She leant over the counter and looked down. He was so small.

'Okay.'

The rucksack was heavy now, full of the important water. They made their way to the bridge, their footsteps echoing as they climbed the long metal stairwell. Misted sunlight through the scratched acrylic glowed in the painted azure tunnel.

Turning the corner at the top. What if she found a blue metal lady camouflaged against the walls? What if the lady stepped out, blocking their way? Electromagnetic currents flowed into her armpit from the radio. She stopped.

'What, Mama?'

'I don't know. Wait.'

Feet mounting the bottom of the stairwell on the other side: not just one set of feet — several. And voices, human voices this time, talking in low tones. They might be friendly. Then again, they might not. The footsteps were climbing, growing near. The people would turn the corner onto the stairs on this side any second and see them.

'Who are they?' Jed whispered.

The footsteps stopped suddenly.

'Hallo?' A man's voice. 'Anybody there?'

She flew then, pulling Jed back down the stairs three at a time.

'Run!'

The footsteps pelted after them. 'Wait!'

She streaked towards the automatic doors, the rucksack clanking, dragging on her shoulders, and skidded round to the bike.

A clattering on the floor tiles in the atrium. They'd be on her any second. A man with an NYPD cap, a body under a blanket with a shock of greying hair, a blue metal lady.

She threw Jed into his seat and began to scoot, one foot on a pedal. The footsteps were outside now.

'Hey! You! Wait!'

He was right behind her. Another voice, a man further back.

'We're not going to hurt you!'

She threw her leg over the crossbar and raced away. She didn't stop until she was back on the fibreglass lanes. Her lungs burned. The bike ate up the wide grey road. Her feet were two pistons.

She looked behind. No one. Her ears were ringing. What if she'd made a mistake? What if those people could have helped?

'Mama?' Jed's voice had a tremor in it.

'Not now. Tell me if that radio in your lap does anything weird,' she said.

The sun burned away the morning chill. The temperature climbed. That sequence of TrincXcode notes, that sustained bass and its overlaid rapid-heartbeat of a melody, that endless music that could build things, that could change a world. It went round and round in her head, keeping time with the clicking bike chain: F sharp major, C sharp minor, time signature moving like water.

The three of them in a line on the bed. Matthew. Jed. Her. Listening.

To the left, a small turret atop a Cotswold-stone house set back from the motorway in a green field. She recognised it. She'd always loved that house. They were getting close. They'd be in Warston before sundown. She must have cycled almost twenty miles already. It hardly seemed possible.

Next to the house, a group of trees, something moving in the middle of them. She came to a halt.

Definitely something there. It moved again, in the shadows. It was big enough to be a person; bigger, thinner. The gait seemed wrong, more like an Agrico-bot. But the bots were all out of power; only the drones were still going. The feeling that she was being watched. That Farmfresh lorry: doors open, then closed. Or perhaps she was imagining it, like the blue metal woman in the service station.

'Can you see that, Jed?'

She heard the rustling of pages behind.

'Ssh. I'm reading *Peter Rabbit*.'

'*Peter*—?'

'I bought it from home.'

'What?'

'In my jacket.'

'Please. Can you see what that is over there?'

He stared hard at the woodland. 'Can't see anything. What did you think it was?'

'Nothing.' She must not lose her grip.

They set off again.

Some hours later, at the roadside with their coats off, the lifeless radio at their feet and eyes on it like a hawk, Jed twitchy and checking around himself every few seconds, they ate their lunch: chocolate bars from the service station and the chickpeas in the dry-bag from the day before. Her ears were ringing. She pulled out the batteries, slid two into Jed's torch and four into the radio. She fiddled with the dials but got no response on any frequency. The torch had a beam almost invisible in the bright light.

'What time is it?'

'Two.'

'Are we nearly there?' His eyes were so like Matthew's.

'I think so.'

A rabbit poked its head up on the verge opposite.

'Here, little bunny.' Jed clicked his fingers. The rabbit bobbed back below ground.

She was still hungry, her back ached and her eyes stung. She stood up, shook out her legs like an athlete before a race.

The Olympics. It was supposed to be the Olympics this year. In Pakistan. It might still happen.

'My bum's hurting.' The bike listed as Jed leant sideways.

'Keep still.'

'Are we lost?'

'No.'

They'd passed an exit a few miles back; it hadn't looked familiar. Now she'd stalled among the endless rows of cars. She might have overshot. Perhaps she should go back to the last turn-off.

'I don't want to travel any more.'

Jed raised the safety-bar on his seat, unclipped the belt and climbed out. He handed her the radio, opened the driver's door of a blue Tesla stranded beside them and climbed inside, closing the door behind him with a final clunk. He sat with his arms folded, staring through the windscreen. She tapped on the window. His chest rose and fell in a sigh.

Across the fields, low buildings painted bottom to top in graduated blues, the highest point sky-coloured and blending nicely into the skyline. Writing ran along one side, too small to read.

The passenger door of the Tesla opened and Jed was running to her, waving something above his head.

'A weapon!'

Something pointed with a short, silver handle. She took it from his hands and brought it close to her chest: an emergency hammer, for breaking windows.

Dad had kept one in his old Saab. He said in case the family was ever submerged in water. She stuffed the hammer into the rucksack.

'Lana ...' said Jed, staring at the blue buildings, eyes narrowed.

'What? What can you see?'

'It says Lana ... something.'

'Laniakea?'

'That's it. There's a drawing of a drone underneath the letters.'

Laniakea. She knew where she was. Exit 18 would be next.

The poster across the way from her that first night, in her neighbours house in London. Laniakea wasn't a place, it wasn't a Chinese youxiu band. It was Hawaiian for 'immeasurable heaven', and it was the name of the company who owned this factory.

She'd known that. She'd known and she hadn't remembered.

'What is it, Mama?'

'This building. It used to be a microchip factory. But it didn't look like this before. They must have knocked it down. This looks completely different.'

'Because they've 3D-printed it.'

'Right.'

'With TrincX.'

'How d'you know that?'

'The way the corners fold over and over each other in triangles.'

She looked, but her eyes weren't up to it.

'Grandpa said TrincX is God moving across the face of the Earth.'

'He did? How d'you remember all your chats? You were only three.'

'I told you, he told me before he died. He said it was terrible and important.'

'Terribly important.'

'No. Terrible *and* important. TrincX is the birth of true Artificial Intelligence, he said. He said when the codes go from general-level intelligence to super-level, it will be only days, Mama, or even minutes, or even seconds. He said that day is going to be one of reckoning. He said TrincX is God's daughter come to walk on Earth, but as long as you've been good to Gaia, nothing bad will happen.'

She thought for a second. 'You know you said that when using TrincX, the algorithm makes the best choice? Like, the one that governs the gas and electricity and water. I've been thinking about it – that one must make the best choice for planet Earth?'

'I guess. Maybe.' He was looking at her expectantly.

'What about an algorithm that makes the best choice for *itself*? Doing what *it* wants to do?'

Jed frowned. 'That's not allowed. It's against the law.'

'But if it had super-level intelligence it could?'

'I don't know.'

There was a falling sensation in her head.

'… super-quick to make.' Jed still talking. 'The Laniakea building.'

'How quick?'

His forehead wrinkled. 'Umm. Two days? Maybe.'

He climbed back onto the bike.

She placed the radio in the rucksack. Her left ear seemed to have lost aural perspective, as though on that side, she was shut in a room.

She put her foot on the pedal.

God moving across the face of the Earth.

The ringing began again, inside her ear. Who had rebuilt this factory using TrincX in two days? Or what had?

'Mama, are you ill?'

God's daughter.

'No. Why?'

'You're all shaky.'

'I'm fine. Nearly there.'

She came off at the slip road then a roundabout. Exit 18. Nearly done it. No military blockade, no one at all. Only a home-made sign on a wooden post, '*Country Fair, this way.*' An arrow left to Rugby, which had the nearest leisure centre. If the army had been through, that's where everyone would be registering. Maybe. What if the army hadn't been here, though? What if Warston had been forgotten? She took the roundabout and turned right.

The road carved between featureless grass banks. Wind turbines turned in the fields beyond, their fins drawing lazy circles in the skyline. Birds swooped and ducked, alighting on the old exchange cables. She felt nauseous, her palms wet, the sweat smarting on two blisters beneath her index fingers. Home: so close she could almost taste it.

They passed the fruit field, more blue Agrico-bots static among the lines of fruit nets, their long picking arms dropped either side like children in a sulk.

A T-Junction, the final turn-off for Warston. There was the horse chestnut tree, its trunk shaped like an ogre. On the corner, the garage had been replaced twenty years before by a small square wind-processing plant, usually humming with electricity, silent now.

Another wave of nausea. Without warning, saliva filled her mouth and her stomach contracted. She jumped from the bike just in time. She could hear Jed retch himself, as sick poured out of her onto the road panels. The puddle at her feet was full of half-digested chickpeas. Her throat burned.

'I'm sorry. Must have eaten something bad.' She wiped her mouth with her sleeve. She felt better.

'Are you going to die, Mama?'

'Don't be ridiculous, it's just a bit of sick.'

'Do you think the soldiers have found Dada? Will it be Southwick and Waters?' His irises burned into hers.

She remounted the bike. 'Let's find Gamma.'

High hedges either side of the lane. Past the abandoned trout farm. Past enormous silos, metal fences, signs: BEE FARM; DANGER OF DEATH; NO UNAUTHORISED ACCESS. She thought of the lilac-painted walls inside, the rows upon rows of hives.

The taste of the honey: rape-flower pollen. Crystalline, flavourless. She'd had it for breakfast a few days ago from the jar in the kitchen cupboard. Now NYPD had it. Perhaps he'd eaten it already. Perhaps he and his girlfriend and the other man had. Perhaps they'd licked their fingers, one by one, afterwards.

The bike rolled on a slow decline. White cottontails hopped out of the way into long grass. A pheasant gandered wildly beside them for several metres, Jed urging it to keep up, before it made a sudden left turn and disappeared into the hedgerow.

At the crossroads the old sign on its vantage point, carved fingers pointing three ways: 'Yelverton 2 miles. West Holden 3 miles. Warston 1 mile.' The land stretched out in front, then fell away steeply before rising again a mile further off at

Sinistral Point. The Point was a hill, patched green and yellow, dotted now with wind turbines, two spindly trees growing alone at the top, branches bent by wind. Long before the turbines had come, she'd sledged down there on a tray. She scanned the horizon: Warston, hidden in the bowl of the valley. It was tarmac, not fibreglass, from here on. Nothing had changed here. Nothing.

Round the bend, down the steep hill, the faded red sign: SLOW CHILDREN P AYING. She'd always found that funny. The bike flew along the approach. Horses stamped their hooves in the high-hedged fields behind the road. Past the strip of land where Dolly Darker once lived, a caravan-shaped rectangle of grass still flattened after all these years. Here was the humpback bridge, the shallow brook beneath. Here was the tiny cross-roads. Here was Warston.

Still. Silent. She must hold her nerve.

The sun shone on the tree branches, wood pigeons called. If she shouted 'Hallo!', her voice would echo round the valley.

Carmel and Stan's thatched white cottage dripped with pink roses just in front of her. She wheeled closer, peered through the leaded windows. She knocked on the door. She opened the letter box, looked through: nothing was out of place.

'Oh God.'

'What is it, Mama?'

'It's—'

'Where is everyone?'

To the right a little way off, the stone shelter of the war memorial. An object on the wooden bench inside: a Coca-Cola bottle on its side. Down the lane to her left, long grass along the verge. The smell of green in her nostrils.

Sheep baaed in a field behind. The breeze swished.

'So quiet,' whispered Jed.

She took him out of his seat, let everything drop on the verge beneath an oak. Her neck was stinging, sweat pooling in the small of her back. Jed's hand snaked its way into hers. His fingers gripped tight, his face grubby in the stark light. She gathered up their stuff. They walked along the lane.

No one here. Calm. Remain in control.

Her parents' cottage. They looked up the path to the front door. She lifted the latch on the gate. They walked up the path, heaving the bike with them. Her mouth had gone very dry.

'Gamma!' Jed yelled at the door. She shushed him. He looked confused.

'Wait here. I'll go and check,' she said.

'I don't want to be by myself.'

'We'll keep the front door open. You sit on the step outside. I'll talk to you all the time, so you feel safe. Okay?'

Jed swung his eyes to the field on the other side of the brook, where horses flicked their tails at flies.

'Okaaaay.'

She kissed him.

The sun beat against the black door. The smell of burning gloss paint. She turned the handle. The square hall revealed itself.

The cottage was unoccupied. She could tell already. She could feel it. Perhaps she, Signy, might not even be here. She might be a reflection in a mirrored universe, all the way to infinity. There might be millions of 'hers', but not all of them would be opening this door in Warston.

She was surrounded by cool terracotta-painted walls.

'Love, I'll only be a second.'

She left Jed sitting on the step, holding XO.

She opened the door to the living room. It could have

been any time – another era, an outdated century. Diamonds of sunlight fell across the seagrass matting. The pretty curtain decorated with roses was pulled a quarter-way across the pane. The cushions on the sofa had depressions in them, as if some-one had sat there not long ago. A half-drunk cup of tea in a white saucer sat on top of the rattan coffee table. The door to the wood-burning stove was ajar, the ashes of burnt logs in the grate. A trapped bee buzzed at the windows. Another bee, free and far from the bee farm. She stared. It was dying, its wings flapping, black and orange body jumping against the glass. The air was stuffy.

Thousands of pollen-drones on the Parkland Walk.

'Mama?'

'It's okay, I'm right here. Going into the kitchen now.'

She crept across the floor, the matting crispy like hay beneath her feet. The kitchen door lay open against the living-room wall.

Maybe something behind it. No.

In the kitchen, the solar wall clock ticked noisily: 3 p.m. A plate covered in crumbs, a butter knife, a half-drunk glass of water on the circular table, the chair pulled out and turned to the side as if someone had risen in a hurry.

She looked through to the playroom: the dartboard; her father's telescope, its lens angled at the carpet.

Mum's radio on the shelf between the washing-up liquid and the telephone. A breeze coming from somewhere, cooling her neck. The back door banged gently against its catch.

Something brushed the back of her thigh and she screamed.

'Jed!' she cried. 'I'm so sorry. I didn't know you'd come in.'

'Where's Gamma? Where is everyone?' His voice was rising.

'Let's look in the back garden ...' Slow motion. '... in case she's in the shed ...' Her body was in slow motion. '... Or the summerhouse.' She couldn't will herself to move faster.

'Why would she be in there?'

'I don't know.'

His breathing grew rapid. 'She might be dead.'

That switched her on. Adrenaline suddenly in her legs.

'No, love. No. She's not.' She shook her head. 'She's not.' She ran through the back door onto the terrace of flagstones. 'Ma? Anyone?'

She wheeled round, back into the house, faster now, taking the stairs three at a time.

'Stay there!'

Jed stood on the bottom step, waiting. She stuck her head into her mum's room, her old room, the spare room, the top bathroom. This uncontrollable shaking.

'Oh God, oh God.'

She flung the rucksack under a bunk and raced down the stairs. Jed had his weight on one foot, silently counting bobbles in the peeling wall paint.

'Where we going?'

'Out!'

She locked the front door and fled through the back door, locking that behind her too. She hurried them around the side of the house and they ran down the front garden, damp grass making wet crescents on their boots.

The Old Bakehouse: Gethin's parents' home, Dylan's two fat ewes munching in the small field.

Her eyes streamed in the sun. She knocked on the door. She tried the handle.

They ran to the back of the house. The large vegetable patch had been pulled apart. A few rotting potatoes lay in the grass. No. She rubbed away their coatings of soil with her thumb and hastily folded them into her T-shirt.

'Mama.'

'We have to keep looking.' This *shaking*.

'I don't *like* it.'

They ran through the churchyard, past the crumbling grave-stones on the slant and into the church.

Dusty Bibles on pews, threadbare velvet prayer cushions on hooks beneath wooden benches. Time slow, then fast, then slow. A cross picked out in stained glass on the lancet window blazing at them from on high. The blue, red, green and yellow panes throwing colours on the stone floor. Thick bell ropes with felted pulls at the church's west end, swinging gently in the wind from the bell tower. The details, all the details. No one here. No one.

They pushed on, to the low wooden door at the back into the rear churchyard. She looked over the fields towards Val and Tenny's farm. Only cows and sheep in the distance.

'Can I collect green pebbles from the graves for my pockets?'

'There isn't time.'

'For luck?'

'*No.*'

A peeling iron gate led to Warston Manor. Why was she taking them there? They had to keep moving. If she stood still, she would see how things truly were. Jed would. How things weren't. Who wasn't. Any more.

Their footsteps on the gravel as they raced round the side of the manor wall.

Past the swimming pool, past the stables. Beneath the long oak-trunk shadows in the drive, she pulled the chain beside the door. A bell jangled inside. She wanted to pee. A dog barked.

A dog.

She pressed her face against the door's ancient glass window;

the huge flagstoned kitchen. A pink nose leapt, misting a circle on the glass from the inside.

'Comet!' cried Jed. 'It's Comet!'

Her head was pounding. The dog scratched at the door.

'Jean wouldn't have left him behind,' Jed said.

Signy turned the handle. The door opened. Comet flew out. He charged through Jed's legs and tore round the driveway, entire body wagging.

She stuck her head into the kitchen.

'Hallo?' The word bounced off the stone floor. 'Anyone here? Jean?'

'Do you think Jean's dead upstairs?'

'Stop saying that.'

'Oh, look.'

Jed's eyes softened. Comet was jumping in and out of the fountain in the centre of the driveway, lapping water. He shook his coat and came to a halt at her feet, where he eyed her dolefully.

All this way. All this way for a dog.

Jed patted Comet's back. 'He's thin, Mama. He's panting. That means he's thirsty.'

The dog was going to make Jed feel safe. Safer.

He cradled Comet's head in the crook of his arm.

'You're coming with us, Cometee. Yes. Good doggy.'

'We haven't finished.'

They ran to the Tithe Barn, Comet at their heels, to look for others, for Pete and Aliza.

She stared out across the land.

No Mum. No Gethin. What makes a place alive? Not nature – humans. Here where the village should be, an empty shell. A void. No.

She stood in the field. She wanted to scream. She wanted

to not care if anyone heard. She wanted everything to come out like sick, like a baby. She wanted not to give a shit about anything.

Matthew wasn't here. Her father wasn't here. Her mother wasn't here. God was moving across the face of the Earth.

She opened her mouth. A hard, hard silent sound. If she pushed any harder, she'd break herself. The tiniest frequency, unmoored, high, a radio unable to find its wave.

'Mama.' Jed tugging at her leg. 'Mummy. Mama. Mum. Stop making noises, Mama, *please*.'

'I'm sorry,' she said. 'I'm sorry, little one.' Jed was crying now. Those big fat round tears he made. 'I was wrong. There's nothing for us here. We have to go.'

'What? Where?'

'I don't know. Rugby first. Then another place. We need to find people.'

His face set. 'No.'

'Yes, love.'

'This is where Dada thinks we've come. This is where he's coming when he wakes up. We can't leave or he won't find us again.'

'Jed.' She couldn't say it. Not now. It would kill him. 'How will we get help for Daddy if we don't find people?'

'He doesn't need help now!' he yelled. 'He's coming *here*!'

'Jed, okay, shush.'

This mustn't happen. Please let this not happen now.

'You *said*!'

'Okay! Yes, that's the truth.'

'Comet *needs* us!' He put a hand on the dog's head. 'We came all this way—'

'Jed—'

'. . . and now you want us to *leave*? Gamma might come

back. Where do *you* think she's gone? Who came to take her away?'

'Stop shouting, Jed. Please. I don't know, I don't know.'

'I'm staying.' He put his hands in front of his face and sat down heavily in the grass. Comet rolled onto his tummy next to him. 'You go. I'm staying right here and waiting for my *Dada*.'

She could hear breathing. It was her son. Her son's breathing. He was here. Alive. With her.

'You know I would never leave you. Never.'

She looked back at the manor. The concert grand, glossy and black, filled the drawing-room window, an icon of a life gone away. She looked down. The top of Jed's head. The whorl of his parting.

'Sweetheart. I'm sorry.' There was nothing for it. 'We'll stay. For one night.'

'Two.'

'We'll see.'

She must grow bigger inside, take up more space, create emptiness. The bigger the gap, the more she could hold the feelings inside it.

They went back onto the lane. They looked in the garage beside Dylan and Mary's house. A wide metal swing door. She yanked at the catch and the door yawned towards her, sliding up and in on its runners. Horse tack and farm tools. It smelt of wax and linseed oil. A small set of makeshift wooden steps led up to the converted room above, impossible to see from the outside. They might come upon a body at any point. What would happen then?

'Stay,' she told the dog.

They climbed the little steps and pushed open the hatch. Sun poured through the Velux. Beneath the sloping ceiling, a single bed against a magnolia-painted wall, a sink, a very old electric hob, a kettle on a rickety table. The air felt hot, preserved.

'We can sleep here tonight. No one can see us.'

Jed shook his head. 'I want to stay in my bed at Gamma's.'

'No, monkey.'

'Why do we have to do everything you say?'

'I don't think—'

'It's non-negotiable.'

He climbed down the steps and left the garage.

'Non-negotiable?' she said, to the space he'd left behind. She ran to catch him up.

They returned to the humpback bridge and made their way along the opposite lane, Jed turning in loops.

'What are we looking for?'

'Supplies—'

'And clues like detectives?'

'Yeah.'

Everywhere was empty, front doors closed or locked. Through the windows, the rooms neat and tidy. She looked at Jed. His eyes were bloodshot.

'See?' she said. 'They've all been evacuated.'

'What does evacuated mean?'

'Made to leave and taken to another place.'

'Why? Did bad men come to their houses too? I want to go to Gamma's and be detectives there.'

Back along the lane and up the path, round to her parents' cottage and its rear terrace, legs flagging. Jed unwound the hose by the outside tap.

'The handle with a trigger, like Gamma said. That's a clue, isn't it, Mama?'

'Yes, sweetheart.'

He turned the tap. The trigger clicked, impotent. He wound the hose back into its housing.

At the far reaches of the back garden, the summerhouse. She peered through the windows: some planks of wood and her parents' obsolete beekeeping suits. The black-netted masks were torn, the white cotton trousers stained brilliant yellow, the smoking bellows dusted and mouldy. A solitary frame rested by one wall, a wedge of wax comb stuck in its corner, each cell a perfect hexagon. She leant against the door, the splintered slats sticky against her forehead.

Tired in her bones. Her poor old bones. Dem dry bones.

The flat in London: the study, its dark blue wall, the square notepad with Matthew's pencil doodles on the desk. He should have hidden in the attic with her.

She unpeeled herself. 'Let's look in the shed.'

The shed was drowning in ivy.

'An olden-days padlock,' marvelled Jed. 'With numbers. Why is it locked?'

She knew the code. 'Move out of the way, love.'

Old bikes with punctures. The usual mess of spades, trowels and trugs inside and something else the size of a lawnmower, sitting beneath a tarpaulin in the centre on the floor.

She swept the cover away.

'MediX,' Jed whispered.

The robot's eyes were closed, its white body clean and shining. In its outstretched metal arm, frozen in position, a dosette box of medication. Jed walked closer, tapped its head. It made a sound like an empty bin.

'Hallo, botty. You awake?'

'It's got no power.' The dosette's tiny compartments were marked with the days of the week. She could see the red and blue pills inside; nanoerythropoietin, nanohydrolate, iron. She tried to prise the lids open. They'd stuck fast.

A red flash, the faintest glint from its robotic eye. She snatched her hand away but it was nothing. A trick of the light. She covered MediX with the tarp, closed the shed and went back inside the cottage.

Mum hadn't taken her meds with her. Would there be doctors at the registration centre? Hospitals must have supplies, emergency generators. Would they have brought the equipment to the people, like Mohammed to the mountain? Would there be anyone there at all?

Time had jumped and they were in the larder, even the dog. The wall clock told her it was only five minutes.

Five minutes ago they were in the shed. Twenty-four hours ago they were in ...

'Peanut butter!' Jed at her elbow. He unscrewed the lid, dipped a finger in and put it in his mouth. His eyes closed. 'Mmm.'

She prised the jar from his arms. There wasn't much. She scooped some out and let it slide down her throat. It was too good.

'We'll save the rest. For dinner.'

The shelves were almost empty.

'But I'm hungry now.'

'We have to make the food last, Jed.'

'Please?'

Jed followed her as she walked back to the kitchen and opened the cupboards.

'You're the one who wants to stay here, remember,' she said. 'We've already had lunch.'

'Those horrible chickpeas? Ugh.' He went back into the larder. 'I don't call that much of a lunch.'

There was the sound of the lid coming off again, the *lap-lap* of a canine tongue.

'Don't waste it on the bloody dog!' She whipped the jar from Jed's hands.

'He's hungry too.' Jed picked up something else on the shelf. 'Is this jam? Why would you make jam out of tomatoes? And, what are *these*? They look like massive bogeys.'

'Caperines.'

'What are caperines?'

'A hybrid of GM capers and something else.'

'What are capers?'

'I don't actually know. I don't think anyone does.'

They were talking. Having a conversation. Keeping their minds occupied. Good.

Jed went back and forth, placing things to eat on the kitchen counter. When he'd finished, he went to the downstairs loo. The smell of sewage.

'It's up to the top with paper in here!'

'Come out then, and close the door!'

Jed came to sit on the kitchen stool. She spun the carousel, the contents circling past: salt; a half-eaten jar of powdered mustard; half a packet of millet flour; a Tupperware container of home-made muesli; a dusty cylinder of multicoloured hundreds and thousands. The best before date read: 2021. She put everything next to the jars from the larder.

She flicked the light switches, turned the taps. She listened to the clock ticking. She fetched the service station radio from the rucksack and placed it next to her mother's radio on the kitchen sill. She put Jed's torch next to that. She stood back, looked at everything.

'We have to go out again.'

★

Comet ran along beside them, tail circling, paws splashing in the brook. He appeared beside her with a small fish still alive in his jaws. He shook it, crunched the backbone and swallowed it whole. Fish. In brook-water toxic with spores of Bovine Staph dropped by beetles during the beetle blight. Perhaps they'd be forced to eat fish too, eventually.

Jed dragged his heels up the lane past Warston Hall, where peacocks screamed in their aviary.

'We could collect feathers?'

'Not now.'

They stopped on the verge near the gates to the hall in front of the old well. She lifted the wooden lid. Fresh spring water lay smooth and dark at the bottom. She hoisted Jed up so he could look inside. Half his body folded into the long drop.

'Can we drink it?' His voice echoed. 'Doesn't it have my disease in it?'

'You don't have a disease.'

'Yes. Bovine Staph.'

'For the last time, you don't have fucking Bovine Staph.'

'Don't swear, Mama.'

She would make a fire, she would use the water to cook things with. Matthew's lighter was still in her pocket. And there was wood. Though flames in darkness might attract unwanted attention.

'How will we get it out?' asked Jed.

She lowered him back onto the grass. She'd forgotten to bring anything to collect the water with.

'We'll get a bucket from Gamma's and drop it from a rope.'

Jed found a bucket under the sink. She cut a piece of blue baling twine from the cupboard beneath the stairs. The twine was shiny, slippery in her hands, and she couldn't think how to tie it properly.

'I know!' Jed disappeared upstairs.

He came back with a book of knots, the pages made of cardboard, two holes punched through the centre of each one. In each hole a piece of narrow rope had been threaded to practise with. The book felt sticky in her hands. She looked up 'bow-line' in the glossary and knotted the baling twine to the bucket-handle.

'There's an encyclopedia of mushrooms up there too,' said Jed, 'with the death-cap and the other one that looks normal but is really poisonous.'

'False morels.'

'How long until Dada comes?'

'Jed. Please.'

'It's not me asking, it's Comet.'

'Tell Comet to be patient.'

'He's a dog. He doesn't know what patient is.'

They made the journey back to the well. She lowered the bucket. It thocked against the wall on its way down and hit the water with a plash. She peered over the edge; the bucket floated. She hauled it out, found a clean rock, dumped it in the bucket's base and sent it down again.

'My tummy's hurting.'

The bucket sank under the water. It weighed a tonne. The twine cut into her hands. The bucket and water appeared over the ledge, sloshing clear and cold. Water from the spring underground. It had to be safe. It had to be. They knelt on the grass and gulped the freezing liquid in cupped hands.

'Let's go and make dinner?'

Droplets glistened on his chin.

She dragged the bucket home. Jed, the dog – her disciples.

★

She shook the metal lighter; hardly any gas. Night was creeping, the air cool. She slung a glance at Jed. He was leafing through a selection of children's books, head bent in the pages, Comet at his feet.

The fire would be made in the brick barbecue at the side of the back terrace. The wood-burning stove in the living room was too small for cooking. In the cupboard beneath the stairs she found a paper box with four brick firelighters and six dry pine logs in green netting stacked in a corner. She set Jed to finding small sticks in the garden and laid out what they had to eat: the old potatoes from Dylan's garden; the remains of the peanut butter; two packets of noodles; the tomato jam; herbs and spices from the carousel. She couldn't decide if she was hungry.

The fire lit easily, the firelighters smelling strongly of burning wool and wax. Flames licked at the tender branches drooping over the barbecue. She placed a pan of water on the metal grille for the noodles and wrapped the potatoes in foil that she'd uncovered in Mum's kitchen drawer. She placed them carefully among the coals. The sun dipped below the cottage roof. Jed was shivering.

'Go and put a jumper on,' she said.

'I'm not going inside by myself.'

'I can't leave the fire unattended, love.'

'Please.'

She followed him upstairs, Comet trotting at the rear.

Signy's old room. She opened the chest of drawers and let Jed root inside. She sat on the bed. She might never get up again.

Dead flies on the sill. A familiar odour: carpet, dust, damp. Her shelf of childhood books. Her old bagatelle board.

Hadn't Gethin once explained the theory of Trinculation using its little silver balls? Dark matter and how the universe was expanding. Two positive forces against a negative one, in a triangle. Something like that. The evolution of science. Things were not always evolving, though. Things could go backwards too. Or sideways. He wouldn't have an answer for that. She wasn't even sure what it meant, this thought. She stared at the circles of rusted pins arranged variously on the green wood. One hundred and fifty points was the highest score with one shot.

'I like this one, Mama, although it doesn't make sense.' Jed was in her brother's childhood T-shirt; a print of a *T. Rex* stalking a digger on its front. 'Dinosaurs and diggers? I don't *think* so.'

'I'm cold too. I need something to wear.'

She went into her mother's room: the tea-stained printed wallpaper; miniature strawberries wound with vines. The bed neatly made, the linen bedspread pulled over pillows. Gardening clothes folded over the back of a chair, a pair of woollen grey socks balled on the floor. In the cupboard she put her nose to her mother's clothes. Everything smelled of hazelnuts.

The air in here felt light. She whistled to rub out the nothingness: F sharp major, C sharp minor. It didn't sound right.

The manuscript paper underneath the piano music. That pad had been brand new. It would stay new forever.

She pulled one of her mother's sweaters over her head; a thick bobbly wool, holes at the elbows, Mum's lemony perfume. She took the sweater off.

The spare room: the shelf of old bottles collected from the brook; a metal horseshoe; a flower press. She checked in the only cupboard: blankets, towels, one of Nana's dresses – navy blue, made of something synthetic with a skirt full of pleats that would never come out. Hanging forgotten for a million years.

All the details, always, suspended in silence. She found a brown fleece in the chest of drawers. This one smelled of lavender bags. She put it on. It was better than the other one. Through the window, the fire glowed.

The potatoes had cooked. The noodles had boiled. She poured the food into three bowls. It was a lot. She should have rationed it. She was ravenous now. Comet devoured his share before she and Jed had even sat on the terrace step. The potatoes were grainy and tasted of earth, the noodles slimy and delicious. Her stomach grew warm.

'This tomato jam hurts my lips.' Jed's head disappeared behind the white ceramic.

'What are you doing?'

'Copying Comet. What's for pudding?'

'Let's go in.'

They left the last embers burning.

She locked the back door, secured the windows, drew the curtains. The trees were losing shape. She stared out into blackness.

'What are you looking at?'

'Nothing.' She turned to him.

He stuck his tongue out; it was electric blue.

She smiled. 'What happened?'

A scattering of hundreds and thousands melting in his palm.

'Can we go to the swing tomorrow?'

'No. We're leaving, like we agreed.'

'We didn't. Gamma might come. And Dada.'

'Jed. We need help.'

'For us?'

'Yes.'

'Why? What's wrong with us? We're okay, aren't we?'

'I—'

'*Aren't* we, Mama?'

'Yes, love.'

'Will we go to Rugby, like you said?'

'Yes. That's where everyone might be.'

'Even Dada?'

'Jed. Enough.'

His head dropped. Comet licked his hand.

There was nothing to do in the dark but think. She lay wide awake on the bottom bunk, Jed asleep on the top, Comet sprawled on a blanket, head-over-paws.

What time was it? Of course the hospital wouldn't have taken equipment to the leisure centre. That wouldn't make sense. She should have gone to a hospital first instead of coming here: the Hospital of St Cross, or that other one in Northampton. They should be elsewhere. Hemel Hempstead. The motorway with Madeleine and Six. Anywhere.

The memory of peanut butter lay somewhere on her tongue. Saliva flooded her mouth. She leapt up, bolted to the upstairs loo and vomited into the toilet. She stared angrily at her tummy. She needed water. The bucket was downstairs. She hissed for Comet to come. He yawned, stretched, got to his feet.

The house was soot-black and silent, the moon hidden behind a large cloud. One owl hooted, another answered. She felt her way down the stairs, a hand on each wall. In the kitchen she dipped a glass into the bucket and swilled her mouth out. She eyed the radios, sitting next to one another on the shelf. She peered through a crack in the curtains: more darkness, the cloud across the moon, a canopy of stars. The beauty of it. There was Sirius, flickering blue and red – the Dog Star. She patted Comet's back. On the way out, she hit the light switch.

Comet growled and his claws clicked on the cork away from her. The hairs rose along her arms. She stood in the living room doorway and followed him with her eyes.

His nose was pushed up against the back door, head lowered, ears down. Her hands felt for the torch on the kitchen counter. She swung the beam into the garden.

A pair of luminous yellow eyes. She crouched out of sight. The torch beam oscillated in her shaking hand. She looked again; the eyes still there. The eyes blinked, turned away. The torch picked out a small, slim body. Another fox. It ran off into the night. Comet licked her ear.

The faintest crackle of static, close by. She got to her feet.

The radio from the motorway. Its dials were alight again. GQOS' voice, very quiet.

'. . . *six hundred and fifty-four thousand and seventy-five divided by two point seven eight . . . six hundred and fifty-four thousand and seventy-five divided by two point seven nine . . .*'

Comet whined. She tapped him on the nose.

Her mother's radio flickered to life. '. . . *two hundred and thirty-five thousand two hundred and seventy-eight point seven seven . . . two hundred and thirty-four thousand four hundred and thirty five point four eight four . . .*'

The numbers ran fast for some seconds. Then both radios went dead at exactly the same moment. She waited. That was it. Nothing more.

She went upstairs, legs still light, and sank into the bed. Her body stank. The duvet billowed up, the soft pillow cradled her head.

Question and answer. The radios had been communicating with one another, she was sure of it. It had to mean something. She wouldn't tell Jed.

Day 9

Two wood pigeons and a yellowhammer calling in a tree outside. She was twelve again, everything all right; Mum and Dad downstairs, Dad breakfasting on goat's-milk yoghurt and grapes, the latest copy of *Astronomy* across his lap, Mum picking through half a grapefruit. Radio 4 blaring, her brother already up and watching television in the other room. Signy would clomp down the stairs to complain about the noise and clomp back to bed again.

Aya feeding the baby. James. Where had they gone to?

'Get up!' Her mother's voice – was it? Time to get up; ten o'clock at least. 'Mama!'

Matthew.

A child, cool fingers shaking her awake. Drool in the corners of her mouth. Jed standing over her.

'You've been asleep for ages. Get up, Mama. I've already let Comet out for a wee. He was whining.'

'What? Don't do that again. Okay?'

'Why not? There's no one here.'

'Just don't.'

She had failed. She had been unconscious while her son had unsecured the doors. She could not rely on herself. The radios talking to one another. She must get herself and her son to Rugby.

'What day is it?' he said.

'Don't know.'

'I think it's Thursday. My Show-and-Tell day. And reading corner.'

'It's Wednesday.'

'No, it isn't.'

'I'm not going to argue about it.'

She dragged her body to its feet. The room spun. She put a hand on Jed's shoulder. Comet's tail wagged the air, round and round; it made her feel sick. The dog's ears were cocked. He looked at her and yawned. White fangs glistened, slick with saliva.

She shuffled to the stinking bathroom and glared at herself in the mirror. Her face was tanned a reddish-brown, as if she'd spent a long time at sea. Beneath her eyes, deep grey hollows. Or perhaps that was her vision deteriorating from the exposure to UV. Perhaps she looked just fine. Beneath her fingernails, black. She leant over the toilet. Spit dripped from her mouth into the bowl.

'My cheek hurts.'

In the light from the tiny rectangular window, the skin around Jed's lips showed itself ugly and swollen. A small boil was rising near his ear. No, no. He was too short to see himself in the mirror. She told him he looked well. They needed a doctor.

They would have a cold wash this morning; the clean water would help his infection, focus her mind. She drew the curtains in the kitchen. Sunlight. Nature sprawling rich with pure purpose, its simple merry-go-round of growing and dying. Lucky thing.

She picked up both radios and shook them.

'What are you doing?' Jed asked.

'Nothing.' She put them down.

They ate some sawdusty millet-muesli with water. Comet had the leftovers but they made him sneeze. He lapped water from a saucepan, flicking it in all directions and flecking the windows of the back door.

'Are you ready?'

The sun hadn't yet had a chance to chase the cold from the air. Naked and shivering, they stood ankle-deep in the dewy grass of the wild garden.

'It's too bright this morning.' Jed squinted. 'My eyes are burning.'

'Don't be silly.'

But her sockets felt hot inside, too. Jed's arms were clutched about his chest.

'I feel ill.'

'You're fine.' He dodged out of reach. ''K. I'll go first.'

She tipped the jug over her head.

The water made her breath catch. Droplets ran off the ends of her hair. Goosebumps. Sunlight. It reminded her of something past, here in this garden; there had been umbrellas and cold water. When was that?

She scrubbed herself hard with her mum's lilac-scented soap. The dirt streamed from her body. Her stomach had grown concave, ribs popping. She grabbed a towel and refilled the jug.

'Your turn.'

'No.'

'Yes.'

'I'm freezing,' he squealed as she poured water on his skin. Gently, she wiped a flannel across his face. 'It hurts.'

'Shush.' She wrapped him in a towel. 'Don't you feel better?'

239

'No.'

She would do water and salt for his cheek, as Madeleine had.

There was a thunderous rumble and two fighter jets streaked across the sky, low to the landscape. A quarter of a second. A sonic boom and two black fuel lines cutting through the blue were all that was left. No chance to shout, wave a towel. They hadn't even moved.

'An olden-days jet,' he said, as if checking he hadn't imagined it.

'Yes.'

'The air force?'

'Yeah.' She rubbed him vigorously through the towel. 'Someone like that. Help must be coming.'

Perhaps that's what GQOS' voice on the radio meant – help on its way.

'Ouch. Why aren't they using the hyper-jets? Did they see us?'

'Get dressed, we're going to Rugby.'

'Mama, but I don't feel well.'

'Get. Dressed.'

She applied salt and cold water to his cuts, which made him yelp, then they dressed in clothes from upstairs. Comet watched from the doorway. She stared through the window onto the lane.

Jed wore her brother's socks. 'They're too big,' he said.

'You'll have to manage.'

They hung from his feet like dogs' tongues.

'You're not the boss of me.'

'I'm afraid I am.'

He huffed and shuffled out of the bedroom. She collected the rucksack from under the bed and they went out of the front door with the dog.

The bike had a puncture.

'Good,' Jed said. 'Now we have to stay.'

She fell back on the porch step and put her head in her hands. Had a person done this? The yellow eyes from last night? The man in the NYPD cap? No. Stupid.

She had to fix it. She had to remember how to fix a puncture. It was a basic skill. How would they be okay if she couldn't accomplish this simple task? Where would she find an up-to-date puncture repair kit for wide tyres?

This was what an apocalypse looked like. A bike with a puncture, a dog, a sick child. This was it.

'Did I make you sad, Mama? Is it my fault?'

'No, love. It's not you. It's never you. We'll go to Val and Tenny's farm and see if there are things to mend the puncture. Tenny's got everything in that barn with the bales and the motorbikes, remember?'

He smiled. 'I like that barn a *lot*.'

They picked their way through the long grass in their T-shirts, past the weir, towards the farm. Her waterproof was tied at her waist. On her legs, Mum's blue cords. She felt closer to her wearing them, like she was sending a message to her, to the universe.

Ahead, the old swing moved gently in the breeze. It hung between two fields in a narrow, fenced patch of land beneath the branch of an oak and above a small stream.

'Can we go on it?'

'No, love, there isn't time.'

'Why isn't there time? Why are you always checking your watch? One swing, then we'll go.'

Jed climbed the low fence. Comet squeezed underneath,

tufts of his white and brown fur left behind on the wood. Nothing to be done: she followed them.

The swing's original log seat had been replaced with a proper wooden plank. The long green rope was frayed. She took a stick and hooked it up, dragging the swing in towards her on the bank.

'Me first.' Jed climbed on and arced across the water. His legs were so short, they stuck straight out over the seat. 'This is amazing, Mama!' Comet hopped from one bank to the other. Jed passed her the rope. 'Your turn.'

'Jed.'

'Just once. You have to. It's so nice.'

The branch creaked as she put her weight on the plank. She pushed off, let her head hang. Higher and higher, that moment of suspension at the top always gave her butterflies. Her hair seemed to float around her face. The swing came to a natural stop. She climbed off. That was it. Pleasure. The end.

'What's that in the water?'

Jed descended the bank, legs slipping on the dry earth.

'We don't have time. Get back here.'

'Just a *minute*.' Flinging off his shoes and socks, he waded in. Something glistening. It poked from the mud in the clear stream. His hands dug in the stream bed. His feet disappeared beneath clouds of silt. He brought out a hexagonal green glass object. 'What's this?'

'A medicine bottle, monkey. Come on.'

'What kind?'

'It's from a very long time ago.' The bottles she'd collected just like this on the shelf in the cottage spare room. 'Put your shoes on.'

'Maybe it was special medicine that made you live forever?' He carried it up the bank and laid it carefully beside her on a

log. 'If we'd had it two days ago, we could have given it to
Dada.'

'It's empty, love.' She ran her fingers over the ridged glass.

'Not completely.'

A tiny water snail had made a home inside.

The sound of small drones brought their eyes up. Far away,
they circled over Sinistral Point. She watched them.

'We're going to Val and Tenny's now, Jed. Put your shoes
on, please.'

'I'm so cold, Mama.'

She felt his head. It was roasting.

'I think I need some of the old medicine from this bottle.'

'You need nanobiotics.'

'Dada says when I'm ill, I need sleep.'

It was true. It had been proven so. She studied his face. She
shouldn't drag him any further in his condition.

''K. We'll go back to the cottage for a few hours. You can
lie down, then we'll try again.'

They returned the way they had come. Crossing the field in
front of Warston Manor, a few hundred yards from the lane,
Comet came to a stop, ears alert.

Voices.

'Gamma?'

'Ssh.'

In the bones of her skull, her tinnitus whined.

Their line of sight was blocked by a thick hedge, all branches.
She took Comet by the collar, and they stalked close to its
sharp edges, keeping low. The dog must not bark.

Heavy-footed steps on tarmac. She pushed her hand into the
wood and created a small hole to see through: three soldiers
dressed in an assortment of camo gear, scarves across their
faces, two with infrared binoculars pushed up on their helmets.

Further off by the humpback bridge, a dark green jeep was parked sideways across the road, its back open and full of things; she couldn't see what.

'Who are they?'

'Quiet.'

A fourth soldier appeared behind the jeep. He was riding her bike. He wobbled on the flat tyre up and down the lane, dismounted and threw the bike into the boot. Heat radiated in her chest.

She pushed Jed onto all fours and crouched beside him.

A person in a black hoodie stepped out of the cottage next door to Mum's, arms heavy with blankets. Two more hooded figures, faces obscured by scarves, came out from Mum's door – one a female, wearing a tattered dress that hung over a pair of grey trousers. The scarf across the woman's face was patterned, green with white bits. What kind of person would do this?

The two people had hold of her rucksack, some duvets, pillows. They made their way down the path and handed everything to the soldiers on the lane. Then three of them trooped back inside the cottage. She counted seven people in total.

She watched as the soldier with her rucksack, left behind with one other, tugged at the drawstring. The contents were dragged out: her T-shirt, socks, Jed's woolly hat. A pair of her pants. The pants were held up to the light, the gusset spread for examination. The man pushed his scarf down from his nose and brought the pants in close. He sniffed, called his friend over. Signy's mouth went dry. They weren't soldiers. They couldn't be.

The second man put the pants on his head. He spread his legs, reached one arm out in front of him, balled his hand into a fist and forced an imaginary head towards his crotch. The other man laughed. She didn't want Jed to witness it. They delved into the rucksack's side-pockets: her penknife, the road map. The knife was opened, the blade tested against a finger, the road map unfolded, studied. They stuffed everything back inside the sack and slung it in the jeep with the rest.

The three people re-emerged from Mum's, her father's telescope wrapped in a blanket, lens poking from one end. The radios. Some of their food.

Comet strained against her hand. She snapped his collar. The dog gave a yelp.

In the lane a fist went up, a gun went onto a shoulder.

Comet barked. The sound echoed round the valley. Signy's fingers lost their grip on his collar and the dog slipped through her hands. He fled around the hedge and bounded towards the people. He arrived at their feet, turned on himself and bounded back in her direction.

The group was on the move towards her.

She sprinted back in the direction of the swing, Jed hanging at the end of her wrist. She was hidden from sight by the hedge, she knew, but had only seconds. Her boots slid down the muddy bank and they tumbled into the freezing water. She struggled to her feet, soaking wet, urging Jed on to the spinney beyond. Once in the spinney, she launched him onto the lowest branch of an oak, vaulted her legs up and over and shimmied after him, higher and higher, until they both disappeared in its many branches.

'I'm so cold, Mama. I dropped my green bottle.'

Oh, for more leaves.

'Hush. Don't move.'

Six figures entered the field. One had stayed behind then, keeping lookout. The man at the front had Comet by the collar. He bent low, whispered in the dog's ear, held one of her T-shirts to the dog's nose. Comet ran about, sniffing the ground. Signy watched them watching the dog. Someone pulled Mum's tub of hundreds and thousands from a pocket, poured the remains into their hand and chucked them into their mouth. She hated these people. She hated them so much.

Comet was close now. He came to a halt at the stream beneath the swing and entered the water. Her hands shook, her fingers cold as icicles. She heard him whine, his paws splashing. A minute passed. The dog climbed out, shook himself dry and trotted back to the group, tail wagging.

The six moved in together. Someone gesturing with three fingers. Infrared binoculars were flicked down, switched on. How cold was she? Almost freezing. She must not move. Jed's teeth chattered above her.

A buzzing growing near. Three blue police drones coming in fast from the direction of Sinistral Point. The six ducked as the drones hovered in a triangle just above them. The group swatted at the air. The drones would find her out next, give her away. Who did they belong to? Who was who here?

She watched the drone cameras draw level with the strangers' heads. The six put their hands up, hiding their faces. The drones were off then, flying at speed. There was a short whistle from the seventh person waiting on the lane. The six turned on their heels and hurried back the way they had come.

She was dizzy. Her arm flew out and she clung to the trunk.

'Jed? You okay?'

'I'm cold. I want Dada.'

'Oh, my love.'

'I lost my green *bottle*.'

'Ssh. It's okay. I'm here.' She squeezed his foot. 'Put my jacket on. You're all right.'

The jacket was wet too. She fed it up the tree. Jed's fingers brushed her hair. He would be more ill later, she knew. The distant throb of a diesel engine travelling away.

They wouldn't be going to Val and Tenny's for puncture repair. They wouldn't be going to Rugby. They wouldn't be going anywhere. Bile rose in her mouth.

They hung like animals in the tree for a long while, the countryside at peace, just the swishing of the breeze around them.

In the dying light they climbed down and made their way home across the field. They were dangerously cold now. Jed's arms were hidden in her jacket's sleeves, wet cuffs trailing the grass. No sign of Comet.

They reached the wall of Warston Manor. Keeping close to the crumbling orange stones, she put her head around one end and scanned the lane, then cut back to the iron gate leading to the churchyard. The high ground gave her a good view of the cottages right up to the humpback bridge.

'We're going through the back field, monkey.'

'I don't want to go to Gamma's.'

'We're not.'

A handful of stars had come out, pricking holes in the sky.

'Where then?'

'Just trust me, okay?'

How could he do that? She couldn't even trust herself.

They went around the edge of the church, safe possibly but too cold at night to sleep in, and climbed the fence at the rear of the graveyard into the damp field behind the cottages. They passed her mother's, the windows coal black.

Jed dug his heels in. 'We need to be going *some*where. I want to get warm.'

'We need to check they've gone first.'

They came out by the well. She'd left the bucket in the kitchen. Those people might have taken it and she would be forced to drink from the brook.

They crept down the lane beside Warston Hall, keeping close to the trees until they reached the crossroads. Deep wheel-indentations ran along the verge here. The tracks curved off the grass, over the humpback bridge and all the way up the hill out of Warston.

'My cheek's throbbing.'

'I'm sorry, love.'

'Will we have to sleep in the woods?'

'No.' She checked up the lane behind.

'I'm sleepy.'

He could hardly get the words out, his chin shook so fiercely. She passed along the lane, hands barely able to make fists now. Jed tripped over something.

The water bucket. A miracle.

'Oh.' Inside the bucket, Jed's otter. 'What are you doing in there, XO? You must be freezing.' He pulled the teddy to his chest. 'Do you think they left him here by accident?'

'I don't know.'

They were in front of Dylan and Mary's now. The front door was smashed in. Splinters of white wood speckled the step up to the porch. The moon's light kissed the outside of the Velux that cut into the sloping garage roof. She pushed Jed up the drive.

'In here.'

She'd expected the garage to have been looted, but the interior was untouched. No one needed a horse saddle or tack or horse brushes. Perhaps the people would return for a second sweep.

They climbed up into the hidden attic room using the

stepladder. She kicked the ladder off to the side in case anyone came snooping in the night.

The room was damp-smelling but not too cold. The base of the sink was covered in a carpet of semi-fossilised bees. They stripped themselves of their wet clothes, found the mattress on the metal-framed single bed and clung to one another beneath two dusty blankets.

'I hate it here.'

'I'm sorry. Don't scratch your cheek.'

'It's itchy.'

'Leave it alone. And stop fidgeting.'

Her throat was parched, her stomach knotting. She felt sick again.

'I'm hungry.'

All their things gone.

'And thirsty.'

There would be nothing for breakfast, lunch or dinner to-morrow. Or the day after. Wednesday. Or Thursday, was it? White-blue moonlight glowed through the Velux above their heads.

'Do you think Comet is hiding in a bush?' said Jed.

'Maybe. Yeah.'

'Do you think he's scared?'

She squeezed his leg beneath the covers. 'He can look after himself, sweet. He's descended from wolves, remember?'

'Yes.' He made a low howl at the moon. 'I wish Dada was here.'

'Warmer now?'

'Sort of.'

She must think like an animal. She must be a hunter now. When Jed finally dropped off, his feet pummelled her thighs.

Day 10

She'd been awake for the entire night. Possibly.

Runnels of rainwater tracked across the Velux. With the rain came angry, darker-grey clouds flying one over the other in the wind.

Matthew.

She leant off the bed and retched. What day was it?

She should collect the rain in the bucket. How safe would it be to drink? Not as safe as the well. The thought of trudging there brought on heavy stones in her legs.

She nudged Jed's shoulder with her foot.

'Wake up.'

'Sleeping. Go away.'

She leapt onto the bed and opened the Velux. Water soaked her head, the wind flattened her hair. The hamlet was still.

'Get dressed, we've got lots to do.'

'Don't feel good.'

Jed shuffled in the blankets. She tugged on her boots, jumped through the hatch to the garage and scoured the shelves: Dylan's workbench; horse paraphernalia; a toddler's rocking horse on top of a heavy chest. She moved the rocking horse to the floor and threw open the lid.

'Jed! Come and look!'

Jed's head appeared above her in the attic hatch. She dragged Dylan's twelve-bore shotgun out carefully. Jed's mouth fell open.

'Woah. Does it use lasers, like the big drones?'

'No, it's very old. It uses shot. And two boxes of cartridges, look, and Gethin's air rifle, a hunting knife and something ... hang on ...' She scrabbled around at the bottom. 'A fishing rod! Folded up.'

'What are we going to do with them?'

'Kill animals,' she said.

'To eat?'

'Yep.'

'I'm not hungry.'

'Oh, love, you have to eat.'

'Will we use the gun to protect ourselves against baddies?'

'That's right.'

'Do you know how to work it?'

'Dylan taught me.'

'When you were little?'

'We used clays as targets.'

'Clays? What are clays? Is it loud?'

'Yeah. Jed, you are never ever to touch this gun, do you hear?'

'Yes.'

'Good.'

She turned the gun over, trying to remember what was what: the breech; the safety catch. She tried to cock the barrel but the mechanism was stiff. She wedged the end between a vice on Dylan's small wooden workbench and pressed down. The gun snapped open. Two black chamber tunnels. Dylan had kept the gun primed; the breech was empty, the chamber clean. It smelled of iron inside, gunpowder. She picked a box of cartridges from the chest, examined the tightly ridged texture of their red plastic covers, the flat golden ends, searching for signs of water damage.

'First, we look inside Dylan and Mary's house.'

'What for?'

'Drugs for you. And matches. Then we'll fetch water from the well.'

Jed listened to the rain hammering on the garage door.

'What about that? Can't we drink the rain?'

'We don't know what's in it. After we've got water, we'll go to Val and Tenny's.'

She pressed the shotgun into her shoulder, rested her cheek on the stock and focused just beyond the barrel. The fit of the gun was still true.

'But those people took the bike.'

'Not for the repair kit, for food. To look for eggs.'

'I want to sleep, Mama. I'll stay here.'

'No.'

'But no one can see me here.'

'You're coming with me.'

'Tenny's farm is too far. It's not safe.' He followed her as she collected their jackets from the room. 'If we find Comet, we won't eat him. Will we?'

She leapt back down into the garage. ''Course not.'

'Good. He'd taste horrid anyway.'

'Be quiet now.'

He jumped from the hatch onto her back. 'Carry me.'

'You're heavy.'

He wasn't really. Not any more.

Out of the corner of her eye, her dad. He was floating, a shimmer, a blur, right there in the garage four feet away. She turned to him but he was gone.

'What you doing?' Jed was right in her ear, arms tight around her neck.

'Did you see Grandpa just now, over there?'

'What d'you mean?'

'Did you see Grandpa, Jed? Get off, you're strangling me.'

'I didn't see anything.' He slithered to the floor, eyes large. 'Was it a ghost? Your eyes aren't right because you haven't been wearing your UVs. And you're hungry. When you're starving you see things that aren't there. You might be going mad.'

'I'm not, love. Don't worry.'

'It's called a hallucination.' He fingered the air rifle. 'Can I take this one?'

'You're too little.'

'But you will teach me to shoot it?'

'Not yet.'

'When?'

'Soon.'

He went quiet.

'When you put the shotgun on your shoulder just now, it wasn't loaded. I thought I should tell you. It could be important for another time.'

She checked the gun. He was right. She pushed two cartridges into the barrel and clicked on the safety.

She slung the gun belt over her left shoulder. The gun was heavy. She grabbed a handful of extra cartridges, sealing them carefully in a piece of rag, and went to put them in her top pocket. Something already there: a piece of paper. She pulled out a rectangle of stiff white card, creased and water-damaged: 'A silent five-day meditation retreat.' A graphic of the moon in the night sky at the top. The paper fluttered in the wind. '... in the beautiful Welsh mountains in sunny June.' She tore the paper into four, let the pieces blow away. She stuffed the cartridges and hunting knife in her pocket and stepped out into the rain.

Dylan and Mary's house; the smell of lamb fat still permeating the kitchen's dirty yellow walls. The black and grey faux-marble floor tiles had lost their white grout and were wadded with mud and food. Everything in Warston – everything – was antiquated, still, like a photograph taken long ago. A wind-up toy hedgehog sat on the shelf above the sink, in its paws a sign: 'Don't ask me, I just work here'. The kitchen cabinets were open, empty.

In the small living room, the remains of a fire. A fire had always burned here, even in the height of summer. On the mantelpiece – Julie's show-jumping mini-trophy, ticket stubs for a Leicester City football match, a baby tooth in a silver box with the label, 'Gethin: aged 7'. Where the Holoscreen would have stood, a space. Those people must have taken it to sell. She stared at the wall.

Jed's money: it had been in her rucksack. But what did money mean now? She hadn't spent a single Lite-card since they'd left London.

In the double bedroom upstairs, the mattress had been up-ended. Watermarks blotted the bed-slats. Beneath that a layer of dust, a pale green valance and Mary's slippers neatly arranged on the carpet. The dressing table had had a going-over. A coral lipstick rolled in an open drawer.

'Look, Mama.'

'Careful.'

'Of what?'

He painted the lipstick on his mouth and smirked at himself in the scratched mirror.

'Jed, your infection.'

He looked clownish. 'I'm Ronald McDonald,' he said. 'He was an American baddie who used to make food that hurt. The Chinese made him go away. It said on *Newsbites*.'

In the bathroom, no medicines; the cabinet shelves were bare.

Jed whispered, 'What do you get if you cross a giraffe with a hedgehog?'

'Tell me.'

'A seven-foot toothbrush.'

'Funny.'

'Mama, I feel hot.'

Through the narrow passage to Gethin's bedroom. Photos of rock-climbers on the walls. A blue bedspread with footballs all over it, the words 'Everton FC' curled across a painted ribbon. The bed was made, the wardrobe open; inside, two hangers and a black leather belt with a silver Batman buckle, as if the room longed for him to never grow old.

Signy combed the pen-holders on the desk. She found a pass-port photo of Gethin, aged around eight, in front of an orange curtain. He was smiling, his top two front teeth were missing. It was the age at which he'd discovered he had Crohn's, and he'd nearly died and the endless treatments had started.

She sat heavily on the mattress, gun at her side. The air felt close. Jed sat next to her. He made a sound, like a chuckle.

'What's funny?'

He sighed. 'Nothing. I was thinking, we've been here four days and Dada's still not come.'

'Four?' She swivelled her body towards him. 'You're getting muddled. Two days.'

He shook his head.

'*Two*, I'm telling you.' Something about his insistence made her angry inside. 'You're getting—'

'I'm better at maths than you.'

'Computing maybe. It's only *two days* since we arrived here.' There was silence. She swallowed. 'Plenty of time for Dada to arrive. Okay?'

'Fine.'

Jed hopped off the bed and crawled under it. She tapped his foot with her boot.

'What you doing now?'

'Just seeing. Looking for treasure. Ah. Found one.' He wriggled out. A blue Bic lighter full of gas. She rolled her thumb over the flint. A short flame danced in front of her. Jed pulled his other hand from behind his back. 'And these.' A pair of UV glasses.

'My little friend.'

She planted a kiss on his head. He put the glasses on.

'There. All normal.' He smiled.

She stared out of the window at the rain. Two days. Two.

'Don't be sad, Mama.'

They left the house and set off with the bucket to the well. When the bucket was full, Jed drank nearly a pint straight off.

'Feel a bit better,' he said.

Another boil was growing near his eye.

Tenny's farm sat by itself next to the canal. They cut across the field, past the swing. She was carrying the gun in front of her. Her tummy ached.

'I'm sad about Comet,' said Jed. 'Comet!'

'Not so loud!'

She saw him glance at her out of the sides of his eyes.

'Comeeeet!'

'Stop that.'

The rain could fuck off as well.

Tenny's white sheep grazed. She could shoot one and eat it. Sheep were safe to eat. They stared at her through their diamond-slitted pupils.

Through the gate into the yard. They went to the hay barn full of motorbikes. It was empty.

'But where have all the bikes gone?' cried Jed.

'Perhaps Tenny and his family took them when they left?'

'Perhaps those people from yesterday.' Jed looked behind himself. 'I'm all wet. Let's go. I don't like it here.'

She didn't either.

'In a minute.'

Chickens clucking in the outhouse.

'Stay here.'

She left the gun against the wall and opened the rotting wooden outhouse door. A stench of chicken shit. The only light came from a square hatch leading to the grass pen beyond. A cockerel strutted in warning at her feet. Two hens scattered outside. The feeding trough had a fistful of grain in the bottom. The birds wouldn't last long on that.

In the rooting tray, seven eggs, two still warm. She carried them carefully out to Jed and went back in.

A lone hen cowered in the corner. It spied her in the door and lifted one foot from the ground.

She lunged but the bird was too quick; it ran for the hatch outside, missed and flew two feet into the air, trapping itself on a perch.

'Jed.'

'I'm not coming in.'

'Fine.'

She clapped her hands and the hen flew forward, right into her arms. She twisted the neck. The chicken went limp. Simple. It was much heavier dead.

They tracked across the grass in the pouring rain towards another rusted barn – a night shelter for long-ago banished cows – with the chicken and eggs in a sack. The barn was constructed of corrugated metal sheets oxidised to a reddish brown, the floor spotted with sheep droppings. It had only three walls, the fourth being an open rectangle like a picture frame that looked out on the empty field to more fields in the distance.

'Go and get dry sticks, monkey, and one long one for the spit.'

'I don't want to go out on my own. And there aren't any dry ones.'

'Look, just there. Those under that sheep-feeding trough aren't too wet.'

He did as he was told.

The eggs would be saved for later.

She sat cross-legged on the floor and stared at the chicken. She knelt on the bird's spindly feet. The feathers were hard to pull, as if they'd been glued in. Jed went back and forth, a pile of damp wood growing steadily by the open wall. Finally the chicken was ready – naked, puny-looking – her hands raw and red.

The fire lit easily with the straw and Gethin's lighter, the damp stalks smoking, making them cough. She sawed the hunting knife back and forth across the chicken's neck and cut the bottom end of the bird away. Chicken shit dribbled out onto her trousers. The meat would need cleaning or they'd both get ill.

'Don't go anywhere near the fire.'

'Where are you going?'

'To wash the chicken.'

A small watery ditch ran along the edge of the field next to the barn, swollen with the heavy rain. She swirled the carcass in the water. The freezing cold felt good on her scratched hands.

Jed was waiting for her at the mouth of the barn.

'I didn't go near the fire.'

'Good boy.'

She pulled out the chicken's gizzards and chopped the legs and wings off. She rammed sticks through the meat pieces and fanned them out to cook. They knelt on the ground and took turns blowing into the fire to keep it alight. The meat began to sear; it smelt incredible – of summer barbecues and bonfire nights. Matthew would be proud. Would have been.

'It *must* be ready now,' Jed said every few minutes.

'You're hungry then?'

It took forever to cook off the pink. Her arms ached from holding the sticks over the flames. She cut into a piece of meat with the knife.

'It's ready.'

They devoured it, hardly chewing, nodding at each other, eyes red with smoke, then sat side by side waiting for the fire to die, their chins slick with grease. Jed let the chicken bones fall at his feet and bent over them.

'Look at that.'

The bones in a familiar pattern.

'Looks like a fish,' she said.

Jed snorted.

There was buzzing in the iron struts above: three honeybees circling.

'More bees far from the bee farm!' she said. 'Hallo, bees!'

'They're lonely, they've lost their friends. Now they want to be friends with us.'

'I'm not sure bees make friends with humans. I like the sound they make though.'

'What – *bzzzzzz*?'

'Yeah – bzzz.' She smiled.

Jed attended to his chicken bones. 'How old was I when all the bees died? Was I alive?'

'You were in my tummy.'

The carpets of bees. A holocaust. She'd cried when she'd seen it on the news, far away in a far-off land like a fairy tale, something happening to other people. Then it had come to Europe.

'People said it was the end of the world but it wasn't, was it, Mama? They made the little pollen-drones and then it was all okay. And now the real bees are coming out again, aren't they?'

'More or less.'

More. Or less.

She looked down at Jed's pattern of bones.

'An infinity sign as well as a fish.'

He looked at her. 'I was wondering when you'd realise.'

'You're not the only genius. Who taught you that? School? Or was it Grandpa?'

'Everyone knows it, silly. You can use it in TrincXcode, instead of triangulate constellations.'

'Constellations? Constellations meaning musical chords?' This she could understand.

'Two of the notes are always the same in TrincX, see? And one note is different. Mathematically, that one note forms the point of the triangle. With the infinity sequence, you can loop the constellations into cycles. Then the programming has a different function.'

'What kind of different function?'

'The algorithm continues learning.'

'And how do you stop it learning?'

Jed smiled then. 'Mama. You just switch it off.'

Constellations. Cycles of notes. No end to them. She wished she could switch herself off. Just for an hour.

They watched the bees chase one another out of the barn. She ruffled Jed's hair.

'Did you know they do a funny little figure-of-eight dance, the bees, just like your infinity sign, when they get back to the hive to show the other bees where the food is?'

'We learned *all* about it in school.' He let out a sigh. 'They're super-intelligent. Like me.'

'Just like you.'

They stared at the rain-soaked landscape.

They trudged back towards the hamlet, bellies full.

'Do animals get sad?' Jed asked.

'What do you think?'

'I think they do.'

'So do I.'

'Why didn't you say, then?'

'I wanted to know what you thought first, so you're not influenced by me.'

'I bet Comet feels sad, all alone.'

Matthew. All alone in the bedroom.

They passed the front of the manor. The grand piano shone like a black star through the living-room window. On an impulse she made a left turn, pulling Jed towards the knot garden and round the back to Jean's kitchen door.

'Miss Yue made us use influencing.'

Made: past tense. His world retreating.

'She did? On other people?'

He snorted again. He was always laughing at her, laughing at her antiquated thinking.

'In coding. The program learns for itself but you have to use influencing. To get it to do what you want. Otherwise, it takes control of itself.'

'But you told me it wasn't able to take control of itself, remember? You said that that was illegal. And just now you said that you can switch it off.'

'*Mama.*' So much frustration in his tone. 'That was different. We were talking about the hardware, the constellation. Influencing is something else. It's the software, part of the stuff you feed into the program. But you have to get past the program's SHIELD system first.'

'To do what?'

He waggled his hands in the air at her. 'To *influence*. Why aren't you listening properly?'

'I am.'

'Getting past the SHIELD is hard. The ones in school have an open SHIELD so we can practise.'

'Right.'

There was a silence, then he said, 'I mean, you'd have to be practically Wolfing Mozart to influence if the SHIELD was up.'

'Wolfgang. What d'you mean? And what's a SHIELD?'

'Never mind. Influencing.' He rolled the word like a sweet in his mouth. 'You don't really get it.'

'You're right. I don't.'

He followed her around the fountain.

'Why are we going here?'

'I'm not sure.'

'Is something influencing you?'

He was teasing her. Her six-year-old thought she was stupid. She'd show him.

'No.'

262

She was going to put her hands on that piano. She was going to touch something she loved, make something beautiful travel through her fingers.

He shook his head. 'I don't want to go in here. I want to go home and lie on the bed.'

'Tough.'

She pushed at the door and stepped inside the manor's flagstone kitchen. The looters had been through here in a hurry: pens, notepad, loo roll, cutlery, all on the floor.

They tiptoed into the panelled hallway. A grandfather clock tocked upstairs beyond the narrow stairwell.

'Are we going to take the piano with us?' whispered Jed.

''Course not.'

He pointed at the stairs. 'Medicines. There might be medicines up there.'

'Yes. Good. Let's go up.'

They were halfway up the flight when he said, 'Is the gun loaded?'

She checked. Of course it still was. Her hands were trembling.

The grandfather clock was on the top landing, pendulum swinging heavy, slow. They found the bathroom: a roll top bath, two sinks. The cabinets were empty.

At the end of a run of deep red carpet, a four-poster bed in the master bedroom, the bedding gone.

Her eyes fell on a shallow drawer without a handle beneath the bedside table. Slipping the blade of the hunting knife into a gap between drawer and frame, she forced it open. Brown pill-bottles, silver blister packs, tabs: tramadol, oxycodone, warfarin. Some amoxicillin.

'Could you swallow these?'

He put the bottle to his eye. 'Too big. What are they?'

'Antibiotics.'

'Antibiotics? They don't work any more.'

'I know.'

She chucked the bottle in the drawer. At the very back, a travel-size tube of colloidal silver gel. '*Best Before: 07/09/2026.*'

Jed peered over her shoulder. 'Not using that.'

'Don't be stupid. Silver doesn't go off.'

She rubbed the gel into his lips and left the room. She caught her reflection in the smoked glass of the mirror hanging in the corridor. Her face was thinner.

Far away, the peacocks screaming.

There were ten bedrooms. They looked in each one, hopeful. They contained nothing of interest save, for Jed at least, one pair of girl's maroon tights balled like a hedgehog.

'I'm taking these.'

'You're going to wear tights?'

He shook his head. 'To keep my jeans up.' He pulled his waistband out. There was a large gap between tummy and denim.

They went downstairs into the drawing room: dog-eared sofas, a chaise, an oriental sewing box with a carved walnut lid on an inlaid desk. She looked inside the box: cotton reels, needles, scissors. She wrapped the eggs in Jed's new tights and put the box in the sack with them.

'What's that?' he said.

A twentieth-century combination stereo with record player, CD player and double cassette decks on a shelf. Extraordinary.

'It's a music system.'

'Music *system*? Like a computer system?'

'No. It's what they were called in the old days. From quite a while before I was born.'

Her eyes slid to the piano, glossy lid propped open. She pressed her cheek to the veneered top. The lacquered wood felt cool and smelled of envelopes. Moisture spread across the side of her face. She peered inside: strings, felt, hammers, dust. She sat on the stool. Yes. Her fingers picked out a Mozart variation.

Jed fell onto the sofa. 'That's Wolfing's "Twinkle".'

'Wolfgang. It is.' She put her hands in her lap.

'Are you sad, Mama?'

'Yes.'

'Because you miss Dada?'

'I miss everyone.'

'Except me.'

'Except you. But I'd miss you most of all if you weren't here.'

'When Dada comes you won't be sad any more, will you?'

She kept her eyes on the keys. 'No, love.'

She played the notes – so close to the front of her mind – with one hand. She looked up. Jed was smiling. The music was right there, at the ends of her fingertips. He was leaning forward.

'That's part of TrincXcode, Mama!'

'I know.'

'That's clever!' At last. Her heart swelled. 'You're clever! How do you do that?'

'I don't know.' It was the truth. 'It's just something I can do.'

'Woah.' His mouth was open. 'Can you play TrincXcode variations? Can you play infinity?'

'Um ...'

She repeated the pattern of notes, improvising cycles with both hands now. The melodies spiralling out, golden, each one folding away from the last like the petals on that rose in Regent's Park. Deep Secret. Exhilarated, her foot found the sustain pedal.

There was a hissing sound from across the room. Jed was on his feet.

'What?'

'Look!'

At the left-hand side of the main amplifier box on the stereo, the green power light flashed. The cassette decks were open.

'They moved,' Jed whispered, 'by themselves. It's like the radio, but now *things* are moving too. The light came on when you played the code. The system switched itself on.'

'No.'

'*Yes.*'

The power light went off. The house seemed to vibrate. She repeated the cycle of notes.

There was a click. Her eyes flew to the stereo. The power button flashed and GQOS' voice, soft, toneless, drifted from the speakers.

'*90 degrees, 16 minutes, 33 seconds South, 65 degrees, 5 minutes, 44 seconds West.*'

The wall lamps flickered. She jumped from the stool and curled her arms around Jed's chest.

'I told you you could do it,' Jed whispered.

Silence. Then: '*42 degrees, 63 minutes, 12.2 seconds North, 73 degrees, 11 minutes, 28.5 seconds East.*'

The lamps flickered. From the kitchen the click of the kettle, the hiss of the water heating inside, like distant waves.

Jed freed himself from her embrace and disappeared to the hall. GQOS was speaking again, reams of co-ordinates, faster and faster, the numbers no longer separated but one unbroken string. Jed returned with a pen and pad and started to scribble. The wall lights flickered. The kettle clicked off, on.

GQOS was silent. Jed's pen hung in mid-air. Ten seconds passed.

The *tick-tick* of the kettle filament cooling. Jed stuffed the scrawled pad into his pocket. She took his arm and ran for the door. He didn't protest.

Later in the room she studied Jed's scrap of paper with GQOS' co-ordinates. He drew close to her.

'What do you think they mean, Mama?'

She shook her head.

'Perhaps the real army's coming to take us home? Perhaps you've called them,' he said.

'Perhaps.'

'I've got a tummy ache,' he groaned, rolled sideways. 'Going to be sick.'

They only just made it to the garden in time. He needed a doctor. He wasn't well enough to walk far. She watched him closely all night. He slept soundly, hardly stirring.

Day 11

Jed covered his eyes. 'Is it dead?'

'Yeah.'

Her hunger couldn't be sated. The eggs they'd taken had been boiled and eaten only an hour ago, and now the shotgun and one of Dylan's sheep lay at her feet, an explosion of claret chunks in the grass.

He made a gap between his fingers. 'Is it sad?'

'It's dead. It can't feel anything.'

'How do you know?'

'I don't.' An insistent whistle rang in her ears.

'What do we do now?'

'Butcher it.' Her voice sounded different – thicker, deeper, as if speaking through rubber.

Discovering Matthew on the bed.

She dragged the sheep to the corner of the field beneath a yew.

'A sheep beneath a yew tree,' she said.

'What d'you mean?'

'Yew. Ewe. It's a joke.'

'I don't get it.'

She set to work slicing the length of the animal's belly. Her fingers looked different too – calloused, puffy. Farmer's hands.

The animal's intestines flopped out in front of her. She stared at the bloody mess and forced herself to feel nothing. This was how you did it. She'd remembered. She picked up the heart, liver and kidneys and placed them on the lid of an upturned salt-lick.

She flayed the rest, laid it open like a gruesome butterfly. Too much meat for two people. Bluebottles fizzled above. She swatted them away but they were persistent.

'Perhaps we can smoke it,' she said.

'What? Like an old vape?'

She pulled Jed's hand from his face. His skin was taut and waxy. A bright red line beneath the surface travelled towards the boil at his ear. How had she not noticed? What kind of mother was she? She left the sheep meat, took his hand and hurried back to the garage.

She combed the shelves. Colloidal silver wasn't enough. There had to be something else.

A box of horse medicine. She didn't know what any of it did. Ketamine: she wasn't giving him that. A vial of iodine, on its side in a tray full of studs.

'Fuck's sake.'

She sat with the vial on the garage floor, diluted a few drops in a tin filled with water from the bucket. She held the lighter flame under the tip of a needle from the manor's sewing box. The point scorched. She gripped it with a greasy tack-rag and dipped the needle in the solution.

'I don't want it, Mama!'

'I'm sorry. Whatever's inside needs to come out.'

'It's going to hurt!'

'Yes. But it'll feel much better afterwards.'

He scuttled to the shadows. She took his hand and led him back into the light.

'Look away, love.'

He pushed her then. She fell backwards.

'I wish Dada was here and not you! I hate you! I wish it was you that was asleep!'

'Stop that!'

She yanked him towards her and inserted the needle in each boil, one after the other. He squealed. She gripped his wrists. An egg-cup's worth of neon goo oozed out. It smelt bad. She tried not to gag. The poisonous-looking liquid slid down his jaw and dripped onto his shoulder. He was crying hard. She dabbed on more iodine.

'I don't like you any more.'

'That's fine.'

Fingers of sun touched the floor. A bee buzzed close by. A bee. Another. She held Jed to her.

'It's okay. You're okay. You're still here.' The swelling had diminished. His face was stained with iodine. 'You look better already.'

'It's sore where you stabbed me.'

'I didn't stab you, I lanced it.'

He threw his arms around her neck. His fingers on her skin were soft as feathers.

A rattling noise outside in the lane. Signy put a finger to her lips. She sneaked to the garage door and looked out.

Her mother's MediX robot was coming down the lane towards them, tarpaulin trailing in its wheels, right arm out-stretched, dosette box in hand. Its eyes flickered. At the bottom of the drive the robot made a sharp right turn towards them. Jed screamed.

'Help me close the door! *Jed!*'

The door's runners had rusted; the door groaned shut inch by inch, cutting the daylight away as MediX rattled on the tarmac.

It was no more than two feet away when the door shut completely and everything plunged into blackness. The wheels came to a stop on the other side.

'Who sent him here?' whispered Jed.

She found his hand in the darkness. She hadn't padlocked the shed door after they'd been inside it. A mistake. No one had sent the bot. It had switched itself on and let itself out.

'*Birgit,*' a cheerful voice piped in an American accent, '*you have not taken your medication for twenty-seven days. I cannot locate a signal from your neck chain. Yours is the closest heartbeat within range. I deduce that you need medical assistance. If you do not need assistance at this time, press the green button, or if this is not you, press the green button and I will reset. If it is a medical emergency, press the red button and I will patch through to emergency services.*'

She lifted Jed into the attic room.

'Stand on the bed and keep a lookout through the window. If you see anything, or anyone, at Gamma's cottage, or coming into the village by way of the humpback bridge, tell me.'

'How am I going to do that?'

'Shout.'

'But I'm too small to see.'

She slammed the hatch closed, locking him in, and pulled the toggle on the garage door.

'*Hallo, Birgit.*'

'Hallo, MediX.'

'*I'm sorry, my software does not recognise your voice. I'm programmed only to respond to Birgit, though I'm detecting low blood pressure and a trace virus. Please wait: verifying.*'

Signy looked across the field to her mother's cottage. No sign of anyone. She pressed the red button on the robot's chest panel.

'*Dialling emergency services. Please wait.*'

There was bleeping and a long, flat sustained tone.

'Who sent you, MediX?'

'I'm sorry, my software does not recognise your voice. I'm programmed only to respond to Birgit, though I'm detecting low blood pressure and a trace virus. Please wait: verifying.'

'Fuck's sake.'

'I'm sorry, my software does not recognise your . . .'

Signy pressed the green button. The robot's head drooped as it shut down to reboot. For a second time, she tried to wrestle the dosette box from its hand but it was stuck fast.

'Can we keep him?' Jed called from behind the hatch. 'He could be our friend?'

'No.'

'Why not?'

'He's about to reset. He switched himself on, and he's faulty. He might switch on again in the night and give away our location.'

'But there's no one here. And what if MediX is like the radios? What if it can do things?'

What if it could do things? Its arms were strong. No, she didn't trust it. Wearily, she stood back. She knew exactly what to do with the bloody thing.

The robot's wheels bumped over the tarmac towards the brook. There were about two more minutes until it reset. She couldn't believe how little it weighed. She shoved it over the edge of the bank. It rolled down the side and crashed into the green water, barely covering three inches of its body. That was that.

She made her way back to the room and fell on the bed. She felt inexplicably guilty. The sheep meat was waiting for her in the field. She must not forget it.

The last time she'd seen MediX working, it had been

administering steroids to her dying father. When he had died, the medical team reprogrammed it to work for Mum. Just like that.

'Maybe it came on when you hummed the TrincXcode notes?'

'What?'

'The robot.'

'I didn't.'

'You did. You hum them all the time, I told you. Like when we were at the manor. You're playing the code, influencing, and things are coming alive.'

'No, love. It could never have heard my humming from that distance.'

'Yes, love. It could. It picked up your heartbeat. Bots can pick up frequencies within the TrincX sequence, if that's their programming, up to a mile away. You're influencing it. Making the system do what you want, instead of what it's programmed to do.'

She sat up. 'Tell me again. What kind of things can you make a system do, just with sound?'

'If you get it right, whatever you like. We might be able to start a car. We might be able to talk to someone through another music system, but not the one at the manor because I don't want to go back to that creepy house.'

Sit at the piano with the ghosts? No; she didn't want to either.

'What if we sang the code, Jed? Would that work? You sing one part and I sing another.'

'Like our own variation? Like Wolfgang's?'

'Yeah.' Finally he'd got the name right. Her son. Self-learning. A perfect algorithm. 'That might work.'

★

She woke to find Jed sitting in the narrow bed, imaginary book in hand, lips moving in the half-light.

'Which one?' she said.

'The Shellfish Giant.'

'Selfish.'

'No. It's my variation. It's got prawns in it.'

'Very funny.'

They got dressed and went outside to search for things to eat: nettles, dandelion leaves, the remains of the slaughtered sheep, which they roasted over a fire inside the church. The wet wood brought thick smoke rolling over the pews, forcing them to wait out in the gloomy porch.

Afterwards, she tried to preserve the last of the mutton by building a smoke-chimney from sticks in the vestry but it caught light, scorching the meat to a crisp. She buried the charred remains away from the garage.

Despite not feeling well, Jed wanted to take Dylan's fishing rod to the brook's edge. He jigged on the bank, impatient beside her, as she prepared the rod.

'Do you know what scurvy is?'

'Yep.'

'It's lack of vitamin C.'

'I know. I just said – I know.'

'We might have it.'

'We don't. Here, you have a go.'

He cast the line. The nylon flew out. It stuck on a branch on the opposite bank.

'Oops. How can you be so sure?'

'I'm sure. Why do you think I'm making us eat all those dandelion leaves?'

She waded across the water and untangled the line.

'Your hair falls out, then your teeth.'

'Yes. We're going to stop talking about it now.'

'Is it as bad as Bovine Staph?'

'Jed.'

'Well? Is it like the plague? Do you get spots full of puss and then die?'

'It's pronounced "pus". Now be quiet, you're scaring the fish.'

On the way back, empty-handed, they passed MediX lying on its side in the water. She looked away.

'Poor Botty,' said Jed.

In the gloaming they collected water from the well, the landscape coated in thin gold light. Jed walked in figures of eight.

'... but Peter hid in a flower pot and Mr Mack Wrecker didn't see him.'

She struggled through the field at the rear of the cottages with the heavy slopping bucket.

Ahead, the sun was an orange lozenge falling into the horizon, surrounded by rose-coloured clouds. A peacock screeched.

'Will it go rusty, do you think?' Jed kicked at the long grass.

'What?' She felt more alone than ever.

'MediX? Lying in the water like that for nearly two whole days already.'

'Two? One day. Not this again, love, please.'

'Two days,' he insisted. '*Yesterday* you put him in the brook.'

'Sweetheart.'

Her tone was sharp, and they fell into silence as the sun dipped further and their shadows grew longer.

'What d'you call a mushroom who tells jokes?'

'I don't know.' She knew.

'A fungi to be with.' He sighed. 'You knew.'

'No.'

'I can tell. You should never lie to a child.' He gave her the side-eye, and walked away. 'Close your eyes, Mama.'

'Where are you going?'

'Stay there. Don't peek. Lean down.' His hands at her ear, breath warm on her nose. 'There.'

Her hand went up to feel. A wild flower in a lock of her hair; petals wet, stalk already drooping.

'Suit me?'

The sun so low now, it made her squint.

Jed's chin lifted. 'What's that? I hear something.'

'We're tired, love. We're imagining stuff in our minds.'

A low hum like an idling motorbike. Jed stared at the line of trees that edged the churchyard.

'Not in my mind. It's there.'

A dark cloud in the air. It was on the move.

'Bees.'

She grabbed Jed by the collar and darted sideways. An angry ball swarmed past them into the darkening east.

'There must be one big hole in those silos,' said Jed. He grabbed her arm. 'Look!'

Another swarm. Another black mass, far quieter, following the bees' trajectory: pollen-drones. She waited until it was out of sight.

'What does it mean, Mama? Are they all mixing together? Are they friends?'

'I don't know. I just ...' What would Matthew say? *Don't worry, it's all going to be ...* 'I don't know.'

Aware of her insignificance beneath the dome of darkening sky, she lugged the bucket home. They climbed the ladder, kicked off their boots. She threw herself into bed.

Through the Velux, black night. The mournful hooting of an owl, the flitting of nocturnal animals.

TrincXcode notes revolved in her head. Evolved. Those triangulate chords moving into figure-of-eight sequences.

Bees hum in the key of C. Pollen-drones hum in the key of nothing; their creators should have gifted them a sound.

She climbed out of bed, feeling for the pad and pen Jed had snatched from the manor. The squares of paper were small and meant for 'Just gone out,' or 'Buy milk!', not composition. She licked around their edges and attached one to the other like Rizla papers. To the rhythm of Jed's breathing she scored two sets of stave lines, wavering and uneven. Crotchets and quavers against the blank white, accidentals scribbled by hand. The notes flowed easily, the music both mutable and fixed. The melodic line, hers. The harmonic line, Jed's. Jed was clever, he would learn fast. After two hours, she climbed back into bed and fell asleep.

In her dream she ate two baked potatoes, four slices of toast, a soapy sweet mango, a bowl of oranges and a plate of calamari. And then she dreamed that she threw it all up.

Day 12

Matthew.

Her body smelled gamey. She stared up at the view: clouds. Her clothes were damp. They should leave, find a human doctor. Or a DoctreX, if they were still functioning. Drugs. They should have stayed with Madeleine and Six; if they remembered her, she hoped it was for more than the jelly beans. She hoped they were surviving.

The music. She dragged her thoughts into a line, splashed her face with cold water. The importance of routine. Though there didn't seem many routines left: Jed's saying please and thank you, an attempt at personal hygiene.

He was already awake, hands fidgeting, fingers looping one over the other. The boil on his face had filled again overnight.

'Get up. We're leaving.'

'Now?'

'First we need to do some things.'

He looked at her beadily, 'What kind of things?'

It took only an hour to teach him his part of the code, though when she began to sing her own at the same time, he lost his way. He laced his hands behind his head.

'It's impossible. I can't read your blobs.'

'You know they're called notes. If you'd agreed to learn an

278

instrument, like I said,' – this was absurd – 'this wouldn't be hard, would it?'

'I didn't *want* to.'

'Anyway, you don't have to read them. You can learn it with your ears.'

'What are those?' He pushed his finger at the paper. 'They're not notes.'

'They're rests.'

'I want a rest.'

'No. Again. It's important. We're influencing.'

'You don't even know what that means.'

'I don't need to, do I? I know how to create the code. We need to learn it so we can go on our journey.'

'To where?'

'To find you medicine.'

'I thought you said there was nothing wrong with me? And how will Dada find us if we leave again? I don't want to.'

'Just sing the fucking music.'

He did as he was told, the harmony echoing the melody like a canon. Like an equation drafted by God's daughter.

'Good,' she said at last. 'You're getting it. Again.'

They went past the well, through the gate into Gethin's uncle Aled's field, heading towards the ridge leading to Sinistral Point. A search for mushrooms. After this, they'd return to collect water and what belongings they had left.

It was hard going, the ground squelching underfoot, the shotgun, safety on and heavy on her shoulder, the cartridges rolling against one another in her pocket. She'd used just one barrel on the sheep. The gun was still armed.

Or was it? She stopped and brought the shotgun around to her front.

'Apple trees!' cried Jed with longing.

She looked up. Aled's orchard garden. A few lonely apples hung from the branches.

'They're cookers,' she said. 'They'll give you tummy ache.'

'Please?'

He wandered through Aled's open gate.

She propped the gun against the fence and made a cradle of her hands beneath the trees for him. Jed heaved himself up, freed one. His body flopped onto the grass. She took the apple from him, scraped her teeth into the skin and spat it straight out.

Jed bared his teeth. 'Bad as spinach?'

Her tongue prickled, hot and bitter. She licked round the inside of her mouth. It was coated in fur.

'Too early.'

'When will the other apples, the eating tree apples over Harry's peacock house, be ready?'

'It's an aviary, not a house. Same as these apples,' she said. 'One more week.'

Any answer was better for him than not knowing.

'How will we know when it's been a week?'

'When they're ripe. But we won't be here then.'

He was silent for a moment. 'Why do things always have to be one thing or another?'

'What?'

'Like – yes or no? Black or white? Dead or alive?' He pulled up a bunch of grass in his fist. 'Why can't they be both things at the same time? Yes *and* no? Black *and* white?'

'I don't know. It's how the world works.'

'Dead *and* alive,' he said, getting to his feet. She made sure not to look at him. 'Sleeping.'

He walked ahead of her out of the gate and up the hill. She

let him go for a second, then picked up the gun and followed.

From the top of the ridge, a panoramic view. The white sky stretched away beyond the rolling landscape.

'See anything?'

'Nope,' he said. 'But I hope we see Comet.'

They were exposed here. The people who'd come to the village: they could be watching. She led Jed quickly along the top of the ridge, above the sloping field bearing the scars of the rabbit warren where Gethin used to set traps. She pushed open the gate to Sinistral Point. At the bottom on the other side, a copse. From inside the copse, buzzing.

'Another swarm,' Jed said. 'What if all the bees have escaped the silos?' He bent to the grass. 'Look! I keep finding things.'. The life-hammer from the car on the M1. 'So weird.'

He held it out to her with both hands.

'It must have fallen out of my rucksack when those people took it from the cottage.' She put it in her pocket.

'They'd come up here with it?' Jed was studying her.

'I guess so,' she said. His gaze didn't waver. 'What?'

'Grandpa's your daddy, isn't he?'

'Yes.'

'And he's dead. Your daddy's dead?'

'Yes,' she said.

He turned away.

The wind turbine poles planted equidistant from one another rose brilliant white from the earth into the dirty grey sky. The village had fought hard to keep the turbines out: a battle they'd lost. Sheep grazed to the side. The wind was strong today. Each set of enormous fins chopped the air to pieces. All that energy; useless now.

At the edge of another field no more than a quarter of a mile away, a flicker of movement. Something blue hidden in the treeline. Her eyes watered. By the time she'd wiped them, it had gone.

'Can we get mushrooms now, Mama?'

'Yeah.'

Fresh movement in the open field: three small animals, perhaps dogs, streaking towards the trees where the blue object had been only seconds before.

'Do you think it might be Comet? Oh, I wished to see him and now I have! *Commmmet!*' Jed's shout echoed around the hills.

'For God's sake!'

'But it might be him,' he protested. 'I don't want him to die.'

'There could be people nearby, you silly boy.'

'Don't call me that.'

'We have to get going. We need to go home and get our things. If you want to eat today, hurry, find mushrooms.'

They searched close to one another at the base of each turbine, urgent, bending low in the shadows of the giant poles. Jed found the first enormous flat cream disc, gills brown and damp and smelling of soil. Their collection grew from one to three.

'One more,' she said. 'Then we're going.'

Dogs barking. The sheep running past her to the opposite corner. A thud on the earth, getting nearer. It took a second for her body to catch up. Bootsteps.

She shoved Jed hard in the small of his back.

'Go!'

He set off, sprinting towards the hedge at the opposite side of the field. He ran fast, dodging in and out between the turbine poles. She could only just keep pace, the shotgun banging against her back. Faster, faster they went, with the sound of other boots gaining ground.

Her sights fixed on the approaching hedge.

'Underneath!' she yelled.

Someone tugging at the corner of her jacket, dragging her back and down. She tried to shrug them off, but a boot to the back of the knees sent her body slamming to the ground. She was face down in the sodden field. She twisted the gun around to her front, swung onto her back and fired with her eyes closed.

A click.

'Oh dear,' said a man's voice. 'Forgot to load?' The gun was wrestled from her. Hauled by the collar, upright now, she sat, legs splayed, in the grass. 'That was a mistake.'

The four cartridges in her pocket. Her hand felt for them.

A man with brown eyes. Next to him, the woman looter from the village: tattered skirt, hoodie, dark green scarf hiding her face; the white bits on the pattern were flowers. Flowers. She was holding Jed by his coat.

'Hold him properly then, Hope,' said the man. A deep, gravelly voice.

'I'm not touching him. There's something wrong with him, look.'

'What?'

When Hope didn't answer, the man pointed the barrel of her own gun at Signy's boots.

'Nothing,' Signy said. 'Nothing's wrong with him.'

'It's Bovine Staph,' said the woman. 'Seen it before. His face is riddled.'

'No,' said Signy. 'It isn't.'

'Nobody touch him,' the woman ordered.

'God's sake.' The man's breath, hot in Signy's ear and smelling of aniseed. 'Get up, then.'

Unsteadily, she got to her feet.

Hope said, 'Go to Mammy now.'

Jed ran to Signy's side.

Something paddling at her calves. A wet tongue licking her hand. Comet.

'Dog yours, is it?' The woman.

Comet gazed up adoringly. He pushed his snout between Signy's legs.

'Not mine. We're travelling through.'

'You're hiding in that little village down there,' said the woman. 'This is your dog. He's been looking for you.' She stared over Signy's shoulders at the rest of the group. 'Told you it were a woman owner that time we was with them two others with the truck – dog's a pushover.'

'It's not our dog,' Signy insisted. 'We're from London.'

'Turn around,' said the gravel-voiced man. He sounded local.

She turned, nudging Jed behind her.

Seven men stood behind them, a similar raggle-taggle of camo gear, helmets, hoods, scarves. Two white terriers in the grass at their feet.

'You're not soldiers, are you?' Signy said. 'We'll give you whatever you want, just leave us alone, all right?'

The man lifted Signy's twelve-bore onto his shoulder and aimed it at a turbine pole.

'Click.' He chuckled. 'You wanted to hurt us, see? Now why shouldn't we do the same to you?' He put his hand into her jacket pocket and pulled out the cartridges. 'Nice.' He examined the red casings. 'Clean. We all need ammunition now. There's bad things going on. You'd know if you'd been travelling.' He cracked the barrel like a twig across his knee and pushed two cartridges carefully into the chambers. 'What else you got back in your little hidey-hole?'

She swallowed. 'Nothing.'

The woman stepped close. 'We'll see about that when we get there. Any more of you?'

'No.'

'You were staying in the house with the two radios?' Her irises were dark, almost black.

Signy blinked. She could smell her dad's cologne on the woman's skin. It had been on the shelf beneath the mirror in Mum's bedroom.

'The radios that talk to each other,' insisted the woman. 'Two GQOS. All the numbers. The co-ordinates. Where d'you get them?'

'Yes,' Signy answered, in spite of herself. 'Like a conversation?'

The woman's eyes narrowed, flicked up to the others and down again.

'That's it, see. Who's making GQOS talk?'

'I don't know.'

'I don't know,' Hope mimicked. 'Where d'you get the radios from?'

'We haven't got time.' The gravel-voiced man. The gun barrel was at the back of Signy's neck. 'Someone grab the kid. I need the Mum to show me where their stuff is. We're going to walk back to wherever you call home.'

Another man took Jed's arm.

'I'm not scared of your disease, lad. Tell your mam I'm not hurting you.'

'He's not hurting me, Mama.'

'Now move,' Hope said. 'Quickest route. No detours.'

Signy led the way between the turbine poles towards the gate at the bottom of Sinistral Point. Rooks were squawking in the trees.

They would be left for dead. Or shot. Or they might shoot

only her and take Jed with them as bait – collateral against food and water. She could pretend to trip, hurt herself. They had her gun. Jed wasn't fast enough. A hot loose feeling spread across her pelvis.

They reached the gate. What was supposed to happen now? Had she not noticed Jed was this ill? Or had she? Had she noticed and then forgotten? She'd been sure the gun had been loaded. What had she been doing all this time?

'Open it.' The gravel-voiced man at her ear again.

She reached for the catch. Silently the gate swung away on its hinges. She shut her eyes. She could just stand here forever.

A loud buzzing. Police drones, perhaps. Let it be police drones.

Three columns of bees swarming and weaving between turbine poles towards them, something peculiar about their movement. The dogs scattering up the field, squealing, rounding on the bees, snapping at the air.

'*Now!*'

A volley of shots into the clouds of bees. The bees still coming. Pollen-drones too, all mixed together. The clank of guns reloading.

Now. It was now.

She scooped Jed into her arms, raced through the open gate in front of her, turned an immediate right and sprinted fifty metres up the side of the next field, keeping tight to the boundary. Shoving Jed into a thick tangle of hedge, she crawled in after him. He was fighting her, elbows in her face.

'Ssh! It's me.' She peered through the branches down the hill.

The swarms hovered a few feet from the group like three black phantoms, the group motionless, shotguns trained.

The columns were pulsing now, oscillating – the bees rising, forming spirals. Her eyes followed as they ascended, the spirals growing wide until millions of drones and insects separated and re-formed as one huge black cloud high above. The looters continued to fire at them until they disappeared into a copse.

Left behind in place of the bees, three armed military drones, identical to the large black one she'd seen at the start of the M1. They had been hidden beneath the others, waiting, suspended in mid-air. For what?

Military drones. Here. In this field.

The army.

The sun came out, bathing everything in brilliant yellow.

A deep hum was coming from somewhere inside each drone. It resonated in her toes.

'Why aren't they silent, like before?' breathed Jed. 'Why are they making that noise?'

All was still, out in the field. The looters hadn't moved. The drones hovered above them, ancient-looking suddenly, as if they'd been waiting there forever.

'What are they doing?' Jed said.

'Ssh.'

From inside the drones' circular bodies, tubes extended outwards from holes, like insects stretching their legs.

Something. Something would happen.

Another volley of cracks. A second round of bullets from the seven guns. The shell pellets pinging off the drones' black exteriors and falling like raindrops, to the grass.

The looters took off then, skidding up the hill towards the ridge.

Shouting.

Back by the gate, the drones, immobile. Then she watched as, in unison, they twisted slightly to the right and, from the ends of a tube on each drone, three blinding columns of green light travelled up the hill after the group. Lasers. Advanced weaponry. The three columns split unevenly, dividing into seven smaller beams. Each beam found its target as seven tiny dots, one on the back of each looter.

Seven into three. Three into seven. The Earth was turning too fast.

A hot white-green light and a hiss like magnesium burning, like a blowtorch on a crisp packet.

Screaming. Then it was over.

The stench of burning flesh. Seven plumes of smoke rising. Dogs barking, lapping the remains.

Jed stayed absolutely still. She did too.

The drones travelled up the hill and hovered above each spot. Another sound from far off, like footsteps in the grass.

The army. The real army. They were coming now. The army that had just murdered seven people.

The army wouldn't have done that. It was someone else. Something else.

They must stay here. Wait. Make not a sound.

She watched as the long black tubes retracted inside the drones, while over the crest of the hill, a motley collection of Agrico-bots, their unwieldy webbed langlauf feet rolling one over the other, tall blue bodies and long drooping arms, made their way slowly towards the smoking piles.

'The blue metal ladies,' Jed whispered.

The Agrico-bots positioned themselves directly above an area of smoking ash, inclining forward, just as they would have done when out sowing seeds, until they were almost facing the ground. The dogs ran further off as the bots' clear seed-funnels extended from their middles and sucked the charred remains inside them.

As the drones hovered above, the operation was repeated

until all the ash had been collected and the Agrico-bots re-grouped in the centre of the field.

Their belly funnels extended once more. They began to dig, each one using its trowel-arm. A dark-coloured liquid was squirted back into the earth from the funnel tubes at their bellies. A noise like a leaf-blower; grey lumps flying down the funnel. The hole in the ground was filled in.

The bots made their way to the apex of the ridge. The mushrooms she and Jed had collected were picked up and placed in the collecting bag at the bot's side.

The drones swivelled and flew a few feet closer to where they hid. She didn't breathe. It was as if they were staring down the slope towards the hedge, right at her.

The drones began to travel further in her direction. She pulled Jed into her, threw the back of her jacket up over both of their heads and put her hands over his ears. His lobes felt cold beneath her palms.

They were going to be obliterated. Burned to nothing.

Singing then, soft and eerie: the TrincXcode harmony. A child's treble. Gently, Jed removed the jacket from her head.

Out in the field, sixty or so yards away, the drones had come to a halt.

'Your code,' he said, stopping his singing for one brief moment. 'They like it.'

The drones were on the move again, closer still, the dogs following, ears alert.

'Sing, Mama,' Jed urged. 'We need both our voices.'

The TrincX melodic line. Yes. Yes. Her mouth opened. The sound must come out.

Two voices criss-crossing like a canon.

The drones stopped again. The Agrico-bots had turned their bodies in her direction. Listening.

On and on they sang, four whole cycles of the code, the drones stilled. On the fifth cycle, the whole mass of them swivelled as one and left suddenly, flying higher up the ridge and over the other side, taking the Agrico-bots and the dogs with them. Their hum diminishing, fainter, nothing.

Her ears ticking.

Green stalks springing from the ground at the base of the turbine poles where the creatures had been working the earth, small and thin to begin with but growing quickly.

Within thirty seconds the stalks reached two feet. Offshoots curled from the mother stalk, leaves reaching away from one another.

'They're making things grow!' cried Jed. 'Are they? I think they killed those people because they hurt us and hurt the bees. I think they're our friends.'

She forced him out through the other side of the hedge.

'Run.'

They hurried along the tree line in the crusted ditches, bodies bent low. They had to get back to the room. Jed was ahead. She no longer had the gun. The drones could be military weapons, or a mutation, perhaps remotely controlled. They might not be able to tell good people from ill. The seven looters had seen these particular ones before.

Her son. Her son. She must protect him.

Perhaps this wasn't real.

The drones could be lying in wait in the lane.

She would cross Warston Hall's field. It meant passing the peacocks in the aviary, which might set the birds off screaming. The far end of the hall's paddock abutted the war memorial, which could be used as a baffle while checking the lane. From there she would lead Jed into the brook and walk back to the garage through the water.

She helped Jed over the fence onto Harry's land. Past the coach house and the crumbling bricks of Warston Hall, entering the paddock, keeping in the violet shadows of the giant oak trunks on the west side. To the east side the aviary; silent, a splotch of bright feathers splayed out across the bald earth near the cage's edge. The birds had starved.

One of Harry's polo ponies was grazing twenty feet away, belly distended. It whinnied and danced over, tail proud. She shooed it away but it returned, nuzzling her shoulder. Its breath was warm and smelled of hay. She leant her head against its damp flank, brown coat hot, muscular. Its lips nibbled her hair.

It was okay. It wasn't.

Jed's hands were squeezing her cheeks. His blue irises right there: '*Mama!*'

'I'm here.'

'Aren't they our friends? The big drones and the bots? They killed the baddies. Why are we running away?'

The world was upside down. A child could accept this. Her child could.

'No.'

He was all she had.

They reached the stone war memorial, the pony trotting with them for a while, hind legs flicking behind itself. She took Jed's elbow and led him against the wall.

'Stay here.' She edged to the corner and poked her head out.

There was the humpback bridge, the crossroads, the entire length of the lane right down to the manor wall. All she needed to do was cross the short stretch of tarmac and jump into the water from the bank.

She returned for him, led him around the side. They climbed down, silent. She put him over her shoulder. He didn't weigh much any more. It was four long strides to the brook, a splash on landing. Dark in here. Branches hung over the water, the brook deep enough to flow into and over her boots, reach her calves. She had to put him down; he gasped as the cold soaked through his trousers.

Into the cool underbelly of the humpback bridge. Jed spotted something in the water and bent at the waist.

Another hexagonal green medicine bottle. He pushed it into his jacket pocket.

A sound on the lane: footsteps approaching fast from the road that led up the hill out of Warston. Not a bot. She pulled Jed to her, squashing herself against the curved wall of the bridge. The steps passed overhead.

Jed sneezed. The footsteps stopped, retraced themselves. This was it. A man or a woman, worse than drones. Boots appeared on the bank. Someone slithered into the brook.

Or better.

Gethin stood before her in the water. They stared at one another.

'G?'

'Sig?'

His head ducked under the bridge, moved towards her. His arms around her neck, squeezing, warm skin on hers. He smelled of himself. Her friend. She'd conjured him: how else could he be here? He held her at arm's length, his face dirty, wild-looking, a wispy beard, narrow frame drowning in a green parka. He carried a large black holdall over his shoulder. He smiled suddenly, his face creasing around the eyes, and took her hands in his.

Jed looked from one to the other, chin lifted.

'Not safe,' she mouthed.

Gethin nodded. She pointed down the brook. They moved off, Signy at the front, Jed between them. She felt Gethin's eyes on her back; when she looked behind he was right there.

She reached the drowned MediX robot, arm outstretched, dosette box still in hand. Her boot snagged on it. The water-logged dosette box fell away at last into the water and floated on the current like a little boat, too fast to capture. On they went until they were opposite Dylan and Mary's house. She signalled for them to stop.

Gethin gestured up the bank, eyebrows raised. She nodded. They scrambled on to the lane and sprinted up the short drive. She pulled the garage door open. They scurried under. Blackness enveloped them. Her fingers felt for Jed.

The click of fasteners. Another click and a torch beam lit the greasy back wall. The beam swung into Jed's face. He threw his hands up.

'Sorry.' Gethin's voice. He was real. He was here. Now.

She pushed them towards the ladder, fingers to her lips, Jed's body shivering in front of her.

Once inside, she leapt onto the bed and lifted her eyes over the lip of the Velux. The lane was empty.

'G,' she hissed.

Gethin's eyes travelling over the dirty sink, the faded peach lampshade lopsided around the broken bulb. He climbed onto the bed next to her. He stared out of the window at the lane.

'The large drones? Here?'

'Oh God, G. Yes. Fuck. Who controls them?'

Gethin fastened the window. He studied her face, eyes narrowed. She caught his hand in hers. His knuckles were sharp. She fell against him, she couldn't help herself, pushing her head into the crook of his neck.

'We saw them and … the drones and the Agrico-bots,' she breathed. 'They seemed to be working together. They were so …'

'I know,' he said. His arms were around her. The air seemed to sparkle.

'Are they military?'

'No.' He took a step away, his hand still sealed in hers. 'Oh, Sig,' he whispered. 'My friend.'

Jed dived into the soggy mattress and burrowed beneath the blankets.

'Don't feel good.'

She stroked the curve of Jed's back through the wool.

'It's all right, monkey.' She looked at Gethin. 'What then?' she asked again.

Gethin's eyes scanning her. 'What's wrong with your boy? He looks bad. Those weals on his face. Is it Bovine Staph?'

'No. No.' She started to cry. 'It isn't. Is it?'

'Look.' He went to his holdall. Three sheets of silver blister packs. 'Nanos. Here, you have them. Give them to him.'

'What about your …?'

'Go on,' he insisted.

'Thank you.' She kissed him on the cheek.

Jed chewed a tablet. 'Ugh.' He fell back on the bed. 'My face is sore. When's Dada coming?'

'Soon, love.' She glanced at Gethin. He frowned. 'G? Tell me.'

'I think …' he said. There was a long silence. 'The AI program, the algorithm, that protects the planet, that runs the electricity, solar power, the bee farms, everything – the Trinculated one …' He ran out of breath.

'Yes …?' She knew what he was going to say next.

'It has control of itself. It has control of the military drones, the Agrico-bots, the MediX's. They're part of it, Sig. They've been harnessed and repurposed. They're the hardware that is going to help carry out the algorithm's ultimate goal.'

She had known this. Her father had been speaking to her ever since they set out on their journey, speaking to her through her son, his words, in code. God's daughter was moving across the face of the Earth.

'Who's behind it?' she said.

Gethin turned to the Velux again. 'Not who, *what*. It. Listen to what I'm telling you. The algorithm. The self-learning module was built to achieve its goal.'

'Its goal is to protect the planet, Mama,' said Jed. 'Remember?'

She remembered. 'It's making the best choice for itself from infinite options.'

Gethin and Jed said 'Yes' at the same time.

It made sense. It all made sense. Dad had been right.

'The algorithm was nine-tenths built by the Chinese, did you know that?' Gethin said. 'The West stole it after the war. I think we were so keen to bring it to market, no one thought to input the correct bookends, the correct safety mechanisms to ensure its constellations came to an organic halt at each stage of its decision making. Now some of us are in its way.'

He scratched his throat. A red welt bloomed at his Adam's apple.

'But . . .' She looked around the room, as if the answer might be contained within its walls. 'I can't . . . Why is this happening now? Why did the system wait till now?'

'The beetle blight would have been its tipping point. We've had it coming. We've been a chandelier, dangling from the ceiling on one frayed metal chain. Now the chain has broken and the program won't stop until it's done.'

She glanced at Jed. 'What does "done" mean, in this context?'

'I don't think it wants us all dead,' Gethin said. 'Humans are a species too, and the algorithm's job is to protect all life.'

'So that's …' She was going to say 'good'. Was it good?

'I think that once it set its ultimate goal in motion, it knew it didn't need to obliterate us all, it just needed to set up a situation in which human beings would do a pretty good job of fucking it up, obliterating themselves.'

The bedsprings squeaked as Gethin sat heavily at the end of the bed.

NYPD. His looting partner. The bomb. The people in Regent's Park who stole their bag. The scammers, the looters, the angry, greedy, stupid, heedless people. Nature had its own way of protecting the planet. Perhaps the algorithm was a catalyst, that was all.

She shook her head. 'But wait, that's only one theory and we can't be certain it's correct. We can't take the risk of exposing ourselves, assuming we're going to be okay because we – Jed, you, me – are not killing things.'

Jed said, 'But we have killed things, Mama. A lot of things. To eat.'

'Yes, love, we have.' She nodded at Gethin. 'We need to stay low, hide, until we're sure.'

'Mmm,' Gethin said. 'How will we be sure of that? How will we know we're safe from harm?'

There was silence. They couldn't be sure. Not without risking their lives.

After a while, Jed said, 'They're helping the bees, Mama.'

'What d'you mean, my heart?'

'The bots and drones are taking the bees back to their true cosy home. They're making endangered and dead things come alive again.' He looked at her, pointedly. 'Maybe the bees will get to use Dada's wooden house, after all?'

This made sense. He made sense. Her son.

'It's wasn't Lau-Chen, was it?' Jed said, after a moment. 'In real life, it wasn't Lau-Chen in Scotland who created TrincX?'

In real life.

'No,' said Gethin. 'Not Lau-Chen.'

A distant buzzing. Gethin grabbed her arm, dragged Jed out from under the blankets and led them up against one wall of the room. They waited as the sound grew near. A small blue drone passed over the Velux, camera pointing downwards. Then it was gone.

She was close to Gethin's face. 'The police drones work for the algorithm too?'

He nodded. 'The program has control of everything.'

'We have to leave,' she said.

'We can't just walk out,' he whispered. 'To where?'

'But, Mama, tell him.' Jed's voice, husky. 'We've found a way to protect ourselves. We *do* know we're safe from harm.' He went to collect the string of papers with the TrincXcode music and gave them to Gethin. 'The drones and the bots. Tell him, Mama. You sing infinite TrincXcode and they stop.'

Gethin's eyes travelled to the notes, back to her face.

'No.'

'Oh,' Signy said. She hadn't thought. She hadn't added events and come up with the sum. Jed had. 'Yes. Yes! It gives us ... control. We think it does.'

'The system's too clever now for influencing from us, musical or otherwise,' Gethin said. 'It's playing with you.'

'Why would it be doing that?'

'Who knows? It's a system that's advanced beyond our cognition.'

'You know that's not logical – *playing with us*. There has to be a reason.'

'"Logical"? Perhaps.'

Signy pulled the folded piece of paper covered in Jed's scrawled co-ordinates from her pocket.

'Look. I improvised some music on the piano at the manor and GQOS spoke these from a radio.'

'Yes,' whispered Jed. 'There has to be a reason.' He leant in and his voice dropped even lower. 'Maybe it likes us.'

Gethin stared at the numbers. He took an Ordnance Survey map and an orienteering compass from his bag, unfolded the laminated rectangles and set the map out flat in front of him. He was silent for a long while.

The Velux had fogged. Condensation dripped onto the bed.

His fingers traced the paper. 'The first set are for Devon.' His eyes flicked from paper to map. He went still.

'What?'

'The second set are here, Sig. Co-ordinates for Warston.'

'Don't be …'

He indicated a line of Jed's writing. 'These others, these lines here, are for places elsewhere in the UK. This one, for example, is in the Shetlands. But these –' the second line – 'are Warston.'

'There were other numbers,' said Jed. 'They came out too fast.'

'Why would they be giving co-ordinates for here?' Her feet disappearing through the floor. 'How does that make sense? Unless it's supporting Jed's theory that we are being protected?'

'It is! It's because *we're* here,' said Jed. 'It might be trying to help Dada find us, too.'

'I'm not so sure. The system communicates with itself. My guess is it's listing areas where humans are still alive.' Gethin's words were coming out fast. 'I mean, if it's a collective hive mind—'

'Okay. But wait. This ...' She pointed at her manuscript. 'This is a version of TrincX. *This* is what controls the ... hardware.'

The drones could be coming for them, coming right now.

'That's right,' said Jed. 'We saw people being killed, didn't we, Mama? They shot at the bees and shot at the drones and then the people were killed. But we didn't get hurt, even though we've killed a chicken and a sheep before. The drones heard our singing and left us. You have to learn it. It makes you safe.'

Gethin turned to her. 'Where?'

'Sinistral Point. The large drones were covered in thousands of bees and pollen-drones. It was ... Looters stole our belongings from the village. That's why we've been camped out here,' she said. 'Two people have to sing the code to make it work. I wish I could show you how well it works on things that use power.'

Gethin pulled a folded GScope from his pocket. He sat on the floor.

'You can.'

Jed put the device in the palm of his hand. His face fell.

'It's dead.'

'Show me.' Gethin touched her knee.

Her fingers ran over the smooth GScope screen.

'Sing it,' he said.

They began to sing. Four cycles of notes in soft voices. Gethin watched with arms folded.

Nothing.

'There. The music doesn't do what you think it does,' he said.

'Ssh,' said Jed. 'Wait. Come, Mama, sing again.'

At the end of the fifth cycle the GScope flickered.

GQOS' voice: '*Hallo Gethin-th. How can I hel … hel … help-p-p?*'

'That can't be right,' he said. His mouth was twitching.

'It can,' said Jed.

Gethin sat back on his knees. 'We might be able to contact someone.'

'Might we?'

'They … All my instincts are telling me this isn't possible, simple composition having the capability to influence. I have a PhD in bloody Trinculation. How can the rules have changed …?'

She reached out her hand, touched him lightly with the ends of her fingers.

'This is how we're going to get food and water, protect ourselves if we leave. Or –' she looked at Jed – 'until help comes. You have to learn it, G. Right now.'

'Ssh.' Jed turned to the Velux.

Another insistent low vibration far away, a deeper frequency from the small police drones. Signy leapt on the bed and prised the window open.

Above the hill-road out of Warston, two of the giant drones were heading away from the village.

'They were right here!' She watched them until they were out of sight. 'G. What do we do?'

'They were here already. You know that?' Gethin looked almost rueful. 'The drones, the Agrico-bots. All the hardware. Waiting for a signal. That's what I've been saying – I don't think it's anything you're doing. I think if they'd wanted you dead they'd have killed you already.'

'And I keep saying, it could be our code that's keeping us alive. You have to learn it.' She pointed at the manuscript.

'Mama, the Scope's gone black.'

Gethin stared at the notes. 'I can't read music.'

'You can learn it the same way as Jed. Call and repeat.'

Gethin's ear was not as good.

'I'm sorry,' he said, head dropping.

'Try again.'

Over and over the notes, until Gethin had a rudimentary grasp of the first five bars.

'I need a break.' He sat back. 'You sing for the GScope again.'

'I've got a headache,' said Jed.

'The medicine will work soon, monkey. Promise.'

Sixteen cycles of the music they sang, while Gethin kept watch from the window. The GScope crackled and hissed. The pixels in the graphene screen came and went like waves on water.

Jed was flagging.

'My head. I can't think properly.'

'Another five minutes.' Gethin dropped back to the floor. 'Please, Jed. For me.'

They sang again. The green band of light around the GScope's camera flashed.

'*Hallo, Gethin. How . . . an I he . . .?*'

'Hallo, GQOS!' Jed said. 'Hallo again!'

'Ah!' Gethin looked at her, eyes alight, and back to the screen. 'GQOS, does your camera work?'

'*I . . . fraid . . . ethin.*'

Gethin shook his head. 'GQOS, can you put yourself into low-T transmitter mode?'

'*Hold . . . minute . . . ease.*' A high-pitched whistling.

'It could be spying on us through the camera,' suggested Jed. She pulled him away from the fisheye lens.

'Keep singing.'

Like a distorted echo, a variation on her own TrincXcode composition flowed from the GScope speaker back out to them. Though it wasn't they who were singing. It was two men.

'Anybody there?' A woman at the other end, over the men's voices, faint but unmistakably human. 'Anybody listening?'

Gethin threw his hands up. 'Hallo? Yes! We're here! Who are you? Where are you?'

'... safe ...' said the voice. '... patterns ... crowding ov ... ing.'

'How many of you?'

'Twel ... men ... omen. Two ... ren.'

'We're three here,' Gethin said. Static at the other end. 'A man, a woman and a child. Where are you? Your location.'

'... hampton.'

'Repeat!' Gethin put his ear to the microphone. 'Northampton?'

'Wolver ...' said the woman. 'Wolver ...'

The line went dead.

They stared at one another.

'Wolverhampton,' said Signy. 'Twelve of them in Wolverhampton. I think she said two children.' Jed let his head fall into her lap. 'How did they know the melody, G? How is that possible? I improvised it.'

'Because it has a mathematical shape?'

He took up the paper again, pressing it close to his face, studying the notes. She could see his lips moving.

'It's golden and infinite,' explained Jed.

Gethin nodded. 'It must be.'

'But how did they know to make it so like Mama's?' Jed's face creased with the effort of thinking. 'Perhaps the algorithm has been *trying* to teach it to us? By playing it on the radio? Perhaps it wants us to learn it?'

'Perhaps,' said Gethin. 'We can't be sure.'

Signy stood. 'Wolverhampton. That's where we're heading.'

'Now?' Jed got to his feet and sank back to the floor again.

Gethin shook his head. 'He's not strong enough.'

'Tomorrow then?' Jed said.

'The nanobiotics take twenty-four hours to work – we need a day to build you up.'

A day. They could all be dead by then.

Gethin returned to his map. His hands were trembling. He took a pen from his pocket and wrote at the top, '*I'm not sure the nanos are going to do it, Sig. He needs proper care. We're going to get him that, ok?*'

She looked into his eyes, so close to hers. She trusted him. Trust. It was the only gift she had left.

'It's two days' travel to Wolverhampton. We'll cross out of Yelverton past Tenny's. I know we can do it. If there are those people and us alive, there'll be others who are too, who have worked out the code like you, Sig.'

To set eyes on other people – hide together, survive together, make plans.

'But with a sick child? And what if it's a trap? What if the people on the GScope are actually looters luring us in? What if it's the algorithm pretending to be human?'

'It's our only option.' Gethin was staring at her feet. 'How long have you been in Warston?'

She thought hard for a moment. 'Six days, I think, if you include the day we arrived.'

'Thirteen,' said Jed. 'I've been counting in my head.'

'Monkey,' she said, 'stop. You know it's not that long.'

'Is.'

He was wrong. She looked at the window. It was growing dark. How was that possible? It had only just been morning.

She climbed onto the mattress and stared out at the lane. She'd been counting too: sunrises and sunsets.

Matthew had died on day six, of that she was certain. On day eight, they'd arrived in Warston. The looters had been in the village on day nine.

She closed the window and looked down.

'When did we begin sleeping here, in this room, Jed?'

'Ten. Day ten.'

'It's ...'

Thirteen days? How had seven days gone missing? What had she been doing, while Jed had counted them away, the lightness and the dark? How could she possibly have got it so wrong? Her body collapsed into itself, arms and legs meeting her chest, like a flower closing at dusk. An apt comparison, she thought as she fell, because now it was night. She landed on the bed.

'You okay, Mama?'

'Yes.' She knew nothing. A whole week could disappear without her noticing.

Jed leant towards Gethin and said in a low voice, 'Mama's really tired.'

She curled into a foetal position, and watched them both, her face turned to the side.

'We're all tired.' Gethin frowned at her. 'Sig, how did you get here?'

'On my bicycle.'

'Your *bike*? Your pedal bike? All the way from London?'

'Yeah ...'

A bicycle. As she said it, she knew he'd been right: how could she possibly have imagined she could outwit a system of far superior intelligence on a *bike*? The system would have killed her already if it had wanted. She had been busy thinking she was surviving, but it had been playing with her. Perhaps, as Jed suggested, it had wanted her to learn to play the code.

Jed was looking at her expectantly.

'We're waiting for my daddy,' he explained to Gethin. 'He's been asleep for a long time.'

She could hear Gethin's breathing.

'You cannot become better than a bird in the future,' muttered Jed.

Gethin leant forward suddenly. '*What* did you say?'

'"*You cannot become better than a bird in the future*",' he repeated. 'We met some people on the motorway and their daughter said she'd seen a blue metal lady, a robot, in a factory, who spoke to her and said it.'

'That's Lewis and Quark.' Gethin's eyes opened very wide. Signy sat up quickly. 'That's a quote from their blog, their weak neural net. It was the AI's attempt at a fortune cookie saying. I used it in my—'

'... article "See How Far We've Come"?' Her heart was pounding again. 'I remember it now! G, oh God, listen. I saw the paint names from their blog, *Burple Simp*, *Roycroft Briss*, hanging around the necks of iCanX in a shop in Camden Town days before that.'

It did mean something. Her theory. It had to.

Gethin was already on his feet. 'Perhaps it's a coincidence.'

'Oh, come *on*. Really?'

'Perhaps it's both?' suggested Jed, from the floor. 'Perhaps it's a coincidence and not a coincidence?'

They turned to look at him.

'It can't be both at once, love,' she said.

'Why not?'

'It just can't.'

'But it means something,' Gethin said. 'It helps me to believe the system might be keeping us alive.'

'Does it? Why would the system keep *us* alive, G? Specifically? What did we do to deserve it?'

'I'm not inside the mind of the algorithm.' Gethin bit his lip. 'Perhaps we have skills it needs? It may want to learn certain ... ways from us?'

'What ways? I'm not special.'

'Not to you, you're not.'

She stared at the backs of her hands, at her palms, her fingers. There were white and liver spots on her skin, nicks across her knuckles, her nails were rimed with mud. She'd created music with these hands. Sound sequences that systems responded to. Perhaps this made her special. Special enough.

Jed took the green bottle from his jacket pocket.

'Yes. Things are going weird. For example, I lost this in a field days ago,' he said. 'Then I found it again. In the brook, just now. How did it come back to me in a different place?'

'That's interesting,' Gethin said.

'It's not the same one, my heart,' she said. 'It looks the same but it isn't the actual one.'

'It is. It had this snail in it, see?'

The snail was stuck to the inside of the glass. Maybe it was the same one, after all. Maybe the system had put it there.

'I'm going to make sure I keep Dada alive.'

'Dada?'

'That's his name – Dada.' His eyes held hers.

He went to the water bucket and swooped the bottle gently back and forth, making the sound of the tide.

'Monkey, don't. We drink that water. The bottle's not clean.'

Jed sighed and carried the bottle to the bed.

'How you doing, Dada? When we get home, I'll show you the house me and Daddy built for the bees, but we have to be careful because bees might be living in it by now.'

Gethin cleared his throat. 'Jed, sir – any chance of a bath?'

Jed giggled. 'You could get in the bucket?'

'Bit big for that,' said Gethin.

Jed climbed under the covers. Signy tucked him in. Gethin took a last look through the window. He took off his sweater, stretched it across the inside of the glass and jammed the two ends into either end of the Velux.

'In case,' he said.

'Can I say *Peter Rabbit* to you?' said Jed.

Gethin got in beside him. 'Be my guest. I haven't seen you for a long time.'

Jed rested his head in the crook of Gethin's arm. 'I'll be as tall as you soon.'

'Careful, young man, with that infection of yours. Don't want it getting worse.'

'Wait. Dada's saying something.' Jed put the bottle to his ear. 'Good idea.' He set the bottle down carefully. 'Dada says you can be my standby daddy if you like?'

'It would be an honour.' He ruffled Jed's hair.

She climbed into the other end of the bed and laid her head down, listening to Beatrix Potter, Jed's soft recitation.

A standby daddy. It felt both wrong and right at once.

She crawled into the opposite end of the bed. Jed was asleep. Gethin moved around next to her.

'What d'you think you're doing?'

He lay facing her. 'Well, you don't expect me to sleep on the floor, do you?'

They hadn't been this close since they were children.

307

She didn't know what to do with herself. She lay on her back, straight as a rod, and stared at the ceiling.

Matthew listening to the World Service through one earphone. Her heart hurt.

'Is this it?'

'What? The dawn of a new age?'

'Yeah.'

'Maybe. The humans that are ready to accept change, that can adapt . . .'

'Yes?'

'Might be okay. I don't know.'

They were both silent for a long time. All was still outside.

'You sent me that email, G, that warning email. At the beginning when the power cut out. I didn't hear from you again.'

'Sorry. I wanted to make contact – every comms system blacked out.'

'I thought I saw your motorbike travelling down my road later that day.'

'Poor Sig.' He touched her shoulder with his fingers. 'That bike fell to bits ages ago. Your imagination.'

'And I thought I saw you in the crowd near Finchley Police Station, when the explosion went off.'

'An explosion? Not me, either.'

'But you were in London? Didn't you hear it?'

'I wasn't in Finchley, Sig. I was at home, preparing to leave. Our minds do gymnastics when under stress.'

'Yeah.'

All the thousands of thoughts she'd had since the day they'd arrived home to find the freezer melting. Too many, each one adding up to almost nothing. Not in the grand scheme of things. Nearly nothing.

'I saw my dad,' she said. 'A vision of him. A few days ago.

It was so real, G. Realer than any Holoscreen.'

Gethin chuckled softly to himself.

'What?'

'"Realer".' He placed his hand on the crown of her head. His palm was hot. 'Brain isn't getting enough Vitamin B.'

'What was he like, my dad? From a scientific perspective? Mostly, I remember him at his desk.'

'Wonderful, Sig. A brilliant mind. Some of his theories still hold water.'

'Yeah. Like the bucket,' she said, and she could hear the click of his lips making the shape of a smile in the darkness. 'I miss him.'

'I miss his two sets of glasses.'

It was a conversation.

The buzzing of a small drone. Gethin gripped her hand.

He threw the covers over Jed's head then lay down again, covering Signy and himself, the sound overhead now, a bright light passing left to right across the window. She clung to the blanket.

'What's it doing?' she whispered.

'I don't know.'

They lay quietly for some minutes until it had gone.

'My eyesight's failing, G. The UV is doing it in.'

'I went to find Stella in Oxfordshire after I left London. I thought I might be able to protect her. My ex-wife. Ha. She wasn't there. I didn't know what to do. I walked here.'

'Walked.'

'I was hoping ...' Gethin continued. 'I mean, this place is so insignificant. Stupid, really. One should never ignore the science.' His voice wobbled. Perhaps he was about to cry. 'We all want to return to childhood in the end.'

'What about your Crohn's? You've given us your nanos, G.'

'I've ways of coping, don't you worry.' He chucked her under the chin. 'I'm beyond happy to see you. Alive. With Jed. I'll do my best to look after you, take care of your boy.'

'Thank you.'

'Don't mention it.'

Rain spattered on the Velux.

Heavy rain another time: she and Gethin crouched under a bush in Harry's paddock playing Forty Forty, hiding from Keller, who was It. They had to make the dash to the signpost on the lane which was Home. Harry's polo ponies grazed in the field, roan heads bent low against the sheeting rain, steam evaporating from their flanks. She'd streaked away from him across the paddock and over the wall of the hundred-year-old war memorial towards the signpost. She'd left him for dead and he'd been caught.

'What happened to Matthew?' he whispered. 'Do you mind me asking?'

'Men broke into our house. There was a fight. I don't think they meant to hurt him as much as they ... Jed and I hid in the attic.'

Gethin squeezed her arm beneath the covers.

'I just can't bear to think of him lying there all by himself.' She pulled the covers tight around her. Tears pricked behind her lids.

Gethin wrapped his arms around himself. Her hunger was loud. Perhaps if she and Gethin stayed like this, side by side, Jed safe at the end of the bed, everything would be okay.

'I don't even know what day it is any more,' he said.

'Neither do I. G?'

'Ssh.' He breathed, long, slow.

She felt his muscles relax. Her eyes returned to his face. He was already asleep.

The Next Day

A journey to make. Maybe. Another one. Not just Jed with her this time but Gethin too – a new tribe. Comrades.

She woke, bleary-eyed, disorientated. Gethin was staring at the sky through the Velux. The upward curve at the tip of his nose like a cartoon drawing of a child; the constellation of freckles on his cheeks, forehead, around his mouth.

Matthew.

'Did you sleep?' She'd made him jump.

'I'm so fucking hungry.'

She rolled herself out of bed.

Jed's voice behind. 'I think I feel better but I'm starving, Mama. My tummy hurts.'

'But it's good you're better,' she said. 'It's really good.'

His welts had subsided. He looked almost normal. They would make plans and survive. She and her son, forever and ever amen. He sat up.

'Teach me to use the airgun? I need to know how.'

'Magic nanos,' she said. She found the blister pack and gave Jed his next dose. 'Would you like me to teach you?'

'No,' said Jed. 'Him.'

Gethin dressed and disappeared into the garage with Jed.

She lay on the bed, exhaled. When was the last time she'd fully breathed out, really emptied her lungs.

Through the window, clouds passing. Then rain.

She climbed on the bed, opened the Velux. The downpour lanced its streams towards the earth. She watched for a long time. The water shimmered, moving sideways and down in the wind. She saw herself and Gethin as six-year-olds; towelling shorts and wellies, climbing the spindly tree on the other side of the brook.

No. She pulled the window shut.

The torch beam swinging to and fro in the garage.

'Load.' Gethin's voice. 'Uncatch the safety. Aim. Fire.'

The sound of metal on metal. Those pellets would be useless against anything but the smallest of animals.

Jed's voice: 'Click.'

She stuck her head through the hatch, watching him take the airgun from the crook of his arm. He pretended to break the barrel.

'Clean,' he said, putting on a deep voice. 'Not going to waste them. There's bad things going on. You'd know if you'd been travelling.'

'Stop that.'

Jed and Gethin squinted up at her.

'It's what that man said,' said Jed.

'I know who said it,' she snapped. 'Stop.'

'Anyway, he's dead now. I am allowed to say *dead*?'

Matthew's body, half-on, half-off the bed.

'Give that to me.'

She jumped into the garage, snatched the airgun from his hands and stomped up the ladder to the room. Jed followed.

'I want to learn the airgun. I want to protect us from looters. I want to make the GScope work,' he said. 'I'm starving.'

'Quiet.'

His cooling skin. The pink-red blood blot spreading.

Gethin entered and peered into the almost empty bucket.

'The well,' she said.

They put on their boots and jackets. Gethin took the airgun.

The sky lowered. They sprinted, Jed on Gethin's back, through the churchyard and across the field behind the cottages, ripping dandelion leaves from the ground and stuffing them in their pockets.

They reached the well. Jed pocketed three hard apples fallen from the tree above the telephone box.

Gethin went on watch with the airgun. She dropped the bucket in the well-tunnel, body pressing close to the wall. A smacking sound as the bucket hit the water. The rope flowed through her hands. She tugged it back over the lip of the well. The weight of it dragged in her pelvic floor. Water slopped onto her boots. Gethin took it from her and they struggled home.

The stink of filthy bodies in the room. Water dripping on the rug. She laid the apples Jed had picked in a line on the floor and pulled the leaves from her inside pocket. Small brown shapes, like sheep droppings, came out with them and skittered across the wood.

'Coffee beans,' Jed breathed. 'In the service station. Remember? In the basket with the tangerine.'

There were ten beans in all. She popped one into her mouth. It tasted bitter, granular. She spat it out in the sink and glugged some water. Gethin touched her shoulder.

'No good?'

Jed stowed the rest in the cupboard beneath the sink.

'Just in case.'

'In case what?'

'You want a coffee, silly.'

They shared the sour apples and dandelion leaves. Jed helped Gethin study the TrincXcode notes. Her hands should have been doing something, preparing for travel. She went to the garage, found some hoof oil on a shelf and returned. She sat on the rug, lubricated the airgun.

'Give me your belt, G.'

Gethin lay on the floor, lifted his hips like a girl, pulled his belt free. She used the leather as a strop to sharpen the hunting knife while he murdered the harmonic line under Jed's tutelage. Her stomach felt small, tight as a clenched fist. The singing stopped.

'Sig.' Gethin waved at her above Jed's head.

A nosebleed, the blood dripping off Jed's chin, spotting the rug. She pinched his bridge and stuffed one nostril with the rag they'd used to wash themselves.

Gethin pulled Jed's lower lids down.

'What does he need?' she said. 'Meat?'

'Not Dad's sheep,' said Gethin. 'They're stuffed with toxins.'

'No,' she said. 'It's the cows that are toxic. We already ate one—'

'Sig, the West imports all its lamb from New Zealand. Surely you knew that? Dad sells his meat to Eastern Europe. They all do. The farmers get a pay-off to keep schtum. No sheep.'

How had she not known that? Everything was toxic. Everything everywhere. She was sick of it. Sick to death.

Gethin jumped through the doorway to the garage. She followed him into the darkness.

'G?'

He emerged from the gloom with a green tarpaulin covering his head and shoulders. It smelt of petrol. The airgun was in his arms. He slung his holdall on his back and put his hand over hers.

'Where are you going?'

'Hunting,' he replied.

'We need to come with you. To sing.'

'No. You two can sing together, here. Tenny's farm has eggs and chickens, right?'

She grabbed his sleeve. 'I don't want you to leave.'

'Sig.' He took her hands. 'Trust me. Please.'

He opened the garage door. Then he was gone. Her friend. She waited in the blackness, before climbing into the attic and standing on the bed to watch him as he travelled away from her through the window.

'Mama?'

'Yes, love?' She jumped down, paced the small rectangle of room.

'Can we sing to the GScope now?'

She didn't feel like it; she didn't feel like anything.

'Sure.'

She looked. The GScope was gone.

'I forgot,' Jed said. 'Gethin took it in his holdall. He put it in the side pocket.'

She sat on the rug and stared at the wall.

'Well then, we'll just wait until he's back.'

She fell on him in the doorway.

'Did you see any drones? Anything?'

'Nothing.' He was wan, breathy. There had been no chickens, only the rooster still alive, too scrawny to bother with. There were four eggs in his pocket. He placed them on the floor. 'They might be rotten inside.'

'But where have all the chickens gone?' Jed said. 'There were so many.'

'Taken by foxes, I imagine,' said Gethin.

They ate the eggs raw, though Jed protested, demanding to know why they weren't able to make a fire inside. She could hardly wait to get the food inside her. The albumen travelled through her throat like snot. Even in her hunger, it didn't taste good.

Jed crunched the shell. 'Wish there were more.'

'Don't.' She took the shell from his hands.

'It's full of minerals,' said Gethin. 'We should eat ours.'

He placed an eggshell in his mouth.

'Ugh!' Why had she copied him? 'It's like eating glass.'

'It's not enough. We need to keep sharp or we'll make mistakes. Jed needs B vitamins.'

'Where are we going to find those?'

'Fish,' he said. 'Not ideal. Better than sheep. I'll cast the line. You keep lookout. We'll go at dusk.'

She didn't want to be out in the dark.

'You need me too,' Jed said, licking dried blood from his nosebleed off his fingers.

'No,' Gethin said. 'You stay here. You should rest.'

'No,' she said. 'Jed, 'course you're coming. We'd never leave you behind.'

The sun sank behind the fields. An earlier downpour had washed the landscape sparkling new in the low light. She carried the folded fishing rod, Gethin the airgun. His holdall was on his back.

'You taking that out again?' she said. 'No one's going to steal your stuff, you know.'

'They might,' said Jed. 'What about the looters?'

'Indeed.' Gethin looked from Jed to her. 'It's all I have.'

'You have us,' Jed said.

They checked in all directions, then sprinted down the drive, skidding along the sodden banks into the brook. The water level had risen and was fast-flowing, eddying green and brown around their calves. Dizzy with hunger, she took the lead, Jed behind her, wading upstream towards the humpback bridge, navigating MediX, the robot's empty hand reaching into the air as if awaiting rescue. Halfway there Gethin stopped, dug into the earthen bank with his fingers searching for worms. A couple of tiddlers went into his pocket. As they set off again he whispered, close to her ear, 'I saw them killing one another.' His breath smelled of pear drops.

She leant into him. 'The drones, the bots?'

'No, Sig. *People*. Tearing each other apart. As a species, we're just …' He held her arm. 'Sometimes I think the world would be better off without us.'

'You don't have a kid.'

She turned her back and stalked away, pulling Jed on with her.

They reached the bridge, their heads ducking beneath the curving bricks. The water was deeper here, dark and gelid, up to their knees. Greater depth meant more fish.

Gethin would have to adapt, would have to learn to accept change, if he wanted to stay with her and Jed. She watched him as he telescoped the fishing rod together until the rod extended over the water. He skewered a worm onto the hook. She watched as it curled and uncurled like a fern. Sometimes even the most brilliant minds needed to be taught the simplest things. A system could not teach a person how to love. Humans were self-learning when it came to that.

Gethin cast into a corner where the brook was calm, waiting for the slightest twitch from the line. She and Jed kept lookout, stepping to the mouth of the bridge, peering over the rim of the bank on tiptoes, eyes on the lane. The only sound was the gurgle of gallons of liquid passing along the narrow channel. She and Gethin had found a dead sheep floating here once, washed downstream in a flood.

She tried to picture Gethin's Oxford. Tearing each other apart. Madeleine and Six in London. Matthew in the flat. Perhaps he had been taken away. Perhaps the drones had sent a MediX to check if he was still alive.

The darkness crept around them. Gethin was only an outline now against the crescent of night sky at the far side of the bridge. He made a slicing movement with his arms. She heard the whirr of the spinner as the line reeled in. The rod bent towards the water in a tight arc. Something large thrashed beneath the surface. Gethin leant back. He tugged sharply on the rod. A huge fish leapt from the water into the air, flipping back and forth, mouth gaping, the hook caught in its cheek.

Gethin waded to them with the fish trailing in the water, still alive and held taut on the shortened line. He hauled the fish to a mudflat at the water's edge.

A brook trout, scales silver and glistening even in the half-light. Gethin handed Jed the rod and moved off to hunt for a rock. The fish was muscular. Her hand went onto its head. Its scales were cool and silky beneath her fingers. It regarded her with one unblinking eye, gill-flaps opening, closing.

Gethin returned with a broken brick. He nudged Signy away, put his foot on the trout's body. Its tail fin slapped helplessly. He lifted the brick high above himself.

Humming.

At the far end of the bridge, something ominous was descending to the water. A dim black shape in mid-air. From somewhere inside it a greenish light emanated, like a hovering firefly. The moon behind a cloud threw its rays on two thin black barrels pointing out towards them. A splash as the brick fell from Gethin's hands.

The drone was barely twenty feet from them and on the move. Behind what she had previously thought was an opaque black exterior, a small black ball was visible, rotating like an undiscovered planet.

She pushed Jed behind her. She crept her fingers beneath Gethin's clothes.

'G!'

'Don't. Move.'

The drone came to a halt above the fish, still flapping on the mud, lowered itself closer. A second source of green light in its undercarriage ran backwards and forwards over the fish's scaly body.

'I think –' Gethin took up the fish with shaking hands – 'it wants us to put it back.'

He returned the fish to the water gently. The trout swam away.

The drone rose up, level with Gethin's head. It was so close to him, he could have touched it. The light from inside seemed to bore into them.

'Now.' Gethin spoke through his teeth. 'Sing TrincXcode now.'

They sang, a hollow sound, their voices cracked, wobbly. The drone hovered.

'Now we back away,' said Gethin. 'Slowly.'

They retreated along the brook, not taking their eyes from the drone, placing their feet carefully, the song uninterrupted. The drone remained at the mouth of the bridge. She could hear its body twisting left and right, as if trying to make sense of what it was hearing.

Signy's foot caught on a sharp, hard object in the water and something closed about her ankle. She fell back into the freezing brook, her melodic line aborted. MediX had her in its grip.

Gethin and Jed struggled to free her as the drone restarted its approach, floating over the water like mist.

'Quickly!'

'*My software does not recognise your ... I'm sorr-sorry but I'm prog-prog ... only to ... pond to Birgit-it-t-t.*'

Those long thin barrels closing in.

'Sing!' Gethin commanded. 'We don't know what it's going to do!'

She felt for Jed's hand. She was so cold now, her voice barely worked. They sent the TrincX duet spooling through the dark. MediX relaxed its hold. Gethin whipped her to her feet.

'Run!'

The dark banks rising, the notes still flowing in between breaths, her chest red-hot inside. She glanced over her shoulder. The drone had stopped beside MediX.

Notes from behind, then. A melodic and harmonic line. Beautiful music. The drone and the bot were singing to one another. Communicating.

Signy, Gethin and Jed mounted the crumbling bank, sprinted to the lane and up the drive. She hauled the garage open. The door closed behind them.

'Everyone all right?' Gethin's voice.

'Yeah.'

'Yes.'

They climbed the ladder to the room. The walls seemed further apart. Jed sucked in lungfuls of air. Gethin got onto the bed. He opened the window.

'Don't! What are you doing?'

He studied the lane.

'Its sole purpose seemed to be to prevent us killing that

trout. It must believe it unnecessary for the fish to die for our survival.'

'What does it think we should eat then?' She kicked the bed-leg. 'For fuck's sake. Is it still there?'

'It's gone.' He stuck his head further out. 'I think MediX has gone too.'

'What? How is that ...? They were talking to one another, weren't they.'

He looked down at her from his position on the bed. 'Yes.'

'We lost the rod and the airgun.' Jed was on his way to the sink. He picked up the green bottle and peered through the glass. 'We're back, Dada. We don't have anything to eat, we don't have any dinner for you. Sorry.'

Gethin took Signy by the shoulders. His fingers were strong. In the darkness, his eyes were two hollows. He said nothing.

Unnecessary for our survival.

The rules had changed. How could she learn them? She leant her head into his neck.

She put Jed to bed; he fell asleep immediately. She climbed in the other end; Gethin climbed in next to her, back turned. She pushed her body up against his, fitting around him in a perfect C. C major and C minor.

'We're leaving in the morning, right?'

So many silences.

'I don't think we should wait any longer,' he said, eventually. 'Jed needs medical attention.'

Her heart dropped into her feet.

'Do you remember,' he said, as if sensing she needed a change of subject, 'when we played that game of chase across the fields, girls against boys, and you were so fast, you caught up with our team – we were all hiding up a tree?'

She remembered. She remembered snagging her wrist on barbed wire, helping her little brother over a fence, and her own blood spraying all over her shirt. She remembered her pride at sniffing the other team out by herself.

'Yeah.'

'God, Sig.' She could tell he was on the edge of dreaming. 'I can't give you any promises.'

'About what? About Jed?'

'About all of us. That we're going to make it.'

When he was completely asleep, she turned the other way.

She woke in the night. There was a great deal of noise outside, back and front, multiple clankings, the squeal of metal on metal, bleeping, the hissing of pistons. She knew this noise. Nobody who had spent any time in the countryside could fail to recognise it.

She sat up. Gethin was already awake and upright, body stiff with listening. At the other end, by their feet, Jed slept on, oblivious.

'Agrico-bots,' she whispered.

Gethin put his fingers to his lips. He got to his feet, pulled the jumper covering the Velux to one side, opened the window a fraction and looked out.

'They're seeding,' he said. 'Their night-lights are on. There are loads of them in lines all down the lane.'

'Seeding?'

'There are two large drones moving backwards and forwards above them all. I think they're overseeing the job.'

'But what ...?'

He shook his head. 'Ssh. Lie down. Be still.' He closed the window and rejoined her in the bed. His breath was hot in her ear. 'We must lie still. Wait it out.'

'What if they come for us?'

'They're on a project that doesn't involve us. I'll stay awake, keep watch. You sleep.'

In what wild world did he imagine she could possibly sleep now?

She was dreaming. She knew she was.

A drone came for her, humming, waking her where she slept. It hovered over her in the tiny room. She buried herself beneath the sheets, curling into a ball, Jed's feet in her chest.

And yet she didn't want to wake.

After a time, the drone's humming quietened. She was pulled from the bed into the air as if she weighed nothing, as if she were a ghost, floating. Her legs dangled. Jed's steady breathing below. She was lowered to the floor. She was on her back. A gentle pressure on her collarbones, though nothing touching her. The drone lowered itself until, on its undercarriage, very close, she could see the word LANIAKEA etched in tiny letters. Beneath that, a drawing of a drone. Like the poster. Like the new factory along the motorway. Her hand went out to touch it.

Words curled like smoke from her own mouth. They hung in the air as perfect spirals. She couldn't read them.

The drone lowered itself further, until its belly touched hers. An electric shock – and yet the drone on her bare skin did not feel like metal at all but warm, textured.

There was a new sound: a Doppler echo, a heartbeat racing fast. Too fast to be her heart.

The drone was floating away from her now, its green light glowing inside. She put her hands to her belly.

The drone at the door. Its outline lost to the darkness. Gone.

Time passing. She, breathing in the black, falling. Her ribs rising, descending.

The Last Day

Pale light quavering.

Quiet outside. Wood pigeons.

Inside the room a bluebottle dived frenziedly against the Velux. Beyond the sloped window, a sky of watery blue. She wasn't lying in the bed next to Gethin and Jed. She was on the floor, rolled up in a blanket.

Gethin was asleep. He was supposed to have stayed awake. It wasn't his fault. She looked at his red hair, falling across his forehead. They were weak with hunger. Staying awake was no longer in the body's lexicon.

A crick in her neck. She touched her belly. She lifted her jumper. The shallow breathing of the others.

The revery alone will do.

When she'd written that poem, perhaps Emily Dickinson had experienced a dream. Not exactly like hers, but a dream all the same: stark, realistic. Every human dreamt. It was how they kept their hopes alive, their fears. She wondered if the algorithm dreamt, the drones, the bots. And if so, of what?

She made her way onto the bed, stepping over Jed's head, and edged open the Velux. The lane was empty. Leaves swishing in the trees. Leaves. There were leaves! Not many, but some.

The Agrico-bots had been seeding. Change was coming.

The three of them were leaving now.

Jed lay on his front in the Matthew position, legs and arms poking from the blanket. His eyes opened, doll-like, unblinking. He turned on his back and rose up from the waist. She thought of the man in the shed on the Parkland Walk.

'I'm hungry,' he said.

'Stay here.'

She climbed down the ladder into the garage. Her tummy was hurting.

Blades of light sheared through the edges of the metal door. She waited for her eyes to adjust and pulled it open a fraction, laying herself on her side across the floor. She peered through the narrow aperture. Her breath bounced off the concrete, warming her cheek. An ant moved in front of her face. It scurried up her neck and over her nose. She swiped it away and went back into the room.

'G.' She shook him awake. 'G. What happened last night after I fell asleep?'

'The noise went on until it got light. Then it stopped. I heard them leave.' His eyes were thick with sleep.

'What noise?' asked Jed.

'Right. We need to re-establish contact with the people in Wolverhampton, before we leave,' she said.

Gethin sat up. 'Why?'

'What if they're not alive? We have to make sure they're still there before we set out.'

He rose and dragged the GScope from a pocket in his holdall.

'What noise in the night?' Jed wasn't letting it go.

'Jed, help me sing,' she said.

'Fine,' he said. 'Don't tell me.'

They arranged themselves around the GScope and began the familiar cycle of notes. The screen crackled.

After a time, different voices. Two women. A greeting.

'Hallo?' An Irish accent over the melody, the word clear this time.

Gethin and Signy exchanged glances.

'Hallo?' Gethin whispered. 'Am I speaking to the twelve in Wolverhampton?'

'No, the University of Galway. Where are you?'

'It's like the Eurovision Song Contest,' Signy whispered and Gethin laughed, properly laughed out loud. In spite of everything.

'Northamptonshire!' Gethin called into the GScope. 'We spoke to twelve people in Wolverhampton yesterday. We're heading there. How many of you are there?'

'Five.' The line went fuzzy. '... gate filter.'

Gethin leant in. 'What? What did you say?'

'Great Filter,' came the voice. '... constellations.'

'Ask about the bees,' Signy insisted.

Gethin flapped at her with his hands. 'Keep singing, Sig.'

The line went dead for a second.

'... vibrate ... frequency ...'

A new set of singing voices joined, blurrier, further off.

'That's them!' cried Signy. 'That's the people in Wolverhampton! I recognise their music, their voices. Hallo? Is that you?'

'... es. Here!'

The screen went suddenly black. No amount of singing could bring it back to life.

And who wanted to bring it back anyway, she thought, this sort of life? Everything was a puzzle. A puzzle and a mess. The end.

'I hate evolution.' Jed's eyes were trained on the Velux.

She let her chin rest on his head. His hair smelled of dog. It made her think of Comet. She wondered if he could be still alive.

They packed everything they had into Gethin's holdall. Jed dressed himself, attended to his boots. They gaped about his ankles. He couldn't manage the laces. She caught him trying to slip the green bottle into the bag when he thought she wasn't looking.

'Not that, love,' she said.

'I'm not leaving Dada behind.'

She pulled the water bucket over. Her breasts felt heavier than usual, her nipples peculiarly tender beneath the rough material of her jumper.

'Put the bottle inside the water. It's better for Dada to stay here, not to be squashed in a bag full of clothes.'

'He's coming with me. I'll carry him.'

She didn't have the will to argue.

She checked everywhere, ensuring nothing was forgotten.

The blank music manuscript. The wooden house. The cats.

'Ready?' said Gethin.

'Bye, room,' whispered Jed.

Gethin slung the holdall on his back.

They squeezed through a gap in the garage door, crept tenta-tively round to the back. There was no sign of the Agrico-bots.

'There are more leaves, look,' she said into Gethin's ear, as she stared at the trees to the rear of the back garden and beyond in the churchyard.

Four police drones overhead.

'They're carrying things,' hissed Jed. 'There, in their spindle arms.'

Her eyes weren't good enough.

'He's right,' Gethin said. 'They've something there. Like rags.'

A small drone dropped like a stone in front of them. It flew past their feet, deposited something and rose steeply skywards.

She looked down at the grass: a grey long-sleeved shirt with yellow daisies. Gethin picked it up. He opened it out. Two buttons missing.

She was in her body and out of her body. She was moving. Her legs were moving her.

'Sig?' Gethin called. 'What are you doing?'

'Mama?'

The drones were swooping and ducking like birds, their gyre increasing as they moved away through the blue. She stumbled after them.

The two buttons. The small drones circling in a holding pattern over the bottom right-hand corner of Mrs Jones's horse field

The septic tank. Mrs Jones's septic tank was there.

She was running now, leaping through the brook. The drones dropped their objects into the tank.

'Stop, Sig!'

'Mama, stop!'

She reached Mrs Jones's field. There was a stabbing pain in her pelvis. She dragged herself the last few yards until she was directly below the drones and close to the edge of the tank. The lid was off. Steam rose from the hole. Gethin and Jed were beside her now.

'Sig? Stop!'

Trousers, shirts, skirts, dresses, socks, shoes, boots, belts, bags, a hairbrush, handbags.

The three of them stood in a line, staring at it.

Life's only meaning, she thought, was within its context, its perspective.

'That was Gamma's shirt, the one with the flowers.' Jed's

voice, tremulous. 'Who do these other things belong to?'

'Dad's coat,' Gethin said.

Jed turned and ran, scrambling under the fence, sprinting back to the garage. Gethin caught him.

'Get off me!' Jed yelling. 'What were all those clothes doing in that horrid hole?'

The pain in her stomach was intense.

'It was nothing.' Gethin spoke for her. 'Recycling. Old clothes no one wanted. Come now, we don't have time. We have to leave.' He turned to her, voice low. 'Sig? Pull yourself together. Tell yourself – it's nothing.'

It's nothing.

She was trying to follow, but there was another arc of pain, a sensation so acute it brought her to her knees.

Jed ran to her. 'Mama? You okay?'

Gethin flung the garage open and dragged her inside. He helped her into the attic room, where she lay unmoving on the rug.

'You okay?'

The two boys leant over her.

'What's wrong, Mama?'

Jed's face filled with worry. With love.

Her hand went to her belly. She let her fingers creep towards her breasts. Her nipples were puffy, larger than normal, swollen, sensitive to the touch. Her hand flew out and she grabbed Gethin's leg. Jed was at the door.

'It's okay, Jed,' she said. 'I'm okay.' She rolled on her side and got to her knees. Her head felt full of water, like the bucket. 'I must be pregnant.' She heard herself say it and knew it to be true. 'I'm pregnant.'

Gethin's head shaking. 'But ... how d'you know?'

The dream: the Doppler, the *heartbeat*. Matthew and she had

had sex that last night in the top bedroom. How many days ago? They had made a baby. They had made a baby and then he had died.

Jed's eyes widened. 'Who put the baby in you? Was it him?' He pointed to Gethin.

She swallowed. 'It was Dada.'

'But Dada doesn't know about his baby.'

'No.'

'Are we going to tell him when he gets here?'

'Yes.'

'I'm going to have a brother or sister?'

'Yes.'

Pregnancy symptoms. After eight days. Or fifteen, according to Jed. No, both those numbers were wrong. It was too soon. It wasn't possible. Was it?

'Sig.' Gethin put his face close to hers. 'Jed's face is swelling again. There's a boil on his arm too. Are you okay to walk? We need to leave. We need to get to Wolverhampton, as soon as we can.'

'It's nothing,' she said, and fell into a dead faint.

Visions of the baby floating inside her, delicate as a porcelain figurine. She was giving birth in a freezing vacuum, the baby only part-human; its body normal, its face a bee's head that stung her over and over when she put it to her breast. She dressed the baby in her mother's floral shirt and threw it in the well. It crawled up the curved wall on all fours back to her and spat brown liquid in her face.

She came to in a cold sweat. She had been moved to the bed. Jed was sitting on the rug, watching her. She called his name. Her eyes closed. She sank back into the blanket.

★

On her side, head throbbing.

She and Matthew had made a baby.

Morning sickness. This shouldn't be happening. Her body expanding, thickening. Not yet.

Gethin leaning over her. 'Sig? Thank God.'

He helped her up to sitting.

'How long have I been out?'

'Dunno. Four hours?'

'I need to pee.'

'We need to go now.'

'Yeah.'

Jed approached, wary. 'I love you, Mama.'

'I love you too, sweetheart.' Her hand on his knee.

He patted her belly. 'Hallo, baby. Can you hear me in there?'

She made her voice high. 'Hallo, Jed.'

Gethin was going through his bag.

'Put these in your pocket.' He chucked the pack of nano-biotics at her.

'Why don't you take them?'

'Just do it, will you.'

She knew why. In case.

'What's its name?' Jed asked her.

'I don't know yet.'

If it was a boy, she would call it Matthew.

Him: she would call *him* Matthew.

'Why not?' He stroked her hair. 'How will Dada know to come to the Wolverine place?'

'We're wasting time,' Gethin said. 'Let's go.'

'Mama, look at the window.'

Green tendril-shoots had found their way across the edges of the window frame. A prickling at the tips of her fingers.

Gethin was at the door. 'Hurry.'

She got to her feet, stared at her ankles in her boots, laces trailing. She thought of Michelle in her fluffy dressing gown. She climbed down the steps into the garage behind Gethin and Jed. Gethin heaved the door open. Grudging daylight bleached the darkness to pale green.

Green: that wasn't right. The sky was sickly, as if the hamlet had been moved overnight and repositioned in a wood.

Jed stepped out onto the drive. He looked back in wonder.

'Gaia,' he breathed. 'Mama, look! God's mummy. She's awake.'

She stepped over the threshold.

In the lane in both directions, shrubs and plants overflowed along the verge: dark and light greens, yellows, saplings, lilac flowers. Perhaps she would wake any minute, Jed beside her on the bed.

To her left, Virginia creeper and ivy climbed the walls of her mother's cottage, the bricks beneath barely visible, spindly shoots reaching beyond the top floor windows, suffocating the building. In the field across the lane, the septic tank was invisible now beneath a scramble of bushes.

'Four hours you say I've been out?'

'I promise you, Sig.'

She looked back at the garage; its roof snarled with green. The ivy had grown right across it, dropping out of sight on all sides, its tiny disc-like projections suckering to the tiles. Perhaps nature would engulf them. Like a wave.

Gethin gave her a look she couldn't fathom.

'It's happening.'

'What's happening?'

'*It.*'

Change. He meant change. Her hand went to her belly.

They made their way swiftly to the rear garden. This was

what had been going on in the night. This. The square lawn was hidden beneath more shrubs and delicate saplings that reached Jed's shoulders. The daylight burned her eyes. In the vegetable patch the earth was freshly tilled, the soil rising and dipping in soft troughs and furrows, and in each one different vegetables grew: oversized carrot-tops, their bright green fronds waving merrily in the wind; creamy-white hearts of cauliflowers among dark, thick leaves; at the back of the patch the stalks of runner beans, like long ears, wound around vertical canes of bamboo driven into the earth and joined together with baling twine.

Jed said, 'This is what they want us to eat instead of fish!'

'Don't touch them,' she told him. 'We don't know what chemicals have gone into them.'

'But they made these for us!'

'No.'

Her bladder was bursting. She crouched next to the house, overshadowed by the ivy-covered gable, the metal life-hammer jabbing at her from her pocket. Frothy urine puddled at her feet. She seemed to be always peeing. She stared down at the dark yellow liquid. This was all she was: a collection of organic matter thrown together – samples of cells, DNA, quanta. Her life meant nothing more than the potatoes in Jed's hands, the ivy on the roof.

Her fingers went beneath her jumper. A baby in there. A tiny bean. Smaller than a lentil.

Jed kicked up potatoes with his boot.

'I'm going to take some anyway.'

'No, monkey.'

'Yes. We're starving.' Too late. He and Gethin were already collecting, Jed chewing on a carrot. He looked up. 'Delicious.'

Gethin said, 'Let's go.'

They scaled the low fence of the churchyard, the baby

pushing at her pelvic floor. Greenery dwarfed the gravestones and the front wall of the church. The clock on the spire poked its hands through strangling creepers. Using the gravestones as baffles, they scurried round to the west side of the church, where they would have a view of the fields leading to Tenny's farm. Beyond Tenny's one of the many gated roads led to Yelverton, barely two miles away.

Life was exploding; where the manor's grass fields should have been there were spiral-shaped arrangements of ferns, almost tropical.

'Golden,' breathed Jed. 'Infinitely golden.'

Through the trees, the swing-field visible, the top half still grass, sheep grazing, the bottom half a tangle of spiralling bushes like hair that had been combed in the wrong direction. The bushes were sharp, vicious-looking. Brambles – giant ones.

Murmurations of starlings in the sky. Holes from a freshly dug rabbit warren pockmarked the ground to their right.

Jed tapped her thigh. Their eyes met.

'Look.'

In Mrs Jones's horse-field, a tree had grown out of the septic tank, fruits hanging down, green ones, teardrop-shaped. A tree that had not existed minutes ago.

'A fig,' said Gethin.

A fig tree. Her mother's shirt growing into the sprawling roots, the cotton perhaps threaded through the trunk.

They hurried across the manor field, picking their way between the ferns, the manor's ancient walls, the tithe barn, alive with vines. They crossed to the swing field, those spiked bushes blocking the path. A tiny passageway half a foot wide ran between the bushes and the hedge at the boundary of the field.

'Up here.' Gethin led the way.

Backs to the hedge, progress slow, until they reached the

end – a new wall of brambles rising, snarls of sticks and prickles, high as her head. They stood in its shadow.

'Wait there.'

Gethin trampled a path through. He returned to collect them, led them to the other side.

They were in the grassy half of the field now, the landscape almost normal here. Those three fluffy sheep glanced up, grass cuttings hanging from their mouths.

She looked over her shoulder then followed on, stumbling towards a spinney at the other side, one arm protectively on her belly. Down the hill beyond the brambles, the swing hanging in its strip of land. Vines grew around its ropes.

They threaded between the trees.

Behind them, a rustling, a branch snapping.

Nothing there: birds, the wind in the trees, the sound of their own breathing. High above, crows' nests dotted the sky, black blotches against the blue. She gulped in air.

The spinney led into Tenny's sheep field, here too, lush with ferns. Ahead, the farmhouse drowning in ivy.

Behind the shed, the small chicken run had been enlarged to encompass the entire backyard and a low hedge had been laid as a boundary fence. In the centre, hundreds of chickens pecking at vegetable scraps.

'The Agrico-bots have done all this?' she said.

'The system,' corrected Gethin. 'The system has.'

A system: a set of things working together as part of a mechanism or an interconnecting network; a complex whole. This system had enlisted simple machines for complex tasks. Humans had been doing this for centuries. Now the human system had broken. A new one was taking its place.

They made their way around the side of the building onto the bridge over the canal.

'We must have come the wrong way,' she said.

'But there's Tenny's house.' Gethin frowned. 'This *is* the bridge?'

The gated road to Yelverton should have led off from here. Instead, there was a large wood of densely packed, fully mature pine trees. The wood stretched lengthways in both directions, as far as the eye could see. The unmistakable scent of pine needles in the air. It looked dark inside the wood, almost black.

'I'm scared, Mama.'

'It's okay. We've got to do some travelling to get to the people we spoke to. Let's pretend we're Alice in Wonderland.'

'Alices,' Jed said.

'What?'

'Three of us – Al*ices* in Wonderland.'

Gethin had already walked on. They hurried after him.

An eerie quiet. The forest floor thick with glossy needles, nothing else. In sections the soil had been turned, perhaps to drive the trunks in. The ground seemed unstable, shifting beneath their feet like water as they walked deeper in.

Jed ran his hands over the bark of a tall, thin pine.

'What chemical is the program using to make this grow so quickly?'

'I don't know, love,' she said. 'A new one certainly.'

'This wood goes on forever.'

'Don't say that.'

'The road to Yelverton should be only half a mile from the bridge by Tenny's farm,' said Gethin. 'By going forward in a straight line we'll eventually come to it.'

'What if it's not there any more?' Jed said.

They moved on silently, the view the same in every direction.

'We should have met the end of the gated road already.' She slowed, rested her head in her palms.

The sound of a drone beyond the treetops. Jed looked up.

'What if it drops something else at our feet?'

'We'll retrace our steps to the canal,' Gethin said.

They turned back, walked for a minute.

'It all looks the same,' she said.

'We're lost,' Jed announced.

'No,' said Gethin.

'Mama?'

'G, are we lost?' She put a hand on Gethin's arm.

'I …'

She waited for him to finish.

On they went. They could have been travelling in circles, though she had a strange sense the land was steadily climbing.

'It's been an hour,' whispered Jed.

'No.'

'I've been counting in my head.'

'How are we ever expected to make it to Wolverhampton?' She leant against a trunk and looked up – a sea of green above, like standing in the shade of a huge umbrella. How long since she'd seen so many leaves? 'We can't even make it as far as Yelverton.'

'Mama, my disease is hurting.'

She fed him a tablet from the blister pack in her pocket.

He chewed with his eyes screwed up. 'How big is my sister at the moment?'

'Or brother.' She hated this endless circular forest. 'Tiny.'

'It's a girl. Will she grow?'

'In nine and a half months.'

'What if she grows really quickly like these trees and the plants?'

'She won't.'

'How d'you know?'

'Nine and a half months is how it works,' she said.

But the rules had changed, hadn't they? Eight days – or fifteen – or another number? She'd eaten eggs, meat and plants that had fed off land fertilised by the machines. It might work differently now. The baby might arrive far sooner than normal. The thought made her throat close.

Gethin stared at the floor.

'Mama?' Jed was studying her face.

'What?'

He placed his ear to her belly. 'Don't worry. The baby's talking.'

'Don't be silly.'

'It's a secret.' Jed sat up. 'What's that sound?'

Signy stilled her breathing. A faint trickling close by. Jed leapt to his feet.

'Wait, love! Wait for us!'

She ran after him.

The land led downwards. In the cleft of a shallow dip, a stream. It emerged from below ground, feeding through a slender channel to their left.

'Safe to drink,' Gethin said.

They dropped to their knees, scooping up handfuls of water, cold and sweet.

'If we make tracks this way, the water will lead us out,' she said.

They set off downstream.

Some time later, the stream widened. Daylight shone ahead two hundred yards or so beyond gaps in the trees, pushing its way between the dark trunks, picking out details on the forest floor: fallen branches; a shrub sprouting infant shoots; a stilled object farther off at the very edge of the wood. It was large enough to be an adult, slumped. Or a child. Her hands tightened into fists.

'It's your rucksack, Mama.'

'My heart, the people who came to the village took my rucksack. Remember?'

'And now it's here.'

Gethin blinked at her. 'It does look like a rucksack.'

They crept towards it.

'Sigsigsig!' Gethin's voice, a susurration. He gripped her arm.

The Karrimor logo, the stain on the right-hand pouch, the broken fastener at the base. She stared. It could be a trap.

'See? Yours. How did it get here?' Jed said.

She went close, lifted it up. It weighed nothing. She clicked the catch and upended the sack. A piece of dark green material floated out. A scarf. With white flowers on it. She put it to her nose. It smelled of woodsmoke and distant perfume. Her father's Eau Sauvage, fresh and bitter.

Signy let the scarf drop.

'It was that woman's at Sinistral Point.'

'Hope,' said Jed. 'That was her name – Hope.' He stamped on the scarf. 'Go away, Hope.'

She pulled the rucksack onto her back. The feeling of it hanging there was comforting, familiar.

'Maybe the drones took your bag from the bad men's jeep?' suggested Jed. He fiddled in his pockets. 'Where's Dada? I forgot him! I have to go back!'

'No, Jed. We're to keep moving.' She fixed her gaze on the daylight ahead. 'We can't possibly go back. We're finding our way to the people now.'

Jed wailed. Gethin put a hand over his mouth but he twisted away, voice rising.

'And where's XO? You've left him behind too!'

'Ssh,' said Signy. 'We didn't have time. I'm sorry! I have the life-hammer. Look!'

'I don't care about the hammer!' he howled. 'Where's Dada? I want Dada! Are we even going to see him at Wolverine? Why do you keep taking things away from me?'

He stumbled towards the edge of the wood. He was faster than she was and the gap between them grew quickly. He went out beyond the tree line. She picked up her pace, Gethin at her side. They shot out into the light.

The lid of sky opened above them. Jed had his back to her, still as a pillar, on the cusp of a field of unnaturally tall yellow rape.

She didn't recognise the field, the rape, or the season they seemed to have found themselves in. The terrain was flat, the rape surrounded by leafed trees on the far side. Jed's head inclined. Perhaps he was crying. Everything he loved had gone. Except her.

She grabbed the hood of his raincoat and spun him round. The front of his jacket was covered in butterflies. They'd settled like a sea on his arms and chest, their neon markings like the cat's-eyes on those endless fibreglass roads of the motorway.

'Beautiful,' he breathed.

He raised his arms and the butterflies took off, alighting on Gethin's jacket, her jacket, soundless as paper, wings flickering, bright yellow rings that opened and closed, opened, closed.

Bees buzzed in the rape. Small blue drones above.

'My God,' Gethin said.

Something rustled deep in the rape. It was heading towards them, the giant crop stalks bending like trees in a breeze. The buzzing grew loud.

'Bots!' hissed Jed. 'Agrico-bots!'

She must take her son back into the wood. She looked over her shoulder.

More Agrico-bots coming at them from the trees. Too many to count. They stepped out from the sides of the trunks, each bot covered in a coat of bees. The butterflies flew up, gathering in the air above. Five huge military drones arrived overhead and hovered higher up than the butterflies. Jed clung to her.

She turned again, to the rape. More bots cut through the yellow flowers, accompanied by their own cloaks of bees. There was that dronal humming again. It was deep, intense; it shook the earth beneath her feet. The air smelled strongly of pollen. The bots were close now, indistinguishable from one another, their gait as clumsy as ever, but there seemed now a strange regality to their tall, spindle-like bodies. Thousands of pollen-drones were mixed in among the bees, like the shadows of bees, like the future, but here in the present, now.

The bots' two lines closed in, facing one another either side. An army on manoeuvres.

'Don't do anything,' Gethin said. 'Don't sing.'

A moment. Everything everywhere, absolutely still.

A swinging motion and the bots were moving again, this time weaving among one another in a figure-of-eight shape: slow, synchronised.

'They're dancing.' Jed's voice, so quiet she could hardly hear him.

'They're not interested in us,' Gethin said. 'I told you.' The bees and the pollen-drones in the air, swooping and regrouping, the bots still locked in their dance. He turned to her. 'They think as a collective. Watch.'

'Like bees,' she breathed. 'They must have a hive. Their drone-hub, their home, where is it?'

'Hives. Hubs. Homes. There will be more than one colony.'

Thousands upon thousands of them digging underground, she thought, burrowing their way into buildings, seeding new life.

Jed put his hand in hers. 'They're leaving.'

A number of bots were returning to the rape, thin upright backs disappearing among the tall green stalks. Bees, pollen-drones and butterflies followed above the yolk-coloured flowers. The remainder departed to the wood.

The three of them were left alone. Gethin's eyes were glassy.

'I've seen that dance in London.' He shook his head. 'They're communicating with one another. I think they know about your baby.'

She let the rucksack fall at her feet.

'How would they know that?'

They could have tracked her on her journey to Warston – the drones, the algorithm. She'd scented her way like an animal peeing everywhere, Matthew's unknown baby growing in her stomach. The movement in the trees, the lorry door that was open and then closed. They could know. They could.

Gethin's hands were shaking. She watched them.

'Let's stay calm. We have to keep moving,' he said.

'Mama?'

'Yes, my love?'

'Maybe they want you to raise a baby that can look after Gaia?'

She looked into his face. 'Maybe.'

It was the best thing anyone could have said.

'Will they want me to do that too? Look after Gaia?'

'Yes, monkey.' Her heart was aching so. 'How could they not want you to help as well?'

'These shapes they're planting things in. The Golden Ratio

isn't a natural phenomenon, Sig.' Gethin was already on the cusp of the rape. 'Did you know that? It's a mathematical construct humans drew up to give shape to the impossible. The program is creating its own constructs, beyond Fibonacci, beyond the ratio. That's evolution. What do we know, really? Nothing.' He plunged into the green stalks. 'Hurry.'

They ran after him.

The rape reached above their heads. They fought their way between the stalks, faces aglow with green-yellow light. A blizzard of pollen spores, trails of frondescence in their wake. She put her jumper over her mouth.

Jed was flagging, his body drooping. Gethin held him up by one elbow. Onwards in a straight line.

The edge of the field. Through the stalks, a wide verge at the side of an A-road. It was thick with Agrico-bots flip-flopping their langlauf feet along the tarmac. Dotted in between, MediX machines, WaitreX, DoctreX, an iCanX or three. Drones, big and small, floated above the lines of machinery. Every robot on the road was equidistant, precisely aligned, travelling in one direction. An endless procession of hardware.

She knew this place. The T-junction leading to Warston. Yes, there was the horse chestnut tree with the trunk in the shape of an ogre. They had travelled no more than a mile since they'd left the room.

The bots were all heading towards the motorway, towards the Laniakea building. Their strangely familiar bodies cast shadows on the road. The low humming from the largest drones vibrated through the road panels, snaking its way into her soles.

Something else was coming now, clack-clacking along the line. Blurry at a distance, it grew close until there was no mistaking what it was.

Mum's rusted and broken MediX.

Its beaten body squeaked on the fibreglass, its right arm outstretched in its dosette box position.

The shirt. The fig tree. The MediX.

Gethin was whispering something. Something about not being able to travel on the motorway to Wolverhampton. Something about going another way.

Signy's axis of vision was wrong. She was capsizing. The Earth was turning too fast again. Something pulling her.

'Mama!'

Jed jerking her arm, Gethin and her son, dragging her backwards into the rape. Saving her. No, taking her sideways, Jed's free arm karate-chopping the stalks in front of him.

It was the same time. It was now. A grassy field dotted with black and white sheep and one black ram, its beady eye upon them, the rape far behind now. She had no memory of leaving it. Pines rose in the distance on a slow incline to what might have once been somewhere she knew. The trees stretched as far as she could see.

Jed and Gethin running. So was she, feet drumming the earth. The empty rucksack flopped on her back. Where had the sun gone? It was drizzling.

Jed's heels flicked in front of her; this one, that one, this one, that one. The two boys were faster than her, a long way ahead suddenly. Her feet pounded, loud as hooves. The earth trembling under her weight.

A sound. Something behind her, fast and light. The ram. She just had to make it to the trees. She looked back.

Not the ram.

It was coming at her, its solid rectangular mass, floating across the field. A BinX machine, its large hoover tube hanging off its right side. Her mind had too much space in it, had the time to register its incongruity here. She thought of the pages of dinosaurs in the encyclopedia in Jed's room.

Her eyes fixed on its form.

'*Mama!*'

'Jed! Keep going!'

'Sig!' It was Gethin's voice, cracked, raw.

'Take Jed, G. Do it!'

Ten feet from her, the giant machine came to a halt. It had a hum that was deeper than gravity. Or perhaps it did not. Perhaps she imagined it.

Its casing was midnight blue. How had she not seen that before? So many things she didn't notice. Bees and pollen-drones darted across its body. It was a tower in open space.

She listened for the sound of Jed's feet. Please, God, let them have reached the trees.

The BinX moved forward.

'What do you want?' Signy cried.

'*We want only what is right,*' came GQOS' voice. '*I've got a new hose for the garden you'll like, Jed. It's got a trigger. I've got to go back to the doctor tomorrow about my kidney.*'

The sound was tinny and far off, as if someone were trapped inside a metal room.

'How are you doing that?' Her voice echoed against the machine's body.

'Gamma? Is Gamma inside?'

Jed standing behind her. He had stayed.

'Sig, step away.'

Gethin too. He had learned. The mathematical formula for love. A human was a self-learning system.

A vast empty space in her mind. The machine vibrated through her feet, up her legs into her skull.

'Jed,' she said. 'You have to go now.'

GQOS' voice was clear as a bell. It was singing. TrincXcode, reams of notes, blending one over the other.

'Please don't hurt my son,' she said. The music ceased.

Jed K. Maurice is your son.

'Yes, yes. Jed K. Maurice is my son.'

A high ringing began in her head. She stared at the machine's impenetrable side. This was the future. The future was now.

An artificial brain, a neural net, a code, assimilating, assessing. A knowledge of things she had no knowledge of. And some she did.

'Jed? Are you there?'

'Yes, Mama.'

'Then we have to sing now.'

Their song began, Jed's line a counterpoint to hers. The infinite TrincXcode. The Golden Ratio – how could it not exist? It existed right here, in this music.

The BinX hovered closer still.

'It's okay, monkey.'

Who said that? Was it her? A roaring in her ears.

'Your science cannot save you but your science is beautiful.'

'I don't—'

'You cannot become better than a bird in the future. The words mean both nothing and something, and all things in between. This is the elegance of your quantum theory.'

'... please.'

'You are not chosen, and yet you are. The capacity of human thinking knows but cannot understand this simple binary code.'

Her hand crept into her jacket. She threw the life-hammer with force in front of her. She didn't know why. It arced through the air, its metal point flying towards and striking the machine's body with a dull thwang. The hammer fell to the grass.

'*Do not be afraid,*' it said to her. '*You are nothing. You are everything.*'

Signy felt a pulsing in her solar plexus.

'*See how far we've come.*'

Her heart. She was tipping, free-falling. She was on her back. The view became all sky. Rape pollen drifted from the air and settled on her face.

Three large drones flew into her peripheral vision and asserted themselves directly above her.

'Jed?'

'Mama?'

'You have to go.'

'Get up, Mama.'

'Go.'

'But—'

'Go!'

'But, Mama. Come!'

'Yes, you go now.'

Her words muzzy, far-off. They didn't sound like words at all but a series of vowels. Her thoughts soapy, melting, not unpleasant, like a warm blanket around her ears.

What comes after may be better.

To make a prairie it takes a clover and one bee . . .

Alive and dead. Matthew. Matthew's baby. If she could just fly out of her skin.

The BinX was very close now. She could reach out a hand and touch its wide expanse of rectangular navy-blue. Its surface had a sheen. Beyond this, all that greeted her was her own reflection.

Her hand made contact. A rushing sensation at her third eye, flooding her body. She imagined seeing deeper, beyond the

347

fascia, to a series of balls rotating within, the universe as two mirrors in front of her.

A tall young woman walking naked through a wood, un-blemished skin, her hands brushing at the trunk of each tree, keeping a watchful eye on flora and fauna. The woman's gaze turning, the knowing in it ablaze. Signy having to look away. The ringing in her head unbearable.

Raining now. Rain dripping on her face, running into her mouth. A grey cloud floating in the shape of a fish or infinity.

She was ropes floating free beneath water.

'Get up, Sig.' It was Gethin. 'Get up!'

'Mama, look! Look!'

Two sets of footsteps moving away from her. They were leaving her behind. She turned to see them go. Her son, her son.

But Jed was still there, Gethin too, fleeting figures moving left to right across the field towards the perimeter of the wood.

Towards a band of people. Coming out of the tree line to meet them.

Men, women, children.

Jed ran forward. She watched him as he fell into the embrace of an older woman, her gait familiar, his body twisting round to point at Signy, his face bunched. He was trying not to cry.

She watched Gethin as he clasped the hands of an older man, hugged him. She watched them; they were talking, the man making shapes with his hands, gesturing into the wood.

'Mama! Come!'

'Sig!' Gethin was shouting. 'Come! See who it is!'

They were moving towards her. All of them.

She counted. Twenty-seven. Twenty-seven human beings. Three women had heavily rounded bellies. Pregnant. Babies coming.

And then Tenny, Mary, Dylan, Jean, people from the village. Not all but some. Jed was hopping on one foot, calling out, something about Laniakea, something about food and sleeping.

And then her mother. Mum. Right there in front of her, moving towards her, looking well, healthier than she had for years, her arms open in greeting.

'Signy, my darling!' she cried.

The shirt. The fig tree. The MediX. Not symbols of death. Of hope.

'Get up, child!' Her mother coming closer, closer. 'They won't hurt you. We've all been kept safe in the Laniakea building, by the machines. There are more of us! It's all right, my love. You're going to be all right.'

'I'm going to be all right,' she echoed.

Matthew, his child in her belly. These people here, waiting to take her somewhere, wanting to keep them safe. They had been both chosen and not chosen. She had. Gethin. Jed. A simple binary code she couldn't understand. It didn't matter.

GQOS spoke. '*Go,*' it said. '*Be free.*'

She sat up. The drones hovered above.

'*Gaia needs you,*' said the machine. '*You are necessary, all. More than wise, you must be kind.*'

'I will. We will.'

She got to her feet and ran to embrace the people she loved.

Acknowledgements

This book would not have happened without the help of many brilliant individuals, and I would like to thank the following people for their inspiration, time, talent, kindness and support: Marcus Gipps, Steve O'Gorman, Brendan Durkin, Melissa Hall, Laura Macdougall, Olivia Davies, David Nicholls, Lisa Hilton, The New Scientist, Tim Urban and Andrew Finn, James Lovelock, Nick Bostrom, lewisandquark, Tess David, Chloe Seager, Alice Lutyens, Dixie Linder, Rowan Routh, Carrie Cracknell, John Hopkins, Fiona Walker, James D'Arcy, Victoria Shalet, Roger Hyams, Albyn Leah Hall, Anne Rabbit, Emily Bliss, Jessica Weetch, Megan Walsh, Pascal Harter, Sarah Flax, Richard Skinner, the Faber Academy, and all my fellow Faberites.

Last but by no means least, I would like to thank John and Kit Stevenson, for always being there.

Credits

Susannah Wise and Gollancz would like to thank everyone at Orion who worked on the publication of This Fragile Earth in the UK.

Editorial
Marcus Gipps
Brendan Durkin

Copy editor
Steve O'Gorman

Proof reader
Patrick McConnell

Audio
Paul Stark
Amber Bates

Contracts
Anne Goddard
Paul Bulos
Jake Alderson

Design
Lucie Stericker
Joanna Ridley
Nick May

Editorial Management
Charlie Panayiotou
Jane Hughes
Alice Davis

Finance
Jennifer Muchan
Jasdip Nandra
Afeera Ahmed
Elizabeth Beaumont
Sue Baker

Marketing
Lucy Cameron

Production
Paul Hussey

Publicity
Will O'Mullane

Sales
Jen Wilson
Esther Waters

Victoria Laws
Rachael Hum
Ellie Kyrke-Smith
Frances Doyle
Georgina Cutler

Operations
Jo Jacobs
Sharon Willis
Lisa Pryde
Lucy Brem